Thoughts of Vandalism

Acknowledgements

Thank you, God, for everything. Thanks to my family and friends for their love and support.

The information on the 24th Infantry Regiment of the Korean War, the "Deuce Four," came from The Military Channel's, *Battlefield Diaries: Last of the Buffalo Soldiers*. Thank you Military Channel for this documentary chronicling the events, medals, and honors of the Deuce Four as well as the discrimination and disrespect these soldiers faced.

Thoughts of Vandalism

Kerwin Frix

This is a work of fiction. Names, characters, places, and events are either the product of the author's imagination or are used fictitiously.

THOUGHTS OF VANDALISM

Copyright © 2013 by Kerwin Frix

Frixbird Press

PRINTED IN THE UNITED STATES OF AMERICA

1

The Arrest: November 2002

"I wish Darth Vader were my father," I declared innocently at dinner as I scooped up a spoonful of three-bean salad. I had just recently outgrown my second-grade fetish of thinking that only black men were good-looking. Now, as a third-grader, I found a man dressed in black and wearing a helmet to be appealing. I was only eight years-old, but I was very attracted to the idea of a powerful, bad man reaching out to his only son, requesting that Luke Skywalker come to join him on the Dark Side. Certainly that was love, wasn't it? It was only once I chewed my final wax bean that I realized that no one in my family had responded to my comment. I was surprised at the silence because I had thought my statement would have been met with approval: *Yeah, it* would be *cool to have Darth Vader as a father!* I certainly did not expect my father's grimace and cold stare across the table towards my mother.

I was also probably the only third-grader in my elementary school with crushes on Forrest Tucker from *F-Troop* and Chuck Connors from *The Rifleman*. If you have no idea who either man is, all you need to know is that Forrest Tucker was over fifty and Chuck Connors was over forty years-old when they starred on these shows. *Red flags, anyone?*

So as I sat at the dinner table happily waving my Freudian red flag as if I were standing on a sidewalk along Main Street watching *The Future Dysfunctional Women of America with Man Issues* march in a parade, my little flapping piece of cloth went unnoticed as usual. But then again, who could possibly notice my tiny, solitary red flag when my twin brother, Matthieu, was sitting across the table wielding his multiple red flags, dive-bombing them like Kamikaze planes into his meatloaf, beets, and three-bean salad then setting them on fire?

Matthieu and I were kind of like the seriously fucked-up *Wonder Twins*. Obviously, he would be Zan and I would be Jayna, although sometimes I also got to reprise the role of space monkey, Gleek. Instead of turning into forms of H_2O as Zan did, my brother would transform himself into a variety of natural disasters. He would succumb to his roller-coasting emotions as if we had just activated our Wonder Twin powers as we pressed together the knuckles of our closed fists. "Form of: a tornado!" Matthieu would proclaim. I, on the other hand, would have to turn myself into something that would appease his force of nature. So as he twisted in a circle and spun out-of-control looking for things to fling into the air, I would incant, "Form of: a trailer park!"

It might be these random circumstances of my youth that eventually led me to be hand-cuffed in the backseat of a police car only two-hundred yards from my house. It might also be these random circumstances that caused me to date a loser which led me to being hand-cuffed; a loser that I hated for being himself and also for having an extremely small penis; a penis so small that I thought he could've at least had the decency to apologize for it. I kept imagining a day that would never come, so to speak, when he would say to me, *I'm sorry that I am so dissatisfyingly small.*

I used to be of the camp that believed, *Size doesn't matter; it's what he does with it.* I can tell you that anyone who believes that has never had sex with somebody smaller than six inches. Somehow, though, The Loser really hadn't seemed embarrassed that his penis was the same size as my pinky finger. In fact, it reminded me of that joke when one whiny person tells another person all her petty problems. The non-whiner would rub her index finger and thumb together and ask, *What's this?* The whiny person would shrug and say, *I don't know.* The non-whiner would then respond, *I'm playing the world's smallest violin.* Well, it's not the world's smallest violin. It's the world's smallest hand-job and I was the one giving it.

I did notice that The Loser had some of those natural male enhancement pills from GNC underneath the sink at his house. He played them off as belonging to his roommate. So why when he moved in with me a few months after this hellacious night did I find those same pills underneath my sink? Maybe more importantly, why weren't they working?

As I sat in the back of the police car willing myself to keep my mouth shut, which was near impossible since I was drunk *and* dressed like a hooker (although I have no idea why being dressed as a hooker would affect my ability not to speak), I tried to think of other things to distract me from my present nightmarishly humiliating circumstances. Unfortunately, the only thing I found myself doing was questioning why I left a dysfunctional relationship with a guy with a really big dick to move away and get involved in a dysfunctional relationship with a guy with a really small dick.

Right now at two a.m., the only big dick in sight was the police officer sitting in the front seat. I sighed. I knew that it wasn't fair to call him a big dick. He was just doing his job. Still, I couldn't be completely objective about his and my roles at this time of the morning due to my circumstances and inebriated state. After all, he was the reason I was shackled in his backseat. Besides, of course, my being drunk, driving drunk, and crossing the double yellow line on a wide right turn right in front of a police car that I did not see because my peripheral vision had temporarily diminished.

When I had moved to Chattanooga back in July, I had been so optimistic. I was going to make a new start; become the Mary Richards who would toss my crocheted hat up into the air in the middle of downtown because I had in fact made it after all! And downtown was exactly where I was headed for my new start with a criminal record.

I was also less Mary Richards and more Happy Hooker because I was wearing a shiny black plastic miniskirt with a large zipper up the front, knee-high black leather boots, a trashy Guess shirt, and a fake fur coat. I had been dressed for a Halloween party, post-Halloween, that I hadn't even wanted to go to in the first place. The only reason why I had agreed to go was due to the immature whining of The Loser. "But you said you would go," he insisted maniacally. "You promised. You promised." He sounded like *Rain Man*. The only thing that he didn't do was rock rhythmically back-and-forth in his seat. Exasperated, I had sighed and acquiesced. I had immediately regretted it as soon as we arrived at the party, if not during the drive across town. He insisted that he would drive, and once we entered the party filled with more losers, I insisted that I would get drunk.

3

In my buzzed state, I secretly or not-so-secretly sneered at everyone there and found a place on the couch far away from The Loser because I was suddenly embarrassed to be seen with him. When I sat down on the couch, I sat next to a guy whom I was not the slightest bit interested in and we started talking. I have no idea about what. But I ended up laughing; he ended up laughing; and The Loser ended up jealous. We left the party. Apparently, I had humiliated him in front of all his friends by talking to Couch Boy. Apparently in this group of social rejects, Couch Boy was also The Ladies Man, The Male Whore, who had ruined many a fabulous relationship between fools.

I realized that I had segued in my train of thought. Originally, I was thinking back to when I moved to this town in the summer. My best friend, Marais DuBois, had come to visit me and we sat on my front porch drinking wine into the early hours of the morning. Around two a.m., we saw a police car pull over a small truck at the darkened gas station across the street. Immediately curious, we scurried over to some shrubbery at the front of the yard, hid behind it, and watched and listened as the officer spoke to the driver who was apparently under the influence.

Although we could not hear the driver's side of the conversation, we could deduce his responses from what the officer said. The police officer was not with the Hamilton County department, but from the local department of Red Bank, my small incorporated town. "So you are going straight home?" the officer asked the driver sternly. Apparently the driver assured him that he was. "If you don't go straight home, I'll shoot you," the officer told him. Apparently, this was a bargain the driver could live with. I realized that it was also one that I was willing to accept and I broke my vow of silence.

"One night, this summer, I witnessed one of the Red Bank police officers pulling a guy over and he was driving intoxicated," I explained. "The police officer let him go and just said that if he didn't go straight home, he'd shoot him. Why won't you let me do that? I just live two-hundred yards up the road. I can even see my house from here."

"I'm not with the Red Bank police department," he responded nonchalantly as he continued to write information down on his small clipboard. "I'm with the county."

4

"Oh," I said, my attempt at a legal argument stymied.

"Would you like to go ahead and take the breathalyzer?" he asked me again. This was the third time he had offered. And this would also be the third time that I would refuse. "It's really better for you if you go ahead and take the breathalyzer," he explained.

I knew that the laws had changed since the good 'ol days of high school when you could refuse the breathalyzer and hire a slick lawyer to get you out of trouble because the police had no "proof" that you were actually drunk. But I knew that I was drunk. I just didn't know on a scale of 0.0 to 4.0 how drunk I was. So why establish it for a court of law? Wouldn't that just make it worse for me?

The officer placed the clipboard down on the front seat beside him and started the ignition. I felt my stomach sinking. This was really happening. I had really believed that, somehow, I was going to get out of this situation without getting arrested for real. How did the daughters of politicians handle this? Oh yeah . . . the answer was in the question. How did the heiresses handle this? Oh yeah . . . they had hundreds of millions of dollars thereby making them exempt, not from the laws of the land, but from the punishments of the land. So then, how did middle-class girls like me handle this? Oh yeah . . . we went to jail.

As the police officer turned the car onto the road that led to the jail which was only a few blocks away from where I worked, reality began to sink in. I really was going to jail. I was going to have a mug shot and get fingerprinted. I was going to be locked in a cell and have to do forty-eight hours. And I wasn't going to the local armory where I could sleep on a cot in an old gymnasium and alternate between playing *Chinese Checkers* and *Old Maid* with my fellow drunks while we served our time. I was going to have to tell my mom.

My bottom lip began to tremble and a tear rolled down my cheek. I was presently living my worst nightmare; the worst nightmare that was within my control, that is. Being tortured and murdered were by far worse nightmares, but getting a DUI or not getting a DUI was under my control. And also unlike my good 'ol high school days, MADD had made it impossible for redemption, at least in this world. Once you got a DUI, it stayed on your record forever, *until death do you part*. If you were a lawyer or a doctor, it was

5

no big deal to have a DUI or two. But if you were someone like me who still found employment by filling out a generic application and *maybe* occasionally including a résumé, it was humiliating because there was that disconcerting line on the form: *Have you ever been convicted of a crime other than a minor traffic offense? If yes, please explain.*

Another tear slid down my cheek. *Please explain what?* was what I wanted to know. *Why I was dating The Loser?* I had no legitimate excuse. *Because I felt as if I were stuck,* was the only answer I could deduce. I had not made many close friends in just the short time I had been here—well, no one close enough to call in the middle of the night to bail me out of jail. I really had no one else to turn to except The Loser when I needed help or just needed help getting arrested.

We drew closer to the jail and the cuffs felt tighter and tighter around my wrists. I could feel them cutting into my skin. As uncomfortable as my arms were as they remained secured behind my back, what was more disconcerting was that my plastic skirt was inching its way up around my waist and obviously I had no way of remedying the situation. In this cop's eyes, I'm sure that I had already shown my ass, but I sure as hell didn't want to show him my thong underwear.

By the time we pulled into the parking area that was right in front of the Intake door, I was crying and could not even wipe away my tears. The police officer opened the back door and in between sniffles I told him, "I need help pulling down my skirt." He called for a female officer and she stepped over and kindly helped me pull my skirt down and gently helped me out of the backseat. At this moment, I was appreciative of her kindness. "Thank you for being so nice," I told her as I sniffled.

However, once we entered and went to the table in the center of the room where I was surrounded by police officers and other criminals sitting on benches, my attitude began to change for the worse. I was scared and when I got scared, I got angry. However, the police officers did not know of my attitude adjustment and had generously un-cuffed me due to my recent good manners and perceived humility.

"I'm going to give you one last chance to take the breathalyzer," my arresting officer told me. "Will you take the breathalyzer?" he asked sternly.

"I want to make a phone call," I said firmly. And thus began the show-down between me and the po-po.

"Will you take the breathalyzer?" he asked again. I could tell his patience was waning, but I wasn't easily intimidated by authority figures.

"I want to make a phone call."

"Will you take the breathalyzer?" he yelled.

"I want to make a phone call. I am entitled to make a phone call!" I shouted back, letting all in the holding cell know that I was fully aware of my legal rights as a citizen of the United States of America. And in a fatal move of obnoxiousness, I pulled my cell phone out of my purse and began pressing buttons.

"Put the phone down!" my arresting officer instructed me.

I continued to reiterate my right to make a phone call and stubbornly refused to release the cell phone. As a result, the kindly female officer of a moment ago twisted my other arm up behind my back to the point where it felt as if she were going to break it.

"Go ahead, break my arm. That's what I want you to do," I encouraged her as I antagonistically continued scrolling through my phone book, knowing that I was not actually going to press the *Send* button because I knew I would really be in the shithouse if I did. My reverse psychology worked and she let my arm go. Another officer grabbed my phone and then pushed me into the unisex bathroom off of the holding cell and locked me in. Right before the door slammed shut behind me, I heard my arresting officer yell, "Bitch!"

At first, I paced back and forth in front of the toilet filled with righteous indignation (me, not the toilet), but then I got a brilliant idea that I had learned from one of those forensic crime shows. This girl who had been abducted and taken to her abductor's trailer had pressed her fingerprints all over the bathroom, even behind the toilet, to prove that this man was the one responsible for kidnapping her. I thought it would be a good idea for me to press my fingertips all around the bathroom walls to prove that I too had been locked into the bathroom for an indefinite amount of time, practically kidnapped and falsely imprisoned by the local police.

I went from cement block to cement block pressing my fingertips onto the wall. However, as I began to sober up, I realized that it only took seconds, maybe minutes, for me to leave fingerprints all over the bathroom, proving nothing about the length of time that

I was locked in it, just that I had been there. With that awareness and with the realization that the police had probably been watching me on video the whole time and thought that I was a total nutcase, I began to get depressed.

Finally, I sat down on the floor and resigned myself to wait. After what seemed like hours, the bathroom door was unlocked and I was finally released from my solitary confinement. The female police officer was no longer kind to me. She grabbed me around my bicep and clinched my arm in a tight grip. Then she shoved me onto a bench and hand-cuffed my right hand to it. I held my face in my left hand until I felt another body sit down beside me. I looked up to see a twenty-something guy with a black eye and a smirk as he saw me hand-cuffed to the bench.

"What're you in for?" he asked.

"DUI," I told him. "You?"

"Aggravated assault," he said. I noticed that his arms were folded comfortably across his chest. *Aggravated assault and he wasn't even hand-cuffed?* I glanced around the room at all my other fellow criminals. No one else was hand-cuffed to the bench except me. *I fought the law and the law won.* A second wave of depression swept over me. *And now I'm hand-cuffed for being a bitch. Who's the loser now?*

2

I had always believed in God. However, I had not had much faith in organized religion. My lack of faith in church communities began from the time that my family joined an incredibly snotty, cliquey, hypocritical church after we had moved to Tennessee. As you can probably guess, a nice, accommodating Girl Superhero in the form of an Appeaser and a Boy Personified Natural Disaster do not mix well with self-centered, pompous assholes who can smell *weakness*, at least *weakness* in the eyes of the world, and want to kill it dead just for sport. Or maybe not kill it dead because this was church for Chrissakes. They just preferred to alienate, belittle, and torment those perceived to be weaker in order to appear even more powerful and domineering.

I remembered one time in high school when my mom and I were cleaning out a cabinet we discovered a church bulletin from when we had lived in North Carolina in the 1970s. The bulletin told of an outdoor service where members could dress casually and *Morning Has Broken* would be sung by the congregation as it was strummed on an acoustic guitar. I had smiled at such a pleasant thought. Why couldn't churches now be more like that? I would love to sit outside in the grass, feel part of a loving community, sing folk songs, and ride the peace train.

Instead, the Sunday mornings of my childhood involved Academy Award-winning performances where I starred as an opossum, pretending to be asleep no matter what my parents did to wake me, in order not to have to go to Sunday school and church. The boys and girls that we had Sunday school class with all lived in a different part of town than we did; had more money than we did, or at least dressed and acted like it; and they all went to school together. Matthieu and I were outsiders.

Matthieu was luckier than I, though, because anywhere he went he was a force to be reckoned with, be it a forest fire, a tsunami,

9

or an earthquake. People may have been irritated by him, but he was all in their faces whether he wanted to be or not and whether they liked it or not. I, on the other hand, had been trained to *go with the flow* and instructed, *don't rock the boat*. If I ever became angry or resented my brother's outbursts and disruptions to the family, I was denied the ability to express my raw emotions. "No, no." I would be chastised. "Don't upset your brother further. It's just going to make things worse." Don't upset my brother? I'm just going to make things worse by being allowed to express myself instead of being forced to repress myself?

So the role of suppressor and appeaser I had become. When the Sunday school girls were hateful and mean to me, I just smiled and tried to be their friends. When they smirked and looked down at me for the hand-me-down clothes that my mother insisted on receiving from an older neighbor whose fashion sense *sucked*, something I knew even as an eight year-old, I was confused as to why they were being so unkind to me. I was nice to them. Why weren't they nice to me?

"Your brother is such a weirdo!" one girl snarled at me during a discussion of *love thy neighbor as thyself*. I was stunned by her rudeness, although I would quickly learn that these kind of comments would barrage me on a daily basis, often times many times a day from different classmates and "friends." I was unsure of how to handle a situation such as this one because both of my parents were Turn the Other Cheek-ers. Or were they Trained Defenseless Victims? Either way, my brother and I learned how to be successfully victimized and tormented by mean people. Instead of defending ourselves, we would take our lumps, eventually believing their hurtful words to be true, and descend into a Zen-like state where we became one with Charlie Brown.

"Vandelyn Devanlay?" An officer spoke from above my head, interrupting my thoughts. I looked up and saw one of the police officers who previously had been stationed behind the desk instructing me on what fun thing we were going to do next. "It's time for your photo." I sighed as he bent over and unlocked the cuff that was attached to one of the slats in the bench. He also unlocked the other handcuff and let my arms go free. As he led me over to the mug shot station, he stopped me in front of a high-tech machine. His eyes lingered on the letters in my name as he looked at my paperwork.

"Hm," he said. "All the letters in your first name are the same as in your last name except one. Ever notice that?" he asked. I cringed internally as I also waited for him to notice that my initials were *V.D.* He didn't.

"Yes, sir. My parents are word jumble enthusiasts." My sarcastically deadpan comment just slipped out as it always slipped out. Unfortunately, this wasn't the time for a sarcastic comment. *Please don't handcuff me and lock me in the bathroom*, I silently pleaded. Thankfully he chose to ignore me. He instructed me on where to stand and told me to look directly at the lens. In a matter of seconds my mug shot was taken by a computer and a copy would even be printed out and placed with my belongings as a souvenir from the evening.

As he led me back to the holding tank, another officer approached me with an orange jumpsuit. Since this was just merely "jail" until you called a bondsman to bail you out and a friend to pick you up, no one was required to wear a jumpsuit. I looked at it as the officer extended it towards me.

"This is an all-male jail," he explained. "We have no cells for women. Due to the way you are dressed, you might feel more comfortable putting this on over your clothes."

"Thank you," I said as I accepted the jumpsuit. I was allowed to step back into the bathroom and zip it up over my clothes. I felt appreciative of the jumpsuit, but I was surprised by the concept of an all-male jail, not that I was disappointed to have to remain up front in one of three holding cells in the main lock-up area. But this was the only jail in the city. Did only men commit crime in this town?

When I exited from the bathroom, I was led to one of the aforementioned holding cells and was escorted into a jail cell that had the cell door propped open. A few other young women were surrounded by bars with me. I guessed that most of them were in for the same reason that I was: DUI. Of course, they probably thought that I had been arrested for prostitution.

I was tired, unhappy, and bored. All I wanted to do was sleep some of those emotions away. So I lay down on the hard bench and did my best to slumber. Instead of counting sheep jumping a fence one-by-one, my thoughts tumbled topsy-turvy in my mind like clothes in a dryer.

One particular thought came to prominence: how had my life ended up here? I focused on it and it faded away into an inky darkness; disappearing like the predetermined answer on the triangle in a *Lucky 8 Ball*. Since I had no predetermined answer, my mind wandered in order to find one. Its starting point the logical place: birth.

3

All babies are miracles. And all parents should look at their newly born offspring as miracles. Thankfully, most of them do. I know my mother was one of those parents because I've seen the photos taken when my parents brought us home from the hospital. My father was holding the camera while my mother cradled me and Matthieu in her arms. I was swathed in a yellow afghan that she had crocheted in anticipation of my arrival. Matthieu was swathed in a store-bought blue blanket because my parents hadn't realized they were pregnant with twins. Sometimes when Matthieu was really angry, he'd blame all his problems on the fact that he'd come home from the hospital in a store-bought blanket while I'd come home in a lovingly crocheted blanket. (And just look at how well my life turned out.)

As my mother sat outside on the patio furniture with her babies gathered in her arms and the bright sunshine smiling down on all of us, I could see her loving, enamored, adoring gaze at my innocent cherubic self. I theorized that she was wondering what amazing gifts I would possess; what loving times we would share; her great hopes of a wonderful life for me filled with happiness, joy, and success. Maybe she was even speculating about what great firsts I would achieve. I'm sure that she did not imagine that I would be the first in my family to get arrested for DUI which was no minor feat since one branch of the French side of my dad's family were alcoholics who also possessed valid driver's licenses and owned cars. Or at least they had licenses and cars before they all died from cirrhosis of the liver.

The one drunken twig on my mother's side of the family, my mom's great-uncle (who also happened to be a lawyer), George Washington McCurry, was known to ride through the center of town on horseback so inebriated that he'd fall off and hit the dirt road when he finally passed out. But of course he wasn't arrested for anything; the kind townspeople merely strapped him back in the

13

saddle as the horse trotted our family's own "George Dubya's" drunk ass back home.

But a DUI was not my only family first. I also was the first to be diagnosed with Human Papillomavirus (HPV) and not only was I diagnosed, I also carried one of the toughest strains of the virus. As in the hardest to defeat. Both by the age of thirty! Happy! Happy! Joy! Joy!

My first visit to the OB/GYN occurred when I was seventeen, almost eighteen, in a time when my vagina was so happy, healthy, and fresh that it could've starred in a Noxzema commercial. I had absolutely no desire to go to a gynecologist, but my mother was very vaginally conscientious and knew it was time for me to have an examination. I went to a male OB/GYN and was so nervous I could only inhale shallow breaths. Tu-Tu, the name I affectionately use to refer to my precious little pink tart, was even more nervous than I. She had only been exposed to my boyfriend, Kyle White, which had been happy times, and now I was going to have to expose her to a stranger. Not so happy times.

When my turn arrived, I was led back into the examination room. As I sat waiting on the table, my body folded into a shape that only Origami could design, my anxiety rose. The paper robe was wrapped tightly around me because my body was freezing cold despite the fact that my underarms were sweating. Finally the doctor entered. After much instruction and encouragement, I finally scooted down to the end of the table. However, I had worn my old school hiking boots that weighed about five pounds each. One false move by this M.D. and I was going to clang his head like a pair of cymbals.

Even though the procedure was not painful, just mildly uncomfortable and embarrassing, Tu-Tu's feelings were seriously getting hurt. What had she done to deserve this? I was also questioning why I had to expose my most vulnerable inner core to a complete stranger just because he had a couple of extra initials after his name. And not only that, my mom had to co-pay him. And the irony of it all was that if I told my mom that Kyle would've done this for free, she would've been pissed.

Then I realized how ridiculous my thought was about Kyle checking out Tu-Tu. I definitely wouldn't want him peering into her insides. He was a smart guy, but he was completely in the dark about the inner workings of the female genitalia. Kyle once asked me, "If

14

it's not that time of the month so you don't have a tampon in, but you go swimming in a pool, what prevents your vagina—" he said those last two words really fast— "from drinking up all the water?" I told him, "She's a *vagina*. Not a throat!" And another time when we were talking on the phone, he was doubtful about whether or not PMS was real. He thought it might be a made-up excuse. I responded, "Yes. You are right. It is totally made-up. Those nationwide ad campaigns for Midol exist just to see how gullible men really are." He never mentioned PMS again. Although those thoughts of Kyle were distracting me from my gynecological circumstances, they were not able to prevent my blood pressure from rising, my cheeks from flushing, and my resentment from building.

I seriously did not like being vulnerable and this was about as vulnerable as I had ever been in my life. The only thing keeping my back flat against the table and my boots in the stirrups was the female nurse standing behind the doctor, peering over his shoulder. I felt secure that she was watching his every move like a hawk.

And then suddenly the greatest indignity had occurred without warning. Just when I thought the procedure was over, just when I had begun to feel a sense of relief that I hoped would turn into a feeling of peace, he stuck his thumb up my ass. It probably wasn't really his thumb, but it felt short and fat like a thumb. Maybe he just had short fat fingers. Or maybe it was because my anus was not used to being violated and I merely had a tight little bum hole.

In any case, I didn't care how many medical degrees he had on his wall, it's still downright rude for him to stick one of his digits up into my sphincter without consulting me or at least warning me first. I imagined an etiquette class where I would teach OB/GYNs how to properly address their patients, preferably starting with, "Pardon me, but . . ." before performing this procedure. At the very least they could say, "Pardon me, butt."

Finally, he told me I could push back against the stirrups and sit up. He didn't have to tell me twice. I scooted back and realized how lucky the doctor had been. If I hadn't been so stunned, he would've received an uppercut to the jaw from my hiking boot.

As I was securing my paper robe around my body, he asked if I were on birth control. My cheeks colored. When would this embarrassment end? I shook my head no. He went on to say that if I chose to get on birth control, I could do so without my parents' knowledge. It would be my choice. I told him, "OK. Thanks." and he and the nurse left the exam room.

I ripped the robe from my body, shoved it in the garbage can and quickly donned my bra and panties. As I pulled on my jeans and shirt, I thought about his proposal. Although I appreciated the information, I really thought he was unrealistic. What did he mean my parents wouldn't have to know? I was living off an allowance. I had no idea how much birth control cost, but I was pretty sure it would cost most of my allowance. My mother gave me an allowance to help me learn how to manage my money. So what was I going to do when I asked her for ten dollars so I could go to the movies? She'd say, "What happened to your allowance?" And then I'd say, "Oh. I spent it on my monthly prescription of birth control pills." That would not go over well.

After I finished dressing, I left the room, grabbed my examination receipt from the plastic container attached to front of the door, and met my mom at the payment counter. As she pulled out her insurance card and check book, I had to wonder: did she really believe that I was still as innocent as the day I was born?

4

If you are ever trying to slumber, I don't recommend attempting that feat on a jail cell bench because it's not going to happen unless you are dead tired. I was dead tired so I did manage to sleep for what felt like forty-five minutes; however, once dead tired wore off, discomfort took over and rendered me wide-awake.

I sat up from the bench, wishing that I were home in bed, and realized that I really needed to start calling bail bondsmen to spring me from this joint. Since I and the other females were in the holding cells up front, our cell doors remained opened and we could pass freely through the doorway and walk up to the counter.

The officer behind the desk watched my approach with appraising eyes; his eyes weren't appraising me, but rather seemed to be appraising what I might do. I guessed he had observed the show-down hours ago and was preparing himself for my attitude.

"I need to call a bail bondsman," I said. "How can I go about doing that?" I was exhausted and deflated of any ego. I just wanted out.

"The list of bonding companies is hanging on the wall over there just above the phone. You can just dial 9 and then the number. It's a free call."

Something helpful in jail was *free*? *Really free*? Or would my phone calls just be added to my court costs as if I were staying at a hotel with itemized charges added to my bill? I walked over to the phone and looked up at the list of companies and their phone numbers. I was still so new in town that I had no knowledge of which bonding companies were better than the others. I picked one in the middle of the list and dialed.

A man answered by announcing the name of the bonding company. "Hi," I said. "I need to get bailed out of jail." He took my information and told me he'd get working on it. "When will someone be down here to get me out?" I asked. He assured me it would be no longer than an hour. I was thankful. Now all I could do was wait.

And wait was what I did. When an hour was up, I returned to the phone and redialed the number. The same guy answered the phone. "It's been an hour," I reported. "Is someone on the way?"

"Someone will be there in thirty minutes," he told me. For some reason I believed him. When thirty minutes passed and my name was not called to be released, I returned to the phone. The same guy answered. "We're still working on it." This conversation was starting to sound like my last dysfunctional relationship with The Big Dick.

He actually has a real name, but when he and I first started our flirtation, Marais and I had nicknamed him The Big Dick, or TBD for short, because his dick's reputation had preceded him. *TBD* then turned into the pseudonym, *Thibodeaux*, because TBD began to sound like *Thi-bo-deaux* to our ears. It was also more fun for us to call him that.

Anyway, after four years of on-and-off "dating" (if I could even be so bold as to classify our relationship under that term), I learned that Thibodeaux couldn't keep his word even if it were clipped to his sleeve like a mitten. Therefore, any promises Thibodeaux vowed to me were consistently left unfulfilled and all that remained was a metaphorical shoebox overflowing with I.O.U.'s. Somehow this bondsman was just the same. He kept promising results and in the end I was left at the curb waiting on a ride that would never show. So I did to that bail bondsman what I did to Thibodeaux. I quit calling him and decided that if he actually did follow-through on one of his "promises" he would be left waiting at the curb looking for me.

I dialed another company. A different man answered, of course, but he made the same promise. "Look," I said cutting through the potential B.S. "I've already waited for a couple of hours for a bondsman who kept telling me that someone would arrive soon and it still hasn't happened. If you're going to do the same thing to me, would you please go ahead and tell me so I can call someone else?"

"I really will be there within an hour," he assured me. "Probably the other company was hesitant to bail you because you've only lived in this town for a few months. They probably see you as a risk. But our company doesn't see you as a risk."

"Well then why didn't he just tell me that?" I complained although this man would have no way of knowing the answer.

"I don't know," he replied. We hung up our respective phones and I walked over to the desk and asked if I could borrow a phone book. The desk sergeant handed one over to me and I walked back over to the phone. I didn't have Tod's, formerly referred to as The Loser, cell phone number memorized because I always just speed-dialed it from my cell phone directory. I didn't know his home phone number because I rarely ever called him at home and it too was on my speed dial.

As I ran my finger down the column of last names, I prayed that it would be listed in his name and not his roommate's because I did not know his roommate's last name. I was relieved to see Tod's name followed by his phone number printed on the page. I dialed. It rang and rang until the machine picked up. *Crap!* I hung up and dialed again, hoping for a different result. None came. I shoved the phone back onto its hook, returned the phone book to the desk, and memorized the seven digits. I'd try back in a few minutes.

I dialed and redialed Tod's number at fifteen minute intervals only to hear his answering machine telling me to leave a message. My irritation was increasing like a balloon attached to the nozzle of an unsupervised helium container. Just as it was about ready to pop from the pressure, my presence was requested at the counter and my frustration deflated. I smiled. My bail bondsman had arrived and in a finite amount of time I would be out of here. It wasn't quite the magic of Cinderella anticipating the meeting between herself and Prince Charming, but it was as close as I was going to get on this particular Sunday morning.

As I waited, I contemplated my situation with Tod. Tod Savoy was a guy that I met through a female client, Taylor Kazakov, who came into our salon. Taylor and Tod had gone to high school together for one year in a very small town about an hour away called Bean Field. Bean Field is located just a few miles away from Dayton, the town that hosted the Scopes Monkey Trial in the 1920s and inspired the movie, *Inherit the Wind.*

At that time, the people of Bean Field, fearful of new ideas and jealous of Dayton's notoriety, were appalled by the notion that humans' acceptance of evolution was evolving. As a result, the town decided to host its own trial against evolution (no persons were actually tried, only the concept) which became known as the Monkey-See-Monkey-Do Trial. I never heard the actual details of that courtroom drama, but I envisioned a courtroom with a papier-mâché gorilla dangling over the heads of Southern Baptists wielding sticks and yelling, "Piñata! Piñata!"

Taylor had revealed this little known fact to those of us at the salon also adding that the Bean Field trial was the reason her grandfather hadn't been accepted into Harvard. I mean, had he even had a chance? What were the odds that both Grandpa could go to Harvard *and* Uncle Jed could find black gold while shootin' for some food? When she saw our befuddled faces, she went on to explain that for a number of years after the Scopes Trial, Harvard would not accept any applicants, no matter how intelligent and qualified, from Dayton or Bean Field.

I discreetly raised a dubious eyebrow at Taylor as I mulled over this being the reason her grandfather had not become an Ivy Leaguer. It sounded more like a convenient save-face excuse to me. Kind of like in the 1980s when my high school choir had the opportunity to sing in Europe and many parents declined sending their children, citing "Terrorism." (In those days, terrorists were hijacking planes, but letting the passengers live.) However, most of us suspected that it was a convenient save-face rather than having to explain that they didn't want to spend a couple grand for the trip.

Taylor was three years older than Tod who was thirty-seven, making her forty. When I first met Taylor, she was very outgoing, loud, and she had chatted at me, which I suspected was her way of befriending me. She had not left a good impression. While Donna foil-highlighted Taylor's hair, Taylor babbled endlessly about her career as the vice-president of "Big Cig" which was of one of the three insurance companies in town, her second ex-husband, and her daughter before moving onto chatter about her present husband, Martin Kazakov. "He's not an architect," she admitted to someone or no one at all.

Puzzled, I had asked, "Was he *supposed* to be an architect?"

She answered, "His family gives him a hard time about it. Apparently he had natural ability for it, but chose not to pursue it. He is descended from Matvey Kazakov, the famous Russian architect who designed a couple of royal palaces."

20

I made sure to yawn and stretch after this gratuitous comment. She reeked of "I am oh-so very important and my life is oh-so dramatic." And how could I forget this part: "And I make a fat salary which makes me oh-so rich." I assessed her to be a small-town girl with something to prove. My suspicions were confirmed when I discovered she had been divorced twice and married three times by the age of thirty-four. It struck me as ironic too because Taylor had been insinuating into the conversation what a strong female she was; how ambitious and dominating she was in a "man's world." If that were really the case, why was she flagging down the Man Bus after every divorce and leaving her previous marital vows and marriage licenses at the curb as if they were unclaimed baggage?

To Tod's credit, he moved from Toronto, Canada to Bean Field when he was fourteen years-old and only stayed a year before returning to Canada to live with his mother. His father is a medical doctor, a GP, but when he was in Canada, he had been an OB/GYN. Apparently he couldn't specialize in the United States without taking more medical courses since the standards between the two countries were different. So he just decided to be a General Practitioner instead.

When I first learned this information regarding Tod's father, it immediately reminded me of a story I had heard on *Unsolved Mysteries*. Only a year or two before, I had seen an episode of *Unsolved Mysteries* searching for a Canadian OB/GYN who was wanted for a rape charge. It was thought that the offending physician had moved to a small town in the United States; somewhere where he was under the radar.

I jumped to the logical conclusion that Dr. Savoy was a likely suspect since Bean Field was quite a Podunk little town. Besides, why else would somebody move not only from one country to another, but from a large cultural city to a small sheltered town known for its exploding crystal meth trailers, teen pregnancy, and citizens who felt compelled to post the Ten Commandments signs in every other front yard because their love for religious legalism was greater than their love for the kinder, gentler Jesus?

Of course I hadn't mentioned this suspicion to Tod or anyone else for that matter, nor had I even visited Bean Filed to confirm any of my presumptions or to meet his father and scope him out to determine his propensity for criminal behavior. (Although one

Sunday when Tod and I were taking a scenic drive, I did *attempt* to go to Bean Field. When we entered the county and saw a homemade billboard with the words, "Go to church or you're going to Hell!", I pointed at the sign and told Tod, "No way am I going into this land of dueling banjos!" and I made him turn the car around.)

"Vandelyn Devanlay? Please come with me," an officer instructed me. I knew I was on my way to freedom.

My first act of liberation was to be allowed to remove my orange jumpsuit. I stood in the center of the jail happily wearing my scantily-clad outfit and followed the officer through a door that led me into a corridor. He deposited me in front of another counter manned by a couple of police officers. I was handed two paper sacks: one with my fake fur coat in it and the other with my purse and paperwork from my arrest. I pulled out the coat and put it on as the officers told me to continue down the hall, out the glass door, and figuratively into the arms of my bondsman. I couldn't help but smile.

As I walked towards freedom, I opened up the other bag and saw my mug shot staring up at me from a sheet of 8.5 x 11 paper. I was so impressed that I paused in the corridor. My photo looked hot. Feeling "hot" hadn't been easy for me to feel these last few months because I hadn't been able to work-out like I used to and was now sporting love handles rather than the concave stomach and tight abs I once had.

My police photographer had captured a sly expression on my face rather than one of total despair, grumpiness, or irritation as were the looks of so many mug shots. I looked a mix of mysteriousness and mischievousness. Why couldn't the DMV do excellent work like this instead of their usual trademark photography of making relatively attractive people look like a warning against inbreeding?

I shoved the paperwork that included my court date as well as the photo shot back into the bag and pulled out my purse. I immediately removed my cell phone, noticed that it had been turned off, and pressed the power button. After a few seconds, the screen revealed that I had five new voice mail messages. My stomach lurched with a mixture of relief and dread. At least Tod had been concerned enough to call. (I doubt if Thibodeaux would've bothered after a fight. He would've just put the blame on me and slept through the night with a clear conscience.) But what were his messages going to tell me?

Although I wasn't completely happy with Tod, I really didn't want to be part of yet another "We have to talk" conversation. Why not just cut to the chase and say, "I'm breaking up with you." I tossed the phone back into my purse and continued down the hallway and out the glass door.

The cold November air greeted me and I wrapped my fake fur tighter around me because walking out of a police station in a short plastic skirt, revealing top, and high-heeled, knee-high, black leather boots on a Sunday morning (was it even still morning?) screamed hooker. Then again, a newly-released female inmate wearing a fake fur coat on a Sunday morning screamed hooker too.

"Ms. Devanlay?" a voice spoke to me from my left. I turned towards it and saw a light-skinned black man standing a few feet away. "I'm Alvin, your bondsman."

"Hi," I greeted him with a smile. "Thank you so much for getting me out of there so promptly. I am so ready to go home."

He gave me a soft smile and said, "No problem." Then we got down to business. We quickly went over my paperwork which included showing me my court date and telling me what would happen if I didn't show up for my court date.

"Oh I'll be there!" I promised him. No way in hell was I going back to jail or racking up more criminal charges. Although he gave me a small smile, he had an expression in his eyes that seemed to say he'd heard that one before. I guess criminals weren't known for their strength of character or for keeping their word. (Funny, isn't it, that Thibodeaux didn't have a record, but I now did? He so fit the profile.)

Alvin then asked me for my credit card. He made an imprint of it and charged $500 against it, which really sucked. I had money to pay off the bill in my savings account, but using it to pay off my bond wasn't exactly what I had in mind. Alvin assured me that once I did appear in court and the case was finished, my card would be credited back the $500. That helped ease my anxiety a little, but a $500 credit on a Master Card was less valuable to me than $500 cash.

"Do you need a ride home?" he asked.

"Yes," I sighed, feeling a bit deflated. Freedom was not free, as my first few minutes from jail revealed to me. Then I remembered something from my paperwork: my car was impounded and I recognized the towing company. It was just across the river from the jail and was on the way home. Having been towed before, I knew that I needed to retrieve my car ASAP. "Actually, do you mind taking me to the impound lot so I can get my car? It's just right across the Market Street Bridge on Cherokee Boulevard before you get to the tunnel."

"No problem," he said as he led me towards his car parked at the curb.

The drive to Cherokee Boulevard was only a few minutes. Alvin and I chatted about pleasant small talk during the brief ride. I thanked him for dropping me off as he idled in the parking lot of the towing company.

I shut the door and glanced over at the locked gate of the twelve-foot chain-link fence topped with barbed wire. I quickly spotted my 1998 Lexus ES300 imprisoned behind it. I sighed as I pulled open the glass door and grudgingly entered the facility. Once again, I pulled out my credit card, charged the $80 impound fee to it and stepped outside to wait for the man to unlock the gate.

Once he had swung the gate open, I hurried down the gravel drive, unlocked the front door, and slipped my key into the ignition. As I cranked the engine, I felt a little less anxious than I had in the past twelve hours. At least I was free, driving my own car, and on my way home. However, my ear drums about exploded because I had been playing my music so loudly during my pissed off drive home the night before. Marilyn Manson's, *The Fight Song*, blared from the speakers.

I quickly turned the volume down to an acceptable level and quietly drove my car out of the impound lot. I glanced at the clock on the dash. It was two o'clock in the afternoon. I shook my head in disgust at how long I had stayed in jail. The only thing that made me feel better was the fact that my twelve hours would be included in my forty-eight hours as "time served." If twelve hours had felt like an eternity, I couldn't imagine how thirty-six were going to feel.

5

As I drove through the tunnel and headed down Dayton Boulevard towards my house, I thought about food first and the rest of my life, second. They actually had fed me in jail. A male inmate dressed in an orange jumpsuit that matched mine had brought me a tray with lunch. Instead of eating any of it, I merely scooted the food around on the plate with my fork like a sulking child. I didn't want any of their jail food and at the same time it made me sad to reject it.

For some reason, I kept thinking about the faceless persons who had prepared it. I thought about the young man who had kindly brought it to me, even though he was just doing his inmate duty. And I couldn't help but be a little surprised at the dessert that was included: a Mayfield Dairy Ice Cream Sandwich. I loved ice cream sandwiches and was impressed that the jail actually offered such a treat, especially impressed that it was a "name-brand" treat and not some generic imitation. For some reason, though, I still couldn't bring myself to eat it. I just stared at it as it grew softer and softer, becoming mushier as it lost its cool and heated up to room temperature.

When the same inmate came back by to pick up our lunch trays, I told him thank you and felt slightly depressed as I had watched my plate of uneaten food disappear through a door with a stack of other lunch trays. Maybe the warden had lobbied hard to get his inmates such a nice treat and here I was snubbing it as some passive-aggressive form of protest. I tried to make myself feel better by thinking that maybe it still could have worked out for good. Maybe some other inmate got my ice cream sandwich as a second treat instead of it just going straight into the garbage.

As I drew within a mile of my house, I passed the familiar places: the Sav-A-Lot grocery store, the Dollar Store, the local little food joints, and all the churches. It was crazy the number of churches of differing denominations on this road within walking distance of my house: Presbyterian; Baptist; Methodist; Church of Christ; and even a Chinese church. The only major ones missing were the Catholic and Episcopal churches, but they were only a short drive and one road away. (And the Mormon church? I'm sure there was one in town, but only God knew where.)

As I passed the differing brick houses of worship, I felt something drawing me towards them, even towards the Baptists which I thought were by far the scariest of all the main-stream denominations. (I didn't know enough about the Church of Christ to be afraid of it, although I suspected that I would be.) When I was in high school, the Baptists had been the ones in my hometown protesting outside a movie theatre showing *The Last Temptation of Christ*. Kyle and I had stopped by to speak to the protesters and find out their position. Well, Kyle had stopped to listen to them and see what they were saying. I had stopped to argue.

As we spoke to one freaky member who merely kept quoting scripture instead of giving any personal insight into his beliefs, Kyle grew weary and bored. I grew more hostile and sneering. Who cared if Christ had a lustful thought when he was on the cross? What did it matter? The whole message of the protesters could have been summed up in one sentence, "You're going to Hell if you see this movie." Really? As long as no Baptists will be there, sign me up! But I was pretty sure that the road to Hell was paved by Baptists.

It was pretty much at that moment that Kyle put his arm around my shoulders and drew me close into his chest. "Come on, Vandalism," he said, "let's go." I loved it when he called me by my nickname. Since our private high school did not use superlatives because we were all supposed to be equal, Kyle had created one for me inspired by my personality: The One Most Likely to Commit a Felony Based on Principle. So he had played with the pronunciation of my name and called me Vandalism (even though it was only a misdemeanor) whenever I bulldozed my way into a situation that seemed like it might need police intervention. Eventually.

Remembering hateful Christians was like a protective force field for me and the Baptist Church seemed to wither before my eyes. The remaining churches kept some of their appeal; I could appreciate their attractive facades, but could not imagine myself behind their closed doors. Although my family and I had found a more pleasant church to attend years after those miserable first church experiences, I had attempted church once as an adult to see how it felt. I had wanted to feel uplifted and warm and fuzzy on the inside when I left, but all I felt was empty and untouched. I couldn't tolerate the idea of giving church another try. Dressing up in my Sunday Best? Hated it. Wearing panty-hose? Hell no! Invited to Bible-study with sweet young mothers and wives who acted like docile little does? Barfalicious.

Although I was not a fan of organized religion, I still had a glimmer of hope about God. I never read the Bible, couldn't quote one scripture that didn't involve one of the Ten Commandments, but I knew that Jesus had liked social outcasts and misfits like me. He had even been good friends with an ex-prostitute. I figured that some of the male parishioners (most likely the married ones) wouldn't mind hanging out with a real prostitute for half-an-hour and at a loss of twenty dollars for a lightning round of fellatio, but be caught dead with an ex-prostitute as a member of the church congregation? How dirty!

For the record, I don't believe in whores. I think somebody's sex life should be his or her own business. Besides, I had noticed way too often the double-standard between men and women, but then again, who hasn't? I was even more disgusted by the double-standard between women. I remembered when I was in a sorority, some of our upstanding church-going sisters would politely state about certain rushees, "She's not well respected." And then we'd all know she was some free-wheeling high school slut now recognizable by her name and face. The understood ruling? We are better than she is. Stay away from her and do not let her near your date.

Another time during a date rape awareness program involving my sorority and a fraternity, we watched a video where a drunk girl and guy were dancing at a frat party and making out on the dance floor. One of my beautiful, popular, non-virgin, alcohol-imbibing, high-society sisters from some very old money spoke out in that loud, clear, resonating voice of hers that carried across the large room: "What's she doing kissing him on the dance floor?" Then she laughed. I figured that she laughed because she knew she'd kiss a guy on the dance floor if she wanted to and never be held to the same "low class" standard she was attributing to the girl in the video.

27

That was the first time I truly understood that whores who only thought *other girls* were whores went around calling whores, "whores." (Except, of course, for the male whores. To be called a male whore, a guy had to sleep with *everybody*. As in, become The Equal Opportunity Whore who believes, "It's all pink on the inside," sleeping with many women of all races, shapes, sizes, and ages and at least flirt with a boy if not "experiment" with one. However, the aforementioned alleged "male whore" at the party last night might be the exception to this rule. He seemed like a guy who would've been lucky to sleep with up to two women in his entire lifetime.)

Of course, to be called a female whore the process was much simpler. You merely had to hook-up with a couple of guys (and you didn't even have to go all the way), be a girl people loved to trash talk, and let the rumor mill do its work. Hence the whores-whores-"whores" dynamic.

I pulled into my driveway and did not bother putting the car into the garage. I hurried across the patio to the kitchen door and unlocked it. My kitty cat, Mack, was there to greet me with his persistent and adorable, *Mew! Mew! Mew!* I picked him up and held him close while kissing his sweet little two-year-old face. He purred in response.

Mack was a stray that Thibodeaux and I had found outside his apartment complex. Thibodeaux had actually discovered him one morning when he had stepped outside to take his dog to pee and poop. I was still lying naked in bed. "There is this little kitten outside who is meowing like crazy," he told me. "It's really cute." I was intrigued. I got dressed and Thibodeaux and I went back outside to check out the kitty.

Sure enough, an adorable orange-and-white tabby had his head poked through a space between banisters in the stairwell and was staring down at us mewing his little heart out. His mews seemed to be saying, "I need a home. I need love. I need food. Please pick me up." My heart ached for the little kitty and my heart had never ached for anything except my masochistic relationship with Thibodeaux.

Thibodeaux raced up the stairs and picked up the kitty. After he sat him down on the sidewalk outside of the apartment door, Thibodeaux hurried inside and brought out a few pieces of Carl Buddig ham. He dropped a thin slice onto the concrete while I

28

petted the kitty. The kitty just looked at the ham. Thibodeaux picked the ham off the hot sidewalk, cracked the door open, and a black muzzle appeared. He tossed the slice of meat through the crack above the doorknob, the dog nose went up, and the door slammed shut. Thibodeaux attempted to feed the cat a few more times, but the cat didn't want the ham. The ham then disappeared into the open crack of the door and was never seen again.

While I was loving on the kitty, my heart was aching, and my fear for the kitty's future grew. Thibodeaux and I lived in two different apartment complexes that were within a short walking distance from each other. Some young families and college students lived in our buildings along with a few older retirees. Just down the street from our apartments were lower income housing and a high school. I was afraid that this sweet little pussy cat might meet up with a cruel individual.

The thought of this stray kitty looking for a safe home and instead ending up with an abuser frightened me and sickened my stomach. "I'm going to take him home. I'm going to adopt him," I said. My decision made me feel good and worried at the same time. What was I doing saying that I was going to take care of another living thing? It was enough just taking care of me. I'd have to buy cat food and litter and take him to the vet. How was I going to afford all that *and* my bar tab four nights a week?

"Really? You're going to adopt him?" Thibodeaux asked me eagerly. I could tell that he was impressed. I had done something to impress Thibodeaux? That made it even more worth my while.

"Yes," I said firmly, letting all my worries flutter into the deep recesses of my brain.

I picked up the kitty, put him in my car (which involved the kitty crawling under the foot pedals; then I put him in the back seat which involved him crawling into the front seat and once again under the foot pedals; then I put him in the hatchback of my Eagle Talon pleading with him to lie down and be still. When I finally backed out of the parking space, I saw the kitty cat's head poke up from the hatchback as he struggled to climb out, and I prayed that he would remain contained.), and immediately drove him to my mom and step-dad's house to see if they would like to add him to their collection of adopted stray kitties. They declined.

I hopped back into my car, this time with the kitty in a

borrowed cat carrier and took him to my apartment. I poured him a bowl of water and placed it on the kitchen floor. He lapped up water with his little pink tongue and then wandered out into the living room. As the cat cautiously explored my apartment, he was uncharacteristically quiet. This was so weird to me: A little being walking around my space. I patted his head and told him that I would be back in just a few minutes. I hopped back in the Talon, drove down the street to the grocery store and bought a cat pan, liners, litter, food, and two little plastic pet dishes. I hurried back to the apartment, met all of my kitty's needs, and tried to decide on his name.

When I was growing up, our dogs had names that were fitting for pets: Brownie, Socks, Lady, Toby, that kind of thing. I had always been amused by people who named their animals "people names" such as Bob and Susie—which is why when I entered college and met the first human being I'd ever known named Toby, I unintentionally stared at him in disbelief and accidentally blurted out, "Toby? But that's a dog's name!" However, at this time I was twenty-eight years old, single, and this kitty cat was my first ever pet in my adulthood. I named my orange-and-white tabby, "Liam."

The name Liam lasted on the kitty for about six hours; it took me that long to figure out that cats and "Liam" don't mix. I changed the name to one more suitable: Mack. The next day, I called the vet and scheduled an appointment. Although I knew it was the right thing to do—take Mack, have him examined and given the proper shots—I was a bit stressed when I received the bill. It was around $100. I could afford it, of course, because my job as a bartender was pretty lucrative. However, I couldn't help doing the math on how many Wild Turkey 101 and Sprites that would have bought me.

Mack was no longer interested in being squeezed tightly against my chest. His purring had ceased and he wiggled from my arms. I put him down on the linoleum kitchen floor and headed towards the dining room where my answering machine and telephone resided on a chair. I saw the button was blinking rapidly which meant I had multiple messages.

I was glad to see that Tod was concerned about me, but my index finger hovered over the flashing red button with some trepidation. Did I really want to hear what Tod had to say? As I had mentioned before, I was not happy with Tod. He was tolerable, but he did not bring me joy (and pain) as Thibodeaux had. Instead, he brought me occasional irritation coupled with general stability in the form of a traditional boyfriend.

At age thirty, totally confused on where I had made a wrong-turn when it came to guys and had followed the yellow brick road into the land of dysfunctional relationships, I decided that my judgment on guys was way out of whack. So instead of trusting myself, I trusted the traditional behaviors of my youth. A healthy boyfriend asked a girl out on a date. The old-fashioned date: dinner and a movie. He introduced her to his friends because he actually wanted her to meet his friends. And upon meeting Tod's friends, I wished that he had actually hidden them from me. They were the type of people that tested my gag reflex: Mainly young married (or singles desperate for marriage) "crustless white breads" (either by birth or by pretension and sometimes both) who believed in money, marriage, and monogamy (once you found your "soul mate" in grad school, law school, or business school, that is. All previous collegiate "shacking up" experiences were null and void). After about five years of marriage, they were humorless pieces of dry, stale toast whose conversational topics revolved around preschool selection, IRAs, 401Ks, and hefty mortgages in the "right" neighborhoods.

Unlike Tod, spending time with Thibodeaux was always fun and interesting. However, I couldn't help but notice that Thibodeaux was usually withholding from me in some way. He would never allow himself to get as close to me as I wanted him to get. That was part of the pain. Our relationship was dysfunctional for that reason and for others. Some of the other reasons were that we never behaved as a traditional boyfriend and girlfriend. Sure, we'd go out and do things together, but it was rarely like a typical date. I doubt that he referred to me as his girlfriend, even when we were only seeing each other.

Thibodeaux was a good Southern boy who was "raised right" in the sense that he gladly paid when we would go out on our unofficial dates unless I volunteered to pay, which I did now and again. But our relationship was founded on lust and had developed from that shaky foundation. We had grown closer over time and had a closeness that was held on loosely to but not often let go (unless one of us decided to, which both of us had done on-and-off over the years).

However, I knew that something was not right between us in our "relationship." I could look back on my high school relationship with Kyle and see that. To some, that might sound silly using a high school relationship as a guide, but not when it came to me and Kyle. We had never been in love, but we had really cared for and respected each other. Kyle was everything that was great to me in a guy: nice looking, smart, funny, smart ass, strong, secure, kind-hearted, fun, and protective of me. Simply put, Kyle was a well-rounded man of character even at the age of seventeen.

Thibodeaux was decidedly lacking in at least three of those attributes: secure, kind-hearted, and protective of me. Oh yeah, and generally lacking in character. I attribute his lack of character to being insecure. For example, if Thibodeaux and I were hanging out together and someone new came along, he would forget about me and try to impress and befriend the new person, be it male or female. I figure a secure person wouldn't care what some stranger thought. Nor would a secure person ditch his friend or girlfriend for the approval of some stranger. That was also part of the pain: being second best to anyone he barely knew.

Remembering Thibodeaux's flaws, I quickly pressed the button to hear what Tod, a guy who once valued me above others, had to say. The first message came in the middle of the night and he was irritated by my irresponsible departure, sternly telling me to call him when I got home. The second message was less severe and more worried. The third message told me that if I didn't call him in the next fifteen minutes he was going to come looking for me. The fourth message told me that he had recruited Taylor to drive him around and he was heading for my house. The fifth message was full of worry and concern because he was outside my house, I was not home, and hours had passed. The tension started to leave me as I heard him reaffirm his care for me. Maybe Tod was an OK guy and I was just messing things up because he seemed "normal." I wasn't used to "normal."

About a year ago, when Thibodeaux and I were on hiatus from each other, I went out on a few dates with a "normal," emotionally healthy guy. His parents were still married and still loved each other (how wacked was that?); he and his younger sister were very close (again, wacked); he was working on his Master's degree at the university; and he was even a Big Brother to a little boy in the Big

Brothers Big Sisters program. He would go hang out and play video games and spend time with his Little Brother at least one afternoon a week, if not more. He was an all-around happy guy who saw the world as a joyful place. I had absolutely no idea what to make of him. Until that one day when he came in after class and sat at my bar and revealed his fatal flaw. As he sat there conversing with me about innocuous topics, he casually asked me, "What's your cat's name again? Carl?" My eyes narrowed into slits and I backed away from him. Carl? Carl? *Carl?!* Nobody, and I mean *nobody*, calls my cat Carl and expects to have another date with me.

The answering machine finished and the tape rewound itself. I was just about to step back into the kitchen and open the refrigerator when the phone rang. I picked it up on the second ring. "Hello?" I casually asked.

"Vandelyn!" Tod's voice rushed through the phone. "Are you OK? Where have you been? I've been worried sick about you!"

"I've been in jail," I chirped with a smirk on my face. He gasped. I gave him the brief run-down as I pulled a Coke out of the fridge and took a swig. I also pulled out a slice of cheese and folded it into little squares. I popped one square in my mouth and then followed it with another as I finished my story.

"I thought something like that might've happened. I'm just glad you weren't killed." Me too. I was wasted last night when I was driving. Part of the road back to my house from Tod's apartment was winding and had a drop-off on one side that was only protected by a guardrail. It would have been so easy for me to die, wreck, get hurt, and kill or maim somebody else. I shuddered. "Would it be OK if I came over now? I think we need to talk."

Ugh. My stomach dropped. "If you are going to break up with me over this, just do it now." There. I'd said it. And I found myself hoping that he wasn't going to do just that.

"We just need to talk, Vandelyn. That's all." He sounded serious again.

I sighed. "OK. Can you be over here in about thirty minutes? I need to take a shower."

"I'll see you then," he said and we hung up our respective phones. I stepped into the hall bathroom and grabbed a cotton ball and dampened it with baby oil which is what I used as make-up remover and removed what little make-up was left on my face.

33

In the world of Esthetics of which I was an esthetician, baby oil was considered a no-no. And it wasn't just a no-no, but a reason to shun others if it were even mentioned in a salon and spa. Of course I would recommend the more expensive, natural, earth-friendly Aveda product at work, but at home and on my budget, baby oil was the all-purpose winner in my book.

I stripped out of my outfit somewhat surprised that I had left it on this long and hopped into the warm shower. As I lathered my hair with shampoo and washed my skin with a peach-scented body gel, I began to feel a little happier and not so worried about my circumstances. I quickly rinsed, dried off, wrapped my hair in a towel, and brushed my teeth.

A few minutes later I was dressed in jeans, a long-sleeve shirt, and socks. After I had blown my hair mostly dry and applied a moisturizer to my bare face, the doorbell rang. I walked across the kitchen floor and slowly opened the door. My anxiety level increased slightly as Tod entered the kitchen.

"Hello," I said, letting him pass by me before I shut the door.

"Hey," he said.

"Let's go into the den," I suggested. He trailed behind me as Mack walked up to us and meowed.

Tod picked up Mack and petted him as he said, "Hi, pussy cat." We both sat down on the couch at opposite ends. Mack jumped out of his lap and sashayed across the worn carpet and headed back into the hallway.

"What's up?" I asked ready to get this conversation over with.

"We need to talk about what happened last night."

I was starting to get irritable. "OK. What about last night?"

"What were you doing leaving me and going over and sitting with Stan?" Yuck. I was sitting with a guy named Stan? Last night was worse than I thought.

"Oh yeah," I said. "Stan is your friends' version of the male whore. I don't know why I went over and sat by Stan." Besides of course for the reasons that last night I had been embarrassed to be seen with Tod; been embarrassed to be at that party with a bunch of tool bags. "Is it that big of a deal that I talked to him?" I knew that all we had done was talk and sit on the couch in full view of everyone. Wasn't that allowed at a tool bag party?

"I don't like him. He flirts with every girl I date. He's an asshole."

"OK. I agree he's an asshole." Along with most of the people there last night. "So why is he still part of this crowd of friends you hang out with?"

"Shelley and Mike, the couple that hosted the party—"

"You mean Raggedy Ann and Andy?"

"—yeah. Them. They work with him. I guess most of us know the same people." OK. So what does this have to do with me? "What was wrong with you last night? You seemed like you were in a really bad mood before we even got there."

"I was in a bad mood. I was tired from work and running around after work trying to find a costume and coming up empty. It's not easy to find something to wear to a Halloween party post-Halloween. Everything's sold down, picked over, and then I had to rush home and throw something together from my closet. I really didn't want to go to the party and I felt like you made me go. Then when we were finally going back to your house, you pick a fight with me saying how we should break up; that it's been fun, but we just aren't working out. And all I can figure is that you are saying that because I went over and talked to some random guy I don't even know on the couch!" My voice was rising with exasperation.

"I know. I'm sorry I said that. I shouldn't have said anything then. I should have let it go until today when we could have talked when we were sober. It's my fault that you got the DUI."

As much as I would have loved to blame him totally for my arrest, I knew that it wasn't true. "It's not your fault that I got the DUI. I made a choice to drive. I am responsible too." It didn't make me feel better to take the high road, but for some reason, I just knew that I had to accept my role. Although, it didn't help that he picked a fight with me right before we got home. "So what do you want to do now?" I asked.

"Maybe we could start over?" he suggested.

"Sounds fine to me," I agreed. *Maybe Tod wasn't so bad*, I reiterated to myself. Maybe I was just still so out-of-whack that I couldn't recognize a good guy. Maybe we could be OK as a couple. Somewhere deep in my heart, my gut, and my vagina was a feeling that I should end this relationship now. However, I didn't know to listen to those cues anymore because what I had been attracted to in the recent past had been unhealthy. So if my instincts were actually warning me off a guy, wouldn't it stand to reason that they weren't reliable either? "I'm starving," I told him. "Are you hungry?"

"A little. Where do you want to go?"

"Mexican."

We went to a Mexican restaurant that was just down the street and slid into a booth. I ordered a quesadilla and a margarita. (Tod was driving.) He ordered fajitas and a beer. We chatted some more about "Us" until it started to make me lose my appetite and then I suddenly remembered a question I wanted to ask Tod. "Why didn't you answer your phone? I called you at home multiple times when I was in jail."

"That was you?" he asked. I forgot that Tod didn't have caller I.D. Even if he had, I guess it wouldn't have mattered anyway since I was calling from jail. "I was afraid to answer." Then Tod suddenly seemed to remember something. "Oh yeah. Taylor said you hit-on her at Sonny's." Sonny's was a really cool bar in an old motel on Martin Luther King Jr. Drive. I had temporarily forgotten that a small group of us had gone there after the party. But it was all coming back to me now. Except for the part where I hit-on Taylor. I dropped my fork against my plate. It made a loud clanging sound.

"Excuse me?" I was annoyed. First I was accused of flirting with Stan and now I'm accused of hitting-on Taylor?

Tod chuckled as if it were no big deal this bombshell he had just dropped on me. "Everything's cool. I think she was actually flattered."

My anger was rising and Tod was completely clueless about how pissed off he was making me. "I did not hit-on Taylor." This group of people must have had no social lives before they met each other. Apparently they could not differentiate between talking and making a move on somebody. "When did this supposedly happen?"

"In the bathroom at Sonny's."

OK. Yes, last night I was drunk, but I also had a good memory for a drunk. Taylor was one of my least favorite people of Tod's group of friends. Of course I had barely met any of the other people at the party last night, but going by my ability to judge and assess tool bags, there were probably worse personalities in the room than Taylor's.

However, Taylor had surprised and impressed me last night with a side of her that I didn't know she had: smart ass. She had attended the party dressed as road kill. She had on a leopard print dress stamped with faux tire tracks. I thought it was the first glimpse of a personality that resembled some of my friends' wacky personalities back home.

As I drank more, I became chatty with her, and felt a girl-bond thing going on with her. Apparently one woman's girl-bond is another woman's lesbian come-on. I distinctly remember chatting her up in the bathroom at Sonny's while slurping on a Turkey 101 and Sprite while she giggled conspiringly with me.

"Yeah. We talked in the bathroom at Sonny's. Last night was the first night she resembled any of my friends from back home and we were laughing and stuff. But if she thinks that's me coming on to her, she's a moron."

"She said you tried to kiss her."

"*What?*" It came out as a scream. Let's get some things straight. I have no problem with homosexuality in general or with lesbianism specifically. Sure, I'd read the poem, *Muff-Diving into the Wreck*, by Adrienne Rich and liked it. Sure, I, like most girls that I knew, had that occasional fantasy about girl-on-girl action where I was one of the girls. Sure, one of my best girlfriends, Jarrett, and I had discussed that if we ever decided to kiss a girl, we'd choose to kiss each other.

With all this said, no matter how cool I thought Taylor was last night in my drunken fog, I had never found her to be attractive, and I *know* I did not try to kiss her. Not even the teeniest, most dissatisfying penis could make me want to turn to her in sexual desire. "I did not kiss her. I did not *try* to kiss her. She's a total freak," I said.

Tod mistook my disdain at Taylor for being a total liar for me being homophobic which brought a smile to his face and led me to roll my eyes. I was done arguing this point, so I let it go, lest I end up on the "Thou doth protest too much" wagon.

I ended up having a total of two margaritas before we left the restaurant and Tod dropped me off at my house. Something about him made me like him better when I was buzzed. I thanked him for dinner and we hugged goodnight in the car. We even gave each other a little peck kiss. I explained to Tod that I was really tired and just wanted to go home and go to sleep. Alone. He understood.

Since we had gone to eat mid-afternoon, I still had most of

my night to enjoy to myself. I filled Mack's food bowl and flopped down on the couch. One of my most favorite things about my job was that I had Sundays and Mondays off. I thought that Sunday was the best day to have off and to not have to go to work on a Monday just made Sunday even better. Plus, on Saturdays the salon was only open until four o'clock. It was like I got two and a half days off in a row.

So tonight I turned on the television and adjusted the antennae so I could receive the PBS channel as clearly as possible. I only received about four channels through the antenna which meant that I now watched *Friends*, a show that I had originally despised upon sight and had never previously seen.

The main point of contention was these twenty-somethings who had a nice, spacious apartment in New York City and who only worked average jobs like me. (I was later informed by one of my clients at the salon, Jennifer, that the apartment was rent-controlled, as if that explained everything.) I knew what my average job paid and as you are already aware, I can't even afford cable. The ridiculous thing is that I moved to this town to *save* money. Somewhere in the universe The God of Irony was laughing so hard he was peeing on himself.

I didn't find it to be as amusing. I was living in my deceased grandparents' house which meant I was living rent-free. In theory, this should imply that I was saving a few hundred dollars every month. In reality, I was scrimping and barely getting by. One-third of my paycheck went to my car payment. One-fourth of my paycheck went to COBRA. One-fifth of my paycheck went to my student loan from law school (of all places) and most of the remaining fraction of my earnings went to phone, cell phone, car insurance, and utilities. Note to self: Utilities in a house, especially during the summer and winter, cost a lot more than an apartment's.

COBRA was the real culprit, or bitch, as I preferred to call it. However, when I was really pissed at COBRA, I used a name I reserved for only the most special of occasions, "Cocksucking Bastard." What COBRA was to me was a henchman for the mob offering "protection" for my property. It was as if I were giving money to the mob to maintain the status quo and to not exercise its option of busting my kneecaps. What my relationship with COBRA entailed was me paying COBRA hundreds of dollars a month and in return it used that money to buy postage to mail form letters that said, "Coverage denied due to preexisting condition."

A recent visit to my OB/GYN quickly informed me of this lesson which meant I was paying COBRA for the visit while also paying a couple hundred for my physician and lab work out of my own pocket. To be clear, I was paying for one doctor's visit *twice*. However, I couldn't *not* pay COBRA either because it used fear-based power to worry me about all the other life-threatening diseases that could fester within my body while reminding me how much worse my quality of life would be if I didn't have insurance while festering.

This vicious circle is the adult version of the children's visual game, "What's wrong with this picture?" It is also a version of Russian roulette for those of us middle-class dreamers who chose to follow our hearts instead of playing by the rules of the universities, government, and Big Business. "Playing by the rules" meant becoming employed in certain industries with big benefits while working our way up the corporate ladder into big bucks and power suits. Basically, get your degree and catapult it into an acceptable salaried titled position, *or else!* I heard the *Or Else!* message loud and clear to people like me—the working, uninsured, middle-class-"poor" American population: "Die, middle-class, die!"

Of course, my preexisting condition was catalogued as Human Papillomavirus or HPV. Personally I was beginning to believe that my preexisting condition in the eyes of the insurance companies was actually my vagina. In the course of my relationships with various insurance companies, I had health insurance policies that only paid for visits resulting in normal pap smears and I had health insurance policies that only paid for abnormal pap smears. Interestingly enough, whichever type of pap smear result that I had, the insurance company magically never seemed to cover it. And, yes, I do mean "magically" because only a sleight of hand could leave me wondering, "How'd they do that?"

My resentment would then build to the point where I would start griping about how birth control was only sometimes covered by insurance while Viagra was always covered; how guys carried HPV and passed it to girls, yet society and the medical community primarily viewed HPV as a female's problem and responsibility; and how unfair it was that girls had to squat to pee in the woods while boys could do it standing up.

I was distracted from my thoughts, though, as a new PBS program started: a documentary on Chris Whittle. I picked up the remote and turned up the volume. Chris Whittle is an entrepreneur from Tennessee who created Whittle Communications in my hometown of Knoxville, then started Channel One which was educational programming, and then developed the Edison Project.

As far as I could tell, he was a dreamer who had managed to make a living by pursuing his dreams. I envied and respected him for that. Whittle Communications was also the great white hope for myself when I was getting ready to graduate from the University of Tennessee. Rumor had it that Whittle was also a Liberal Arts major. Therefore, unlike most other big businesses, I figured that his company would appreciate the value of my well-rounded education. However, all my initial dreams for good, solid employment with my English degree dissolved when Whittle closed down shop a few months before my graduation date.

As a result, I was left with the option of exploring the job placement center located within one of the undergraduate administrative offices. I had walked up to the counter and asked where I could find employment information for graduates in English. The woman behind the counter pointed at a filing cabinet and told me that the bottom drawer was for the Liberal Arts majors and each degree had its own file. That sounded reasonable enough.

I squatted down on the floor, pulled out the drawer, and walked my fingers down the labeled tabs until I found English. I spread the folder apart and noticed that it was quite thin. I pulled out an 8.5x11 pamphlet. On the cover were pencil drawings of a fireman and a policeman that were sketched in the styles of 1950s cartoonists or propaganda artists. The heading at the top of the pamphlet said: *What can you do with that English degree? Become a fireman or a policeman!* I had nothing against policemen (well, not yet) or firemen, but was this some kind of a joke? Had I gone to four years of college, studied literature and pursued an English degree that also included an emphasis in writing only to have no outlet for utilizing my well-rounded analytical skills and strong writing and communication skills?

I dropped the flier to the floor and completely removed the folder from the cabinet. I peered upwards between the folder's flaps as I pinched it by its skinny little spine and shook it to see what else

40

would fall out. Nothing. Absolutely nothing. I placed the fireman/policeman flier back into the folder and filed it back into the cabinet for some other poor English major to discover and later weep. No wonder Chris Whittle had started his own business. He hadn't wanted to be a fireman or a policeman either and apparently no one else was hiring people like us.

6

After the Chris Whittle documentary was over, I walked into the kitchen. Mack was stretched out across the kitchen table licking one of his paws. I wiggled my fingers into his soft fur while gurgling baby talk at him. He stopped cleaning himself long enough to look at me, paw still poised in midair. He looked so adorable. I immediately snatched him up off the table and held him close.

"Who's mommy's little baby? Who's mommy's little baby?" I cooed in his ear as I gently rubbed his fur. "You're my little baby!" I exclaimed as if he didn't already know; as if he'd never heard this exchange before. And then I made some unintelligible mommy-to-baby noises. Mack purred loudly in response and I squeezed him tight and kissed his forehead multiple times before letting him jump back down onto the table.

I opened the refrigerator and pulled out a big 'ol bottle of wine that was still three-quarters full. I had felt so uncomfortable, guilty even, the first time I brought an alcoholic beverage into my grandparents' house after I moved here. Although my grandfather had run moonshine up and down the mountain during Prohibition and was once chased by revenuers from whom he managed to escape by jumping his Model-T over a large mud puddle while the revenuers drove through it and got stuck (so totally cool and so totally *Dukes of Hazzard!*), my grandparents had never been drinkers and did not approve of drinking.

I surreptitiously poured myself a glass of wine as if trying to hide it from their eyes peering down at me from heaven and walked into the dining room where my CD player was. One of my favorite things to do on Sunday nights by myself was put on music, get a little tipsy/drunk, and dance around the dining room and living room. I considered myself to be a fabulous dancer, even if only in my own mind. But seriously, when Jarrett, Marais, and I went out to clubs, I could shake my hips and grind my bones to DMX's *Up in Here* and look as good if not better than the next club chick.

However, my most favorite song was also the most challenging for me to dance to: Monster Magnet's *19 Witches*. Yet, despite my inability to dance justice to the song, I inserted Monster Magnet into the CD player, tapped to song number seven, and shook my bootie (and, by default, my love handles) to the music the best I could. Then I'd sip some wine, repeat the song a few more times, and drink some more.

Next I'd switch to *Battle Flag* by the Lo Fidelity All Stars and then I'd repeat Rob Zombie's *Never Gonna Stop (The Red, Red Kroovy)* for a few times. For my grand finale, I'd insert Nashville Pussy's CD into the CD player and listen to it from beginning to end; the end being my favorite song, *Fried Chicken and Coffee*. By the time I'd get to *Fried Chicken and Coffee*, the bottle of wine was usually empty, my last glass full, and my body would stumble around the room, rocking as best it could, while intoxicated. Then I'd go to bed, wake up the next morning, and suffer from a hangover.

When it comes to music, I am totally uncool in the eyes of others (Thibodeaux) who hate radio and enjoy relatively obscure (at least to people like me) bands. It was Thibodeaux who took me under his wing and introduced me to Nashville Pussy. Thibodeaux thought it was totally cool that I bought the Nashville Pussy CD upon his recommendation, which in return made me feel totally cool. And as it turned out, I really did like their music.

As a matter of fact, about a year ago when Thibodeaux and I were on hiatus again, I was spending a nice, quiet, sober evening at home, petting the pussy cat, listening to the college radio station (Thibodeaux's influence again), when I heard the DJ announce a contest: "Caller number two will receive two free tickets to see Nashville Pussy at Blue Cats." My ears perked up, but I had issues with calling into a radio station. For some reason I felt self-conscious. It was partly because of my name. It was unusual and I'd never met any other Vandelyns in my lifetime. Anyone listening would know it was me if they recorded my call-in. I wasn't embarrassed to want free Nashville Pussy tickets; I just didn't want to hear myself on tape (for fear of making an ass of myself) unless I had a more anonymous name such as Jennifer. Then listeners would never know *which* Jennifer. Besides: *Caller two?* The tickets were probably won before I could get over to the phone and dial.

A song came on and when it ended, the DJ announced once again, a little more desperately this time, "Win two free tickets to Nashville Pussy. Just be caller two." The tickets still weren't won? Were all Nashville Pussy fans bashful and shy like me?

I finally got my nerve up to call the radio station and dialed the number. It rang, the DJ answered and I said, "Am I caller two?"

He said, "No. You're caller one. Can you hang up real fast and call back?"

After winning the tickets, my next concern was who to take. I wasn't going to invite Thibodeaux because we were "done." (Allegedly.) Marais didn't hate Nashville Pussy per se; she just hated any band that plays any type of music like theirs. Jarrett wouldn't like them either, but had she not gone home to visit her family, she probably would've gone with me. My friend, Jen, who was living in Toronto, probably would've hated them too, but she might have gone just for the hell of it had she been here.

Actually, upon further reflection, my love of Nashville Pussy and other hard rock bands was pretty much my love alone which is why I went by myself to the KISS/Ted Nugent concert a year or so ago. (Thibodeaux and I weren't on the outs then. Thibodeaux just pretended not to hear me when I mentioned it to him. After the fact, he claimed ignorance and insisted that had he known, he definitely would've been there.) That tour was supposed to be KISS's last concert with the original line-up. (It wasn't.)

Ted Nugent came on stage first and I laughed my ass off during one song where Ted called any and every democratic politician that he could think of (male and female) a "whore." As you already are aware, in my world, either everyone's a whore or no one is a whore so I am all about equal opportunity "whore" name-calling. The only way that song could have been improved was if he had extended his "whore fest" to include the Republican and Independent parties because all those politicians (as well as all political groupies) are whores too.

At the time of this Nashville Pussy concert, my newly acquired friend, Jenni-Fer-Furr, popped into my head. Jenni-Fer-Furr and Thibodeaux had a fling during one of our hiatuses. Well, Thibodeaux had a fling; Fer-Furr thought it was something greater.

Jenni-Fer-Furr got her nickname from me due to the "sex kitten" maneuver that she used on Thibodeaux. She introduced herself to him as "Furr." I admit Thibodeaux does exude sex appeal like nobody else; both men and women have been known to purr while merely standing in his presence. Therefore, I excused the "Furr Purr" at first. However, I knew something was up when Thibodeaux told me, "Her name's Jennifer, but she said for me to call her *Furr*. Boys like a girl named *Furr*."

I just rolled my eyes at him and said, "Well, try not to cough up a hairball."

Since we were on hiatus and on "friend" level In the Time of Furr, I focused my attentions on a hot younger guy from work and let Thibodeaux play with his ball of string. A month or so later, Thibodeaux and I found ourselves once again together shacked up in his bed. It was around two a.m. and we had just finished having sex. Then there was a knock at the door. It was that cute knock, you know, the knock to the tune of: *Shave and a haircut, ten cents!* Thibodeaux looked at me and I looked at him as if we were two people caught naked in bed while someone's girlfriend was knocking on the door in the middle of the night.

"Ignore it," he said.

"Okay," I agreed. We lay in bed naked and quiet.

Another knock rapped against the door. This time it was a normal knock that seemed to say, "Hi! I'm here. You must still be asleep and didn't hear the first cute knock."

Thibodeaux and I both lay still in bed, hoping the knocker, whom we both knew was Jenni-Fer-Furr, would go away. I was beginning to suffer from bouts of inappropriate giggling. Then the angry pounding on the door started.

Instead of getting dressed and doing something to protect myself in case Fer-Furr broke down the door, clawed at me, and started a cat fight, I hid under the covers and giggled. When she came over to the bedroom window, banged on it, and started yelling through the closed shades, "I know you're in there! Why don't you act like a fucking man and come out and be straight up with me? I know you're not alone!" I pulled a pillow over my head and laughed uncontrollably into the sheets.

Thibodeaux jumped out of bed and ran naked into the living room, making sure that every lock he had on the door was in use.

Then he came back to bed and apologized.

"Sorry about that. I haven't hung out with her in a few days. I thought she knew what was up."

When we finally went to sleep and woke up the next morning, Thibodeaux walked me out to my car. Apparently Fer-Furr had come prepared or she had come back during the night with sidewalk chalk. On the sidewalk outside Thibodeaux's front door were the words "Act like a fucking man!" written really big.

Then as we approached my Eagle Talon, we passed his car. Apparently she had dumped a pile of sludge on the roof. At least I hoped that was sludge. Thankfully, she had left my car alone. I kind of grimaced at Thibodeaux as I nodded my head towards his car and said, "That sucks." He nodded his head in agreement.

Then I started laughing all over again. "I'm sorry for laughing," I said. "But that really is too funny."

He leaned his head over the sludge on his car and sniffed it. "Oh my god," he said, wrinkling his nose. "It smells like shit."

Thibodeaux forgave Jenni-Fer-Furr pretty quickly for what became known as "the log cabin that Fer-Furr built" because he knew he was at fault. However, he did describe to me the humiliation of driving to the gas station with a pile of shit on the roof of his car; the embarrassment of speeding between stoplights trying to dislodge it; having to sit in the drive-thru car wash while the high-powered hoses sprayed the pile of shit down from the roof onto his windshield and then blew it back and forth across the glass, smearing it right before his eyes. Then when the brushes came down he spoke of his disgust as the bristles picked up the poo and splattered it across his car and the stall. After the rinse cycle finished, he said he hauled ass out of there, afraid that the car behind him was going to be pissed if the driver saw the poo-covered bristles coming at him.

Of course, it took Jenni-Fer-Furr a little bit longer to forgive Thibodeaux and me (even though I hardly knew her) for our alleged betrayal of her. Eventually, though, she did and I discovered that she was actually pretty nice when she wasn't taking a dump on a car roof or using children's sidewalk chalk for deviant purposes.

I picked up the phone and gave her a call. She wasn't home, so I left a message on her machine telling her about the tickets, which night, and to call me back if she wanted to go.

On the night of the concert, Jenni-Fer-Furr and I cut to the front of the line, acting like the big-shot poseurs that we were. Once we grabbed drinks and claimed a spot on the dance floor, the first band, Dick Delicious and the Tasty Testicles (I'm not kidding), came out to play. Although some of the songs sounded a bit on the inappropriate side, the music was fast-paced enough for me to dance to. Fer-Furr, for some reason, was not as taken with the band as I was. After they were done, the lead singer walked up to me and handed me a free CD because, and I quote, "Your dancing gave me something to look at while I was up there singing." (See? I told you that I was a good dancer.) I was pleased, but Fer-Furr was not impressed.

Then Nashville Pussy took the stage. I noticed that the older tattooed blonde was no longer with the band; she was now replaced by a sweet-faced, pretty young girl who looked to be about nineteen. However, the other three members were the same. Of course I danced my ass off. Fer-Furr wasn't really into the music so she sat at a corner table and sipped on a cocktail or two.

When the show was over and Nashville Pussy was packing up, I got a brilliant idea. In the trunk of my car was the box of T-shirts that Jarrett and I had made during a "business venture." Our business was the making of T-shirts; our company was called "Tuff Muff." As a result, our first batch of T-shirts had our logo on them: Tuff Muff. Now then, Jarrett and I totally thought our T-shirt concept was fabulous. It was so kick-ass, smart ass girl. How were we to know that the female population in my hometown did not identify with kick ass, smart ass, Tuff Muff girls?

For the most part, guys liked the shirts more than girls did (well, except for Thibodeaux). One surprise was that the T-shirts created an open dialogue between the sexes. One guy asked me, "Tuff Muff? Does that mean it's hard to get into or that it's like a Brillo Pad?"

When Thibodeaux saw our T-shirts and their logo (we had two styles of twenty shirts each), he merely asked me and Jarrett, "What are y'all doing? Starting a lesbian softball team?" Of course, to his credit, he did purchase one (he said he knew of a lesbian he could give it to) and we even made him pay full price. However, we did run into one guy who wanted to wear one. We gave it to him for free to help with our promotion. (It didn't help.) Thibodeaux pretended to be irritated. "You gave a stranger a T-shirt for free but you made me pay full price?"

That's when Jarrett jokingly told him, "Don't be such a bleeding vagina."

Thibodeaux wrinkled his nose in mock disgust while I snorted with laughter. "That sounds like it should be an Irish expression," I said. "You know like 'Jesus wept' or 'Christ on a Cross.'" Then to demonstrate, I said in what was intended to be an Irish brogue, "Don' be such a bleedin' vagina."

Unfortunately for those within earshot of me, mimicking accents was not one of my strong suits. Whenever I attempted the sing-song accent from India, it came out British. Whenever I attempted a British accent, it came out Japanese Tourist. Whenever I attempted a Japanese accent, it came out Irish brogue. Whenever I attempted Irish brogue it came out Swedish.

So there I was performing my "brogue" to Jarrett and Thibodeaux and it actually came out sounding like this: "Ja. Don't be such a bleedin' vagina. Ja." Jarrett started laughing. Although I could tell that Thibodeaux was amused, he gave me the furrowed brow and scrunched up face that implied my imitation was so painful for him to hear that he was wondering how he and I had even managed to become friends.

I walked over to Fer-Furr's table and saw that she was engrossed in conversation with a cute guy. "I'll be back in a second," I told her. "I've got to run out to my car."

"Okay," she had said. "By-the-way, this is Justin. Justin, Vandelyn." Justin and I spoke our hellos and then I hurried outside to my car, popped open the trunk, and removed two shirts, one of each style. When I returned to the dance floor, I walked over to the stage entrance in the back corner and waited. A minute or so later, the young female member stepped out probably to grab some piece of equipment off of the stage.

"Hi," I said. "I thought y'all were great and I wanted to give these shirts for you and the other girl."

She smiled at me and accepted the shirts. "Thanks," she said.

"No problem," I told her as I turned and walked away. Maybe I'd get lucky and those girls would wear our shirts when they played another concert. What cool, free exposure! I headed back to Fer-Furr to tell her what I'd done just as Justin was standing up holding their empty drinks in his hand.

48

"Would you like another drink, *Furr*?" he asked her. She nodded and I raised my eyebrow.

After he walked away, she said to me in a low voice, "If you are ready to go, I think I am just going to hang out here for a while." I took the hint. Since Fer-Furr had driven her own car and met me at the club, I knew she was fine on her own.

"Yeah, I am a bit tired," I said, which wasn't untrue. Justin returned to the table and he and "Furr" leaned their heads in close together and resumed their conversation.

"Nice to meet you, Justin," I said. "I'm going to head on home."

Justin looked up at me and said, "Yeah."

I smiled at "Furr" and waved my good-byes. As I headed out to my car, I thought about "Furr" and her mysterious ways. When I reflected back on that night, I realized that evening was the closest that Jenni-Fer-Furr and I would ever come to being friends.

Soon enough she bonded with a girl named "Velvet" and then they coupled up with a girl named "Chastity" to finally form their own hell-raising holy trinity. Jarrett, Thibodeaux, and I would see them from afar every once in a while and on those rare occasions, I'd say something smart ass like, "Look. There's Jenni-Fer-Furr, Velvet, and Chas-Titty."

But of course, Thibodeaux could do me one better. He always referred to them as Helen Keller's daughters: Furr, Velvet, and Corduroy.

7

Ow! Ow! Ow! Although Mack was standing on my chest and meowing at me, telling me it was time for his Monday morning loving, his presence had nothing to do with the pain I was feeling as I lay in bed. My head was killing me from all the wine I drank last night.

I petted the pussy cat while my head throbbed. A few rubs of fur later, I set the cat to the side and struggled out of bed and into the kitchen where the generic ("generic" had become my "name brand") ibuprofen sat on the counter. I took a couple and chased them with water. I was fortunate that I rarely got headaches, except of course for the self-inflicted ones, so two ibuprofen should do the trick.

I grabbed a Coke (for the taste of it) from the fridge, poured myself a glass of water (for the hydration of my headache) from my Brita water pitcher, and took my drinks into the den. I plopped down on the couch, picked up the remote, and channel surfed through all four channels looking for something to watch.

On *Montel*, a twenty-year old couple was having a paternity test done to determine if Joe-Bob was actually the father. On the forty-something-feminine-side of the *Today* show, the topics of conversation included organic vegetables and "how to kiss." Since I bought generic canned vegetables because I could buy more of them for a dollar, I really couldn't relate to some chick that was willing to pay four dollars for a carrot. As for kissing? I already knew how to kiss. Actually, not only did I know how to kiss, I knew how to lick my tongue along the whips and curves of Thibodeaux's tribal tattoo as it wrapped around his bicep, savoring the salty taste of his skin on my lips.

What the hell was wrong with these forty-something women and their conversational topics? What happened once women got married/became "successful"/had kids? Did they trade in their gray matter for marshmallow fluff? I was beginning to think that *The Stepford Wives* was totally misunderstood.

The next channel was showing an episode of *The Beverly Hillbillies* (need I say more?) which is why I settled on the least of the four evils. I chose to watch *The Voices: The Show for Women*. I thought the title was the worst because it conjured up images of Sybil and her personalities' voices reverberating throughout her head. I wondered if this title was meant as a subliminal message from Hollywood suggesting to the general public that women were crazy.

The show's opening credits were simple. The black "V" that represented the "voices" came spinning out of the background, came to a stop right-side up, and the empty part of the V was filled in with pink, basically making it a pink triangle. I wasn't sure if the producers of the show quite got what this meant, but still, it was by far the edgiest part of the show. Then a taped male voice firmly announced, "The Voices: The Show for Women!" as if this show handled only razor-sharp topics that were strong enough for a man but made for a woman. I sat back, sipped on my drinks, and let the show begin.

The concept consisted of a panel of four women sitting at a long news desk who had a list of topics to discuss, but apparently no script. I guessed that the "from the hip" perspectives were "racy" and "avant-garde" from the network's perspective, but somehow the topics and opinions continued to be as typical and tame as an article from Red Book. I sighed but continued to watch the foursome: The journalist, the smart one, the funny one, and the sassy one. (The sassy one had just recently replaced the dumb one. The dumb one had gotten hired because she was dumb and then, strangely enough, was fired for the same reason.)

The first topic was instigated by the journalist (the one who seemed to actually come to the tapings with a prepared speech, a neutral Mid-Western accent, and perfect posture) and she discussed politics. (I guessed this would be the "strong enough for a man" segment.) However, the discussion quickly disintegrated into a cackling henhouse. One voice could be heard above all the rest. The sassy chicken squawked, "What I don't understand is why Hillary Clinton didn't leave her husband! What are other women going to do now if their husbands cheat on them? She needed to be a role model for the rest of women in this country!" (What was this?

51

WWHD?)

Some of the audience giggled; some gasped; some made agreeing noises and clapped; I just went deaf. What person with any intelligence would think that Hillary would leave Bill? Hill-Billy is a political machine moving faster than Jeb Bush's voting machines can trick Florida Democratic constituents into voting for his brother. With speed like that, infidelity can be overlooked and forgiven quicker than I can ask, "Aren't all male Democrat politicians whores?"

Well, aren't they? FDR? Whore. JFK? Whore. The remaining male Kennedys? Whores. Oh, excuse me. One is a convicted murderer and another was an alleged rapist. The *rest* were whores. And what about the married Democrat who smiled at the cameras every time he was questioned about his mistress, the missing intern? He was probably so relieved when the news channels started covering 9/11 because they had something else to focus on besides his cheese-dick smile.

Don't get me wrong. Male Republicans aren't any better. They are just a different breed claiming Family Values one minute and then soliciting a male intern via email the next. (OK. That was *one* Republican politician. I'm guessing the rest just don't know how to use email.)

And what about Kenneth Starr wasting taxpayers' money investigating Clinton's possible infidelity as a reason for impeachment? What was Clinton guilty of? Improper use of a cigar? For possibly getting laid by someone other than his wife? (*There's* a newsflash: *Democrat president has sexual relations with someone other than his wife.*)

I imagined the Barnum and Bailey ringleader announcing, "Welcome to the American political circus! In the first ring, the judicial branch, we have: whores! In the second ring, the executive branch, we have: more whores! Last but not least, in the third ring, the legislative branch, we have: almost as many whores as self-centered pompous assholes elected to positions of power! And *that*, ladies and gentlemen, is a lot of whores!" Besides, as often as JFK banged other women (I was pretty sure that it was he who put the *Jack* in jackhammer and jackrabbit) nobody ever considered impeaching him. And what about today's Republican executive branch? Didn't we have blatant commingling of Dick and Bush in

52

the White House at this very moment? Why wasn't Kenneth Starr-Fucker sticking his nose into the Oval Orifice now?

So forget about Hillary. Personally, I thought the woman who deserved a lot of respect was a former *Baywatch* star who had her husband arrested after he hit her. I thought that took a lot of courage to stand up for what was right and show other women not to take that crap off of any guy. However, I doubted this demographic panel of "professional, intelligent, middle-to-upper class successful women" would ever give a woman like her a crumb of credit. They'd just dismiss her as a brainless bimbo not worthy of their time. I'd also guess that at least half this panel of women would claim ties with "feminism" despite the fact that they looked down on other types of women, say bleach blondes with savage tans whose professional careers included *Playboy* centerfolds and unauthorized releases of their sex tapes. I guess some girls count and some girls don't. Wait a minute. That's how the rest of society thinks too. What a coinkidink!

8

Tuesday morning, I leaned against the concrete wall on level four of the parking garage and looked out over Market Street as I waited for Donna to arrive. Across the street and adorning the boarded façade of an old building was a large triangular-shaped 1970s blue neon sign with white lights stating, "Nick's Liquors." I loved that sign. Every day when I saw the sign, I would think about how I needed to bring my camera with me to work so I could take a picture. And every day I would forget to add it to my bag. *Tomorrow*, I kept telling myself as I drew my winter coat around me.

"Vandelyn!" a voice shouted at my backside. I turned to see Donna parked a few spaces over from my car, grabbing her purse out of the passenger seat. Every morning, I stopped by the salon, dropped my belongings off, and checked the book to see if Donna and I had any appointments first thing in the morning. Fortunately today, neither of us had a nine o'clock so we could enjoy a leisurely walk to Mercury Salon and Spa. The Mercury Salon and Spa was quite an edgy sounding name to my ears, especially for a place that saw its share of roller-sets every day. However, Donna and I sometimes referred to it as the Black Hole because some days where we worked was less red hot salon and more dark, life-sucking abyss.

"Hey, Donna. No nine o'clocks."

"I know," she said. "I already stopped by to check before I parked."

I walked over to Donna's car, a cute little four-door economy car with a metallic auburn paint job that became extremely vibrant in the sunlight. I had once commented on the cool color of the car. Donna had admitted that she hadn't really cared much about the make of her car; that she had actually fallen in love with it because she loved the color of it. "It'd make a great hair color," she had told me. Donna was all about her hair color. In the few months I had known her it had been a white blonde, a deep brown, an auburn shade with highlights, and various incarnations of red. I once asked her what her natural hair color was and she told me, "I have no idea."

Donna pulled a cigarette out of her purse and lit it stating, "Let's take the stairs."

As Donna and I chatted about her eight year-old son, Derrick, and her estranged husband, Tony (I didn't mention my arrest because I hadn't felt up to discussing it yet), I thought about how much I loved the walk to work, even on the cold days as long as they weren't bitterly cold with the wind whipping around us. On those days, Donna and I would take the free shuttle from the parking garage that traveled a route downtown and dropped us off directly in front of Mercury. One of the perks of Mercury was that the owner and head stylist, Kitty Francis, paid for our monthly parking passes to park at the Choo-Choo parking garage. I was definitely appreciative of the free parking because it saved me from having to pay a meter all day long or pay at a lot. On my miniscule budget, every last untouched penny in my pocket helped maintain the Bargain Basement lifestyle to which I had grown accustomed.

As we continued our brisk stroll down Market Street we both turned to each other at the same time stating, "How cute." In front of Warehouse Row, one of our local downtown tenants, Roy, sat on a bench. At his feet stood a four-pronged aluminum cane and also a cute little puppy attached to a leash. Roy sat on the bench, his head drooping, and his eyes looking at the puppy while holding the bright pink leash held loosely in his hand. At the sight of us, the little pup immediately jumped off the ground and began yapping.

"Hey!" Donna chirped. "When did you get a puppy?"

Roy looked up and seemed to be startled by both the puppy's yapping and the fact that someone was actually speaking to him. He seemed unsure as how to handle the attention. I squatted down on the ground by the puppy and scratched her head and ears. "She's adorable!" I think I even squealed. "What's her name?" Donna had also joined me at Roy's feet beside his cane and loved on the little canine.

Roy recovered from his initial shock or shyness and said, "Tippy. Her name's Tippy."

Donna asked him again when he had gotten her. He slowly

told us that a businessman who worked downtown had bought him a puppy and given her to him just a few days before. Then Roy retreated into silence. I thought that was pretty cool for someone to give Roy a puppy (especially a guy in a suit) since Roy was one of the "invisible people" who lived downtown in the old Patten Hotel.

The Patten Hotel was once a family-owned, upscale hotel in the heart of downtown that had been turned into public housing apartments a decade or more ago. *The poor Patten Hotel*, I thought. A once majestic hotel reduced to a mere hovel in the same manner once-glorified WWII battleships were sold for scrap metal. No matter how amazing you might be at one point in your life, your time is going to come. Roy was one of the many tenants that occupied a room in this once-glorious haven. Donna and I loved on the puppy a few seconds more and then said our good-byes while Tippy strained to the end of her leash wanting to chase us and exert all her pent-up puppy energy.

As we continued to walk our route to the salon, Donna and I chatted about Roy and his newfound puppy. It made us happy that someone had been thoughtful to Roy. We discussed our surprise that a business person would be kind-hearted enough to notice someone like Roy and want to help him out. After my law school experience (a place filled with megalomaniacs whose desires to zealously defend their clients were not inspired by a morality of "right and wrong" and earning justice for the people they were representing, but more about feeding their own inflated egos), I was pretty cynical towards anybody with a career that involved making good money and trying to impress people with their material success.

Not that I was really any better, though, when it came to mingling with the masses. Until today, I had never spoken to Roy in my life, although I had noticed him immediately when I first started working downtown during the summer. Then again, how could someone not notice Roy? Every day he used to pass by our large front window pushing his old grocery cart filled with aluminum cans while wearing what looked to be his interpretation of lederhosen. Roy's warm weather uniform consisted of green shorts, a light tan short-sleeved shirt, brown leather shoes with dingy socks, and a dark green hat that I could have sworn had a feather sticking up from its brim. He had no cane back then; I guess he used his shopping cart for support. Funny thing was that Roy wasn't very old either; at the most, mid-fifties? His brown hair and mustache had very little gray in it, if any, from what I could tell, but his thick glasses and stooped-over appearance gave him an elderly appearance and fragile quality.

I wondered what his life was like living in the Patten Hotel, now the Patten Towers, with an extended family of other tenants all in similar circumstances. I wondered what most of the tenants general lives had been like to end up in situations of living alone off of disability checks, every day the same. I mean, even if I had suddenly found myself with a disability and a monthly government check I still wouldn't live there. But then again, I felt that I had other options. Maybe its tenants didn't.

As Donna and I passed Patten Towers, one of the tenants, Iggy, was standing on the corner smoking a cigarette. An ambulance was parked on the side street with its siren off, but its lights flashing.

"Hey Iggy!" Donna called out. Iggy was around my age and had a crush on Donna. Periodically he would stop in to ask the price of a men's haircut. He was interested in cutting off his waist-length hair and donating it to Locks of Love, but he wasn't quite ready to do it yet.

"Hey!" he hollered back with a big grin on his face.

"What's going on?" Donna asked referring to the ambulance.

Iggy shrugged. "Don't know. Maybe Sally had another seizure." Sally was a woman who looked like a hobbit. She was also known to have seizures so severe that she was also the only pedestrian I knew of who wore a bicycle helmet. She was nice except for the time that I saw her walking down the sidewalk in front of the salon and she yelled at me for no reason. Of course, after noticing that the grocery bag she was carrying was filled with prescription bottles large enough to contain horse pills, I figured the reason was self-evident.

Before Donna and I could continue on our way toward the salon, Iggy yelled out, "So, Donna, when are we going out?"

"Never!" she yelled back. Iggy laughed as he waved good-by. We did the same. As we rounded the home stretch, we passed our favorite location, The Public Library, which was across the street to our left, and then crossed over MLK Jr. (which used to be 9th Street) to enter our block. Across the street at the other corner of MLK Jr. was the historic Read House, a hotel dating back to the Civil War. The walls in its lobby were lined with portraits of Civil War generals (or sergeants or whatever) although I had never really stopped to read the brass plaques at the base of each frame. I just remembered General Lee's picture was hanging in there. The other soldiers all looked alike to me.

The Read House was also rumored to possess a ghost from the Civil War times since the hotel had been used as a hospital for injured and dying soldiers. However, the ghost was not one of the soldiers, but it was of a woman who was said to either be a nurse or a prostitute. (Funny, isn't it, when a fuzzily recollected story of a woman is involved, it goes something like, "She was either a professional career woman or a hooker. I can't remember exactly which.")

Sharing the sidewalk with us on our immediate right was Morgan Stanley, the pay parking lot, and then Cup'A'Joe before we arrived at Mercury Salon and Spa. On the other side of the salon were Feinman's Fine Hats (which was now owned by a Korean family who bought the business after Mr. Feinman retired earlier this year) and The Convenient Mart which was run by a self-possessed-man-of-few-words named Jusef, who went by "Joe."

In fact, the first time that I had heard Joe speak was when one of the Patten Towers tenants tried to use a sack full of pennies to buy a six pack of beer. "No way am I counting all those fucking pennies!" he had spat. "Get out of my fucking store!" After the man left the store, Joe grabbed the beer and mumbled unintelligible words that were intermittently interrupted with a "heh-heh-heh" laugh. It was slightly scary.

Despite Joe's reserved personality, Donna and I had become friends with him over time. We quickly saw his softer side the first time he brought his mother to work with him. She'd sit quietly behind the counter with a smile and her presence kept Joe from cursing as much. Soon enough, he was inviting us over to his house for a swim in the swimming pool in his back yard. "It is an inground pool," he had assured us in his staccato-accented voice. "It is not one of those redneck above-ground pools." One night he even met us out for drinks to celebrate my birthday. He had generously bought all my Wild Turkey 101 and Sprites, often times bringing me a refill before I was half-way finished with the drink I held in my hand. (Coincidentally, I don't remember riding with Donna back to my house or throwing up on the floor beside my bed.)

I came out of my thoughts as Donna yanked the door open to the salon, causing the little bells attached to the door to smack against the glass rather than tinkling to let Kitty know that someone had arrived.

"Hello Kitty!" Donna yelled out in her booming voice.

Donna obviously had a strong personality, but I wanted to confirm it with my homemade psych test. I deduced that adults with strong personalities were once kids who pressed really hard when they colored. I wanted to see if Donna could help prove my theory.

"Donna, when you colored as a kid, did you color softly leaving white spaces or did you color really dark with no white spaces?" I already suspected the answer: no white spaces.

She had answered, "I colored so hard that I had wax flakes from the crayon on my paper. Why?"

I told her my theory. I also revealed that I colored lightly— with white spots between the color—while rotating the crayon's tip as I colored in order to keep it with a nice long point. She told me that when she'd colored, she'd worn the tip down to a nub and sometimes used such force that she broke the crayon in half. I shook my head in mock disgust although I could still remember my childhood disappointment at finding inch-long broken crayon stubs with flattened tips in my elementary school's crayon box.

This morning in my usual style, I smiled a "soft-presser's" smile and said hello to Kitty in a much more reserved manner than Donna's and headed back to my room to put on my smock. We had recently changed our dress code to all black with all female employees wearing a black Asian-inspired smock as our top. Since most of my clothes were black, I was cool with this new development. Since I had also been raised in private school where a uniform was mandatory, I loved the idea of wearing a smock that was actually kind of cute. I would usually wear my own black shirt to work and change into the smock once I arrived. The change of clothes allowed me to be "incognito" during my walk to work and during my lunch hour, giving me a feeling of freedom during my off-the-clock time.

I walked back up to the front and sat down at the reception desk since we were in between receptionists at the moment. Kitty couldn't hire a receptionist that lasted for more than a few months. It was as if she had no clue about how to hire someone with competence, professionalism, and a pleasant demeanor.

The first receptionist at my time of employment was a country woman named Minnie who was probably only in her mid-fifties, but, like Roy, seemed so much older. (Not a good look for a salon and spa offering services for improving one's appearance and wellness.) Her eyeliner was always running down from underneath her lower lashes and she had the wrinkled mouth of a long-term smoker who was also wearing ill-fitting dentures. She was a nice lady, but she couldn't remember how to schedule certain services and often screwed up the booking schedule.

One slow day at Mercury, I had sat up front in the empty reception area talking to Minnie. At the time, she was telling me about her knowledge of natural healing and internal cleansing products. Now this topic of conversation did interest me. Despite the ungodly amounts of toxins in my body via my alcohol intake, I was very interested in being healthy. As a matter of fact, before I moved, I had been in great shape despite my partying lifestyle. So I was intrigued by Minnie's knowledge of how to detoxify one's body—until she mentioned removing the worms attached to one's intestines.

"Worms?" I had asked. People had worms? *I* had worms?

"Sure," she had responded. An overweight middle-aged man with a large, protruding gut just happened to walk by the front windows at that moment. "See him? See how large his gut is?" I nodded. "He probably has worms this big—" she used her hands to demonstrate a measurement of their largeness—"attached to his intestines."

"*What?*" I was horrified. I was still unable to comprehend the worms attached to the inside of me much less the gargantuan ones inside of him. "And detoxifying my body will get rid of these worms?"

"Oh yes. Of course you'd want to only do it over the course of a weekend when you had a few days off because you are going to be on the toilet the whole time. But my daughter has been good about detoxifying my grandson and when he had surgery last year, the doctor said he'd never seen such clean intestines in his whole life."

"So no worms," I reiterated.

"Right," she had said. "No worms."

"But you are serious. We all have worms inside of us."

She nodded and said, "Yes. You know when a woman has a C-section, they pull her intestines out and put them on a table so they can get the baby and there are all these worms wiggling about. It's no big deal."

"And if I detoxify my body, these worms will come out in my poop?" I remembered one of my good friends from high school and college, Lacey Anderson, had gotten a tapeworm from her cat. She said that she had to take medicine to kill the tapeworm and how she saw parts of its tape-measure-like body in her poop. I didn't think I could handle standing up, turning around to flush the toilet, and seeing dead worm parts in the bowl.

"Sure," she said as if it were no big deal. "Actually one time I went to a natural healing meeting at the Town & Country restaurant and one woman sitting next to me at the table started scratching her face. I asked her what was wrong. She said she didn't know, but that this incredible itching had just started in her cheek. All of the sudden, I saw a worm poking its head out of one of her pores. I didn't tell her what was going on. Turns out she had been doing a detox and one of the worms had gotten loose in her body and just decided to come out of her face. I just told her to come with me to the bathroom and then I pulled the worm right out of her pore."

I shuddered. I wondered what one did with a worm that pokes its head out a pore. Flush it down the toilet? Name it? See if it saw its shadow and called for six more weeks of winter? Maybe I'd let the worms stay where they were after all. I hadn't had the courage to ask my doctor on my next visit about the worms because I felt as if I were in a Catch-22. If we really didn't have worms inside of us, I'd look stupid. If we really did have worms inside of us, I'd look stupid *and* I'd have to deal with the fact that I had worms. So one day on our way to lunch I repeated the conversation to Donna to get her perspective. All she had to say was, "Minnie is one loony toon." Ever since that day, though, Donna referred to lunch as, "Time to feed the worms."

Donna had a nine-thirty haircut and I had a ten o'clock brow wax. Since I was still relatively new to the salon, it took longer for me to get booked-up which meant I spent some of my time up front playing receptionist. Donna was always good about helping out and we would alternate shifts when possible. So far this morning Kitty

61

had been booked since seven o'clock with regulars, especially with the roller-set and wash-n-style crowd.

As I headed back to my room, I passed the shampoo bowls and the hair dryers because they were right across from my door. One older lady (Mrs. Halliwell, a dentist's wife who was waiting for Kitty to shampoo her) was talking to another older lady (Mrs. Mitchell, a business man's wife who was waiting for Kitty to undo her long-since-dry hair rollers) about her recent trip to the beach at Destin, Florida. As I entered my room to check my wax and muslin supplies, I heard Mrs. Halliwell say, "I just love the ocean down there at Destin. It's so pretty."

Mrs. Mitchell couldn't just agree or make a polite comment. Instead she said, "It's not an ocean. It's a gulf. There is a difference. I used to be an elementary school teacher and it drove me crazy when someone did not know the difference between the gulf and the ocean!"

Mrs. Halliwell was as taken aback as I was. I'd never heard anyone get huffy about the ocean versus the gulf before. "Well, I'm sorry," she said. "I didn't really think about there being a difference."

"Well, there is!" Apparently Mrs. Mitchell was not going to let it go. Fortunately or not so fortunately for Mrs. Halliwell, depending on how you want to look at it, another older lady, Mrs. Dobbs (I didn't know who her husband was, but he must've been "somebody" because they lived on the East Brow of Lookout Mountain), breezed down the hall past the shampoo bowls. She recognized both Mrs. Halliwell and Mrs. Mitchell and stopped to chat.

"You sure do look nice," Mrs. Halliwell commented to Mrs. Dobbs.

"Thank you."

"Are you going somewhere special?" Mrs. Mitchell asked.

"Well, I have a luncheon that I am going to this afternoon. It's the Red Hat Society! It is such a hoot!" she laughed. "I went to my first meeting last week and had such a good time."

"I've not heard of the Red Hat Society," Mrs. Mitchell said.

"Me neither," Mrs. Halliwell agreed.

"It's for women like us who have spent most of our lives volunteering, raising families, fundraising, and who now say, 'Tough! We're not sacrificing ourselves for everybody else anymore. It's our turn to do what we want!'" Mrs. Dobbs was joyous.

"How do you belong to this group?" Mrs. Mitchell asked.

"Well, it's something you have to be invited to," Mrs. Dobbs explained.

"I've never been invited to a group like that," Mrs. Halliwell commented. Apparently she wasn't going to be invited today either.

"Well, it's a lot of fun!" Mrs. Dobbs cheered and retrieved her coat from the closet at the end of the hall and dashed off. Kitty rushed up the hallway, thirty minutes behind as usual, ushered Mrs. Mitchell to her stylist's chair up front and asked Donna to shampoo Mrs. Halliwell when Donna finished with her client.

I went up front, retrieved my brow wax client, Jennifer Atchley, and reclined her back in the facial chair. As I applied the wax, I asked Jennifer where downtown she worked. She told me, "Big Blue." (In addition to Big Cig, Big Blue was another of the insurance companies in town. Big Un was the third one.) Big Blue had acquired a four-story building that used to be a department store in its hey-day further down on Broad Street. Even though I liked my job as an esthetician, I found myself envious of people employed in "regular" jobs that involved a desk, a salary, and benefits.

"That's cool," I commented. "You like it?" She smiled at me as I attached the muslin to the wax.

"Oh yes!" she chirped.

"I bet you get health insurance for cheap," I said. I couldn't help but comment on the health insurance angle since I was getting ripped-off every month by COBRA.

"We have great insurance and it is so inexpensive for employees of Big Blue!" She quoted me a ridiculously low price that probably also included her dental and vision. I ripped the muslin strip from her skin, yanking the desired hairs from their follicles. "Ouch," she said.

"Sorry," I lied.

"Why don't you give me your mailing address and I'll send you a package on our different policies? We have some really affordable ones that you can choose from based on your individual needs."

Now I was remorseful and happy at the same time. "Thanks!" I told her. After I finished shaping her brows, I gave her my information and sent her on her way.

A few minutes before my and Donna's one o'clock lunch break, the door jangled open and in walked one of Donna's clients, a young lawyer named Chris. He was nice, but I could still sense the class distinction that he thought existed between us. For example, one day when Donna and I had gone to lunch at a diner around the corner, Chris had walked in to get his lunch as well. He stopped by our table to chat briefly. At the time, I had my Cobb salad in front of me, and although I was starving, I left the salad untouched because Donna was still waiting on her meal. Donna noticed that I wasn't eating and questioned me on it. "You haven't gotten your food yet," I explained. Chris' eyes widened with new appreciation. While Donna was laughing at me for my "extreme politeness," Chris was impressed. "Wow," he commented. "Most people don't know to do that." What I wondered was did he actually mean "most people" or "most people such as Donna and me" (a.k.a. "service industry people") who were presumed to be less educated and therefore less aware of proper etiquette than say he, a successful lawyer?

"Hey Chris," I greeted him as he held the door open for his wife and infant child.

"Hey, Vandelyn. I wanted to bring my wife by so you and Donna could meet her and our daughter. This is my wife, Cara, and this is Mary Katherine."

I smiled. "Hi. Nice to meet you." Cara didn't say anything to me, but she gave me a half-hearted smile and held Mary Katherine close to her chest as if I might have some contagious disease that would render her daughter unmarried and working for a living at the age of thirty.

Donna stepped from around the corner with her purse and coat and bellowed, "Vandelyn, get your coat. It's time to feed the worms! Oh, hello, Chris. I hope you don't want an appointment right now because I'm going to lunch. And who is this?" Chris introduced his wife and child again. Cara looked at Donna and me as if we might be descendants of the Read House ghost and she was unsure of which legend to believe: were Donna and I women with legitimate jobs (the way Cara was looking at us, I knew she'd never classify us as "professional career women") or hookers who gave her husband blow jobs for tips in the back room?

Donna sand-blasted her way through the introductions and probably didn't even notice that Cara kept a safe enough distance

64

from us so as to not encourage anything more than a cold politeness between her husband and us. I excused myself from the reception area and returned to the esthetics room to grab my purse and my coat. When I entered the lobby, Chris and his family were gone and Donna was ready to go.

After Donna had let the salon door slam shut behind us, she said, "Did his wife have a corn-cob stuck up her ass or what?"

I had paused to look into Feinman's Fine Hats window and ogle a Kangol hat that I adored. It was tan angora and oh-so cool. It was also forty-three dollars. But Donna's statement was enough to startle me out of my longing.

"Definitely has a corn-cob stuck up her ass," I agreed. "She must think that we are giving Chris sexual favors."

"She's fucking nuts," Donna said as we passed by Joe standing out on the sidewalk talking on his cordless phone, a typical activity for Joe when the convenient mart was slow. We waved at him. He nodded his head at us.

"She's also twenty-six, has health insurance, could easily afford that Kangol hat I love, and she doesn't even work; doesn't even *have* to work. While I, on the other hand, work forty-hours a week and still feel like I have one foot in the gutter."

Donna looked over at me with a sympathetic gaze. "Sucks, doesn't it?"

"Just a little."

When I got home that afternoon, I parked my car in the garage and walked to the mailbox to collect the mail. I was surprised to find five envelopes addressed to me from DUI attorneys. I knew they were DUI attorneys because "DUI" was stamped all over the outside of the envelopes, apparently to let me know that they specialized in this particular defense. I wasn't ready to talk about my experience with anyone yet, but apparently these attorneys were ready to broadcast my circumstances to anyone and everyone who might come in contact with these envelopes. Now even my mailman knew that I had gotten a DUI. What if I had lived at home? Or what if my mother or a relative had dropped by to see me and saw five envelopes from DUI attorneys? Once again, my theory that lawyers were a bunch of assholes was confirmed.

I unlocked the side door and entered the kitchen, dropping

the mail onto the table. I stopped to pet Mack as he meowed up at me from a kitchen chair. The only good thing that had come out of the shock of seeing five envelopes of potential legal representation was that it prompted me to look for an attorney. First of all, I was most definitely not going to hire any of those lawyers who had solicited me. Since I didn't know who was respected and affordable here, I knew I needed to call my only real friend from law school, Kate Bethel-Greenblatt, and see if she had any referrals.

I know that saying Kate was my only real friend from law school might sound odd to some, but I would hazard a guess that anyone who thought that was sad hasn't attended law school. Basically, Kate was the only one from law school that I could trust. For those of you who don't know, law school is basically a very exclusive, arrogant fraternity and sorority mixer that lasts for three years. Although the desire to be ranked in the top ten of one's class is most important to the A-type personality which so dominates law school student body, it is also important to "see and be seen" in social events, rubbing elbows with those who have already passed the bar, then later sucking face with fellow 1Ls in a bar. Therefore, it is common for law students to be seen in large groups laughing and socializing with each other as if they were friends, but I would not trust certain other law students as far as I could throw a Black's Law Dictionary. And I'd only throw a Black's Law Dictionary if I had a chance of hitting a law student, namely Elizabeth White Bean, in the head.

Elizabeth White Bean was that annoying law school type that claimed to be a "liberal" and allegedly wanted to help the "victims of society." In reality what she wanted was power and notoriety just like every other law student and every other politician. She was That Girl who was offended by every slight she viewed as sexist and she was the only person on the planet unfamiliar with the cliché, "Choose your battles." However, she was not really concerned about "equality for women" in general. She was only concerned with superiority for herself specifically. One day in our small Women and the Law class (which consisted of seven females and one male), our discussion got off track. It veered into a monologue from White Bean (as I liked to call her) speaking vehemently about the importance of class rank in law school. Someone asked if it were really all that important. She answered, "Yes, it is important! I need to know where I am compared to the rest of you in order to see who I'm better than and who I need to beat!"

Another time at a small get-together, White Bean brought a friend of hers from high school who was visiting for the weekend. White Bean introduced her in the same way she introduced everybody with whom she chose to associate: by his or her résumé. "This is my friend, Tara. Tara graduated from Georgetown, *magna cum laude*, with a degree in finance. She now works in New York City for Bear Stearns." Then White Bean glanced around the small group of women of which I was included and determined which ones of us were worthy to introduce to Tara and which ones were not. "Tara, this is Melissa. Melissa is a 3L who will be working for one of the biggest firms in Nashville. Also, Melissa's mother is a State Supreme Court judge. And this is Rachel. Rachel's Law Review article will be published next month and she has an internship with a federal court judge in New York this summer. Maybe you two could get together when Rachel gets into town?" White Bean was beaming as she played matchmaker between the women who could accelerate her career. Although I was on Law Review and was a 2L representative for one of White Bean's committees, I was not significant enough to be worthy of an introduction. Maybe she realized that I secretly hoped to have a ring-side seat the day that Lady Justice ripped off her blindfold, grabbed her scales, and used them to bitch-smack White Bean in the face.

Even though I knew what kind of person White Bean was, I still found myself expecting some sort of human decency from her. When I chose not to return to law school, I called her and left a message on her machine telling her that I would no longer be the 2L representative; that I was sorry to leave, but she would need to get a replacement. Although it was not necessary, I thought basic decorum would have prompted her to call me back. I thought she might have called to say she was sorry to hear about my leaving and thanks for letting her know in advance. Instead, she acknowledged nothing.

It was then that I remembered a story that she told us during one of our Women and the Law classes. She told us about a "sexist" experience that she had in college when she was on some Ivy League school's prestigious debate team. It was all male except for her. All the guys on the team loathed her. One guy on the team told her one day during practice, "I hope you never get into a position of power.

If it ever seems like you might be in a position of power, I will find a way to bring you down, even if it means telling everyone that you are a whore." I could hear the cold-blooded anger and resentment in that male student's voice even as White Bean retold the story.

White Bean told this story as if the only reason this situation had occurred was because she was a woman on an otherwise all-male team. I had to wonder about that. Of course the "whore" name-calling was definitely uncalled for and sexist (what male politician could ever be scandalized for allegedly being a "whore" in college?), but maybe, despite his inappropriateness, he saw her for what she was: an egocentric megalomaniac who pretended to care about the welfare of others in order to catapult herself into a position of power. White Bean was just another wannabe lawyer hoping to slither her way upwards into power through the cracks in the legal system.

I shook the cynical thoughts from my head as I grabbed a Coke from the fridge and headed into the den with my purse. After relaxing on the couch, I pulled out my cell phone and scrolled through my phone list until I found Kate's phone number. I pressed *Send*. Kate answered on the third ring.

"Hey Kate!" I chirped. I surprised myself with this need to sound perky, as if everything in my life were going great. "It's Vandelyn."

"Hey, Vandelyn. How are things going with your new career?" she asked.

"Fine. I really like what I do." This statement was mostly true. "It's nice to be somewhere new, doing something new." What was I saying? Did my brain think that I was being interviewed? Must put positive spin on all topics? "How are things with you and Sam?"

She hesitated only for a split second and then said, "They're fine."

"OK, Kate. What's going on?" I asked.

"I am so frustrated," she sighed. "I'm sorry. You've just caught me at a bad moment. I just got off the phone with Sam. This weekend, which is Sam's weekend with his daughter, we were going to surprise Rebekah with a trip to New York. Sam's got to go there for business next week, so we thought we'd all go up there for the weekend and Rebekah and I would fly back together on Sunday. Well, Sam just spoke to his ex-wife about it, *as a courtesy, to be considerate*, and she tells him that Rebekah won't be able to go because

68

Rebekah already has plans—which involve a manicure, pedicure, and haircut—as well as a one-hour session with a tutor to help Rebekah with her Chemistry homework. *On our weekend!* She is scheduling appointments for Rebekah on our weekend without even consulting us about what our plans might be!"

I could hear the frustration in her voice. I was pretty appalled myself and it wasn't even happening to me. "That is so wrong," I said. "When my parents got divorced, my dad apparently thought 'divorce' meant you split from everybody in the family, including the kids. I hate to see a man who actually wants to spend time with his daughter be denied it by her mother. Or not so much denied, but treated as if he were merely a sperm donor. But then again, my father would have been honored to be thought of as only a sperm donor. It would have saved him a lot of money." Thinking about my father caused some of my own hurt and anger to bubble. I tried my best to ignore it as I always did when it tried to reach the surface. I could not deal with the pain. At least, not right now. Or maybe ever.

Kate was still absorbed by the situation. "It's not that I don't want Rebekah to get tutored or get a haircut or anything like that. But why does it have to happen without us being part of the discussion?" She sighed. "I'm sorry, Vandelyn. You didn't call to hear me vent. What else is going on with you?"

I took a deep breath. "Actually, I am calling you to see if you can recommend a good attorney. I got a DUI over the weekend and don't know who is good here. Do you have any ideas?"

"Wow, Vandelyn. That's awful. I'm sorry to hear that." She paused for a moment as if deep in thought. "I don't know of any attorneys there, but I could ask around." She got quiet again as if she were thinking some more. "Hey! I have an idea. Remember our Trial Practice professor, Mitchell Overton? The very successful criminal defense attorney? He knows attorneys in many different cities and I'm sure that they are all good. Why don't you give him a call?"

"Good idea!" I agreed. Mitchell Overton was one attorney that I actually liked. He was funny and down-to-earth and actually congratulated me on leaving law school. He said, "I think you could have been a good lawyer, had you wanted to be. But you are smart for leaving if you know it's not what you want to do. A lot of people don't have the courage to leave once they're in and realize that they hate it." He also had a good relationship with his students, telling them that they could give him a call with questions any time they needed to; if he wasn't able to take their calls right then, he would call them back. And he always did. "No chance that you happen to have his number, is there?"

"I do have it." Kate paused for a moment and then located his information. I pulled a notepad out of my purse and wrote down the number as she read it to me.

"Thanks," I told her. "And good luck with this weekend. Is there any chance that you can work it out?"

"I think so. I hope so," she sighed. "God will work it out. I guess what really burns me, is *why* she does things like this. It isn't just about her trying to 'take care' of Rebekah; she schedules things like this during our time *on purpose*."

"She's angry about something else," I agreed. "Ever notice that the arguments people have are rarely about what they are arguing about at that moment?"

"Only all the time," she said as I felt her smile into the phone. "Because that's what I do for a living." I had to smile myself. After we hung up, I snuggled into the couch, kicked off my shoes, and sipped on my soda. I thought about something that Kate said: God will work it out. I actually admired her belief in God. Apparently she had a solid, happy, tight-knit spiritual upbringing in the synagogue whereas I had an unstable, unpleasant, please-fall-through-the-cracks-so-we-don't-have-to-deal-with-your-problems upbringing in the church. Was Jewish spirituality just different than Christianity— besides, of course, the obvious differences? Was it just more *real?* Was there just more love, care, concern, and honesty?

When I was in eighth grade, I was good friends with a girl named Sarah Mertz. She was a year younger than I was and I remember how much fun I had whenever I spent the night at her house. Her mother was a trip. She spoke so candidly about everything. Sarah was embarrassed by her mother, but I thought Mrs. Mertz was so funny and cool. Mrs. Mertz was always making observations about things that no WASP that I had met would ever dream of mentioning. Such as the time she mentioned that against a tan body, pale breasts looked like fried eggs. And then there was the time she came into Sarah's room and confided in us about the "horrors" of her menstrual cycle. "Girls," she giggled. "My period was so heavy this month! I bled through a tampon, a pad, *and my pants!*"

One time when Mrs. Mertz was driving us to the pool, Sarah was bragging about her lack of armpit hair; something I envied because if requested I could grow a crop under each arm. "You are so lucky!" I told her. Mrs. Mertz added, "Oh, don't feel bad, Vandelyn. If Sarah is like any of the other women in our family, she'll be like a gorilla under there any day now." Sarah's usual response to her mother's revelations was pure mortification. However, I thought these conversations of uncensored truths were fabulous.

One day, Mrs. Mertz asked my mom about my father. With some melancholy, my mother revealed to her in a quiet voice that they were just recently divorced. To my mother's surprise, Mrs. Mertz responded with a robust, "Congratulations! How wonderful for you!" which made my mother laugh. Mrs. Mertz then told my mother about her pending divorce to Mr. Mertz: "When I married Lenny, I didn't realize that I was going to be his *second* wife, behind his mother! She's always holding Lenny's inheritance over his head; he'll do anything for her to keep his inheritance intact, including ignore me." My mom had always liked Mrs. Mertz, but after that day, I think she loved her.

Until I met Mrs. Mertz, I never knew there could be such healthy honesty within a family. As my young mind grappled with what made the Mertz family different, my thirteen year-old brain focused on the only difference that I could discern: religion. I asked myself, "Is Mrs. Mertz the way she is because she is Jewish?" If so, I *loved* Judaism. Judaism made you honest. Judaism let you talk about reality. Judaism didn't hide from problems. Instead, it exposed them—which was so unlike my life at home: pretend to be happy; pretend nothing is wrong; don't tell the truth about your feelings, about your pain; don't confront the issue. Then, when your soul starts to die, ignore it. The message I heard was a manic, panicked, *Don't! Don't! Don't! Pretend! Pretend! Pretend!* The only message that I wanted to hear was a calming, *Don't pretend.* Stop pretending. I had spent my whole life pretending. How was I going to learn how to stop now?

71

9

In the middle of a witty repartee between Phoebe and Chandler on *Friends*, my home phone rang. It was Tod. "Hey," he greeted me. "Sorry it's taken me so long to call you back." I had called him late afternoon from work. "We had to work a little late tonight."

"That's okay," I said

He continued. "I wanted to see if you wanted to go grab a drink and a bite to eat."

"I'd love to," I agreed. I had been debating about what to make for dinner. My stand-by was homemade bean burritos which were great in my eyes, but if someone else saw one of my burritos, he'd probably find it a bit repulsive. I'm not much of a culinary chef.

"I am on my way home now. Do you want to meet me over at my house and go from there? You can spend the night so you don't have to worry about driving."

"Okay," I agreed and we hung up.

Tod lived in North Chattanooga in a house that was really close to Frazier Avenue where all the cool eclectic places to hang out were located. Although I wasn't far from them either, just a couple of miles, Tod was a couple of minutes. I went into my bedroom and flung open my closet and tried to decide what to wear. I grabbed a pair of faded jeans, a Ralph Lauren long-sleeve cotton collarless blouse with skinny vertical stripes of pale blue and white, and began to get dressed. As I slipped a brown leather belt through the belt loops, I looked at my boring choice of outfit and sighed. I used to wear hot little outfits when I would go out for dinner and drinks. I used to be able to wear short skirts that showed off my legs; I used to be able to wear cropped tanks that showed off my tight abs. Now I dressed like Martha Stewart before she went to prison.

To my greater chagrin, I noticed that the jeans felt a little tight, but I walked around the bedroom and did a few squats in the attempt to loosen them up. I figured that these jeans had just been washed and not yet worn and would relax as the evening went on. What I hadn't immediately considered was that maybe they were just tight; that maybe I might look like that poor girl in law school that I used to refer to as "Camel Toe" whom I felt sorry for because she was not skinny and her jeans were so tight they appeared to be rearranging one of her more personal body parts into a hoof.

I became perplexed as I considered the possibility that I might enter a public place tonight looking like a pre-prison Martha with a nasty case of camel toe. I returned to my closet to check out my post-love-handle clothing inventory. It was all pretty boring, but with Tod and his crowd what did it matter? The females in his crowd actually wore khaki pants with front pleats (gross!) that buttoned at their natural waists (gag!) and considered that to be fashionable. Of course they also thought the Tommy Hilfiger clothing hanging in their closets was "haute couture."

Without casting too critical an eye at my outfit (although I did check for camel toe and the verdict was in: no hoof), I zipped up my brown leather pointy-toed boots, grabbed a small bag, and added some clothes to throw on tomorrow morning as well as a few toiletries. Then I picked up my sweet little baby, Mack, loved on him, gave him a few kisses, and told him that mommy would be back in the morning. Then I left a light on for him, set the alarm, and headed over to Tod's house.

I parked on the street in front of the house, making sure to keep the driveway clear for Tod and Ted's cars to go in and out. It was already dusk as I shut my door and pulled my coat tightly around me with one gloved hand while holding on to my bag with the other. The autumn leaves rustled under my feet as I hurried up the driveway to the covered front porch and rang the bell. Tod pulled the door open for me and held it as I passed into the front room.

"Is Ted here?" I asked as Tod pulled me into his arms and kissed me. Ted was Tod's roommate and the actual owner of the house that they shared.

"No," Tod told me after he released me. I tossed my coat and gloves onto the couch while Tod stood in front of me freshly showered and dressed, his brown hair still a little damp. Tod was an attractive guy in a regular sort of way. Unfortunately, my attraction to him came and went kind of like an outbreak of herpes. I couldn't help but notice how odd it was to date someone who was technically attractive, but was still someone I did not consistently find to be attractive.

"Is he already out looking for virgins?" I asked.

Tod laughed. "Yeah. He's got to get out pretty early to catch the virgins."

"Yeah," I agreed. "Too bad he's about twenty years too late."

Ted was a couple of years older than Tod (probably somewhere around Taylor's age) and had never been married (neither had Tod). As long as I'd known Tod, Ted had never even dated anyone. Ted was like that pint of unflavored, uncultured (he definitely wasn't cultured) yogurt sitting in the dairy aisle: although it didn't taste very good or look very appealing, it probably wasn't bad for you, but it was still likely to sit there alone on the shelf until its expiration date came due. (Unless, of course, a woman with a yeast infection walked by. Then she might pick him up. But I still couldn't quite make the connection. Maybe that was because a woman with a yeast infection still needed culture.)

In addition to Ted's blandness, he had this irrational desire to date and marry a virgin. This is where the "twenty years too late" came into play. I did not know of any forty year-old virgins except for Morrissey (and for all I knew he might be fifty by now). Although I did suspect that Ted was a homosexual male in denial (hence the unattainable quest for his holy grail: a virgin female; however, I doubted any gay men would desire him either), I still found his expectations to be ridiculous, almost to the point of offensive. I mean, what was "wrong" about dating and marrying a non-virgin? Most girls that I knew had traded in their virginity around the same time that they turned in their learners' permits. Unless Ted was willing to be arrested for soliciting minors for dates, I wasn't sure how he was going to meet a virgin.

However, I do admit that I knew one girl in college who was still a virgin, but she probably wasn't anymore. And as far as I know, she was the only college virgin who wasn't in an engaged-to-be-married relationship. So the best case scenario for Ted was that he would have to find a twenty year-old to date. I could already tell him right now, "That ain't gonna happen," unless he comes into a lot of money and develops a very aggressive terminal illness. Was that a price he was willing to pay for a virgin?

Tod and I walked down the hall together. I tossed my bag into his bedroom and he stepped into the open doorway of the hall bathroom, the only bathroom in the house, and sprayed a squirt of cologne onto his hands and rubbed it into his cheeks. I leaned up against the door frame as he fluffed his thick hair with his hands. As he stepped forward to exit the bathroom he seemed to notice my outfit for the first time.

"You look like a cowgirl," he said.

A tingle of alarm zipped up and down my spine. I had just entered into *Oh Shit!* mode. *A cowgirl?* The only time I ever tried to look like a cowgirl were those times I had no Halloween outfit, had to improvise, and deliberately exited my closet looking like a cowgirl.

"No, I don't," I contradicted a little too vehemently. First stage of *Oh Shit!* mode: denial.

I stepped into Tod's room and walked over to his full-length mirror to check. Tod followed me into his bedroom assuring me that my look "wasn't a bad thing." I stopped stone-cold in front of the mirror and examined myself.

"Oh my god," I breathed with the dawning realization that I looked like a corn-fed prairie girl, minus the braids. "I look like an escapee from *Dr. Quinn Medicine Woman.*"

Tod laughed, thinking that I was being funny. What I was doing was spinning into panic mode—this was a new experience for me because never before had I gone into panic mode over clothes. Then again, before I grew love handles, I never would have been caught dead in an outfit such as this one. And now I was at Tod's house and all I had was a small bag of clothing to choose from. I scrambled over to the bag while Tod protested that I looked fine, great even. (He was so lying.)

I looked at the pants and shirt: both black; they fit properly; and I felt my best when dressed in black. Only one problem: I was wearing brown boots and I had forgotten to pack other shoes. Wearing an all-black outfit with brown boots was just like Ted's relationship with a virgin: ain't gonna happen. So I improvised. I removed the Ralph Lauren blouse and threw it in the bag. I pulled on the black shirt, noticed that it was one of my Tuff Muff shirts, and smiled. Much better. I felt like myself and the brown belt and brown boots didn't matter because they blended with my faded blue jeans. I vowed then and there that I was not going to dress like a pre-prison Martha ever again, even if my worst outfit still looked better than those women dressed in high-waisted, pleated khaki pants.

10

If I thought that I had already overcome my greatest obstacle of the evening by fixing my corn-fed-prairie-girl-look, I was so sadly mistaken. I now found myself at a table for ten blowhards and I was one of the blowhards just because I was sitting with them. Life was not good.

To my left was a newly dating couple, at least by my observation. They were late twenties. She was blond and giggly and he was arrogant and annoying. Obviously these two blowhards were submitting their mating calls to each other and liking it. I personally was hating it; my only antidote a bottomless glass of Wild Turkey 101 and Sprite.

At this exact moment, the male of the species (of whatever species they were) was snapping his fingers, demanding that a server appear immediately. Apparently he had a problem with his chicken wings. As a former server and bartender, I wanted to smack him for snapping his fingers and acting all important and demanding (this was part of his mating call, I was sure of it). The blonde was so wide-eyed-impressed by his air of authority that she quit giggling for a few moments.

When no server magically appeared, the male then mumbled about how bad the service was and how the server was not going to get a tip. I had had a few drinks by this point and I was beginning to get ornery towards assholes. I glanced around the bar that was so busy every server was totally slammed. Under the circumstances, our server had been very attentive. Obviously this particular blowhard had never worked in the restaurant industry (or any service industry for that matter) and was unable to discern between a slacking server and one that was working his ass off to give the best service he could while simultaneously being in the weeds.

When the server reappeared during one of his laps around the restaurant trying to accommodate his patrons, the blowhard pulled him over to complain that his chicken wings were too big.

"Obviously these chickens were on steroids"—the blonde giggled—"or some kind of growth hormones. I am not eating them and I want them taken off my bill. Also, this lovely lady across from me would like another glass of wine. Her glass has been empty for a few minutes now."

His chastising manner of superiority was chafing my ass more than Camel Toe's blue jeans chafed her inner thighs. I had to look away and distance myself from these two as much as I could. Even though I didn't even know who they were, I felt guilty by association. I so wanted to tell the server, "I don't really know any of these people at this table and from what I know of them, I don't even like them."

I turned my back to the blonde and glanced across the table from me where Ted was sitting. He was involved in a conversation with the guy next to him, Bruce, about dating. Ted was listening as Bruce lamented about his dating situation.

"The women my age"—Bruce was in his late thirties, almost forty, I would guess—"I'm not really interested in for a long term relationship." I rolled my eyes and downed my drink. Ted nodded sympathetically. I shook my head in disbelief. Was this another forty year-old guy looking for a virgin?

Somehow I managed to control my sarcasm enough to ask, ever so innocently, "Why is that, Bruce?" I braced myself for another virgin conversation.

"Because I want to have kids and the older a woman gets, the more likely it is for her to have Mongoloid children."

"*Mongoloid?*" I asked, stunned. *Mongoloid?* Was this guy for real? Did he go around saying *colored* as well?

Bruce continued to enlighten me with his condescending Biology 101 lesson. "Yes," he confirmed. "The older a woman is, the older her eggs are, the more likely it is that she will give birth to a mentally retarded child."

"How old was your mother when she gave birth to you?" I asked. "Eighty-five?"

Tod laughed and the server magically appeared to ask if I would like another drink. I gave him an enthusiastic yes. Bruce stared at me. Ted ignored me. They were probably using their knowledge of me to support their theory of needing to date younger women who were more likely to be less smart ass (their terminology, I was sure, would include the word, "bitter") and less drunk. I tried to present myself as rational and reasonable.

"Seriously, Bruce. My grandmother was thirty-eight and forty-one when she had my mom and my aunt. They were perfectly healthy babies and that was back in the forties," I explained. Bruce was not listening to me anymore. He turned back to Ted and continued talking.

Oh well. Getting snubbed was my theme for the evening. When I said hello to Shelley and Mike (a.k.a. Raggedy Ann and Andy) when we first arrived, Raggedy Ann totally ignored me. Raggedy Andy had behaved in a civil manner and returned my greeting. Of course, next to Raggedy Ann was Stan, the alleged male whore. Tod had snarled at him. Although I ignored Stan, he still acted as if I had slept with him and couldn't quit calling him after the fact. (Now that I thought about it, that's probably what he was telling people.) I snapped out of my thoughts when Taylor turned to Bruce and joined in his conversation of dating women his own age.

"You can't date some woman your own age who's a non-virgin and never been married!" she yelped. "A girl who has been dating for twenty years is probably so loose that you could drive a VW Bug up her!"

How crass! All the blowhards at the table laughed except me. I narrowed my eyes and glared at her. She did not notice. I decided that night that Taylor was just like that girl in my sorority: always quick to put someone else down, or make fun of other people's lifestyle choices that differed from hers; always making sure that she was going to be viewed in a favorable light—if being a bully were a favorable light. And let's face it; in this crowd of corporate achievers and wanna-bes, bullies were the "winners." High school may be over with, but the "popular kids" are still out there, trying to one-up themselves over everybody else and I was stuck at a table of them.

High school had been a bag of mixed emotions for me when it came to assessing the in-crowd. Although I was pretty much happy in my school status and with my group of friends, I was messed-up from youth. Growing up in my family, the messages that I received on a daily basis from the outside world was that the way we did things, the way we were, *who we were*, was "wrong."

It was even as if my dad agreed with Those People when it came to our family. Apparently we weren't good enough for him, even though we were flesh of his flesh. My dad was a man who put his needs first over anyone else's in our family. I remember one time when I was in fourth grade, my lips were so chapped that they hurt. I needed lip balm desperately to the point that I was practically crying for it. I told my dad what I needed. He reacted as if I were just being whiney and told me to quit licking my lips. Apparently, it was not a necessity for him to find a nearby drug store and buy some fifty-cent lip balm to alleviate his daughter's misery.

So my father's "dysfunction" was that he didn't love any of us as much as he loved himself. My brother's "flaw" was that he was ADD at a time when that diagnosis was unheard of. Therefore my brother spent his first two decades misbehaving, acting inappropriately, being teased, harassed, and bullied EVERY DAY as a result. My brother was everyone's verbal punching bag and all he ever did in return was be nice.

I remember vividly a day in sixth grade when a pretty boy popular guy in my class stopped me on the sidewalk just to make fun of my brother to my face. He and I were alone as he made his obligatory derogatory comment. I tried to laugh it off, but my face betrayed me. Tears were welling in my eyes and as I tried to pretend to laugh, my lips were twitching downwards revealing that I was about to cry. The pretty boy didn't move, but stared at me. As I was still attempting to pretend, unsuccessfully, that his words didn't bother me, he spoke again as if making a scientific observation.

"You don't like it when I make fun of your brother, do you?"

"Oh, it's no big deal," I lied, fighting back a sob.

His eyes lingered on me for a moment and then he continued on his way. And although that pretty boy was an arrogant ass for other reasons during the rest of our school career, he never did make fun of my brother again.

Many years later, when I was in college, that pretty boy's mom worked in one of the university's administrative offices. She was so friendly and nice I had to wonder how she had produced a pretty boy asshole. Even though I had a low opinion of her son, I politely asked her about him because I felt I should. She proudly shared with me that he was also an English major and that he wrote poetry. I was stunned. It took all the self-restraint I possessed for

80

me to not yell, "That asshole writes poetry? For who? Andrew Dice Clay?" It was much, much later that I recalled his one moment of human decency. Maybe, just maybe, that asshole had a soul after all.

With my mother, things were different. She is a kind woman who was always strong when she needed to be strong for the family. When it came to being strong for herself, however, she was not as invincible. She would assume the worst about herself if she felt someone were criticizing her. And there I was, the littlest freak in our family's shop of horrors. Although I might have been the closest to "regular" or "normal" in our family, with my quiet and shy demeanor, I never had a chance. With all kinds of emotional bombs being dropped around me and on me, I grew up just as messed-up as everybody else.

Therefore, when I saw the popular kids in high school, even though I didn't like them, didn't respect them, didn't want to be them, there was a part of me that wanted to be included by them because the popular kids were "normal," yes? If I were included in their circle, then I would be normal too and no longer messed-up.

"Normal" people were like this: their fathers valued them; put them first; would've bought them Chapstick had their lips been red and cracked. Their brothers were athletic stars who dated the prettiest girls and knew how to behave. Their sisters were cheerleaders and top students who never felt awkward and shy. Their mothers were socialites with an over-abundance of self-esteem. And of course, they were always rich so they never felt the stresses of money problems.

I wanted to be somewhere I was valued, respected, and not beaten down and treated like a reject. To be treated badly by others hurt a lot. To hear people make fun of my father, my mother, my brother, hurt a lot. To have people make fun of me hurt a lot. But those "normal" people never seemed to hurt at all. Most of all, they never seemed to be in any pain when they were making fun of others. Actually, they seemed to be quite happy as they inflicted the pain.

As I grew older, I remembered who those mean people were: they were the popular kids whose fathers bought them things; whose mothers belonged to the right clubs; whose brothers were stars; whose sisters were considered pretty whether they really were or not. And they were all mean people who seemed to feel no pain when they caused injuries to others.

It was then that I diagnosed my Stockholm syndrome. As soon as I quit identifying with my oppressors, I realized that I never wanted to be like any of those people ever again. Instead, I became the reverse-bully, sticking-up for the little guys and the underdogs who were made fun of and put down. With these thoughts fresh in my brain, that night I began to feel that Taylor Kazakov might be the total embodiment of all these mean people from my past.

11

"Jennifer Patel is here to see you." I looked up from where I was cutting strips of muslin on my facial bed to see Donna standing in the doorway of my facial room.

"Okay. Tell her I'll be right with her." Donna returned to the front and I picked up the muslin strips and lay them on the table beside the wax pot. Jennifer Patel was one of my more outrageous clients whom I saw once a month to wax the dark peach fuzz off of her cheeks. She always had something shocking to tell me about her life whenever she came to see me.

Her parents were from India and came to be husband and wife as the result of an arranged marriage. They were quite happy, but were still traditionalists in their thinking. According to Jennifer, her parents told her that she would only get her inheritance if she followed through on an arranged marriage as well. "Not going to happen," Jennifer told me without too much concern during one of her appointments. Jennifer's family lived in Memphis and she had come to Chattanooga to get as far away from their watchful eyes as she reasonably could.

"Do they know you are dating someone?" I had asked her then. I knew she was dating a basketball player.

"No," she said. "As far as they are aware, I've never dated anyone in my life."

"Really?" I was incredulous. "And they believe that?"

"They are really naïve people. I've been sneaking out of the house since I turned sixteen and could drive. I've been dating college guys since I was in high school."

"And they never found out? You never got busted?"

"Never," she told me.

While Mr. and Mrs. Patel were old-world traditionalists,

83

Jennifer, their youngest child (they had three kids: Shilpa, Ravi, and Jennifer), was a packaged product of the unscrupulous part of American culture. In high school, she lied to a college guy she was dating about needing an abortion. He gave her the money, no questions asked, and she used it to go to the mall to buy new clothes and shoes. I thought this was the worst thing I had ever heard and told her so. She just kind of shrugged and laughed it off. Then I realized that it wasn't the worst thing that I had ever heard. I knew a fraternity boy in college, a pompous ass named Yancey, who told me that one guy in his fraternity was a date rapist. (Of course he didn't tell me who it was.) Yancey's perspective was that although he agreed (without overwhelming conviction) that date rape was "wrong," he himself wasn't "into" date raping girls (as if it were a hobby that a young man might pick up, such as tennis or golf). It never occurred to him that he was condoning his "brother's" behavior by not reporting it. He felt no guilt about being privy to this knowledge and doing nothing about preventing another criminal act from occurring against another unsuspecting young woman.

Jennifer also told me about attending Hindu Temple. Apparently, in order to enter the temple for worship, everyone had to remove their shoes. If Jennifer came out after the service and found a better pair of shoes than the ones she had worn in, she'd slip on the cooler pair and leave her old ones behind. "Jennifer!" I had squealed at her. "You stole shoes from someone at your temple?" She had just giggled. Although I did like Jennifer, her lack of conscience startled me. I decided that the only thing saving her from becoming a sociopath or a psychopath was the fact that she consistently revealed her lack of morality.

I walked up front and met Jennifer in the lobby. "Hey!" I smiled at her. "How are things going?"

She popped up out of the chair and I noticed she had a package of recently developed photos in her hand. "Great!" she smiled. "I've got a picture to show you."

"Cool," I said as I led her back to the facial room. She lay down on the facial bed and I wrapped her head to keep her hair out of her face, just like I did for facials. I applied the wax to her skin and ripped it off with the muslin strip. Jennifer was used to this procedure so it caused her no discomfort. While I waxed her cheek, she held the photos up above her face and began to flip through them. I continued waxing and did not pay attention to the pictures.

"OK," Jennifer said. "When you are done waxing, there is a picture I want you to see."

"OK." I agreed. I applied the last little strip of wax and removed the remaining hairs. I gently rubbed some after-wax lotion on her skin and removed the towel from around her hair. She sat up and handed me one particular photo. As soon as my eyes focused on what I was seeing, I went slack-jawed.

"Oh my god," I gasped.

Jennifer cackled with laughter. The photo was of Jennifer's boyfriend lying on her dorm room bed. He was completely naked with an erection. Although I had never seen anything so huge in my life (Thibodeaux used Magnum condoms, but he was not endowed like this, thank goodness), I had heard rumors about the existence of such penises. Just a glimpse of this photograph would have sent Tod's penis crying wee, wee, wee all the way home.

"Does he have any idea you are showing this to people?" I asked. She ignored me.

Instead she said, "Isn't that amazing?"

I had to agree. "Yes. That is amazing."

As I handed the picture back to her, I realized that my right leg was not only crossed over my left, it was wrapped around it. It was as if Tu-Tu had gotten the word out through my synapses that said, "No. No. No! No entry! Too big!" I had to agree with Tu-Tu and Goldilocks: that one too big; this one too small. Where was the one that was Just Right?

After Jennifer left, both Donna and I had small lulls in our schedules before lunch. "Do you mind to watch the front for a few minutes? I need to make a phone call."

"Not at all," Donna said as she settled into the receptionist's chair, a romance novel flipped open across the appointment book pages. As she began to read, I returned to my facial room and shut the door. I opened the closet door, grabbed my purse, pulled out my cell phone, and dialed Mitchell Overton's law office phone number. His receptionist answered. "Overton Law Firm."

"Hi. This is Vandelyn Devanlay calling for Mitchell Overton. Is he available?"

"Does he know what this is regarding?" she asked.

"Well," I began. "I am a former law student of his and I just

85

got a DUI in Chattanooga and I needed to know if he could recommend an attorney for me."

"Hold on, please." I held on for a few moments and then the phone was picked back up.

"This is Mitchell Overton," the voice said.

"Hi. This is Vandelyn—"

"Well, hello Vandelyn!" His friendly greeting roared through the phone lines. "Martie told me a former law student was on the phone, but she garbled your name." I nodded my head through the phone. If someone had not heard of a "Vandelyn Devanlay" before, I could see that happening. "But she said you needed some advice on an attorney?"

"Yes," I sighed. "I got a DUI over the weekend and I am still new in town. I don't know who to go see."

"I know one guy down there who is supposed to be very good. His name is James Peters. He used to be a prosecutor, but now is a criminal defense attorney, including DUIs. I'll see what he can do. What's the best number where I can reach you?" he asked.

I gave him my cell; told him it was fine for him to leave a message; and that I really appreciated his help. He rang off with a sincere assurance that he would call this attorney today and get back to me as soon as he had some information for me. I thanked him and we hung up our phones.

I was hopeful about this prospective attorney mainly because he was a friend of Mitchell Overton's. But the fact that he used to be a prosecutor before becoming a defense attorney was a flip-flop that was oohed and aahed over in law school. A former "good guy" now working for the alleged "bad guys" was considered quite an advantage to defense attorneys because a former prosecutor knew all the state's methods and tricks. I so hoped that this lawyer would be a great fit for me and get me out of my legal mess by poking holes in the state's case against me. It didn't really occur to me at the time that he might be just another asshole.

12

The following Monday morning, I headed down McCallie Avenue for my appointment with my potential lawyer, James Peters. Actually, if the price were right, I was sure that he was going to become my lawyer because what other choice did I have? Thankfully, when Mitchell Overton returned my phone call, he told me that he had pulled a few strings for me. He had told James Peters that I was a personal friend of his. He asked if "James" could alter his fee a little to accommodate my income level. Apparently "James" agreed because I had transferred two thousand dollars of my hard-earned money from my savings into my checking account this morning. I only had a couple of thousand left after this withdrawal and hoped that Mr. Peters (I could not imagine calling him "James" as Mitchell Overton did) would not have changed his mind about giving me a discounted fee.

I slowed down as I approached the old five-story office building and turned into its drive. The parking lot behind the building was surprisingly full. I found a spot in the back and walked towards the front of the building to catch the elevator to the fourth floor. As I pulled open the glass door, I noticed that the bottom floor held a little coffee shop and diner. I passed the diner's entrance and continued over to the elevator. I pressed the up button and waited for the doors to slide open. As I slowly rode the elevator up to the fourth floor, I found myself a little nervous. I really wasn't sure why. It wasn't like I was going to the doctor's office. He was just an attorney that I was going to hire to help me get out of my legal problems, best case scenario, that is.

The elevator doors dinged open and I stepped out into the narrow corridor. It was painted a depressing industrial gray-blue color. All of the doors were gray-blue as well. When I got to the attorney's office, the door was no different from all the others. It merely stated the number "404" and a plaque read, "Law Office." I grudgingly pushed the door open and stepped inside, not sure of what to expect. All the chairs in the waiting room were already occupied. Although I was right on time for my appointment, I was filled with dread of having to stand around a glum office waiting to meet with my defense attorney on my day off. At the far end of the small waiting room was a cut-out window in the wall where the receptionist would greet the clients from his or her desk if there had been a receptionist. What was sitting at the desk was a gruff middle-aged man with a mustache. A pretty blonde, probably early forties to his mid-fifties, stepped out into the waiting room from another room, probably her office, and guided a waiting client back with her. She had flashed me a quick, kind smile and shut the door to her office behind her.

"Vandelyn Devanlay!" the man barked from behind the receptionist's desk. His use of my name was so aggressive and hostile that I, along with the others in the waiting room, was startled by it.

"I am Vandelyn Devanlay," I responded, puzzled by his abrasive demeanor. The remaining clients averted their eyes as if glad that I were the one he was yelling for and not them. The man stood up from the desk and stomped to the back. I followed because I did not dare not to.

We entered his office and he shut the door behind us. "So. You are a friend of Mitchell Overton's?" he interrogated me.

"Yes. I was a law student of his."

"So tell me, how much am I charging you to defend you against a DUI?" Although his voice still had an edge to it, his tone was a bit softer now, as if he were somewhat amused.

"Mitchell Overton told me two-thousand dollars." I was trying to keep my voice solid and steady, but I felt as if I were in an alternate universe where anger management was an incurable disease.

He stared unblinkingly at me for a split second. Then he snorted. Then he laughed uncontrollably as if I were a comedian so hilarious and talented that I might have my own show on HBO.

"Two thousand dollars," he repeated with disgust. "Two thousand dollars."

He shook his head in disbelief and sat there for a few moments. I continued to look at him. My irritation was beginning to rise. I knew that two thousand dollars was very cheap for a DUI defense, but to me it was still a lot of money. I could not afford to wipe out all of my savings account just for this defense. James Peters was pissing me off, but no other attorney would do it for less than four thousand, I knew that for sure. So I just sat in my chair and waited, hoping that this jackass would not renege on his agreement.

He sobered up and started speaking very matter-of-factly. "Here's what I want you to do. I want you to type out everything that happened that night. Where you were, what you were drinking, and what happened when you got pulled over and arrested. I also want you to take photographs of the intersection where you were arrested. Take as many pictures from as many angles as you can. I want you to bring this information to me by next week, as soon as possible," he instructed me.

"OK," I agreed. I could handle that.

"Did you bring your paperwork with you?" he asked me.

I pulled out everything that the police and bondsman had given me. He left to make copies. While he was gone, I wrote out my check to him for two thousand dollars. He returned and handed me my papers. I stood to meet him and handed him the check.

"When we go to court, I want you to 'make yourself pretty.' You are a pretty girl so let's play up on that. Look professional. I'm sure you know how to dress after being in law school." I nodded.

He opened the office door and I walked out into the tiny corridor that led to the lobby. Once I crossed the threshold into the waiting room, James Peters returned to stand behind the desk of the nonexistent receptionist.

"Next!" he bellowed.

I saw a few clients' eyes blink, startled once again by his abrasiveness.

"Next!" he yelled again.

Only a second had passed and the remaining clients seemed confused on who was next in line.

I grabbed the doorknob as I heard Mr. Peters yell one last time, "NEXT! GODDAMN IT! WHO'S NEXT?"

As I let the industrial blue door shut behind me, the only thought in my head as I pressed the elevator button was, "What an asshole."

13

When I arrived home, it was around noon. I was grateful to have what remained of my day off to myself. I parked my car in the garage and walked down to the mailbox to see if the DUI envelopes were still trickling in or to see if any more interesting mail had come my way.

When I removed the mail from the box, I was glad to see that no more attorneys were courting me for business. I was even more pleased to see a large manila envelope addressed to me with Big Blue's return address. I strolled across the patio and entered through the kitchen door. I tossed the junk mail onto the kitchen table, removed my coat, and relaxed on the couch in the den with Big Blue's envelope in my lap. Mack leapt up onto the couch and of course lay across the envelope. I stroked his fur and gently pulled the envelope from underneath him, disturbing him as little as possible. He meowed at me to let me know that he found my movements to be slightly annoying, but then repositioned himself.

I opened the envelope and removed the informational packet. Jennifer Atchley's business card was paper-clipped to the front page and a sticky note was attached from Jennifer, stating that I hoped I found the information to be helpful and to give her a call if I had any questions. I was already feeling warm and fuzzy on the inside. That feeling dissipated as I scanned over the different insurance packages. They were definitely more expensive than what Jennifer was paying Big Blue as an employee. The plans with the lowest deductibles cost twice as much as I was paying COBRA. The asterisk at the bottom of the page informed me that a "preexisting condition" would not be covered until twelve months had passed. When I got to the price ranges that were less than my monthly COBRA payment, the deductibles were huge.

I was getting confused by the statement at each plan

informing me that coverage would kick-in after the deductible was met. What did this mean? That I had to pay all of my doctor's expenses up front until I paid enough money to doctors to reach a couple of thousand (or more) dollars in one year? That couldn't be right, could it? I wasn't sure. If that were the case, it would almost have me wishing for serious illnesses just so I could finally meet the deductible and start getting "paid-for, quality healthcare." Thankfully I was a person who rarely got sick. My only serious illness centered around my OB/GYN visits due to my HPV. I had surgery in June (just before I quit my previous job) while I still had legitimate health insurance (as opposed to COBRA). Therefore, I went to the OB/GYN four times a year to keep an eye on the pre-cancerous cells that kept threatening to develop in my cervix. Even with four visits a year, my out-of-pocket-medical bills (not including payments to COBRA) were probably only around $700 a year. If I understood this correctly, it didn't make any sense to switch to another healthcare plan. As long as I was healthy, maybe I was better off without health insurance altogether. However, I knew that I was not willing to take that risk.

Although I had convinced myself that staying with the evil that I knew was better than switching to the unknown that might actually be worse, I still continued to scan the different plans. I started focusing on two columns: the non-smoker versus the smoker. Fortunately, I was a non-smoker, which meant that I got off cheaper than the smokers. I did feel sorry for the smokers, though, because if I were struggling with the cheaper price, a smoker in my position would be really stressed out by the price differential (and would therefore smoke more, yes?).

The thing that made me laugh, though, was that every time I walked down the sidewalk past Big Blue, a large passel of Big Blue employees were always standing out front wearing their badges, taking their smoke breaks. (This sight also caused me to want to change their name to "Big Cig" rather than "Big Blue" because of all the lit cigarettes out front.) I bet their smoker-employee health insurance was still cheaper than the crappy insurance that they were offering me at the non-smoker "discount." I thought it was pretty hypocritical of Big Blue to make us pay for their employees perks.

But isn't that they way of big business? The Exxon Valdez came to mind, but I boycotted Exxon so I didn't give them any of my money when they raised their gas prices a few cents so they wouldn't have to pay for the environmental damage all by themselves. Luckily for Exxon, there are enough assholes in the world who hate do-gooders, such as one of my high school guy friends who decided he would only buy Exxon oil *because* it damaged the environment. I think he actually smiled every time he saw a penguin covered in oil sludge.

I, on the other hand, had no problem with smokers as long as they weren't blowing cigarette smoke directly in my face. I was one of the few non-smokers who was actually for smokers' rights. I mean, since when is a landing in a stairwell by an open window a "designated smoking area" just because it has a plaque stating so? And what about that awful glassed-in room at the airport where tobacco addicts have to stumble through an inhumane smog-filled 20x20 space just to puff on their cigarettes while we non-addicts pass by on the way to our boarding gates, glancing over at them as if they were animals in a zoo?

I was also one of the few people who thought it was ridiculous that Joe Camel had to be removed as a logo for Camel cigarettes. Supposedly "Joe Camel" was enticing minors to smoke because he was a cartoon character. When I was a child, I'd go to restaurants with my parents and ogle the cigarette machine that was usually located in the lobby or by the restrooms. I knew exactly which kind of cigarettes I was going to smoke when I grew up: KOOL or Camel Lights and that was way before Joe Camel was even created. My choices were derived from my love of Kool and the Gang and my fascination with Egypt. My eyes were always drawn to the picture of the camel standing in the desert in front of the pyramid. And guess what? Even with my positive perceptions of KOOL cigarettes and the allure of Camel's cigarette packaging, I grew up to be a non-smoker. Could it be that people have the ability to make their own decisions about their lifestyle choices despite clever marketing tactics? Could it really be that an individual could outsmart an advertising exec? Go figure.

In law school we had studied the history of cigarettes and the lawsuits against the tobacco companies. I was on the side of the people until the year 1965. That was the year that cigarette packages had first been labeled with the warning, "Cigarette smoking may be hazardous to your health." When I was in elementary school, I remember flipping through a magazine with a friend of mine and coming across a cigarette ad. On the page was the distinct warning from the Surgeon General. I was not exactly clear on who or what the Surgeon General was, but his statement that cigarettes were hazardous to my health sent a chill down my spine. My friend and I knew that this warning was serious business. We probably took it so seriously because our parents had taught us that certain activities were meant for adults only and not children. Both her parents and mine were non-smokers who told us that smoking was not good for us and we heeded that message (except for my freshman year of college when I went through a brief period of smoking when I drank).

So I was all for people who had not had the benefit of the Surgeon General's warning suing the tobacco companies for false advertising ("Feeling tired? Unpopular at parties? Need help studying? Light up a cigarette!") and failure to acknowledge the health risks of tobacco. Up until 1965. After that, I felt no pity. What had happened to people taking responsibility for their own actions? Why was it always someone else's fault? If they knew that smoking was hazardous to their health and they picked up a cigarette and smoked it, are not they ones responsible for accepting the consequences?

I was so tired of the "it's not my fault-it's somebody else's fault" society that we have become. I thought it was ludicrous every time I saw a self-deprecating R.J. Reynolds tobacco commercial, post-lawsuit, that let the audience know that it sold cigarettes, but no one should buy its product because it might cause cancer or other health risks. I pictured R.J. Reynolds as Eeyore. His head would be hung low, his eyes down, his tail missing, stating, "I have a product, but don't ask me what it is; don't buy it from me, because it'll probably kill you. Ho-hum. Nobody likes me."

Not that I liked big business that exploited little people for its own financial gain either. I just think that both sides should accept responsibility up to a point. Otherwise, where does it end? Could I sue Marilyn Manson for my trouble with the law? Blame my fight with authority on the fact that his CD, more specifically, *The Fight Song*, was playing in my car at the time of my DUI arrest? Could I sue Wild Turkey for making 101 proof liquor so enjoyable? The bartender for serving me even though it was I who approached the bar, asked for a drink, and paid for it with my own money? Should I sue Tod for picking a fight with me that night? Get an injunction against Raggedy Ann and Andy for being totally lame and throwing a Halloween party so crappy that the only way I could survive it was under the influence? Subpoena Stan for being an alleged male whore and for habitually hitting on Tod's dates? If I could blame all these varying factors for my present circumstances, exactly whose fault was my DUI arrest, if not my own?

I sighed and cast the envelope and Big Blue's paperwork onto the coffee table. I lay there for a few more minutes and petted Mack as he purred loudly. As I remained on the couch, I knew what I had to do. I needed to go ahead and take pictures of the intersection and type up the events of my DUI on my computer and print them out. It wasn't what I wanted to do, but today was the best day for me to do it. I knew I would feel much better once it was done and turned in to the asshole lawyer.

I gingerly removed Mack from my lap and placed him on the couch after I swung my legs off of it. Of course, now that I had disturbed him, he jumped down off the couch and hurried off into the hallway, meowing his displeasure as he went. I unsuccessfully dusted the fluff off of my jeans and headed for my bedroom closet. I pulled my camera bag down from the top shelf, removed my camera, and sat down on my bed.

After turning the camera on, I saw that I had a couple of pictures left on the roll of film. Mack had followed me into the bedroom and had wandered into the closet, inspecting an empty shoe box. I watched as he pawed at the tissue remaining in the box, pounced on it, and then stepped into the box. He looked so cute. Since I had my camera poised and ready, I snapped his picture. Then he lay down in the box, curling up into a little ball. I smiled and took another picture.

"You are so adorable," I cooed at him as I stepped over to scratch his ears. He meowed a thank you. I took one more picture of his face as he looked up at me from the box and the film began to automatically rewind. I sat back down on the bed, removed the used film, and replaced it with my last roll of new film.

"All right, Mack," I told him, "Mommy's got to go take some photographs, but I'll be back soon."

I grabbed my freshly loaded camera and the film that was

ready to be developed, hopped into my car, and drove down to the corner where I had made the wide right turn that had led to my arrest. Fortunately, a drug store was on that corner so I parked my car in its parking lot and walked out onto the sidewalk.

I took numerous shots from that spot at various angles and from the sidewalk across the street. I still had more film to use, so I drove a fifty yards down the road to the spot where I had actually been stopped by the police in front of the pretty brick Presbyterian Church. I took a few pictures of that location.

With a few more pictures left in my camera, I drove to the gas station across the street from the front of my house and took some pictures. Even though it was late fall, it was a sunny, pretty day and my grandparents' house looked so cozy and homey. The pictures of the house were just for me to have, not for Mr. Peters, and I smiled the whole time I was taking them. I ended up not using all thirty-six shots, but I figured I had plenty of photo "evidence" for my defense. I hopped back in my car, drove down to the drug store, and dropped both rolls of film off for one-hour development. Then I returned home and typed up my drunken-driving arrest experience in as much detail as I could recall. Fortunately, I could recall a lot of details from beginning to end.

It was about an hour later when I sat back in my chair and reread my four pages of writing. I made a few corrections and then hit the print button. I had not realized how tense my body had become until I was finished typing and slouched back in my chair. It felt good to be finished. Now all I had to do was pick up my film. Once I had the film, I could hand over my work product to my asshole attorney and hopefully help him help me from getting convicted. I removed the four pages from the printer, stacked them nicely, and paper-clipped them. I set them to the side of my desk, grabbed my purse and keys, and returned to the drug store to pick up my film.

Once I was back at home and all comfy on my couch, I pulled open the large white envelope that held one of my rolls of film. It was the roll that I just took that afternoon. I checked out all the angles, wrote a brief description on the back of each relevant picture, and separated Mr. Peters' copies from my own. I dropped his copies into the white envelope and kept my pictures in the smaller paper package that held the negatives.

Next I opened the other white envelope. I was pretty interested to see what had been developed. I was notorious for starting a roll of film during one season and then completing the roll three seasons later. What would be on here? Thanksgiving? Christmas? Summertime? Thibodeaux?

I smiled as I glanced at the first picture. It was from Christmas. Mack and I were still living in my apartment and he was playing with an ornament on the small tree that my mom had given me for the living room. How cute! I kept flipping and smiling at each picture: Mack in my closet; Mack out on my apartment balcony; Mack playing with the fresh flowers I had placed in a vase on my glass coffee table. As I flipped, the seasons and locations changed from my apartment to my grandparents' house, but one thing remained the same: Mack. Mack out in the front yard; Mack lying in the empty bird bath; Mack peeking his head through the bushes. All the photos made me smile and were adorable, but when I got to the end of the roll, I scratched my head. Not one of the thirty-six photos had a human being in it. All of the thirty-six photos had Mack in it.

I remembered a woman, Jan, that I worked with in an office one summer when I was twenty. Whenever Jan would pass by my desk, she would stop and talk to a fellow co-worker, Betty, whose desk sat right behind mine, about Jan's two cats. Betty also had cats. I had no pets, was in college, and my life revolved around partying and socializing during the summer. I would hear Jan tell Betty all about her cats' escapades and dote on them as if they were her children. (Jan was over forty, unmarried, and childless.) Every time I heard one of Jan and Betty's conversations, I thought, "That's so sad that all they have are their cats. What old losers." I knew that I would never be like that in my entire life. But ten years later, here I was with thirty-six pictures of my adorably sweet pussy cat and only of my adorably sweet pussy cat. Had I become like Jan and Betty? Was I now a woman who loved her pussy too much?

I sighed and decided that I needed to email Marais. I clicked on the internet connection and went straight to my account. Email was the greatest thing ever when it came to me and Marais. We could talk anytime; tell each other anything even in the middle of the night without having to pick up the phone. Not that we didn't love talking on the phone to each other, because we did. But with her coursework in graduate school, her free time was very limited. If we got to talking on the phone, we could end up talking for hours. So we reserved phone calls for the weekends and emailing for whenever we felt like it. I especially loved it for small tidbits such as the one I was going to send her.

TO: French Sistah
FROM: French Cracka
SUBJECT: Do I love my pussy too much?

I just got a roll of film developed and it was 36 pics of Mack and no one else was in the pictures. Should I be worried?

I hit the send button and relaxed back into the chair hoping that Marais would actually email soon. I hadn't talked to her in a few days via email or phone and was looking forward to some banter with her. Marais had moved to Atlanta a little over a year ago to start graduate school at Emory. I was glad to be a few hours closer to her now, but I still had not had the chance to go visit her down in Atlanta since I'd moved this summer and I missed her.

It was amusing to me now how close we had become because our friendship arose from the unlikeliest of circumstances. She had moved to Tennessee from Philadelphia, Pennsylvania our freshman year of high school. Her father, Dr. Abraham G. DuBois, had been recruited by the historic black college in town for the position of president and he had accepted the job.

I remember Marais when she started high school. She and I didn't have any classes together, but our lockers were close together because they were assigned alphabetically and we would smile and say hi on a daily basis, sometimes chatting a little here and there. By the time we were juniors, we still didn't know each other very well because we ran in different circles, but we had still been friendly. And then sometime during our junior year of high school, everything changed. Every time I would smile and say hi to Marais, she would give me a cold stare or just ignore me. Then she narrowed her group of friends to only include girls that weren't white. And then her group of friends started to wear necklaces that had large pendants in the shape of Africa hanging from them. Whenever I would pass any of them in the hallways, they would glare at me.

Being treated as less than equal, being discriminated against because of the color of my skin, was really unfair and it really started to piss me off. I was getting pretty irritated by and angry about their behavior. But instead of confronting them with it which I was sure would turn into me being accused as being some kind of racist, I swallowed my anger, and simply made snide comments to my friends, which had they been overheard might have been perceived as hater remarks: "What about if I went around with France around my neck?"; or "Why is Marais even wearing Africa around her neck? She's a French descendant just like I am. Not to mention that we are all Americans!"

But I wasn't a racist and I was offended by even being thought of as such. My parents had told my brother and me about the segregation and racism that existed when they were growing up; they told us how wrong it was to treat people differently because of how they looked on the outside. What was important was who they were on the inside. Not only did my brother and I obey their words, we also knew in our hearts that we should "never judge a book by its cover." Although I was not trying to judge anybody by their exterior, I was hurt by Marais' blanket judgment of me; for holding me accountable for something I had never been a part of. I was angry at being treated as if I were "Whitey" or "The Man."

In all honesty, though, I didn't even know who "The Man" was when I was sixteen. I only really found out about "The Man" six years later when I was hanging out with a thirty year-old guy, Frank, who worked at my favorite bar and had been a teenager in the seventies. One night I asked him "What's up?" and he smiled at me and said, "Not much. Just working for The Man." Puzzled, I said, "What?" He had to explain to me what The Man was. He used it in examples such as, "You know, *The Man is keeping me down.*" I shrugged. He continued, "You know, *The Man.* The boss man. The government." I now understood and said, "Ah," with dawning enlightenment.

So there I was, a sixteen year-old representative of The Man without my even knowing it. Apparently the existence of my white face in the hallway was enough to create hostility from Marais and her posse so I thought it only fair and equitable that I return some of the hostility. One day when Marais was removing books from her locker between classes, I very deliberately said, "Hi." My greeting was a little louder than was normally acceptable; it may have even been a little forceful, but I was determined that she make some sort of response. She ignored me. So I turned to face her profile and said, "Hello, Marais." I admit that it came out just a tad sarcastically. She glared at me and turned to walk away. I was really pissed now. "What's your problem?" I demanded. I think I may have even slammed my locker.

"Excuse me?" she snipped as she turned to face me, her shoulders squaring up for a fight.

"You heard me," I said. "What's your problem?" The bell rang signaling the start of class. A few students watched us as they slowly passed through the doors for the start of various classes.

She wagged her finger in my face. "*I* don't have a problem, but *you're* going to have a problem if you keep talking to me that way."

"Is that so?" I smirked. "What are you going to do about it, *sistah*?" At that precise moment, the Dean of Students, Mr. Archibald, walked up to us in the hallway and called us both into his office. We were both issued demerits; our parents were called; we were told that we had to stay after school for a parent-student conference; then he allowed us to return to class. I had to enter my classroom late and my fellow classmates stared at me as I took my seat. Their eyes questioned me about what I had done wrong and estimated how much trouble I had gotten into for doing it.

My mom was calm when she entered the Dean's office, but her eyes and the expression on her face when she looked at me told me she was really angry and I was going to have a lot of explaining to do. Mom took the seat beside me; Mr. Archibald sat at his desk; Marais, Dr. DuBois, and Mrs. DuBois sat in chairs opposite my mom and me. The parents were calm and impassive while Marais and I folded our arms across our chests and alternated between huffing with indignation and casting glares at each other.

Dr. DuBois broke the silence. "I will not tolerate racism," he said firmly yet calmly.

Mr. Archibald agreed. "We do not tolerate racism at The Private School either." I so wanted to yell that I didn't tolerate racism either and that's exactly why we were all sitting in the office right now, but for once in my life I kept my mouth shut.

"Nor do we," my mother said. "I would like to hear exactly what happened today. From Vandelyn and Marais."

"She called me a *sistah*," Marais tattled on me with a smirk.

99

My eyes narrowed at her. Of course she went straight to the part of the story that made me look bad. Of course, I had said it and it did make me look bad so I really couldn't get too mad at her for her strategy. She gave me a sweet smile knowing that she had started with a strong offensive.

"Here's what happened," I began. "I said hi to Marais. She ignored me. I then said *Hi, Marais* and she ignored me and glared at me. Then I got frustrated and asked her what her problem was."

"You didn't say hi to me to be friendly. You were saying hi with an attitude!"

"An attitude?" I huffed. "What about your attitude? We used to speak and be friendly with each other. And now for no reason that I know of, you and your friends glare at me as if I were Whitey or something." I realized that maybe I shouldn't have let that *Whitey* comment slip out, but as they say in law school, you can't unring the bell. I kept going. "If I wronged you or your friends in some way, why don't you tell me what it was so I can apologize? I never meant to do or say anything to offend you," I explained. As I got to the last two sentences, I noticed that my original indignation had fled. We were at the heart of the matter now. I did not want to be her enemy. I actually realized that I wanted to be her friend. I looked at her, sincerely apologetic.

Marais wavered and she glanced over at her mom and dad. "Well, Marais?" her mother gently prodded. "Did Vandelyn do something to offend you?"

Marais turned away from her parents and looked down at the floor, twisting a strand of hair around her finger. "Well, no," she admitted a bit reluctantly. Then she glanced up at me with some ferocity and said, "Except for that *sistah* thing!"

"Marais," her father cautioned.

"Okay, then. No." Marais flopped her body forcefully into the back of the chair and huffed. Then she looked over at her parents again and pleaded, "But how am I supposed to know?" Tears immediately welled up in her eyes and she fell into her mother's arms and cried. My mother and I glanced at each other, puzzled. *Know what?* What exactly was going on?

Mr. Archibald filled us in. "There have been some reported incidents of racism at our school." I was stunned.

"Marais heard a student telling a racist joke to another

student and laughing as she passed by them. One of her friends, Sasha, heard another student refer to Sasha as a 'spook,'" Dr. DuBois told us. "When the students were confronted, they denied it." *Of course they denied it* were the unspoken words that I was sure we all added on after the end of his sentence. My jaw dropped open and I made a face of disgust when I registered what he was telling us. I then understood what Marais had meant when she had rhetorically asked, "How am I supposed to know?" Some people hid behind smiles the same way Klansmen hid behind white satin hoods.

"That's so wrong!" I said. I couldn't believe we still had racists in 1988! Racists that had only been born in the last decade! I registered an even scarier thought. Were these racists the children of affluent leaders in our community?

Marais had returned to an upright sitting position and was blotting her tear ducts with her perfectly manicured fingertips. Her mother handed her a tissue. Marais dabbed her eyes, then her nose.

"I am so sorry to hear that," my mother said. "I understand your concern." She turned to me and rubbed her hand across my shoulders in a loving manner. "It is very important for people to be respectful towards others. Always. Even if we feel as if we have been treated badly," she explained to me. I nodded, my head hung a little lower because I knew she was referring to the *sistah* comment.

"Yes. Mrs. Devanlay is right," Mrs. DuBois agreed in a firm voice as she turned towards her daughter. Marais nodded her head.

Dr. DuBois leaned across his wife and patted his daughter's knee. "Remember," he murmured in a soft voice that we could all hear because the office was so quiet, "what Dr. King said." She nodded again as she stared at the floor and then quickly raised her eyes to meet his. They all three smiled at each other. It was a connection so tender, so strong, that I suddenly ached to be a part of it. But at that time I wasn't a part of it. However, my mom and I looked at each other and smiled our own connection. Looking back on it, I think that was the best worst day of my life. I sighed. Now I had a new worst day of my life and I doubted that it could ever be made "good."

I pushed my chair back from the computer and logged out of my internet account. I glanced out the window and saw the bright sunshiny day. Even though it was cold outside, I knew that I should put on some exercise clothes and go for a walk or maybe even a run like I used to do. It would be good to get some fresh air and maybe try to walk off a love handle or two.

After I changed clothes and put on my coat, I stepped outside and walked the ten yards to the end of my road and waited for a break in traffic. I hurried across the highway and started walking on the sidewalk in front of the gas station, heading in the direction of town. As I walked, I smiled as I appreciated the small, local storefronts. The air was cool and crisp; sometimes the wind would whip across my face, but my knit cap (something that I used to refer to as a "toboggan" until Marais started laughing because up north, a "toboggan" is a sled) kept my head pretty warm.

I walked past the dark brick Presbyterian Church and smiled at its cozy exterior of steeples and a carved, arched wooden door. As I continued, I observed the small building at the bottom of the grassy slope catty-cornered to the Presbyterian Church that housed the Chinese church. Its modest wooden sign was written in English as well as in Chinese characters. I continued and crossed the intersection with the drug store and passed by another small set of locally owned shops and the offices of a dentist and an eye doctor. Tucked down a side street was the large brick Methodist Church. It was beautiful as it stood back from the main road surrounded by a large grassy field. I turned my eyes away and continued down the pavement. I arrived in front of the Baptist church and paused. The Baptist church was larger than the Presbyterian, but about the same size as the Methodist. However, the Baptist church also had a decent-sized building adjacent to it that was its community center. I saw a few people laughing and smiling as they entered its doors and I had to admit that I was intrigued. I thought about how nice it would be to have somewhere warm to belong where people welcomed you with open arms and acceptance.

Then I quickly shook my head as if to dispel my thoughts. What was I thinking? Weren't a lot of Christians hateful, judgmental, and known for rejecting people like me; people who have actually lived a little and made some mistakes? Then I remembered some other things. Some denominations didn't allow women at the pulpit. Others stood on the side of the road, holding posters covered with gruesome photographs of bloody fetuses "in the name of God."

My initial goodwill turned into a glowering stare as my heart started beating a little faster. I turned on my heel and continued walking with dark thoughts hovering over my head. As little as I knew about the Bible, I knew a little something about Jesus that I learned as a child. I knew that Jesus was kind and loving. Jesus wouldn't tell women that they couldn't preach. Jesus wouldn't stand on the side of the road holding perverse photos meant to inflame, anger, and hurt others. Jesus would have held women's hands as he loved them, hugged them, cried with them, *helped* them. He would not blow up clinics "in the name of God." I glowered some more and then I picked up my pace so I could leave that darkness behind me.

The wind picked up speed as I hurried along the sidewalk to a new sightline. Across the street I saw the Junior High and that made me smile. This school building was the same one my mother had attended when she was growing up. At the time, though, the Junior High was actually the High School until they built a new high school a couple of decades or more ago. I stopped on the sidewalk and gazed at the school. It was surreal to stand here and imagine being back in the 1950s; envisioning my mom walking up those very steps into school, heading for her locker, and then for class. I blinked and turned away and continued down the sidewalk. Once I passed the costume rental shop and then the Church of Christ, I turned on my heel and headed back towards home. When I drew near the Baptist church, I looked across the street at the small strip mall with the Sav-A-Lot grocery store and the Dollar Store. Both parking lots were dotted with cars; people were coming and going from both businesses, saving some money and living their lives.

By the time I got back into my house, my nose and cheeks were pink and cold. I shed my coat, pulled off my hat, and flopped down on the couch, enjoying the warmth of my home. As I lay in silence, my eyes staring up at the plaster ceiling, I wondered what I had accomplished with that walk. Not much. I knew my pace hadn't been quick enough to burn off a love handle. And now I was burdened with a reminder of how awful religion was. I had been told that Jesus had come here to love us and help us and even *save* us. Now all that was left from his visit was lousy religion; religion that was used to oppress and judge those that Jesus actually came to help: the poor, the needy, and the lost souls.

How could a group of people supposedly so "knowledgeable" about God be totally clueless about the very point of his existence? I could hear all the Good Christians smug in their self-righteousness: "Well I might gossip now and again, but at least *I* don't drink alcohol!" or "I was a virgin until I got married, unlike *her*!" What did they think heaven was? The Department of Motor Vehicles and God, the Head Civil Servant? Did they think St. Peter used the DMV points system when it came to our various sins? One point against your record for gossiping; two points for imbibing; three points for premarital sex; five points for being a "whore" (if you're a woman. If you're a man, it's only one point); ten points for being gay (for all those Good Christians who think homosexuality is a sin) or having an abortion. What would happen if you got twelve points against you in one year? Would your life be revoked?

I shook my head, mentally flipped-off all the religious folk, and told them telepathically that as far as I was concerned, *they* could all go to hell. With that newly encumbered burden freshly released, I smiled as I closed my eyes and took a nap.

14

I awoke to Mack standing on the top of the couch, leaning his head down into my face, and meowing at me. As I moved, he backed away, still meowing, and ran off into the kitchen. I followed him. He stopped at his food bowl and fussed at me. "Okay," I told him. "I understand." As I reached for the food bowl, he became fussier until he saw me scoop out a nice mound of cat food. Then I poured out his water dish and refilled it with fresh water. Mack was now a contented pussy, crunching on his cat food and lapping up his fresh water.

Now that he was satisfied, I returned to the computer and logged back into my email. I was happy to see that I had a new message from Marais.

TO: French Cracka
FROM: French Sistah
SUBJECT: Re: Do I love my pussy too much?

Yes, you should be worried because the "pussy" (and you know I hate that word) you refer to is your "kitty" . . . as in, cat. Not your "kitty" as in, Tag That! Haha. A year ago, we would have been talking about whether or not Thibodeaux (or Loverboy depending on whether you and TBD were in or out—no pun intended) loved your pussy too much or not enough.

But I am glad to hear that you are well, happily domesticated, and slowly but surely turning into the cat lady. Got to go to the library for research! Love you.

I smiled as I logged out of my account again and turned off the computer. "Loverboy" was how we referred to our vibrators. Although the name in itself was appropriate, that name really came from the 1980s band, Loverboy, because one of our guy friends pointed out that Loverboy's song, *Lovin' Every Minute of It*, sounded like it was about a vibrator. Just thinking about how apropos the lyrics were made me giggle out loud, but it sounded hollow to my ears because I wasn't really happy. Marais did not know of my DUI yet and her assumption that I was well and relatively happy depressed me. She knew that I had been going out with a guy named Tod, but I didn't mention him a lot so she either thought we were no big deal or over. How far off the mark those two concepts were. I knew that I was going to tell her about the DUI at some point, but I just wasn't real excited about broaching the subject. She would be sympathetic and not judgmental, of course, but the thought of discussing that situation with others just made it seem more real and that much more of a downer. So I immediately focused on a happier topic: my vibrator.

My vibrator and I had only been together for a year or two. Marais was actually the one who introduced us. Somehow her vibrator had bit the dust (I tried not to think about the how and why of that too much) and she and I went to the sex store together to pick out a new one. During the ride over, I decided to purchase one as well since Thibodeaux and I were on-again-off-again on a regular enough basis. I thought this would give me a healthy outlet when we were on the outs and prevent any potential sexual frustration from building up inside of me.

Once we entered the sex shop and showed our I.D.s to enter through the door labeled "Treasure Trove" that led to the goodies, I glanced around the various models and found myself cringing inside. Some of them were downright scary. I pointed to a model sitting with a ramrod straight posture—something that I had never been able to achieve since often times I preferred slouching—and stared at it. "What's that thing at the base of it?" I asked Marais. The vibrator in question came in various colors of the rainbow and they all possessed a "thumb." It seemed so unnatural for a dick to have a thumb. So I clarified the problem for Marais: "It looks like a thumb." She leaned in close to me and whispered, "That's not a thumb. That's a butt plug." My first gynecological experience popped into my head where I remembered a brief invasion of my privacy by a short, stubby unwelcome digit. I wrinkled my nose and involuntarily squeezed my butt cheeks together. No wonder I had mistaken it for a thumb.

I scanned other shelves and everything else was just too scary. I did not want some gargantuan penis inside me. The only gargantuan penis I had ever liked was the six-foot "Captain Pecker: The Party Wrecker" inflatable penis that was also a punching bag. A guy friend from the restaurant where we worked had drawn my name in the Secret Santa pool and bought that for me back when I was a bartender. One of the cooks immediately blew it up (which made for interesting pictures) and we all had photo ops with it during the Christmas party. Afterwards, I reclined the passenger seat and drove Captain Pecker home to the house that I shared with Toronto Jen and another girl, Lee. For amusement purposes, we kept Captain Pecker in the living room except for once when Lee's mother made an unexpected visit and I found Captain Pecker stuffed horizontally between my bed and the wall.

"Do you actually use one of these crazy looking ones?" I asked Marais.

At first she hesitated, which was a little surprising because there was no "Too Much Information" when it came to our friendship. Then she answered, "No. Actually I just use the basic kind."

"Yes," I sighed with relief. "Basic. I just want something basic." She led me over to the most basic vibrator in existence. It was pink; six-inches; not too big; not too small; it didn't even bother to look circumcised or uncircumcised. A Ken doll would've been jealous, but no man would be. (Except maybe Tod, now that I think about it.) It was hardly the accessory to great porn videos, but that was OK because I had no plans to make a porn video. It was also relatively inexpensive too. So Marais and I made our selections, paid, and left the store happy.

I felt a little naughty and excited when I returned to my apartment and removed the vibrator from its packaging and thought about using it. Of course I went to the bathroom and grabbed the alcohol and a cotton ball and cleaned it first. No way was I going to put some piece of plastic straight out of its box and into mine. Cleaning the vibrator was kind of an odd experience because it brought up memories of sixth grade music class where we all learned to play the recorder. Since each class shared the instruments, the music teacher soaked the recorders in alcohol to sanitize them.

As I sat on my bed, I realized that I looked more like someone polishing a trophy. After I was done rubbing the molded plastic with alcohol, I held the vibrator in front of my face and giggled with slight embarrassment as I flipped the switch into the "on" position. Nothing happened. That's when I realized that I had forgotten to buy batteries. I closed my eyes and absent-mindedly tapped the tip of the vibrator against my forehead as I chastised myself. *Amateur.*

15

Later that evening, I sat down in the den with a plate of freshly nuked bean burritos and turned on the television. I adjusted the "rabbit ears" and proceeded to eat my dinner. Mack curled up next to me on the couch as a program on Aaron Feuerstein, the owner of Malden Mills which was the manufacturer of Polartec, began. My bean burritos quickly became of secondary interest as I placed my plate on the coffee table after eating a few bites. I was totally intrigued by Aaron Feuerstein as his life unfolded before me. First of all, his mill was pretty much the only one left in the Northeast (and in the United States, for that matter). Most of the other mill towns had become abandoned as the corporate world turned its back on the American workforce and made a run for the border (or overseas) because labor was cheaper and, I presumed, environmental standards were more lax.

Sometime in the mid-1990s, Malden Mills caught fire and burned to the ground. As a result, Aaron Feuerstein was issued a large insurance check. Instead of taking the money and running like so many lesser men (and women) are apt to do, he continued to pay his workers their salaries even though there was no mill and therefore no work, and rebuilt the mill. My heart soared with this newly imparted information, my faith in humanity temporarily restored. When he rebuilt the mill, he built it with the latest technology and didn't scrimp or cut corners like others might have done in order to keep their own pockets lined with a little more green.

Banks reluctantly threatened to call in the loans that he owed, but due to Mr. Feuerstein's strength of character, they found ways to extend his payment due dates. Complete strangers who had heard about Mr. Feuerstein's remarkable moral code would send him checks to help him pay off the creditors attempting to call in the loans. He appreciated the concern of others willing to help him and his workers and turned the checks over to the banks in order to help save the mill.

As I watched the story develop, I witnessed the love his employees had for him because he did the right thing by them. Polartec was constantly under the threat of bankruptcy—business analysts would consider Feuerstein's ethical plan to be a mistake— but he stuck to his beliefs which were inspired by his Jewish faith. I was amazed and filled with hope at the same time.

The interview continued into the Feuersteins' home which consisted of him and his wife and a ton of books. They were videotaped relaxing on the couch, each reading a book, while stacks of books lay on the floor and on the tables around them. I wished I had money to give to them. I even found myself sending a prayer up to God asking that Malden Mills be saved because Mr. Feuerstein deserved to "win." He was a CEO (I would later read somewhere that someone said this stood for "Chief Ethical Officer") who actually cared about people and their welfare rather than his own personal gain. I was sure that any one of his employees would have taken a bullet for him. Heck, I think I would've too and I'd only seen a documentary on the man.

I finished my bean burritos and told Mack after the program ended, "That's the kind of person I want to be." He looked up at me and I could tell that he believed me. Actually I looked deeper into his green eyes and saw a flicker of light that revealed that Mack also believed *in me*. That meant a lot to me coming from a cat since they were notoriously fickle and rarely believed in anyone other than themselves.

I continued to speak my thoughts, "Just wait, Mack. Someday, some way, *somehow*, our lives are going to change for the better. We are going to make a positive difference in the world just like Aaron Feuerstein!" It was an ambitious statement—Mack and I both knew it. Even so, his green eyes never left mine and I knew that he was up for the challenge. I really wasn't sure how I was ever going to be somebody like Aaron Feuerstein since I was just a Joe Schmoe wallowing in my own misery, but I was determined to try as best as I could, one millimeter at a time.

16

The next day at work started off quirky at best and degenerated from there. It began routinely with Donna smoking, us walking and talking and saying hi to Roy and Tippy as we headed on to work. However, instead of Roy and Tippy remaining on the bench as usual, they stood up to join us in our walk. It's not that we minded Roy and Tippy's company—well, at least I didn't. It's the fact that Roy moved at elderly man speed whereas Donna and I usually walked at lightning speed. If Tippy hadn't been confined to her leash, I was positive that she would've buzzed past us at warp speed.

So there we were: Donna and I trying to get to work; Roy trying to continue a conversation; and Tippy tugging at her leash, yapping at our heels. Donna felt no sense of duty to be polite about the situation. She just marched on. I, on the other hand, felt compelled to crane my neck over my shoulder and explain to Roy, "Sorry we can't walk with you—" we were at least five paces ahead, "— but we've just got to hurry and get to work." As I spoke to him, I was surprised (and slightly amused) to see that in one hand the four-pronged aluminum cane was sticking straight up in the air, all four prongs reaching for the sky. The other hand of course held the leash with which Tippy was yanking him along.

Roy did not seem to register what I was saying and continued performing his geriatric shuffle while speaking in his muted voice that was so quiet, I could not even understand him. When I glanced back around, Donna was yards ahead of me and all I could do was say, "Sorry, Roy. I don't mean to rush off and leave you, but we've got to get to work." Then I turned back around and hurried to catch up with Donna.

Once we entered the salon, the quirkiness continued. Kitty was thirty minutes behind as usual. As I walked down the hallway towards the facial room where I stored my belongings on the floor in the closet, Mrs. Franklin hurried towards me, the high heels of her spectator pumps clacking along the black-and-white tiled floor; her fur stole draped casually across her shoulders. She was seventy-five years old, had been a ground-breaking partner in a downtown accounting firm, and was always professionally and elegantly attired. Today she wore a tailored red suit and that added to her naturally zealous personality. She flashed me quick smile and called out good-by to Kitty and continued her speed walk out the front door and headed for her office. Kitty, who had just finished styling Mrs. Franklin's hair moments before, hurriedly grabbed her next client, and escorted her to the shampoo bowls.

I entered the facial room and stuffed my belongings in the closet and checked my facial supplies. The door to my room was open and I could hear Kitty and her next client talking. "Don't you work with Mrs. Franklin at the accounting firm?" Kitty asked. I opened a door to the cabinet that held my waxing supplies, making sure I had back up wax, and was startled to hear the client say with a sigh, "Yes. I do. But she only works part-time because she is so old. She thinks she's such a big deal still because she was a partner in the firm. She can't hardly hear anymore and she talks so loudly on the phone to the few remaining clients that she has who aren't dead already. It's like she doesn't know that she's irrelevant."

I slammed the door to the wax cabinet shut and spun around. Who was this woman at the shampoo bowl?! Kitty was towel-drying the woman's hair as the client continued to grumble and complain, this time about her aspects of the job at the accounting firm. Although Kitty and the woman were oblivious to me in the facial room, I narrowed my eyes at them. Kitty had said nothing to contradict the woman's assessment of Mrs. Franklin. Instead, she had made assenting, agreeing noises as if Mrs. Franklin were some doddering, slightly senile old lady instead of acknowledging her to be a hard-working woman who had become partner in an industry that was typically male-dominated way before women were achieving such titles. Most women of her time period were usually secretaries or Girl Fridays (whatever the hell Girl Fridays were). Nothing against secretaries or Girl Fridays, though. They were just doing the best they could to work at a career within the confines that Society allowed them.

I shook my head to shake out the absurdities that Society created. Society was supposed to be the element that created the standards for others to follow and as far as I could tell, Society was a whore and an asshole rolled up in one. Society dictated what was appropriate for women to do and not to do. Society confined men to more rigid and unyielding roles than women (except when it came to having sex). In return, Society paid men more money and gave them more respect. Society oppressed races that differed from its majority, deeming minorities to be less intelligent, less worthy, even less attractive. Society adored people with money and social standing and considered them to be better than people with less money, or God forbid, people who were actually poor or lived off modest government checks, such as those who lived in Patten Towers.

Society would not approve of Roy (except for that one "Suit" who gave Roy his puppy), at least not according to its rigid rules and ideas. It didn't matter that Roy was a decent human being. It didn't matter that Roy was nice and took good care of his pup. Roy lived off government checks and public housing. Society would go to church on Sunday and then complain the remaining six days of the week about the use of its tax dollars to help people in poverty to live somewhere other than the street. Society would say that people like Roy were "wasting" their lives as well as the taxpayers' money.

What was wrong with this picture that Society had drawn for us and that we had stamped with an $A+$ and a smiley face? I almost laughed at how messed up the world was that we willingly created for ourselves. Was I just crazy for seeing things this way? Or were we all just crazy for buying into the drivel that Society was selling by the truckload?

Right now, I knew that Society would never accept my criticisms of it as valid because I did not have money. "If you had money," Society would snicker, "you wouldn't be critical at all. You're just envious." And that was how it looked, wasn't it? That I was merely of the sour grapes? Well, it wasn't sour grapes. I believed what I thought. I hated being in debt and wanted out of it. One day, maybe that same day when my character (or dare I say, "My faith?") became as unshakable as Aaron Feuerstein's, I would have plenty of money. And I wouldn't be foolish with it. I wouldn't buy pretentious stuff and try to be one of the Joneses. I would continue my self-discipline of having absolutely no credit card debt. I would live within my means, share generously with those in need, and live my life not with Society's stamp of approval, but with Mr. Feuerstein's ideology in mind. *Ha, Society! Just you wait and see!* I taunted. I knew that Society was laughing at me, thinking that it knew better, thinking that I was just as weak as all its other converts, but I drew a line in the sand and double-dog-dared it just the same.

17

As I prepared the facial bed for my next client, I thought about my earlier mental tirade against Society. I was glad that it had only been a rampage inside of my head and not one that I verbally exposed to other people because I didn't think that there were too many people who would get what I was saying. Why should they? I wasn't exactly raging against the machine. I bought a freaking Lexus, for crying out loud, and for all the wrong reasons. (Actually, what were the right reasons? It was really reliable, but so was a Honda Civic hatchback.) I also wasn't burning my social security card, donating all my material goods to charity, or even living in a tent as a means of protesting society's values.

In fact, the only person that I knew of who had lived in a tent was a dominatrix named Cassie. I had only met Cassie a couple of times when she was partying over at a house that I was hanging out at too. It was the summer that I had finally decided to leave law school for good. I had taken a wills and estates class the first session of summer school to give law school one last shot. Although I had done well in the class (I earned a B+), I knew it was over. I had also started going out with this guy Kenneth who was totally sexy and hot (and, unbeknownst to me, dealing with a serious drug problem instead of the recreational one I thought he had) and I often found myself over at the house that he shared with another guy, Wayne.

The house that Kenneth and Wayne lived in was a total dump, but that didn't stop the parade of Society's orphans from feeling at home. Actually, the three of us were fraternal triplets of sorts from Society's castoffs. Wayne was a semi-depressed drug dealer. He was outgoing and funny most of the time, but sometimes he just sat in the Papasan chair, deep in a funk, and smoked bowl after bowl like the caterpillar in *Alice in Wonderland*. I knew that he was contemplating how a guy with great computer programming skills had ended up as a dealer in a crack-head world such as this one.

Kenneth was a former productive member of society who originally used drugs recreationally, but now found himself on the downward spiral towards Junkiedom. I, who had been handed so much law school "reality" over the past two years, was grateful for the company of people unaccepted by Society. They were a lot more interesting and entertaining than a roomful of 2Ls who worshipped Society and everything it stood for.

One night, Cassie, Wayne, Kenneth, and I were all hanging out drinking in the funktified living room. Wayne and Cassie were also high on pot while Kenneth had snorted some coke. I just stuck to beer. It was this night that I learned about Cassie's job as a dominatrix. I also learned that she was a single mom with a five year-old daughter and that she lived in a tent.

Cassie's job intrigued me. She got to work when she wanted and she didn't have to get naked with strangers for money. She just carried her trunk of goodies with her in her car and apparently had an abundance of pleather outfits that she wore with coordinating accessories, depending on the client's needs. The best part of her job, I thought, was that all her clients requested of her was that she urinate and defecate on them.

I thought about my impending student loan debt incurred from four semesters of law school. A woman could get paid pretty good money not to have sex with men but just to pee and poop on them? It didn't sound great, but it did sound not so bad. Maybe I could tie them up first so I could make sure they kept their hands off of me and then literally go do my business. A smile tickled my lips as I imagined whipping politicians, lawyers, COBRA insurance execs, and maybe even a couple of law school professors with my riding crop, lashing them into subservience. The idea of defecating on Society's golden boys pleased me immensely: knowing their dirty little secrets while the rest of their unsuspecting peers idolized them in the newspaper's society columns. My snide fantasies had been interrupted by Wayne's voice cutting through the air.

"Yeah," he said in response to some part of a conversation that I had been oblivious to. "Can you believe Cassie's sister and brother-in-law took in Shelby, Cassie's daughter, and won't give her back to Cassie now?"

116

"What?" I asked.

Wayne turned towards me and continued. "Cassie's brother-in-law is a *lawyer* and Cassie's sister is a *homemaker*." He said the words "lawyer" and "homemaker" with total disdain. I nodded in agreement. "They don't think it's good for Shelby to live with her mother. They think they are better parents than Cassie. Actually they think they are *better* than Cassie!"

I was appalled. Go figure that an asshole lawyer had to be in the mix. I shook my head in disgust. "I can believe it! Lawyers are such assholes and I should know!" I exclaimed. They knew that I had attended law school. "That's such crap! Just because Cassie's a defecating dominatrix who lives in a tent and gets high and drunk, they think she's not a good mother to Shelby?!"

That was the year I was so liberal that I was stupid. It balanced out, though, because that was also the same year that one of the prominent televangelists was so conservative that he was stupid. (Or was he so conservative that he was stupid year after year after year?)

A few months after I expressed my disgust at Cassie being called an unfit mother by her accepted-by-society family members, a certain nationally known preacher spoke out against the Teletubbies. For some inexplicable reason, he called the purple one a homosexual. First of all, his homophobia annoyed me. I'd had friends, acquaintances, and relatives who were gay. This might come as a shock to some, but gay people possess goals, ideals, and values very similar to straight people. The defining difference between gay and straight people was which gender each found to be attractive: the same sex or the opposite sex. What's the big deal about that? The only other difference between the two was that random gay people were a lot more fun to be around than random straight people (see any time spent with Tod's friends as proof). Secondly, a Teletubby, no matter what his or her color, was a figment of the BBC's kooky imagination and was designed to entertain babies and young children. They were never intended to be sex objects. So exactly what crack pipe of perversion was this preacher-man smoking?

Although Teletubbies were completely non-sexual, I had to say that if I absolutely had to pick a sexual Teletubby, it wouldn't the purple one; it'd be the red one. Toronto Jen received the red Teletubby for her birthday as an inside joke from a guy she was seeing. She brought it over to my apartment to show it to me. When I pulled the string at the back of its neck and heard what it had to say, I glanced over at Toronto Jen and raised an eyebrow. She nodded her head because she'd heard what it said too. "It's supposed to say, 'Big hug,'" she explained. To our ears, though, it sounded like "Big cock." We replayed its message over and over and all that red Teletubby ever said was "Big cock." I had to admit that at this time in my life, I felt a certain kinship with that red Teletubby.

I glanced up as I heard a knock on the door. "Your client is here," Donna told me.

"OK. Thanks," I said and Donna retreated to the front of the salon. I followed her out and retrieved Jenny Markman from the reception area. She was a regular of mine, a college student who wisely spent more money on taking care of herself than getting drunk every night. I say "wisely" because I was the beneficiary of her decisions. She was also a college student who knew how to tip appropriately as well, which made me doubly glad to see her. And she was nice too. Nice was probably more important than the other qualities that pertained to me making money, but nice didn't pay the bills. I shut the door to let her change and get settled under the blanket on the facial bed.

After a minute or two, I knocked on the door to make sure Jenny was ready for me and started her facial. Normally I did not like to talk during the facials because they are very relaxing services and are more enjoyable when the client (and I) can get lost in our thoughts or, in the client's case, drift off to sleep. But Jenny did like to talk and as long as she started the conversation, I would respond and keep up my end of the conversation.

She started off by telling me about her sweet and considerate boyfriend. I made agreeing noises and then mentally compared and contrasted her boyfriend to mine. I kept pointing out to myself that Tod was a nice guy and technically attractive. Even so, I could not figure out why I wasn't all that interested in him. What was worse was knowing that I was going to stay with him because my circumstances were dire enough as they were. He liked me and I liked him most of the time and he was my only ticket to anything resembling a social life. As I heard myself admit to my reality, a reality that sounded a lot like me using another person, I was not proud of myself. So I changed tactics and reiterated to myself that I was not using him because I did like him. Really I did. Really, really, I did. Jenny brought me out of my thoughts. She was telling me about how her mom had taken a leave of absence from her job and was coming to town to visit her soon. I guess Jenny's point of telling me that was to talk about her mother's upcoming visit, but I found myself curious as to her line of work.

"What did she do for a living that she took a leave of absence from?" I asked as I removed a warm towel from her face.

"She was an engineer for IBM," she told me. I was impressed. I did the math on Jenny's mother's age and realized that her mother was a bit ahead of her time in her pursuit of a career that was typically dominated by males. The practical side of me once again envied those people with "normal" jobs; people who worked from 8-5, Monday through Friday, earned vacations, had 401Ks, and also received health benefits.

"Wow, Jenny. That's so cool. Why would she leave a great job like that?"

Jenny was quiet for just a moment and then she said, "Did you ever hear about the serial killer in the Midwest? The one that buried his victims' bodies underneath the floor of his barn?"

My heart froze, but I kept massaging Jenny's face. "Yeah. I kind of remember hearing something about that," I admitted. I couldn't recall many details of the case, but I'd heard that much at least. I was afraid of what she might reveal. Had that man killed someone in her family? Why hadn't I kept my mouth shut?

"Well, she was dating him." I remained silent from the shock, but I kept massaging. I didn't know what to say. "They were dating long-distance—actually they were engaged. They met at a conference and of course she had no idea that he was a serial killer or that he could even be such a thing."

"Oh my god, Jenny. That's awful. Is she doing okay?"

"Well, that's why she took the leave of absence because that really threw her for a loop, you know? I mean, since they dated long-distance it was probably pretty easy for him to show her only what he wanted to show her, but it still has freaked her out and has caused her to question her ability to judge other people's characters. It's been pretty hard for her."

"I would say so," I agreed. I massaged her earlobes and then worked on the muscles in the back of her neck. "Hopefully she's not too hard on herself, though. Like you said, it's much easier to hide things when you are dating long-distance." She agreed and then closed her eyes as if to go to sleep. She remained like that for the rest of the facial, which was fine with me. I hoped that she was thinking more pleasant thoughts, maybe something to do with her own happy, healthy relationship. I knew that I was thinking about my relationship with Tod once again.

Why was I trying so hard to force it to work? Because after dating Kenneths and Thibodeauxes my own judgment was off. Kenneth had been a junkie rather than a fun-loving partier and I hadn't seen it until it was almost too late. Thibodeaux was a withholder and would never let me in. Tod was like a large puppy that was always happy to see me; who did normal things with me like ask me out to dinner and take me to the theater; he also tolerated my lesser qualities such as my orneriness. (Of course, I was usually only ornery when I was with him and his friends.) That's why I was trying to make it work because I was trying to get my good judgment back. And wasn't being with someone like him, a productive member of Society, someone who played by all the right rules, the way to get my good judgment of character back? The only reason why I didn't like him was because he was "normal," right? Because I was used to dysfunctional and had become my own kind of junkie for it? Or at least that was what I guessed.

It never occurred to me at that time that my judgment about Tod had been correct. I did not realize at that moment that just because someone seemed "normal" didn't mean they were the right person for me. It didn't occur to me that maybe I should have dumped Tod after the Halloween party which actually was the response I had been heading towards during our drunken fight. Had I not been arrested for DUI that evening, would I still have remained with Tod? Or would I have just moved on?

After the facial was finished and I walked Jenny up to the front desk where Donna was waiting to accept her payment, I returned to the facial room and stripped the bed of its sheets and threw them in the washing machine in the back. I folded the blanket, lay it on a shelf in the closet, and returned to the front. Donna handed me my tip which I then folded and placed in my pocket.

"When's your next client?" I asked her.

She glanced down at the reception book open in front of her

and said, "I've got a men's haircut in just a few minutes and then we can go to lunch after that."

As soon as Donna stopped speaking, the front door jangled open and Donna's client walked in. She greeted him, escorted him back to her chair, and I moved over to the reception desk. Kitty's remaining clients had been waiting somewhat patiently for their turns as they sat in the reception area flipping through issues of *Town and Country* magazine.

I took the opportunity to flip open my library book that I had just begun about honor killings in the Middle East. Immediately I had been hooked by the story about two young women who were in their mid-twenties and had never even dated or been kissed due to the restrictive culture that was still present even in modern times. Although I was very early into the book, I knew that one of them would die from an honor killing and that she would be killed by her own father. I was thoroughly engrossed and lost in another world where women had little to no freedom when the jangling of the bells attached to the door startled me. I looked up to see a young woman and a young man in their very early twenties standing in front of me.

"Hi!" the girl said enthusiastically. I smiled at her and returned the greeting as my eyes flickered back and forth between both their faces. The young man reminded me of a frisky golden retriever, bounding about every few steps with a grin on his face. I suspected something was a little off with him, which was confirmed when the only noises that came out of his mouth were yelps and moans.

His sister began talking at a rapid pace, still smiling. "He's my brother," she explained. I nodded, not sure what they needed from me. "Our mom fed him bleach when he was a baby." My eyes widened in shock and I worked to regain my composure although I was totally appalled that a parent could be so abusive and cruel. "That's why he acts that way." She rushed on to add, "Well, she fed bleach to me too, but I was older so it didn't do as much damage. I just wanted to know how much you charge for a haircut. My brother really needs a haircut soon."

I told her the price and asked if she would like to make an appointment. She declined but thanked me. I gave her a friendly smile, wishing that a kind smile could erase a childhood of misery. As they turned and left, the sound of bells jingling in their wake as they headed down the sidewalk, I realized that they too were Patten Tower tenants. I was still recovering from shock when Donna walked her client up to the counter and accepted his payment. I returned to my room, dropped off my book, removed my smock, and grabbed my coat and purse.

When I rejoined Donna up front, she was already wearing her coat and asked me, "You ready to go feed the worms?"

"Boy am I ever," I said, my sentence loaded with meaning. As we headed out the front door, she asked me what I meant. With her curiosity piqued, I told her about the bizarre and disturbing glimpses into others' lives that I had already experienced that day. When I finished, Donna was as stunned as I was. "Dang!" she said. "And it's only now just lunchtime!"

18

Later that afternoon, when I was deeply involved in the clandestine love affair taking place in the Middle East, the jingling of the door bells snapped me back to reality. I glanced up and saw Jack, one of my favorite regulars, enter the salon.

"Hey, Jack!" I greeted him warmly. He stepped over to the counter.

"Hello, Vandelyn. Is Seabiscuit ready for me?" Jack winked at me and I smiled. He called Donna "Seabiscuit" because he said she walked like a horse.

I heard the water running into the bowl of the pedicure chair and nodded. "Donna's getting it set up right now. Go on back."

He dropped a box of candy onto the counter and headed on back to the pedicure area. I hollered out a "Thanks!" to Jack's backside and picked up the box. It was one of my favorites: Chocolate Squirrels. They were awesome: Loaded with nuts, swirled with a bit of caramel, and smothered in milk chocolate. Even though I did have the love handles, it wasn't because I ate a lot of sweets. I figured that my body was in the shape it was in because of too much drink and not enough exercise. I made a mental note to try and exercise somehow in this freezing weather and opened the box since sweets weren't the source of my problem. I sunk my teeth into the Squirrel and my mouth salivated. From the pedicure chair I heard Jack ask, "How are you, Seabiscuit?"

"Don't you call me that, Jack. I'd sure hate to clip your toenails down to the quick and make them bleed." Donna acted out the love-hate relationship with Jack, but as with everyone Jack came in contact with (except maybe his family), she had affection for him.

Jack's family was a different story. And thanks to this town being of such a small town mentality, I knew the story within a matter of weeks. The bond between Jack and his children was a damaged one. Only in the past few years had Jack and his adult children become closer. Of course the estrangement between them had not prevented Jack's son from inheriting the position of running the family business, nor had it stopped his daughter from building her dream house on Jack's huge lakefront property. But old wounds run deep and apparently when Jack had been married to their mother, he hadn't been a nice man; rumor had it that he had been verbally abusive often and physically abusive once or twice. After he had matured and changed, he publicly denounced his behavior of decades before. A number of years ago at his daughter's wedding that apparently he was lucky to be invited to (never mind that his money paid for it), he toasted his ex-wife: "To a great mother and a wonderful woman who had the misfortune to be married to me." Apparently that one phrase couldn't remedy all wrongs, but it was a start as far as his children were concerned.

Jack's business was the one thing that he had been completely successful. Actually his grandfather had started the business in the late 1800s as a local storefront candy store located downtown. Jack's father then increased the business from a single store and turned it into a local company. Jack in turn had maximized the profits of the company when he took it over in the Fifties after his father's untimely death. Now it was a corporation and distribution center, supplying its candies all over the world. Although Jack was still a figurehead in the company, he was in his seventies which meant that he maintained an office downtown with his own staff (because Jack's mere existence was a business in itself) while his son ran the day-to-day operations out of the office at the corporate headquarters.

What I found to be endearing about Jack was what a down-to-earth person he was. Yes, he was a millionaire many times over. Yes, he had the business skills to create an empire. But not one day in the life that I had ever known him was he pretentious. What may confuse some people is the fact that Jack did own very nice things, but that's not the same thing as being pretentious. He didn't own nice things to impress other people. He owned nice things because he appreciated nice things and could obviously afford them. He even built a warehouse-sized building to hold all the expensive cars that he collected.

One of my favorite stories was when Jack stopped by his

downtown office one Saturday to check on some paperwork. He had been on his way to the minor league baseball game which was being played at the stadium downtown, so he was dressed in jeans and a Chattanooga Lookouts T-shirt. After leaving his office, he headed down the hallway towards the elevator and was stopped by a forty-something lawyer who was miffed because maintenance had not removed his garbage from outside his door. The lawyer took one look at Jack as he approached and mistook him for the janitor.

"Excuse me," he had said gruffly. "No one took this garbage down yesterday and it needs to be thrown out."

Jack stopped and looked at the sack of garbage and then at the man, shrugged, and said, "Okay." Jack picked up the garbage, headed down the elevator, threw the garbage bag into the proper receptacle, and continued on his merry way. I guessed Jack knew that it would only be a matter of days until the lawyer figured out who Jack was and felt completely embarrassed about ordering someone else, especially a seventy year-old man who happened to be a multimillionaire, to take out his trash. (Or maybe that was just my wishful thinking; maybe Jack didn't care at all.) Even so, it was nice to know that even the multimillionaires were sticking it to the lawyers.

I returned to reading my book and I was once again engrossed until Donna and Jack returned to the front counter. He gave her a wad of cash without even having to hear the bill. Donna and I watched him walk out onto the sidewalk and to his car that was parked at a meter directly out front. I inhaled at the beauty of the car. It was a white Lamborghini.

"Wow!" Donna yelped as she observed the car he was getting ready to drive. Kitty's patient clients glanced up from their issues of *Town & Country*, curious as to Donna's outburst, and then returned to their reading. Donna quickly pushed open the glass door and called out to Jack before he could get into his car. I leapt up from the desk and followed her out onto the sidewalk. "Nice Mustang, Jack!" Donna hollered as Jack stopped at the car with his door partway open.

"Thanks," he said, without missing a beat.

After Donna returned inside, I remained on the sidewalk smiling to myself, watching Jack and the Lamborghini continue to be ogled as he drove down Broad Street. Jack was a cool man. Too bad he was forty years older than I was. Then I remembered the crushes from my youth: Forrest Tucker and Chuck Connors. They'd both be somewhere around Jack's age now. When I thought of it like that, an old-man crush didn't seem so bad.

As I pulled open the salon door, the jingling bells jostled my brain back to reality. I remembered my solitary Freudian red flag waving at the dinner table when I was eight years-old. What I did not need was yet another dysfunctional relationship. I shook thoughts of Jack out of my head and suddenly felt ridiculous and a little grossed out. OK. A lot grossed out. *Me? With a seventy-something year old man? Was I nuts?* Besides, he already had a girlfriend— she came in the form of an attractive fifty year-old man-leach, which meant they had a symbiotic relationship: he got sex, companionship, and a bit of eye candy from her and in return she got a house (well, it was actually a condo overlooking the river—on the *opposite* side of the river from where Jack lived. I guessed that for Jack, distance made the heart grow fonder), free travel to exotic places, (limited) access to his credit cards, and free (minor) plastic surgery. Her love of Botox was well known around town. In more upscale, cattier circles, she was often referred to as "Mount Rushmore." However, those of us (Donna and I) who were not accepted into the White Glove Society thought the term "Bo-Ho" was much catchier.

Jack and his girlfriend's relationship might not have been the healthiest of relationships, but who was I to judge? I guess it worked for them. Then again, maybe the term "worked for them" is subjective. Although I really liked Jack, his relationship with her was obviously alluded to in less than glowing terms, at least by other people. His children were wary of the man-leach, because of their love of their father's money or out of their concern for him, I wasn't actually sure. Although the man-leach was probably hoping for a permanent financial arrangement, I seriously doubted that Jack would relinquish his fortune to her. He had spent way too much time, money, and effort creating his empire. I'd doubt he'd be so foolish to let the man-leach take it away from him and his family. Of course Jack never referred to his long-term girlfriend as a man-leach (that was the rest of town), but I'd learned through multiple conversations that she was a professional wife to wealthy men. She and Jack were even seeing their pastor about improving their relationship to marital status. Jack was willing to go, but was not apparently willing to commit.

My eyes refocused on the book in front of me. Tension was increasing because the girl's brother was starting to get suspicious of his sister and her male friend. The brother was looking forward to revealing his sister's "infidelity" (of which there was none) and her disgrace to the family name to their father. I shook my head in disbelief. Was there somebody, *anybody*, in this world who wasn't involved in a dysfunctional relationship? The only thing I found myself being thankful for was that I wasn't going to be murdered by my father for my present dysfunctional relationship (or for any of my past ones, for that matter). It never occurred to me at that time that my dysfunctional relationships might start to kill me in a different way.

19

By the time I got home that night, the book was burning a hole in my bag. I had read up to the point where the brother had wickedly and gleefully reported his suspicions about his sister to their father. At this very moment, the father had reported some good news to his daughter: she didn't have to do any of her chores in the morning. She was pleasantly surprised. The bad news? Unlike her, I knew she wouldn't live to see the morning.

I pulled the car into the garage, leapt out of the car, purse in hand, and scurried into the warmth of my home. Mack greeted me with mews and I loved on him in kind. I checked his food and water bowls, replenished where needed, and then hurried into the den, book in hand. I devoured the remaining pages.

Even though I knew what her fate was, I was still shocked when her father stabbed her to death. I was appalled by his anger and lack of remorse at killing his own flesh and blood over his twenty-six year-old daughter dating a man. And she was still a virgin. Not that non-virgins deserved killing, but all it took was her hateful brother's words to condemn her death. Nobody even bothered to check to see if his words were true.

And her brother? He didn't care either. He seemed to be happy that she was dead. I couldn't fathom this concept. As wacked as my relationship with my brother could be at times, we never wished each other dead. In fact, it was my love for him that caused me to feel so much pain when he was hurting. I was pretty sure it was the same for him. So how exactly does it come to be that a family can so easily replace love with hate?

I remembered a girl, Tabitha, whom I once worked with in the restaurant business. Her father was North African Muslim; her mother, beady-eyed Kentuckian. Tabitha's relationship with her father was tenuous at best due to his old world mentality and conservative ideas about women and how they should behave. "But what about your mother? Being from here, how does she put up with his dominating attitude towards women?" I had once asked her. Tabitha had just rolled her eyes and said, "She gets off on it."

Although her mother might have gotten off on being dominated, Tabitha could not have been farther from her father's ideals. Even when he accepted a job with an oil company and moved his family to Kuwait for a year or two when Tabitha was in high school, she had not conformed to Middle Eastern society.

One afternoon after school, she, another girl, and a couple of guys drove out into the desert to hang out and drink. Unfortunately, the Kuwaiti police happened upon them and became enraged at seeing the two couples in the car together. Tabitha told me that the police called the girls whores (even though no sexual conduct was taking place) and said that if they were going to act like whores, they deserved to be treated like whores.

My eyes widened as she told me how the police were threatening to rape her and her friend. The two guys started freaking out, but Tabitha managed to deter the police by affecting an upper-class Kuwaiti accent, a skill at which she was quite adept (unlike myself). As she gave them some story combined with thinly veiled threats of what her high-ranking family might do to those policemen if they followed-through on the rape, the police apologized, returned to their vehicle, and drove away.

When I was in law school I dated a younger pretty boy from a wealthy family named Whit who was very sophisticated socially. What I mean by that was that he saw people as people, not as genders with certain roles and identities; he enjoyed his friendships with women as much as he enjoyed his friendships with men. One of the interesting insights he shared with me was one time when he went to a strip club with a bunch of guys. While most of the guys were respectful to the strippers, one guy in the group was behaving rather crassly. When Whit asked the guy why he was behaving in such a degrading manner, the guy told him, "You've got to talk to strippers like they are whores. They like to be talked to like that." I shook my head in disgust, pleased that one upper-middle-class guy actually had some sensitivity towards women who weren't in his same social circle. I was pleased that Whit had been disgusted by his friend's behavior too.

What had not gone unnoticed by me over the years is the fact that the allegedly sophisticated upper-crust of society was far from sophisticated, at least by my definition. To me, sophisticated meant having the ability to see the world from a broader perspective, not a narrow one that I associated with ignorance. The irony was that Thibodeaux and his friends, most of whom never entered college, were of a more worldly perspective than some of the J.D.'s and M.B.A.'s that I had encountered in the past few years.

Thibodeaux had been the lead singer in a band. He had seen girl fans in the audience take off their shirts—not to flash their goodies as some might expect, but because they were hot, temperature-wise. Thibodeaux had told me how cool he thought that was. He didn't think it was cool because he crassly assessed that they wanted to "do" him, nor was he the type to jump to the wrong conclusion that they were all whores, like so many socially acceptable, well-educated boys and girls might be prone to do. He thought it was cool that they felt comfortable enough to remove their shirts and dance around because it showed how much they were enjoying his band's music.

What was even cooler was the sophistication of the crowd who respected those few girls' rights to remove their shirts and dance around in their bras without the crowd accosting the young women, acting as if the girls had consented to sexual groping just because they were hot, sweaty, and shirtless. Even though Thibodeaux had some short-comings when it came to our relationship, I was so glad his ability to respect women's rights to do as they pleased was not one of them. To me, respecting others despite what Society might assume their actions to imply is the utmost in sophistication—not the knowledge of what wine is appropriate with a meal or which utensil is appropriate for each course of a seven course dinner.

I placed the book down on the coffee table and stretched. I decided to go and check my email. As I sat down at the computer, I saw the papers detailing my arrest and the envelope of photos resting on top of them. I sighed as the computer booted up. I was due for another visit to the law office of James Peters. But compared to getting stabbed to death by my father, paying the asshole lawyer a visit wasn't so bad.

20

The following Monday, after most of my hangover from my Sunday night dance party had worn off, I left my house, drove down McCallie Avenue, and parked in the lot behind James Peters' office building. I expected this interaction to be much more pleasant than the last because all I had to do was drop off paperwork and photos, then leave. As I rode up the elevator, it occurred to me that neither James Peters nor his wife employed a secretary. So to whom exactly was I planning on dropping off this information? My thoughts of a quick meeting began to deteriorate. I dreaded the thought of having to wait in his reception area until he popped out of his office belligerently yelling "Next!" I wondered how peeved he would be when I cut in line to simply hand him my work product.

When the elevator doors opened, I stepped out into the hallway and walked over to the law office door. I turned the knob and pushed, but the door wouldn't open. It was locked. Even though it was pointless, I attempted opening the door once again. Then I knocked. No answer. I decided that driving to James Peters' office on my day off only to have no one be in his office was worse than having to wait for him and deal with his belligerence. I stood in front of the door for a moment trying to decide what to do. I didn't want to slip everything under the door, assuming it would fit, because as persnickety as this guy was, I could see him saying that he never received it because it was beneath him to bend over and pick up paperwork off the floor.

A man walked around the corner and saw me paused in front of the law office. He apparently had the office next door. "Hi," he said. His friendliness startled me after thoughts of James Peters' hostility. "Are you looking for James Peters?"

"Yes," I said, hopeful that this guy could help me.

"He and his wife eat lunch downstairs in the diner. You can probably find them down there right now."

"Really? Thanks. I've got some paperwork to drop off to him. Do you think he'd mind me handing it to him during lunch?"

"No, not at all," the friendly man encouraged as he unlocked his door.

"OK. Thanks for your help." I got back on the elevator. I was pretty sure that the James Peters that man knew and the one I knew were two different people. The James Peters that I knew would be upset that his lunch was interrupted by a client, never mind the fact that he left me no alternative. I sure wasn't going to turn around and drive back home only to come back later. I also wasn't going to stand around a hallway waiting for him to return from lunch. I knew where he was, so I was going to go find him whether he liked it or not. If he didn't like it, he should pay for a secretary or quit eating downstairs in the diner where he was easily located.

The elevator doors opened and I entered the diner. I scanned the room and saw him and his wife sitting at a two-top by a big window that looked out onto McCallie Avenue. I approached the table. "Mr. Peters," I said once I was standing next to them. I was standing close enough to him and his wife that I could've easily swatted either one on the head with my paperwork without having to straighten my elbow. Oddly enough, Mr. Peters pretended not only not to hear me, he also pretended not to see me. He did not respond and kept his eyes locked on the far wall behind his wife's head. His wife stared at him, obviously expecting him to answer. He ignored her too.

"Mr. Peters," I said more forcefully because I was irritated. "I was told by your office neighbor that you were down here. I am sorry to interrupt your lunch—" (at this point I really wasn't, but thought it best to be polite if only to highlight his rudeness) "—but I have the information you requested that I bring to you *as soon as possible*." I enjoyed emphasizing the last four words as I extended my hand slightly, letting the legal envelope containing the photos and my written account of my arrest cross the plane of the table. Once again, James Peters played deaf, dumb, and mute. But he did take another bite of his sandwich and continued to chew. His wife glared at him a couple of seconds longer and then looked up at me. "Thank you," she said, giving me a smile as she extended her hand to take the envelope from me. "I'll make sure that he gets it."

"Thank you," I said. Then I turned and left. I shook my head in disbelief as I pushed open the diner door and passed through the lobby. As I walked across the parking lot to my car, I found myself laughing as I thought about what an asshole James Peters was. And then about what a dickhead he was. He should have been named Richard Peters, a double dickhead. But I knew as I turned my key in the ignition that it didn't matter whether he was a dickhead or an asshole because those insults were of equal rank to me. By the end of the legal proceedings, though, I would upgrade James Peters to a cocksucking bastard, my insult equivalent of a five-star general.

21

2003: January

Thanksgiving and Christmas passed uneventfully. I went home for both while Tod stayed with his dad for Thanksgiving and went back to Canada to visit his mom for Christmas. I never mentioned my legal plight to my family. When Tod and I celebrated our Christmas together, we exchanged presents. My presents to him were thoughtful, or so I thought. I bought him two CDs: Jackson Browne and Steely Dan. (I thought it was extremely generous of me to buy him Jackson Browne and Steely Dan CDs because I hated them more than I hated Barney, the singing purple dinosaur—and that involves a lot of hate.) He mentioned in passing once that he loved both bands, but didn't know what had happened to his CDs. "Somebody probably took them after one of our parties," he had lamented. *More likely someone stomped them into oblivion*, was my opinion.

Right before we exchanged gifts, however, he held up some prize possessions brought back from Toronto. His Jackson Browne and Steely Dan CDs. "They weren't stolen after all! I just left them at my mom's house!" I had looked down at the two wrapped gifts in my hand and wished I had kept my receipts. "Great," I had commented, my voice flat. He glanced at my hands at the two wrapped squares which were obviously CDs and realized our dilemma. "Oh. Is that what you bought me?" he had asked. He took the presents from my hand and unwrapped them. "These are cool. Really. These have some songs that I don't have on the CDs I own." He saw the expression on my face and with forced gaiety reassured me that my gifts to him were "Awesome!"

Then, as if I weren't feeling inept enough with my gift-giving, he hauled in my presents from his car. He had told me to keep my eyes shut until he gave me the word to open them and I had complied. He had bought me luggage. And then he handed me a wrapped envelope sized box. I opened it. In it was the promise of a ticket to Toronto, Canada for whenever I wanted to go with him and meet his mother and see the sights. I was dumbfounded and chagrined. This was definitely different than exchanging gifts with Thibodeaux. First of all, we only exchanged gifts one year out of four during our on-again-off-again relationship and the only stipulation from Thibodeaux was, "Let's keep it around ten dollars." He gave me a watch that I was sure was a free gift with the purchase of a women's fragrance. (Someone else had apparently received the fragrance.) I gave him a piggy bank and a spreadsheet on how much change needed to go into the piggy bank each week in order to save varying increments of money, all of them greater than ten dollars, by next Christmas.

Ironically, though, Thibodeaux's crappy gift chafed less than Tod's did. I was embarrassed to be so endowed with presents when my gifts to him were so unacceptable by comparison. I was miffed. "Luggage?" I demanded. "You gave me luggage? Who gives somebody luggage after only a few months of dating? And then on top of that, you promise me an expensive plane ticket?" I asked with a grumpy expression on my face.

His face fell which made me feel sadistically good and heart-breakingly sad at the same time. I felt more justified in my anger because I was embarrassed. How could he have led me to believe that a couple of CDs were OK as Christmas presents? CDs of music that he already had in his possession, no less! He gave me no indication that he was going to spend hundreds of dollars on me. At least with Thibodeaux I had been prepared for the outcome and had bought accordingly.

But now it was January. We had survived the exchanging of gifts and eventually I had thanked him for his thoughtfulness and apologized for my rudeness. He continued to act as if my gifts to him were of equal value and significance. I continued to tell him to knock it off.

Today, though, was Martin Luther King Jr. Day. It was a Monday, of course, which meant that by default, I was off. Tod, Taylor, and the rest of their friends that worked in the business world had the day off too. They were all going to go to a matinee movie followed by dinner and drinks. They wanted to know if I would join them. I had curled my lip at the phone receiver when I heard the extended invitation. A day spent with Raggedy Ann and Andy, Bruce, Stan, Ted, the mating-call couple and whomever else sailed on their Ship of Fools? Hell no. Not to mention that thanks to Marais, I really had been educated on the importance of Martin Luther King Jr. Day, despite my high school Honors English teacher's arrogant comment to a classroom of pupils with white faces that "we'll know that equality has been achieved when Martin Luther King Jr. Day is treated the same as Presidents' Day," which of course meant with no deference, no reverence, at all. So I definitely wasn't interested in hanging out with a carload of clowns who reduced the significance of Martin Luther King Jr.'s life and assassination to one of the great employee perks: a paid day off.

In the beginning, I had been pretty oblivious to the battle over the observance of MLK Jr. Day because I had only been in middle school when it started and as a white pre-teen, how aware would I have been anyway? My real education began with Marais informing me of the opposition by some Republicans to even just the suggestion of Martin Luther King Jr. Day as a national holiday; the most notable Republican opponent being a President of the United States. (Ironically, Abraham Lincoln had been a Republican. I had to wonder, was 1863 the last time a Republican president cared about the interests of African-Americans?)

I began to notice the bias against the holiday when I attended LSU my freshman year of college. Martin Luther King Jr. Day was observed, but in a slighted way. The university did not suspend classes for the day in honor of the holiday. Instead, all morning classes were in session, but the compromise was that afternoon classes would be canceled. The slight was obvious to me: most Monday classes were scheduled in the morning hours as opposed to the afternoon. I wasn't sure if it were the state's policy or LSU's policy, but either way, Martin Luther King Jr. Day was treated like a second-class citizen. If that type of back-handed respect wasn't bad enough, what was even more appalling was that it was only in 2000, *three years ago!*, that all of the states of the Union observed it, unlike Grandparents' Day whose legislation deeming it a national holiday was passed without incident by Congress in 1978.

My most memorable MLK Jr. Day was when Marais and I

were in college and we had gone over to her parents' house, which was the tradition, in order to remember and celebrate Dr. King's life and contributions. Marais' father, Dr. Abraham G. DuBois, would always start the evening in their living room with a film projector loaded with a reel-to-reel recording of Martin Luther King Jr.'s, *I Have a Dream* speech from the steps of the Lincoln Memorial in Washington, DC on August 28, 1963. Those invited to the celebration, which included dinner and discussions, were the DuBois family, me, and a small group of students and professors who attended or taught at the historic black college of which Dr. DuBois was president.

When the footage began to roll, everyone in the room became perfectly still. It was so quiet that my muted sips of wine seemed disruptive. Every time I listened to Martin Luther King Jr.'s speech, I got goose bumps. By the time Dr. King started quoting from *My Country 'Tis of Thee*, my hairs were standing on end. When he finished with, "Free at last! Free at last! Thank God Almighty, we are free at last!" my whole body tingled.

As the lone white face, I felt more comfortable remaining silent through the whole speech, but others overcome with emotion released their goose bumps and tingly feelings with "Tell it, brother," heartfelt "Mmmhmms," and at the end, jubilant choruses of "Free at last!" It wasn't until the film reel ended that I realized that I had drained my wine glass in a matter of minutes. While Dr. DuBois broke down the projector and engaged those around him in a discourse about the Civil Rights movement, I poured myself another glass of Cabernet.

Dinner had followed and was a casual affair of homemade dishes set up buffet style in the kitchen and dining room, enabling guests to help themselves and settle into the comfy chairs and sofas in the living room. Someone had turned on the TV and tuned in to reruns of *Sanford & Son*. Under the circumstances I had been rather quiet, talking mostly to Marais and the family members that I knew, partly because I didn't really have anything to add, but mostly because I didn't want to come across like Hoppy, the clueless white police officer on *Sanford & Son* who always tried too hard to fit in with Smitty, Fred, and Lamont and was constantly embarrassing himself with his whiteness.

It was probably because of this paranoia that I secretly kept

137

chugging wine in order to make myself feel less self-conscious. At one point, after watching various episodes where Fred explained what the *G.* in *Fred G. Sanford* stood for, my inebriation gave me the false courage to speak to the group, deluding myself like Hoppy into thinking that I fit in. "Hey, Dr. DuBois!" I called out cheerily across the room to the kindly man, the college president, the host of the party. He looked up at me from his chair, his dinner roll half-way to his mouth. Now that I had his and everyone else's attention, I continued. "What's the *G.* stand for?"

Silence filled the room. Next to me, Marais sunk lower into her cushion on the sofa and hid behind her wine glass. Everyone in the room had already turned away from the television and their conversations to stare at me. From the television set, Fred Sanford took the opportunity to call me a big dummy.

I was mortified and felt my face turning as red as my Cabernet. Just when I was wishing that I would die, laughter spontaneously erupted. Dr. DuBois leaned over into the arm of his chair, his dinner roll threatening to fall from his fingertips as his body shook, thankfully, with laughter and a grin radiated from his lips. Marais smiled, cut her eyes at me, and came out from behind her wine glass. Amongst the roomful of giggles were some comments such as, "We got our own little Hoppy!" Another guest, a female professor, amended the statement to give me a little credit, "Yeah, but she actually got one right!" Someone else said appreciatively, "She's all right; she's all right." A young guy who was probably a student commented good-naturedly, "Guess who's coming to dinner!" Marais, although amused, wasn't about to sing my praises. Instead she leaned over and spoke into my ear, "You can dress white people up, but you can't take them out." In response, I flipped her off by nonchalantly rubbing my nose with my middle finger. "See what I mean?" she said.

This Martin Luther King Jr. Day was a lot different though, mainly because I was here; Marais' parents were there; and Marais was in Atlanta, Georgia. So I decided to have my own solo celebration. I turned on the TV and surfed through all three channels. I was pleased to find some programming that actually related to the holiday.

First, I watched a segment on the Buffalo Soldiers of the Korean War, the Deuce Four, which was an all-black regiment at a time when the armed forces were segregated. After thirteen and a half months of combat, they were the most decorated regiment of the Korean War with two Medal of Honor winners; fifteen Distinguished Service Crosses; 185 Silver Stars; over 2000 Bronze Stars; and over 2000 Purple Hearts. They even got the first victory of the war. Yet, the 24th regiment was disrespected by being labeled as "deserters." As a result, it was deactivated by the Armed Forces in 1951. In return for their service and accolades, these soldiers received no fanfare, no marching band. Instead, they were just sent home.

Next, I watched an interview with some of the surviving Tuskegee Airmen. I was fascinated and uplifted by their success in World War II despite the presence of discrimination, segregation, and bigotry found not only in Alabama, but on a national level as well. Even more inspiring were the men themselves; one man in particular who was a joyous soul despite the difficult times he had lived through.

After the interviews with the airmen ended, the station announced that it was showing *Guess Who's Coming to Dinner* immediately following the documentaries. In its time, I realize and respect the fact that the movie was groundbreaking and progressive in its subject matter. Seeing it for the first time decades later, though, I had found myself blushing with embarrassment every time someone referred to Sidney Poitier's character, John Prentice, as a "Negro." When Joey Drayton, John Prentice's white fiancée, perkily tells her mother that John thinks Mrs. Drayton will faint because he's a Negro, I thought I actually might faint because she called him a Negro.

I'm not exactly sure why the word "Negro" embarrassed me so much; maybe because it sounded antiquated. It made me think of Eddie Murphy imitating white people in *Beverly Hills Cop* or *Trading Places*. In fact, the first time I saw *Guess Who's Coming to Dinner*, the word "Negro" appeared to be volleyed between characters so often that had it been my word during a drinking game, I was sure that I would have died from alcohol poisoning by the end of the movie.

After watching it that first time, I told Marais that the movie's title should be changed from *Guess Who's Coming to Dinner* to *Because He's a Negro* since that phrase was in constant use. She had cut her eyes at me in response and said nothing. It wasn't until I saw the movie for the second time that I had just cause to be embarrassed.

The word "Negro" was only used two or three times tops. Apparently my politically correct whiteness had been overly sensitive to the word making me more like Hoppy than I cared to admit.

I clicked off the television and stretched my arms into the air. Mack peered at me from his cushion on the couch and then closed his eyes once again. I definitely wanted and needed to get out of the house so I decided that I would take a drive up to Point Park, a Civil War battle site and monument on Lookout Mountain, and enjoy the view. Yes, it was really cold outside, but I bundled up in my down jacket and headed out the door.

To get to Point Park, I drove through downtown and into St. Elmo. I glanced up at Lookout Mountain and could see the cut of the Incline track into the steep hillside. As a child, I had been simultaneously thrilled and terrified each time I rode the Incline. It was exciting to ride up in the car, to pass the other passenger car mid-trip, and terrifying to look down at the steep mountain below once we arrived at the top.

As an adult, though, it was much more terrifying for me to drive up and down the winding mountain road with the steep drop-off on one side. Instead, I just focused on the road in front of me and drove at a grandmotherly pace. I drove past Rock City, through Fairyland, and parked on the street alongside the beautiful homes that graced the Brow. I put money in the meter just to be safe, but had learned that in the off season, especially the dead of winter, that I didn't have to pay to enter Point Park, a park that for all of my life until recent years had been free.

I stepped through the stone archway that had seemed like an entrance into a castle to my eyes when I was a child and headed for a few of the cannons stationed at the edge of the mountain. I peered down at the Tennessee River winding its way through the valley below and fixated on the Moccasin Bend mental health facility located on its other side.

During the hot summers of my childhood, I'd stare at the crystal blue rectangular pool on the facility's site and long to swim in its presumably cool, refreshing water. It seemed like a shame for such a pretty pool to go to waste because whenever I visited Lookout Mountain, nobody ever seemed to be swimming in it. Of course no one in his right mind would go swimming on a cold January day, which made me peer closer at the pool's surface because it was located at a mental health facility after all. From what I could tell, though, it remained empty.

I too was alone in the park because nobody in their right mind would be outdoors at a Civil War battlefield on such a frigid day either. I walked back towards the monument and sat down on its steps. It seemed so strange not to be with Marais and her family for their annual celebration. I figured it was probably just as strange for her as well so I pulled my cell phone out of my jacket pocket and called her. As I listened to her phone ring, I pulled my hood up over my head to spare it from the biting wind and snuggled into the down of my jacket.

"Hello?" I heard her say.

"Hey, Marais. It's me."

"Hey!" she said. "What are you doing?"

"Not much," I said. "It just seemed so weird not to be with you and your family that I thought I'd give you a call and see what you were doing."

"Actually, my parents came down here for the weekend so we are spending the day together before they drive back later this afternoon. Can you guess where we are?" I could feel her smile through the phone.

Her question puzzled me because it sounded as if I should know where she was. "I have no idea."

"Stone Mountain, Georgia, of course!" she said with a laugh.

The chills that ran up and down my spine and the goose bumps that followed had nothing to do with the freezing temperatures outside. I gasped. "You're at Stone Mountain?" I repeated.

"Yes. With Mom and Dad."

"Marais," I breathed. "I'm on Lookout Mountain."

"You're kidding." Without waiting for a response from me, I heard her turn to her parents and say excitedly, "Vandelyn is on Lookout Mountain! Right now!" I heard some sounds of disbelief. Both ends of the phone line went silent as snippets of Martin Luther King Jr.'s famous speech echoed in all of our ears: *Let freedom ring from Stone Mountain of Georgia! Let freedom ring from Lookout Mountain of Tennessee!* In the manner found only in Hollywood movies or Broadway musicals, suddenly and simultaneously all four of us started to sing through my and Marais' cellular phones,

"My country 'tis of thee,
sweet Land of Liberty,
of thee I sing.
Land where my fathers died,
land of the pilgrims' pride,
from every mountainside,
let freedom ring."

Afterwards we were silent once more, the words from Dr. King's speech flowing through our brains: *When we let freedom ring, when we let it ring from every village and every hamlet, from every state and every city, we will be able to speed up that day when all of God's children, black men and white men, Jews and Gentiles, Protestants and Catholics, will be able to join hands and sing in the words of the old Negro spiritual . . . .* Before my mind could finish the thought, Dr. Abraham G. DuBois shouted out for all of us to hear, "Free at last! Free at last! Thank God Almighty we are free at last!"

22

If you for any reason thought that I now viewed myself as Super White Girl, the newest heroine in The Halls of Justice, singer of *Kumbaya* and the Terminatrix of Racial Division, you would be sadly mistaken. In fact, as I drove down the winding mountain road, the only mental image I had of myself was of me and my Lexus plummeting through the guardrail into a fiery oblivion. To combat this image, I kept my eyes on the double yellow line and hugged it rather than the non-existent shoulder adjacent to the guardrail and scary abyss below.

Once I reached the bottom of the road to the safe flat land of St. Elmo, I was hot and sweaty from tension. At a stoplight, I removed my coat and brushed away the beads of perspiration from my brow. Only then was I able to reflect on what had just occurred atop Lookout Mountain. What had happened was that the four of us had actually lived part of Martin Luther King Jr.'s dream. How freaking cool was that?!

Although it was a start, our unity hardly cured the racial problems in America because bigots of all colors are sprinkled throughout our society like dandruff across the yoke of a handsomely tailored suit. The non-bigoted rest of us are hardly exempt because we human beings are not perfect and continue to make mistakes. Sometimes we can be unintentionally hurtful even when our intentions are honorable.

Although I knew those types of mistakes were not limited to white people (although throughout our American history, if a minority was present, at some point we oppressed it, raped it, and even killed it), that all nationalities of the world practiced racism, oppression, rape, and murder at some point in time, I knew that I too had blood on my hands.

Of course, I wasn't an oppressor-rapist-murderer. Maybe it

would be better to say that I helped pave the road to Hell with one of my good intentions. Regardless, I think it is always best to come clean because secrets have a way of becoming exposed and our secrets are always dirtier when a third party reveals them.

When I was a freshman at LSU, something disturbing was happening in the state of Louisiana: the election for governor. Normally, an upcoming election would not be disturbing, but this one was because one of the men running was David Duke. I had no idea who the man was until one morning when I was getting ready for class and had the television innocently tuned to *Little House on the Prairie* for background noise.

I quickly jumped to attention when a campaign commercial for the upcoming election began. It was endorsed by an opposing candidate of Duke's and it showed a videotape of David Duke dressed in a three piece suit leading the Klan. If that wasn't scary enough, the meeting took place at night; a burning cross lit the background; and the Klansmen were cloaked by their white satin sheets and hoods.

I was shocked, appalled, and repulsed. A video like this should have ended his political career. All people should have been mortified, horrified, and offended. But they weren't. Despite the video, Duke still maintained a chance to be elected. Even scarier was the realization that people I thought were normal were voting for him. A nice Cajun girl who lived on my floor told me that she voted for him, not because she had anything against black people, but because she was tired of affirmative action and Duke was opposed to it too. (Big surprise. David Duke was opposed to a lot of things, none of them white and Christian.)

In fact, one Saturday morning when I was standing in line at McDonald's for a bacon, egg, and cheese biscuit, I was behind a regular-looking fraternity boy type. He had brown hair, an attractive face, and the look of the average white college guy. Then I glanced down at his shirt. It had NAAWP written across it. Since I had been told that the NAAWP was associated with David Duke, I took a step back from the guy lest he be struck by lightning. When I did, the frat boy noticed the contorted expression of disapproval on my face. Real or imagined, his expression became one of wickedness and I hoped I'd never see him or anyone like him again.

One warm Sunday afternoon during the election campaigns,

my roommate, Allie, and I decided to take our cameras and go downtown and take pictures of Baton Rouge. We went to the Mississippi River and took our photos in front of the Battleship. We stood in front of a sculpture of a man sitting on a cart, playing the fiddle and snapped another picture. We sat on a cannon; stood on a bridge in front of the Governor's mansion; and posed next to a statue of Huey P. Long. Then we went to our favorite places to eat: a picture in front of Piccadilly's Cafeteria, Dumont's Bakery, and Denny's. When we came across a campaign billboard for David Duke, we paused.

"We should take a picture of that as a sign of the times," I said. "One day it is going to be unbelievable that someone like him actually had a chance to run for political office." Obviously I was optimistic that he would lose. Allie agreed with me because she too thought it was appalling. Of course, she was from Louisiana and she was, as she put it, "used to Louisiana being the armpit of American politics."

As we aimed our cameras upwards at the billboard, I stopped before I snapped a photo. "Actually," I said, "why don't you get in the photo. Photos without people in them are just so boring."

So far our photo shoot had consisted of one of us or both of us in every picture. So I took a picture of Allie underneath the billboard and then she took one of me. Confident that we had documented a political travesty, that we now possessed proof of a potential injustice that with our photos could never be denied, we eagerly turned in our film to the one-hour photo shop.

After retrieving our photos, we returned to our dorm room and excitedly tore open the envelopes containing our photos. We giggled as we viewed the photos of us laughing and having a good time downtown and in front of our favorite eateries, but I stopped cold when I looked at the two photos of us underneath the David Duke billboard. Instead of us wearing faces of disgust, instead of us looking up at the billboard and extending our middle fingers, we were smiling. *Smiling! SMILING!!!!!!* Without thinking about it, we had automatically opted for our cute, happy-girl pose that was present in every other picture we'd taken that day.

"Oh my god, Allie!" I gasped. She looked up at my tone of voice. "Look at these pictures of us!" She had not come to her billboard photos yet so she looked at mine.

"Oh my god!" she agreed. We were both appalled by what the pictures seemed to imply. To the casual observer who did not know us, it looked like we actually *liked* David Duke instead of finding him repulsive.

"We've got to correct this as best we can. Get a pen and write an explanation on the back." We both grabbed pens and addressed the issue on the backside of the photo. My explanation was, "This picture was taken to reflect the sign 'o' the times. We're not racists or anything."

To my eighteen year-old brain, my words satisfactorily and succinctly explained our circumstances. To my thirty year-old brain, they sound like they were written by a ditzy Valley Girl (or was that redundant?). Nevertheless, that's what I wrote and what I considered to be a sufficient *mea culpa* at the time. Of course, it is now obvious that it was inadequate, but I had at least tried to right the wrong to the best of my ability at the time.

In addition to my written word, I did call and confess my bad judgment to Marais, which made me feel better to immediately admit what had happened. She thought that I was a complete idiot for not foreseeing the consequences, but she forgave me for my "unintentional blight on humanity," as she called it. She was obviously more eloquent at eighteen than I was.

I had been tempted over the years to destroy those two pictures out of shame, but I decided not to. If one day others found out about the pictures, my word would be my only proof that ill-will had been unintended. I would never want the pictures to be seen by anyone, of course, but at least I could turn the picture over and demonstrate my remorse, however lamely expressed, for that error in judgment.

23

By the time I pulled into my garage, the sky was growing dark. I hurried into the warmth of my kitchen, picked up my meowing kitty cat, and sat down in the den. As I squeezed Mack tightly to my chest, I felt antsy and restless. Mack squirmed out of my arms and I stood up and walked into the dining room. Maybe I could dance around and expend some of this built-up adrenaline.

As I approached my CD tower, I knew that my usual choices of dance music would not do. I wasn't exactly sure what I wanted to hear, so I began scanning the spines arranged alphabetically by artist. I didn't even have to get past the letter *A* to find what I was looking for. My face lit up as my eyes rested on Arrested Development and I slid it out of the lineup.

I hadn't listened to Arrested Development in years. I had even forgotten that I had it. But I immediately inserted the CD into the player, skipped to song number five, grabbed Mack, and began dancing around the living room and dining room, singing the lyrics of *Mr. Wendal* to the pussycat's nonplussed face.

I couldn't help but think about the Patten Tower tenants when Speech spoke about Mr. Wendal. The similar observations that Speech had regarding Mr. Wendal and that I had about Roy struck me. I felt uplifted. Maybe the Mr. Wendals and Roys of the world actually had their priorities straight. Maybe the rest of us were really the lost souls with no real place to call home.

After *Mr. Wendal* ended, I didn't have the patience to wait for song fourteen to arrive so I skipped ahead to it too. Mack was glad for the reprieve and he scurried under the dining room table. He sat squarely underneath the middle of the table, confident that I would not expend the energy to crawl under the table to grab him. He was right.

As I danced around the room to the beat, I thought back to 1992 when this song, *Tennessee*, was released. At the time, I felt pretty sure that everybody on the University of Tennessee campus where Marais and I attended college (I transferred after my freshman year at LSU) loved this song. Not only was it catchy, it spoke of our state.

As a twenty year-old, I felt such pride at my Southern state being included in something so cool as an Arrested Development song. I gushed my enthusiasm to Marais who also loved Arrested Development. I think my giddiness had revealed my inner Valley Girl once again: "Marais! I *love* this song! It's so awesome and it's all about Tennessee! How cool is that? The South, especially Tennessee, rarely gets associated with anything cool!" Insert some squealing in between gushes. I may have even jumped up and down and clapped.

Marais laughed; it was a happy tinkling sound. She was laughing *with me*, I was sure, but soon enough she waved her magic wand of reality and the fairy dust which floated around my head disappeared. "Vandelyn. Have you actually listened to the words?" She was still smiling at me so I knew she wasn't unhappy about my exuberance.

I strained my brain to recollect the lyrics. The song was still too new to me to know all the lyrics, but I felt confident. "Sure," I said. I quoted the chorus about something guiding Speech to Tennessee; something taking him home. That's what had struck me as so cool: Speech's home was my home.

"I don't think you get it," she commented. But she wasn't being unkind; I could still hear lightness in her voice. Then something dawned on me. I threw a hand on my hip and extended the other hand out in front of me in the Talk-To-The-Hand gesture.

"Oh please," I said. "Don't give me the 'It's a black thing. You wouldn't understand' business." I was referring to a popular catch phrase that black students were using on white students anytime they deemed us to be Hoppies, which was occurring more and more often.

"That's not what I was going to say." She paused, "Although, it would not be inappropriate in this circumstance." I rolled my eyes. She gave me a look and then further explained, "He talks about the past sordid history of the South. He talks about climbing trees where his ancestors were lynched." The word *lynched* made my stomach take a sickly turn. "*In Tennessee*," she clarified. Then she threw me a bone after seeing my dejected face. "But he is talking about West Tennessee."

My eyes had hope once again. "Yes," I agreed, greedily taking the bone. "West Tennessee." I paused. "Although, I'm sure East Tennessee was no different." I appreciated her attempt to soften the blow, but we couldn't go on pretending now, could we? "But," I pointed out, "in the song, Speech sounds like he reconciles the past. The song does talk about taking him home."

"That's true," Marais conceded.

"He comes to terms with the past. He is at peace."

"Yes," she had agreed. "He does seem to be at peace."

I time-warped back to the present day in my dining room. Peace. At peace. Speech was at peace with a racist history. He could even call a once painful place, Home. Martin Luther King Jr. had been at peace. The Tuskegee Airmen were at peace. The Deuce Four were finally at peace after fighting forty years to clear their name and get the 24th regiment reinstated in the armed forces, finally succeeding in the 1990s. (How could anyone call those men deserters?) Even Joey and John had been at peace when everyone else in *Guess Who's Coming to Dinner* was freaking out.

I, on the other hand, was not at peace. Not with my past, my present, not even my future. How was I going to become at peace? My life was in turmoil. Suddenly Aaron Feuerstein popped into my head. He had his share of turmoil, yet he too was at peace even though his mill had burned to the ground. He was at peace even though the banks were knocking on his door demanding money. He was at peace even though he could possibly lose everything his family had worked so hard to build. How could he possibly be at peace through all that? As I pondered how others could feel so at peace in the face of adversity, Speech's lyrics to *Tennessee* swirled around my head, reinforcing the three little letters that made me go hmm: G.O.D.

24

"Why are you watching that?" Tod asked me as I stopped my channel surfing to pause on a female televangelist. We were hanging out over at his house so I actually had access to cable television. As uncool as I knew it was to watch somebody preach on TV, I couldn't help it. This woman had been getting my attention for a year or so now, against my will.

I really didn't want to like watching a televangelist. In fact I had enjoyed many a smart ass comment while watching that one lady with the pink hair as she praised the Lord while sitting in a gilded chair adorned with fake rubies. I never could understand why heaven was supposed to be gaudily bejeweled with pearly gates and gold thrones when in actuality Jesus and God weren't into material things. So why did earthly Christians like to think of heaven as a Beverly Hills mansion decorated by Liberace?

Although I was slightly embarrassed to admit it, I answered, "I actually like her. She's really down-to-earth and had a rough childhood. She's not like other televangelists. In fact, I don't even like referring to her as a televangelist. But she's really real." Totally lame. "You know what I mean," I rushed on. "You should watch her sometime. She's really good," I said as I quickly ended my sales pitch.

"I don't believe in God," Tod said in a somewhat condescending tone.

"Really?" I asked a bit defensively, throwing back a little bit of condescension as well. "Why not?" I asked.

"I just don't," he said with a tad bit of superiority.

Personally, I did not care whether he or anybody else believed in God. To each his own. In fact, my dad and step-mother happened to be atheists. For them, their idea of a holy trinity was a stochastic

150

process, a Markov chain, and a probability vector. My father and step-mother happened to be professors of higher math at the Tennessee Institute of Engineering and Science (TIES), formerly known as the Tennessee Institute of Technology (TIT).

My father had a penchant for telling me on those rare times that he saw me about how bad I was in math. This judgment pissed me off of course because a) it wasn't true. I had earned an A+ in pre-calculus and a B+ in calculus; and b) it was a hurtful thing for a parent to say to a child. But I gave it as good as I got. I'd tell him in response, "Yeah, if only I had been good at math I could've worked at that highly respected institution, TITTIES, just like you."

So although I could care less if Tod was an atheist, what did annoy me was Tod's attitude. He spoke to me as if I had just told him that I believed the world was flat or that the moon was made out of cheese.

"You just don't," I repeated with the slightest hint of mockery. "That's a great explanation."

"Oh, okay," he began to speak in a slightly sneering tone. "Please explain to me why you believe in God."

He was really beginning to piss me off. Making me even angrier was that I had no answer for why I believed in God that was good enough to shut down a smart ass atheist. Actually, everything I could think of to say about God, the pink-haired lady and my favorite female televangelist on TV had already said. I already knew the likelihood of Tod listening to anything that they had to say. Somehow Tod had managed to push all of my buttons at once. I pictured myself as a cartoon Frankenstein with steam coming out of my ears while the nuts, bolts, and springs popped from my joints as I self-destructed. I stood up and left Tod's house, slamming the door behind me.

When I got home, I went straight into my bedroom and climbed underneath the covers. I was depressed. Mack curled up on my chest and purred as I rubbed my hand down his coat. What was going on? Why was I always fighting with the love interest in my life? Thibodeaux and I would spar at times; mainly me sparring with him for acting so blasé about our relationship. I'd fight about stupid stuff because the thing that really bothered me, his feelings for me not being as strong as my feelings for him, was never discussed to my satisfaction. Not that I understood our problem in such concrete

151

terms back then. If I had understood clearly that Thibodeaux was never going to be what I needed him to be, why would I have stayed with him? Because I thought I was in love with him? That was exactly the reason.

After I left Thibodeaux for the last time, I called a psychologist and made an appointment. I knew that I had to figure out how I'd gotten so off course in my relationships with guys. I remembered when my mother and father were going through their divorce and my mom said to me, "I really hope our divorce doesn't affect your future relationships with men."

I had been annoyed. "Why would your and dad's divorce affect *my* future relationships with men?!" Freud didn't roll over in his grave that day; he snorted with laughter and peed his pants.

Actually, I don't think my parents' divorce did affect my relationships with men. My dad had behaved like a jerk and I knew it. He had been disrespectful to my mom and had abandoned my brother and me. I had been glad that my mom was divorcing him. I know now that it was my horrible relationship with my father that caused my problems with men.

When I was in elementary school, my Dad gave me a nickname. It was "Dummy." I just remember him saying to me, "Hi, Dummy." I hated it. I hoped he would just quit calling me that. When he didn't, I gathered up all my strength and with tears of frustration in my eyes and anger in my voice, I told him, "I am not dumb so don't call me Dummy!" His eyes went wide as if he had no idea that his nickname was hurtful, but he did stop.

My father wasn't just your basic asshole. He wasn't just a cocksucking bastard. He was THE cocksucking bastard. And since he had not been a stable presence in my life, I was demanding too much from my boyfriends. They weren't just boyfriends; they were supposed to be my saviors; they were supposed to be everything that my father hadn't been and then some. No one could ever live up to that. Not to mention that I was having trouble with my choices in boyfriends.

When I had talked to the psychologist about my problems, I laid everything out on the table because I didn't want to be messed up anymore (obviously, I still need some more sessions). After I described my relationship problems with Thibodeaux, she asked me, "Do you think that love is supposed to hurt?" I knew the correct answer to that. "No," I said. But what I didn't add that maybe I should've added was that it always had.

Love had always hurt in my family so was it any wonder that love also hurt in my other relationships? I loved my mother, but when she felt vulnerable and downtrodden, that hurt me. I loved my brother, but his ADD-inappropriate behavior and people's unkind responses to him hurt me. I had once loved my father, but his selfishness, his lack of care and concern for his family, hurt me. A couple of years ago, I drank a little too much and emailed him as a way to confront him about being a terrible father. Of course he seemed to be clueless yet contrite, acting as if he wanted to remedy the situation. In his rational, clinical, Spock way he emailed me back with "Tell me what you would need me to do to be a great father." I couldn't believe his response. He really had to ask?

I snarled at the computer screen and knew that at twenty-eight years-old, I no longer needed a good father, not like I had needed one when I was growing up. I typed in response, "A good father would not have to ask what he needed to do to be a good father." Then I added, "And never mind anyway because what I needed from you, I needed it when I was growing up."

Not to mention that the list of what it would have taken for him to be a good father would have taken way too long and it would've had to include a list of things that he should never have done in the first place. Does a grown man really need his daughter to tell him, "Don't disrespect your wife"? "Don't abandon your kids"? "Don't call your child *Dummy*"? If the S.O.B. couldn't figure those things out on his own, what help could he possibly give me now?

Man, I was angry. So fucking angry! As I lay in the dark bedroom, I heard a knock on the kitchen door. I ignored it. The knock rapped again. I knew it was Tod and I felt ashamed. I didn't want to see him. I didn't want to see anybody. I just wanted to stop time and hide in the darkness of my bedroom indefinitely. I heard his muffled voice calling my name. The knocking stopped and silence resumed. A minute or so later, I heard him outside my bedroom window.

"Vandelyn? Are you OK? I'm sorry that we fought. I'm worried about you. Just let me know that you are OK." This sucked. I just wanted to disappear from the face of the earth; pretend that I didn't exist. That was now impossible since I had to let Tod know that I was OK.

"I'm OK, Tod," I hollered. "I just want to be left alone."

"OK. Call me when you are feeling better." I could hear his footsteps walking away, crunching in the leaves. I pulled the covers up over my head. For a moment, I wished that I were dead. Not because I really wanted to be dead, but because I didn't want to be in pain. I was sick of hurting. For people like me who knew no way to find peace, death seemed to be the only way to feel no more pain.

25

February

"Guess who my next client is," Donna said to me.

"I have no idea. Who?" I asked.

"Taylor's daughter, Brittanee, with two *e*'s." Donna knew that Taylor got on my nerves. I had never met Taylor's daughter, but I felt for the little girl who had to have that woman as her mother.

"That name is so ghetto," I replied. "With two *t*'s. Where'd Taylor get that name? From a Jeff Foxworthy, *You Might Be a Redneck If* monologue?" Then I felt a little bad because it wasn't the child's fault her mother was a pretentious idiot from the sticks.

A few minutes later, Taylor rushed in with her ten year-old daughter in tow. She was a sweet faced child with light brown hair who must've taken after her father because I saw very little resemblance to her mother's face. Donna greeted both Taylor and Brittanee.

"Hi Donna," Taylor responded, her voice commanding the attention of the few occupants of the reception area who looked up briefly from their magazines. I was sure that Taylor liked having people's eyes on her; it probably made her feel more important.

Taylor was helping Brittanee out of her winter coat and looking around for a place to hang it. I stretched out my arms to take it and she handed it over to me without even a thank you. I guess she thought other people were put on this earth to make her life easier.

"Donna, let me go ahead and pay because I've got to get back to work. Brittanee's dad, Chad, will be by to pick her up around five." It was a little after three now. Taylor must've left work to pick her daughter up from school.

"Vandelyn, could you take care of Taylor's payment for me

155

so I can go ahead and get started on Brittanee? Charge her for a girl's haircut and a partial foil." I tried not to register my shock that a ten year-old girl was getting highlights and instead went through the motions of taking Taylor's credit card and swiping it for the correct amount plus tip.

"Thank you, Vandelyn," Taylor said as she grabbed her card and receipt and hurried out the door. I took Brittanee's coat and draped it over the empty salon chair at the station adjacent to Donna's. Brittanee was sitting in Donna's chair, enjoying the sensation of swiveling her seat to the left and right as she waited for Donna to return with her hair color. I stepped to the back where Donna was stirring the color mixture in a bowl.

"She's getting her hair colored?" I whispered, even though we were all the way in the back of the salon. Our salon was small and it did not take much for sound to reach our clients' ears.

"I know," Donna agreed with a shake of her head. "Who would color their elementary school child's hair?"

"A pretentious idiot like Taylor," I answered. Donna placed the bowl on a small rolling cart, added a stack of foils to it, and rolled it on out to her station. I didn't have any clients for the rest of the afternoon so I sat down in the chair in front of the makeup station that was next to Kitty and catty-cornered from Donna.

While Kitty led her client to the dryer to process, Donna was asking Brittanee about school and friends as she applied the color and wrapped it in foil. Brittanee politely answered with yes and no answers as Kitty called for her next client and led her to the shampoo bowl. Then out-of-the-blue, Brittanee said the darnedest thing.

"You know, most people would prefer to have blond hair than brown hair," she said. As a brown-haired, brown-eyed female myself, my hackles went up. I stepped over to Donna's station to continue the conversation.

"Oh really?" I asked. Donna glanced over at me. I knew she heard the edge in my voice even though I was sure Brittanee didn't.

"Yes," Brittanee said.

"Where'd you hear that?" I asked, besides, of course, from society, the media, white slavers, and Hugh Hefner.

"That's what my mom says." My blood was beginning to percolate. Why would a mother tell her impressionable daughter to buy into society's warped way of thinking? Although in my eyes propagandizing Aryan traits to your own daughter was enough to warrant a visit from Child and Family Services, I was not sure that they'd agree. I had to wonder what Taylor was going to tell her daughter next. That society, the media, white slavers, and Hugh Hefner like big titties? Hey little girl, would you like some big titties for middle school graduation?

I decided to act like a mature adult for once. Or semi-mature. Or the best that I could do. "You have pretty, light brown hair," I pointed out. "Why would you want to highlight it blond?" This question immediately made me giggle in my head. It reminded me of a line from a Top 10 list that I had read in LSU's newspaper, *The Daily Reveille*: "Why would a girl with such pretty blond hair dye her roots black?"

"Actually, my natural hair color is blond," Brittanee said. I so wanted to point out that her natural color was what grew naturally from her head, which apparently was light brown. But she continued. "It's just that there's not enough heat in the atmosphere to keep it blond in the wintertime."

Not enough heat in the atmosphere? On February 1, a tragedy occurred when the Space Shuttle Columbia broke apart on reentry because a damaged panel was unable to prevent the hot gases from penetrating the craft. So, yes, there was plenty of heat in the atmosphere. Unfortunately for Taylor, there just wasn't enough heat in the atmosphere to alter Brittanee's DNA. But I couldn't tell Brittanee that.

So where was a Goode's World Atlas when I needed it? I glanced around Donna's station willing a world map to appear so I could point out Chattanooga, Tennessee's latitude as compared with the much higher, much colder, latitudes of the Nordic and Germanic countries so stereotypically filled with natural blondes who managed to stay blond even with bitterly freezing temperatures chilling their hair follicles right down to their skulls.

I knew exactly who was behind this bit of bogus scientific information. The same chick who claimed her grandfather would have attended Harvard had he not been from Bean Field. Well, to some degree that was true. If being from Bean Field meant that you thought it took heat in the atmosphere to keep one's hair blond, it was no surprise that Harvard wasn't interested in Bean Field High School students.

Kitty was back at her station cutting her client's hair. They were wrapped up in their own conversation, oblivious to ours. I decided to step away from Donna and Brittanee. I realized that it sounded like I was fussing at Brittanee when it really wasn't her fault. She was just regurgitating what she'd been told by her mother for the past ten years of her life. It was Taylor whom I was irritated with, but she wasn't here for me to yell at. And realistically, I couldn't yell at Taylor in the salon anyway without getting fired.

I walked back up to the reception area and sat behind the desk, my brain muddled with thoughts. I remembered all too well my elementary school friendship with a girl named Paula. Paula was a rather plain girl, but she had blond hair and blue eyes. I remember us playing in the backyard of her house one day when she smirked at me and said, "Blondes have more fun than brunettes."

My eyes narrowed and I said, "No they don't."

"Then how come they say blondes have more fun?" I had heard that saying somewhere before, although I wasn't sure where. "They don't say brunettes have more fun."

"So what?" I challenged.

"Remember Smurfette? When she was bad, she had dark hair. When she became good, she got blond hair." I had always hated *The Smurfs*. Now I knew why. Paula continued, "Blondes are prettier than brunettes too."

"No they're not." I defended my brown-haired compatriots.

"Are too."

"Are not," I contradicted.

"Then why are all the models blond-haired and blue-eyed? Even all the Barbie Dolls are blond-haired and blue-eyed."

For the moment I was stumped. Paula took the opportunity to support her claim. "Christy Brinkley has blond hair and blue eyes. And all the other models in magazines have blond hair and blue eyes." It was true. I knew it. Christy Brinkley was a new model at the time and everyone was crazy about her looks. It was also true that every other model in magazines did have blond hair and blue eyes. I was frustrated because the way Paula was structuring this debate, she was going to be right because the media was on her side. Then a name popped into my head.

"Carol Alt!" I shouted. Ha ha! Carol Alt was a Cover Girl model just like Christy Brinkley and she had brown hair. I had thrown Paula a little off of her game, but she quickly recovered.

"She's not even big time," she taunted. "And besides she still has blue eyes." So was this little game of Paula's less about blondes and brunettes and more about her and me?

I then thought of the one woman who in 1981 could trump all, even the blond-haired, blue-eyed Christy Brinkley, at least in a classroom of my fourth-grade peers. "Daisy Duke," I smiled. "Daisy Duke has brown hair. And she's beautiful and tough and smart and cool!" It was my turn to smirk. I had loved the song, *The Devil Went Down to Georgia,* and I felt a little bit like Johnny when the Devil (in this case, Paula) had to admit defeat.

"She still has blue eyes," was all that Paula could come up with, but I didn't care.

"So what?" I challenged once again, this time with even more confidence. "She still has long, brown hair and all the boys think she's hot stuff and kicks butt!" Vandelyn: one. Paula: zero.

My experience was hardly a chapter out of Toni Morrison's, *The Bluest Eye,* but I did know what it felt like to look out into the world at that time and not see yourself reflected back. How can a young child defend her own value when the society around her gives her no validation? That's why Brittanee's regurgitation of her mother's ignorant words irritated me.

My childhood experience stuck with me when I heard that the *Dukes of Hazzard* was going to be made into a movie. Even though I was an adult, I was so excited because I had grown up with the Dukes and had really loved that show. (I still had all of my *Dukes of Hazzard* baseball cards.) Then I saw who was cast as Daisy Duke: a blonde. She was the complete opposite of everything that Daisy Duke had originally been. I was so disappointed that I never did see the movie. What was also disappointing was that the man behind the making of the movie was a guy from my hometown of Knoxville. From what I'd heard, he was also a fellow South Knoxvillian, just like me, who grew up with the show just like I did. In a world full of Paulas, I really wish he had known what Daisy Duke's brown hair, quick-thinking, fearless attitude, street smarts, and beauty had meant to a bunch of girls like me.

26

A little before five o'clock, Brittanee's dad, Chad, entered the salon. Despite the fact that this splintered family sounded like they were contrived on a soap opera (Taylor, Brittanee, and Chad?), I was instantly mesmerized by Chad. He was handsome in the guy-next-door way and had the most amazing blue eyes that I had ever seen. As cheesy as this may sound, they were as crystal blue as the Caribbean Ocean. Really.

"Hi," he said to me as he entered the warm reception area from the cold outdoors. "I'm Brittanee's dad." He gave me a warm smile and seemed like a genuinely kind and decent human being. My body tingled with a good feeling, not a lustful feeling. It was just like a "wow" feeling that I couldn't explain. A wow feeling that I'd never felt with Tod or even Thibodeaux. Maybe it was just those eyes of his.

"Hi!" I chirped. "I think she's done. She's just sitting in one of the station chairs playing a game. Follow me," I instructed him. He followed me to the station next to Donna's and walked over to Brittanee who was playing some kind of handheld game. The resemblance between father and daughter was uncanny even though he had dark hair sprinkled with gray.

"Hi, honey," he said. "Your hair looks nice."

"Hi, Daddy," she replied as she glanced up from the game and then locked her eyes back on the screen again. I stealthily observed how he treated his daughter due to my own personal background. He stepped over to her chair and watched her thumbs pump vigorously.

"Oh, you've almost got it," he encouraged. "But watch out for that—whoops!" Apparently whatever he was warning his daughter about had gotten her anyway.

"Dang!" she said. Then she looked up at her dad and said, "But that's the highest level I've ever gotten to so far."

"Wow! That's great." Brittanee stood up out of the chair and her dad grabbed her coat. Brittanee placed her game down in the chair and let her father help her into her coat. "Do you have any books or anything from school here?"

"No. Mom's got them in her car." Brittanee grabbed her game and they started for the reception area. I followed them back out to the front and then her dad glanced over at me.

"Did her mother already pay? Or do I need to pay?" he asked.

"Mom paid already," Brittanee explained.

"Yes, she paid when she dropped Brittanee off," I confirmed.

"OK, Little Bee," he said affectionately to his little girl, "let's go. Put your hood up because it's cold outside." He wrapped his arm around his daughter's shoulders and started to open the door. Then he stopped. "Actually, Little Bee, why don't you stay here in the reception area and let me bring the car around, OK? I parked around the block and it's too cold for you to walk." Looking over at me he said, "Would you mind keeping an eye on her while I go get the car?"

"Of course," I smiled. "We'll hang out in the reception area together and look out for your car. What kind of car are you driving?" I asked.

"It's a silver Toyota 4Runner." Then he stepped out into the cold and hurried down the sidewalk. I stood next to Brittanee as she stared out the large glass window. As I watched his figure huddled from the cold, I smiled to myself. She had a good daddy. I could tell he'd never call her a hurtful nickname—in fact, he had already given her an adorably loving nickname—and that he'd buy his little girl Chapstick the minute she needed it. Actually, I bet he was the kind of father that would buy Chapstick before she ever needed it. I glanced down at Brittanee's lips and my heart warmed when I saw that there wasn't even the hint of a little piece of chapped skin on them. They were soft, pink, and smooth.

Once I helped Brittanee safely into her father's SUV, I returned to the reception desk and checked out both Kitty and Donna's clients. Donna was done for the day and she was sweeping up the hair from her last haircut.

"I'm going to go out and smoke," she announced. "Do you want to come outside with me?"

"Sure," I said. I grabbed my heavy coat and we stepped outside onto the sidewalk. Donna lit up a cigarette and inhaled deeply.

"Brittanee's dad sure seemed nice," I said, sticking my gloved hands deep into the pockets of my coat. "I wonder how Taylor ever managed to snag him."

"Who knows," Donna said after she had exhaled. "But they did get divorced so I guess she didn't snag him for too long." She took another drag.

"True. Maybe he just couldn't see her for what she was until it was too late," I suggested.

"Possibly. Of course how she is seems pretty obvious to me."

"Me too. Maybe ten years ago she was a little more subtle." A pause and then we both laughed. "Yeah, subtle isn't a word I'd ever use to describe Taylor."

"Maybe it's just that sometimes things change or people change. With Tony and me . . . I don't know what happened between us, but something shifted. We started fighting a lot more and we just couldn't seem to get along." She paused.

I gently prodded her. "So how are things between you now that y'all are in two different states? Did it help for you to move? Or do you think it's making things harder?"

"I know it's harder on Derrick not for him to get to see his dad as often as he'd like. But he knows that I had to get away from my mom." After Tony and Donna had started having problems, Donna and Derrick moved out of their home and into her mother's house. Apparently that arrangement didn't last too long because Donna's mother was crazy or something. A few weeks later, she took Derrick and moved down here, with Tony's consent regarding Derrick, of course. I had never heard the whole story, just snippets.

"Besides, it is cool that Derrick gets to know his aunt, uncle, and cousin better." Donna had moved into a mother-in-law apartment over the detached garage at Tony's sister and husband's house just a mile from where I lived. "He loves playing with Jamal and Jamal's Jack Russell puppy, Teepee. And Derrick and Tony talk quite a few times a week." She paused to smoke.

162

"Do you and Tony talk?" I asked.

"A little."

"Is it helping?"

"Not really. Tony doesn't think he's done anything wrong so right now it's all my fault. So our conversations are not the most productive."

"What did he do wrong?" I asked.

"Like I said. Something shifted. I just felt like he didn't respect my feelings about things; that it was his way or the highway. But he says that I'm the one who has to get my way all the time. I told him that was total crap." Donna paused again. I didn't dare mention to her that she could be pretty stubborn, pretty unforgiving when she wanted to be. If Tony were as strong-willed as she was, I could see what the problem was. Nobody was willing to compromise. "So why did what Brittanee was saying about blond hair get to you? You got something against blond-haired, blue-eyed people?" Donna asked with some amusement.

"Of course not!" I protested. "Some of my best friends are blond-haired and blue-eyed!"

Jarrett, Toronto Jen, Lacey-with-the-tapeworm, my college roommate, Allie, and Jenni-Fer-Furr were all natural blondes with blue eyes. I should also clarify that it doesn't bother me if people color their hair. At various times in my life, I had colored my hair black, red, white blond, and brown with various shades of highlights. I'd even had my hair corn-rowed once. Despite these physical alterations, I never presented myself to others as being anything but a brown-haired white girl. So that was what really bothered me: people pretending to be something that they are not.

"What annoyed me about it was the fact that she's only ten years-old and is already perpetuating stereotypes. What makes it worse is that her mother is teaching her these things. Could you believe that thing about not enough heat in the atmosphere?"

Donna laughed as she stubbed out her cigarette. "Yeah, that was pretty ridiculous." We stepped back inside and sat down in the reception area. We glanced at the clock and saw that it was about time to go. We gathered up our belongings, said good-by to Kitty, and walked out the door onto the sidewalk. After a few moments of silence, I asked Donna a question.

"Do you still love Tony?"

163

She snorted. "Yes! Of course I still love Tony. But what's love got to do with it?"

"Yeah, Tina," I half-joked. "What does love have to do with it?"

27

On Saturday night, Tod and I went out for dinner and drinks. We ended up at a downtown bar called Tundra. It was a daiquiri bar with about eight spinning daiquiri machines on the wall behind the bartenders. My first experience with a daiquiri bar was when I was at LSU. I was amazed at how a person could drive up to a free-standing daiquiri shop that was the size of a Central Park hamburger stand and grab a daiquiri to go from a drive-thru window. It had seemed pretty cool to me at the time. As an eighteen year-old drinker, daiquiris had also appealed to me because they were fruity and smooth. I couldn't really taste the alcohol in them, yet I still caught a buzz. Now that I was a more accomplished drinker, I stuck with my Wild Turkey 101 and Sprite. Not to mention that a frozen daiquiri was less than appealing on a frigid February night.

In addition to Tundra being a daiquiri bar, Tod claimed that it was also a lesbian bar when I had suggested that we go there. "What?" I had laughed when he'd mentioned it. "I've been there plenty of times and I seriously doubt that it's a lesbian bar." I could care less whether it was or wasn't; I'd been to gay bars plenty of times in my life. The crowd at Tundra appeared to be the same mixed crowd I'd seen at bars all over. Lots of college students, older twenty-somethings, and blue collar and white collar after-work types as well. I'm sure that it was a mix of heterosexuals and homosexuals since both do peacefully coexist unless there's a violent homophobe hanging around, but it wasn't like Tundra's clientele was dominated by lesbians.

Now that we were comfortably situated at a table with drinks in our hands, Tod was telling me about Ted's recent plan for landing a virgin: he was going to update the home he shared with Tod. I shook my head. "You've got to be kidding me," I said. "Does he

165

think that dating is like fishing? That you've got to have the right lure?" Once the words were out of my mouth, I realized that for a certain group of people, maybe the women and men in Jack's social circle who consisted of the professional trophy wives and their mates, maybe dating *was* a lot like fishing with lures.

"I guess he figures it couldn't hurt."

"Oh, it could hurt," I said, thinking about the spouses who had murdered their significant others for financial gain of various sorts. "It could hurt a lot. Just tell him not to make the house look too good."

"There's one other thing. Ted told me that I need to move out. He was really nice about it, but he said that girls aren't really attracted to a guy who has a roommate—"

"Correction," I interrupted. "Girls aren't really attracted to Ted."

Tod laughed and continued, "—so I needed to find my own place."

"Oh," I said. "Well, it shouldn't be too hard to find a place around here. There's all kind of cool houses and apartments for rent."

"Yeah," he agreed, but he was lost in thought. "But there's something else. A rumor has been floating around the office that we're going to be downsized. I'm not sure if it's true or not, but if it is, I'm not sure about signing a lease. Most of them are for a year. It's just a thought, but if that happens, I might consider moving back to Canada."

I downed the rest of my drink, irritated. "Move back to Canada?" I demanded. I was pissed off and not exactly sure why. I wasn't in love with Tod. I guess I was just pissed at the thought of being left and having it mentioned to me so casually.

"It's just a thought," he reiterated. "I don't know if anything is even going to happen. Besides, I thought you might want to come with me. Toronto is a really cool city. We could live together and get you a work Visa. It could be really cool. Another thing I thought of is that I also have family in New Zealand. Wouldn't it be cool to live in New Zealand?" My anger dissipated. New Zealand? That sounded awesome. I would love to move to a foreign country whose first language was English (It was, wasn't it?) and had beautiful, warm beaches (It did, didn't it?). Actually, I didn't know that much about

New Zealand; all I knew was that it was close to Australia. I smiled to myself. Maybe I could hop a boat from New Zealand to Australia. Then I could live at the beach and hopefully meet some hot Australian guy. I stopped dead in my thoughts. What a horrible thing to think. I was thinking about running away with Tod with the hopes of meeting somebody else. Maybe I was more like a fish with a lure than I cared to admit.

About an hour later, Tod's friends appeared. Tod had been keeping in touch with them via his cell phone, updating them on where to meet us. It is said that alcohol is a depressant. Tod's friends were more of a depressant to me than alcohol could ever be. I ordered another drink as they all pulled up chairs at our table and at adjacent ones. I had the pleasure of Taylor and some female friend of hers from college, Gina, sitting at our table.

"You're slamming those, aren't ya?" commented Gina. Gina had been at our table for all of three seconds and she was already pissing me off.

"Excuse me?" I questioned her with a raised eyebrow. Taylor was looking around for the waitress who had disappeared with Tod's and my orders a split second before their arrival.

"Let's go grab a beer at the bar and shoot a round of darts," Taylor suggested. Gina agreed and they hopped up from the table. I was relieved.

"Why did you tell them to come here?" I asked warily. "They suck." I did have to admit that I had a buzz, alcohol becoming my version of Wonder Woman's Lasso of Truth. I could tell no lies. Nor could I prevent every thought from popping out of my mouth.

"I guess because they're my friends," he said. The waitress returned with our drinks and I took a slug and used that time to roll my eyes so Tod wouldn't see me. Tod and his friends were reminding me more and more of The Fun Bunchers every day. The Fun Bunchers were what I and my friends called the popular clique in high school because they always had to be stuck together in order to maintain the illusion that they were in a constant state of euphoric bliss, much like our neighbor's dog, Bubbles, was stuck to every male dog when she was in heat. Even though Tod's Fun Bunch was around forty years-old, it was like they couldn't do anything without the rest of the group. In addition to that, this older crowd was always trying to act like they were still in high school: taking pictures at their social gatherings; sending the pictures around to each other via email; being each other's best friends one day then talking about each other behind their backs the next. Oh you crazy, kooky, Fun Bunchers! It's so nice to have you back!

By the time Taylor and Gina rejoined us at our table, Wonder Woman's Lasso of Truth was cutting off my circulation. Gina had been right. I was slamming my drinks and now I was giving Taylor (and sometimes Gina) some intense glares. When Taylor continued to act oblivious to my disdain, I kicked it up a notch. "Hey," I called out to her. My voice might have been slightly slurred, but I was trying my best to act as if I were sober. She looked over at me.

"What's up with you dyeing Brittanee's hair blond? That's so fucked up."

Taylor was miffed. "What did you say?" she asked with hostility.

"You heard me. I said you're fucked up. In addition to that, what's up with telling her that there's not enough heat in the atmosphere? That's total bullshit." I explained to her the problems the Space Shuttle Columbia had on reentry and pointed out that Chattanooga's latitude was a lot closer to the Equator than the latitudes of Nordic and Germanic countries filled with natural blondes.

Taylor did not appreciate my brief science and geography class. As a matter of fact, she was so threatened by my calling her out that she totally went off. She rapidly fired off a whole bunch of sentences that included my name and the word, *Fuck*, used as a verb, adjective, noun, and possibly a present participle.

"Man," I muttered to Tod as Taylor stormed off with Gina following right behind her. Although I was totally jacked up and totally pissed off, I had managed to keep my cool by not responding to her diatribe. "What a fucking bitch!" I hiccuped. "How can she be a fucking vice-president of a fucking company and not even be able to have a fucking conversation without acting like a fucking bitch?"

Tod just looked at me and quietly suggested that it was time for us to go home.

168

28

I woke up the next morning with a serious hangover. Big surprise. But even worse than the hangover was the dark, depressed feeling that was clouding my brain. Whenever I felt this feeling, I knew that due to the influence of alcohol I had said something to somebody that I would later wish that I hadn't. I dreaded finding out what it was.

"Oh, my head," I groaned. Tod stretched in the bed beside me and kind of smiled.

"I bet you feel like shit," he said.

"Yes," I agreed as my head pounded. "I don't remember anything after your friends arrived last night. Did I say or do something to somebody?" I was cringing inside as I waited for the answer, hoping that just maybe this feeling of darkness was wrong for once.

"Well, you pretty much got into it with Taylor. You told her what you thought about her getting her daughter's hair highlighted."

"Oh shit," I groaned. "I didn't."

"You did," he said.

"And what did she do?" I asked.

"She pretty much got totally pissed off, cussed you out, and left with her friend Gina."

"Did anybody else hear it?"

"Probably. But if they didn't, they'll probably hear about it from her today at brunch," Tod said. How reassuring. Fucking Fun Bunchers. Fucking Fun Brunchers. It was corny, but I almost made myself laugh.

"Do you want some breakfast?" Tod asked. He often made a great breakfast of bacon, eggs, and biscuits. When I'm not severely hung over, I like eggs. Right now, though, just thinking about the smell of eggs frying in a pan made me want to throw up.

169

"God no," I groaned. "But could you please get me a glass of water and some Tylenol?" And a toothbrush, toothpaste, some Listerine, a shower, and clean clothes? I shoved the covers off of me and found that I had passed out fully clothed in last night's outfit minus my shoes. I felt like hell.

"Sure," he said and quickly returned with the water and pain reliever.

"Thanks," I said. "I'm sorry, Tod, but I just need to lay here for a little while. I may even need to go back to sleep."

"That's fine. I'm going to go ahead and get up. You rest."

"Thanks," I said as I yanked off my jeans and threw them on the floor. The cool air against my bare legs felt a little better. I pulled the covers back over my body and went to sleep.

A couple of hours later I felt human enough to get out of bed. I brushed my teeth by applying toothpaste to my finger and rubbing it across the enamel. It only helped a little. I splashed cold water on my face and tried to erase the makeup smudges under my bloodshot eyes. Gee, Vandelyn, you look great. I was ready to go home and take a nice warm shower.

I walked out into the living room and saw Tod sitting on the couch watching TV. "Is Ted here?" I asked, hoping that he wasn't.

"No, he went to brunch."

"Oh yeah," I mumbled. Fucking Fun Bunchers. Fucking Fun Brunchers. I almost smiled again. I must still be under the influence. "All right," I said. "I'm going to go on home and take a shower and get something to eat."

"You all right to drive?" Tod asked.

"Yeah. I'm OK. I'll talk to you later," I said.

Tod stood up and walked me to the door. "Be careful," he cautioned.

"I will." I opened the door and stepped out into the brisk air. It was pretty cold, below freezing if I had to guess, but it rejuvenated me. I made my way down the front steps, down the driveway and headed to my car which was parked, as usual, along the curb. I stopped cold as I approached the driver's side of my car which was the side exposed to the street. My car had been egged. A trail of broken egg shells and yolk were frozen to the fenders, doors, and windows. I was so pissed. I could feel my blood pressure starting to

170

rise. I glanced at the other cars that were parked on the street. None of them had been egged. The fact that my car had twelve eggs stuck to its side and no other cars were vandalized meant that it wasn't teenagers out for fun on a Saturday night. It meant that someone wanted to egg my car specifically. Someone who was pissed at me last night. Somebody by the name of Taylor Kazakov.

I turned on my heel and stomped back up the driveway to the house. Man, I was really, really pissed. A forty year-old woman had egged my car! I turned the knob to the front door, but Tod had already locked it. I knocked loudly, releasing a little bit of my anger as I did.

"Hey," Tod greeted me, letting me back in.

"I am so pissed!" I announced.

"What's wrong?" he asked.

"That fucking bitch egged my car!"

"What? Somebody egged your car?" Without even putting on a coat, Tod hurried out to the street. I followed.

"Man," he said. "That sucks."

"Damn right it sucks. I am so pissed. Egg takes off the paint and look at those yolks frozen to my doors and fenders! I am so going to kill her," I vowed. "That fucking bitch. This is so uncool. It is below freezing so how am I going to get my car washed? If what she did damages my car, I am so going to make her pay."

"Hold on a second, Vandelyn," Tod attempted to calm me down. "You don't know that she did it."

"Oh she did it all right," I told him. "Look at all the other cars lined up on the street. None of them have been egged, yet my car has a dozen eggs stuck to it. It's doesn't take Sherlock Holmes or even Encyclopedia Brown to solve this mystery."

"But you still don't *know*." Tod tried to be objective.

"Yes," I practically snarled. "I *do* know. Taylor is responsible for this. And if she didn't throw the eggs herself then she had her little friend Gina do it for her." Tod kept quiet. I threw my belongings into the backseat and climbed into the driver's seat. I cranked up the engine and drove off without even saying good-by again to Tod.

When I got home, I pulled into the driveway and grabbed the garden hose. It didn't really matter how cold it was outside because I had to get the egg off of my car regardless. The spray from the water splashed on me, but I didn't care. I hosed the car until every little bit of egg was off and then I went inside and took a long hot shower and heated up a frozen pizza. I felt so ill from last night's and the day's events that I just curled up on the couch with a mystery and forewent my usual Sunday night wine and dance party. However, I found it very difficult to concentrate on the words on the page because all I could think about was how I was going to get even with Taylor.

29

By Tuesday morning, I was much less angry than I had been over the weekend. Even so, I knew that I had to tell Donna about it first thing. This particular Tuesday morning Donna and I were forgoing the brisk walk to work because it was freezing cold outside and the wind was brutal. Instead, we sat inside the free shuttle bus and waited for the driver, who was smoking a cigarette out on the sidewalk in the station, to board.

"You'll never guess what happened this weekend," I said.

"What?" Donna asked as she took a sip of her coffee.

"Well, to put it bluntly, Taylor and I got into it."

Donna looked up at me from her coffee, her eyes widened in surprise. "Really? What happened?"

"All I did was explain to her that she shouldn't color her daughter's hair and fill her head with propaganda."

"And how'd that go over?"

"Not well. She got really pissed off, and, get this," I paused for more drama, "she egged my car."

"She didn't." Donna was laughing now.

"Oh yes she did."

"How do you know she did it?"

I gave her a look. "Let me see, maybe it was because my car was parked on the street like it always is in front of Tod's house and my car was the only car egged—twelve eggs, mind you—on the whole street. Other cars were parked along the curb, but my car was the only one egged *and* it had the whole carton of eggs splattered across it."

"Yep," Donna agreed. "Sounds like she egged it to me."

"Thank you!" I said, finally glad to receive some validation. "Are women just smarter than men? Because Tod had a hard time

173

accepting that it wasn't just a random coincidence."

"Maybe it's because we know there are no random coincidences; that behind every random coincidence there is a woman," Donna joked. "Actually, it's more like we know what some women are capable of. And Taylor is definitely capable of egging a car even if she is my age and vice-president of a company."

The driver boarded the bus, shut the doors, and pulled out of the Shuttle station. As the Shuttle progressed down Market Street, I glanced over and saw Roy and Tippy sitting on their usual bench. I hoped they weren't waiting for us to walk by, but maybe they had plenty of other people to talk to as well. Tippy was yipping around in circles at a passerby while Roy held the pink leash loosely in his hand and stared down at the sidewalk.

When the Shuttle stopped in front of Mercury, we stood up and departed, walking the few feet to the front door. Donna yanked the door open in her usual hard-presser way and bellowed, "Hello Kitty!" Donna and I stepped through the reception area and into the hair stations where Kitty was busy doing a roller set on Mrs. Franklin. Donna and I stopped, though, when we saw a young woman standing at the previously unoccupied station next to Donna's. She was organizing her hair-styling equipment into appropriate drawers.

"Well, hello there," Donna said. "Where'd you come from?"

"Donna," Kitty sighed at Donna's brusque greeting. "That's our new stylist, Lindy."

Lindy smiled at us and said hello. We returned the greeting. Lindy was a perky twenty year-old, if I had to guess her age, with long brown hair and brown eyes. She was also really pretty; like Dallas Cowboy Cheerleader pretty.

I excused myself to put away my coat and purse in the closet in my facial room and then I returned to the front to check the book. I sighed. Mrs. Donovan was on my book for a facial at 10:00. I returned to my room, filled the towel cabi with warm, damp towels and prepared the station by my stool for the facial.

Since facials were my favorite service to do, I wasn't sighing about Mrs. Donovan's facial for that reason. I was sighing because Mrs. Donovan was filthy rich and cheap, which as I was beginning to learn, was not an unusual combination. Once when I pointed this out to Donna, Donna merely said, "Yep. And that's how they stay so rich." Fortunately, Jack was not cheap.

After years of serving and bartending, I had also learned that women with money and men with money spent it in different ways. As much as the National Organization for Women is not going to like what I have to say, women are usually cheaper than men when it comes to tipping. Not always, but enough that when we servers were sat a table of women, especially a table of women who order salads and waters, we sighed because odds were in our favor that they would leave us a crappy tip. I will say that this was not always the case. I had women customers who tipped well and men who didn't tip well. It was just more of the exception than the rule.

In the case of Mrs. Donovan, however, she had plenty of money. First of all, she was married to a locally renowned heart surgeon. Secondly, she owned the elegant store a block or so away called Divinity Décor & Gifts which sold the unique, upscale gifts and accessories that I presumed Socialites orgasm over, such as Kosta Boda bowls, Mackenzie-Childs glassware, and what I used to refer to as Pucci scarves. Mrs. Donovan corrected me in a less than gracious manner one day after I told her I really liked the Pucci scarf in one of her display windows. "Actually it's an Emilio Pucci *stole*, dear, not a scarf."

Ten o'clock arrived and Mrs. Donovan breezily fluttered in ten minutes later with her Diane von Furstenberg scarf wafting after. I only knew it was a Diane von Furstenberg scarf (not stole) because she announced it upon arrival as she called out hello to Kitty and waggled her fingertips at the rest of us.

She was often clad in the designer accessories that she sold in her store because it was "free advertising" as she put it. Although I was sure that she liked free advertising as much as the next cheap person, I knew that was merely a front. Mrs. Donovan spent a very expensive dime on upscale marketing for Divinity Décor & Gifts. She just liked to have an excuse to flaunt her high-end, exclusive wares. The fact that she could disguise it as free advertising prevented her from being viewed as blatantly rubbing it in our faces.

"I'm sorry I am running a little late, Vandelyn, but I got caught up at work." I escorted her into the room.

"I understand," I said. I pointed to the facial robe, instructed her to change and to then lie down underneath the blanket covering the facial bed. Then I stepped back out into the hall and shut the door behind me. It really wasn't that big of a deal to me that she was running late. I would just tweak the service to make it end on time at 11:00 so she could be on-time for her hair appointment with Kitty, presuming, of course, that Kitty would be on-time for her.

When the facial was over, Mrs. Donovan dressed, and headed for Kitty's chair. Unfortunately, it was still occupied. "I'll just be a few more minutes," Kitty said, but we knew it wasn't true. She was just beginning to undo the rollers from Mrs. Halliwell's hair.

"Oh dear," Mrs. Donovan fretted. "I must get back to work but I really need my hair to be shampooed and styled." I had to agree with her. After giving her a scalp massage while the hydrating masque was penetrating her skin, she looked a mess, despite the fabulous Diane von Furstenberg scarf.

"I can do your hair for you," Lindy piped up.

"Oh, that would be great," Mrs. Donovan said with relief.

Kitty went back to focusing on Mrs. Halliwell's hair. She was probably very thankful that Lindy had started working here today because Donna was busy doing a cap highlight on her own client. Kitty and Mrs. Donovan were friends and I knew that Kitty did not want to disappoint her.

Lindy escorted Mrs. Donovan back to the shampoo bowls, letting her remove her scarf before draping her with the black shampoo cape. Mrs. Donovan held it delicately in her hands as I headed back to tidy up the facial room.

After I cleaned my utensils, changed the linens, put the used sheets and towels in the washing machine and started the washer, I returned to the front of the salon. Lindy was blow-drying Mrs. Donovan's hair, styling it with a round brush as she did so. Mrs. Halliwell was approaching the reception desk so I made a bee-line for it so I could take her money. I wished her a good day as she left and then returned to the salon area.

I took a seat at the makeup station and observed Lindy's technique. Donna's client was seated under the dryer, reading a magazine, so Donna was seated in her chair sipping on a Diet Coke. I could tell she was watching Lindy's reflection in the mirror across the way. Kitty called back her next client and was thankfully back on schedule now that Mrs. Donovan was being taken care of by Lindy.

When Lindy was finished, I was impressed. Lindy obviously had natural talent. Mrs. Donovan's hair looked fabulous. It looked almost as perfectly coiffed as when Kitty styled it herself, which was quite an accomplishment since Kitty had been a stylist for decades while Lindy had just recently graduated from beauty school. I could tell by the expression on Donna's face that she wasn't going to pay Lindy any compliments, though. Donna was competitive and wasn't too keen on having Lindy as competition, or so I guessed. I, on the other hand, was not threatened by Lindy and could not contain my admiration.

"Lindy, you've done an awesome job. Her hair looks fabulous."

Mrs. Donovan was beaming and preening in the mirror. "Yes, my dear, you've done a great job." It was the most sincere I'd ever heard Mrs. Donovan. She tossed her head gently from side to side, watching the layers fall back into place. Then she remembered that she needed to return to work and abruptly stood up. She ripped off the cape, restyled the scarf around her neck, and took off to the front. Mrs. Donovan rifled through her purse for her checkbook as I told her the total. She scrawled out an amount, signed the check with a flourish of her hand, and handed it to me almost at the same time that she hurried out the door.

"Lindy," I said as the bells on the door jingled after Mrs. Donovan's retreating figure, "let me go ahead and show you how we run the register in case you're the one up here when people pay." I handed her the check without glancing at it. She sat down at the desk. "Go ahead and write the amount on today's deposit slip—we keep them in the right hand drawer. Then endorse the back of the check with our stamp." I pointed to the stamp that resided in the same drawer. "Then just put the check in the deposit bag." She did as she was told and then paused.

"What do we do about the tip?" she asked. I laughed because Mrs. Donovan never tipped. It was as sure of a thing as the sun rising in the east and setting in the west.

"*If there had been a tip*, you would pull it and give it to whoever did the service."

She looked at me like I was crazy. "There was a tip."

"No there wasn't," I said somewhat condescendingly, thinking that we were going to have a problem if Lindy couldn't do basic math.

She removed the check from the deposit bag and pointed to the total that was written on the check. It was for five dollars more

177

than the amount that I quoted to Mrs. Donovan. My face colored. Lindy stared at me for a moment and then pulled a five dollar bill out of the drawer. Although I could not help but notice the coincidence of Mrs. Donovan tipping for the first time on the same day that Lindy did her hair for the first time, I'd been screwed enough by coincidence the past couple of days and I wasn't going to let it screw me again.

"Hold on there, sister," I said. "Half of that's mine."

30

March

March fifth was my day of reckoning: my court date. Although I still had yet to tell my family about my situation, necessity required that I share it with Kitty and Donna. When it came to telling Kitty, I gave her as little information as possible, although there was no way around telling her that I had gotten a DUI. With Donna, I pretty much told her the whole story of my arrest, telling it in such a way that we both laughed a little about it, and admitted that I was extremely nervous about my upcoming court date.

So today was now Wednesday, March fifth, and I had "made myself pretty" per my lawyer's instructions, dressed in conservative law school attire, and driven myself downtown for my court appearance. After parking my car at The Shuttle and riding downtown to the courthouse, I met up with Mr. Peters in front of the courtroom. He immediately began talking to me about the case. Our first line of defense was the hope that my arresting officer would somehow forget to show up for the court date and therefore the charges against me would hopefully be dismissed. I really, really hoped that this was how things would work out because I really, really did not want to go to jail. James Peters quickly dashed my hopes for that scenario.

"Your arresting officer is already here," he told me. I wrinkled my nose in disappointment. "I talked to him about seeing if he would agree to lessen the charges against you, but he really wants you to serve all the time you've got coming to you." I sighed. My arresting officer really did not like me. It had been five months since he arrested me and my ability to be a pain in the ass was still as fresh in his mind as if it had happened yesterday. By the way Mr. Peters was talking, I suspected that my arresting officer would have crawled to the courthouse from his death bed if it ensured that justice was served against me.

"Great," I sighed. "Now what?"

"Well, for an additional seven-hundred-fifty dollars, I could ask the judge for a continuance and we could hope that your arresting officer screws up in the meantime. Like maybe he does something unethical or gets busted for something that would ruin his credibility or his career." Gee. Is this what I had to hope for in our criminal justice system? Although I really, really didn't want to go to jail, the thought of hoping that someone else's life would turn to crap so I could be free to roam the streets bothered me. What else would he suggest that I hope for? That my arresting officer get killed in the line of duty before the next court date? Would that keep me out of jail too? And wait a minute, what did he mean, *for an additional $750?*

I gave Mr. Peters a wary look. "I'm not going to pay you seven-hundred-fifty more dollars." I said it without even realizing that I was making my decision. Even so, I knew it was the right choice despite my fear of doing time. Not only did I just want to face the consequences and move on, I also recognized that the officer in question was an upstanding one. Except for the "Bitch!" comment, he had behaved in a very professional manner. I doubted that he would be involved in some illegal activity or impropriety. "What happens if I don't fight it?"

"You just go in front of the judge, he asks you some questions, and you'll get credit for your time served."

A couple of fears peppered my brain. "Is a DUI a felony?" The way MADD was steamrolling over our statutes, for all I knew a DUI was up there with treason, death by firing squad.

"It's a misdemeanor," he told me. My feeling of relief was short-lived.

"They'll revoke my license." I was feeling a bit panicky. "I drove down here by myself. How am I going to get home?"

"Let me go talk to the officer." Mr. Peters hurried into the courtroom and returned a few minutes later. "I talked to the officer. He agreed that you could drive home with your existing license without fear of penalty."

I sighed with relief. Considering how much my arresting officer disliked me, that was pretty generous. "Let's get this over with," I said and we headed into the courtroom.

"Getting this over with" in my terms and the court's terms were two different things. I hoped for immediate gratification so I could get on with my day and, indirectly, my life. But the court has its own agenda which does not include mine or any other defendant's for that matter. I sat down on a crowded bench, one of many crowded benches that resembled a church pew. James Peters disappeared into the front of the courtroom to be with the other lawyers or maybe he just disappeared completely. Maybe lawyers could opt to be paged when their clients' cases were next on the docket and didn't have to waste their time waiting for hours in a crowded courtroom. Who knew? I sure didn't because law school didn't teach practical information such as what lawyers do in court. Instead they teach ridiculous, theoretical situations that only happen in Law-Law Land.

I sighed impatiently as I watched chucklehead after chucklehead appear in front of the court. Why I was spending my morning with a bunch of chuckleheads? Maybe if I had kept control of my emotions the night I was arrested instead of letting them run amuck in a police station, my arresting officer might have been more compassionate towards me. Maybe he would have agreed to reduce the charges against me or possibly even spoken up on my behalf. Maybe I'd be on my way home instead of sitting here in a crowded courtroom biding my time until god-knows-when.

My wishful thinking was interrupted by a new turn of events. Just as I began to think that we were moving right along, the judge was asked to rule on two defendants in a bar fight. Instead of just ruling them guilty or innocent, a court room drama broke out. Apparently the issue being questioned was about fault. Witnesses to the fight were present in the court room in order to help resolve this issue. The scene was set-up; the players were on their marks; and the judge asked questions about what happened when, where the witness was when such-and-such took place, etc. It was thoroughly boring, long, and tedious. Maybe my arresting officer would leave from boredom and forget to come back. Or maybe he had also disappeared with my lawyer only to be paged when it was my turn to stand before the judge.

Finally the reenactment was complete. I had hope that maybe my name would be called before lunch. Unfortunately, the judge looked at his watch and announced, "I have a funeral to attend. Court will resume when I return." He banged his gavel and snuck out the back, the louse.

Those of us who remained, which were quite a few of us still, sighed with frustration. I knew deep in my subconscious that in the big scheme of things, a death was a lot bigger deal than me having to wait a few hours to meet my fate. It was pretty selfish of me and of all of us who were annoyed by the judge's departure for a funeral to be irritated that we were not the center of attention; that our needs were not being immediately met. Maybe that was part of our problem; part of the reason we had been arrested and were present in court today. We were just plain selfish and did not think about others when we made our choices. We didn't care about what was right or wrong. We just wanted things our way no matter what.

That said, I wasn't so selfless yet as to not be irritated that the judge was gone. I just wanted to get this over with. I just wanted to go home. I was tired of sitting on a hard semi-crowded bench. I did not want to leave the court room either because I had no idea when the judge would be back and I sure didn't want to be one of the people who was absent when her name was called.

A couple of hours later, no joke, the judge returned and we continued on in our less than merry way. Finally I was called before the judge. I was nervous because the judge was asking me point-blank, self-incriminating questions; the kind of questions that TV lawyers were always instructing their clients, "Don't answer that." I glanced over at Mr. Peters. He just looked at me and offered me no defense. I reiterate that my law school education was meaningless in this situation because nothing useful in a court of law was ever taught. (But if you'd ever like to hear about Straw Man, Tortfeasors, Unborn Widows, Fertile Octogenarians (or if you just need a good band name), give me a call.) So I did the only thing I could do: I told the truth and hoped for the best.

The best was also the worst in this situation. The judge sentenced me to forty-eight hours at the correctional facility with eleven hours and thirty-eight minutes time served. He revoked my license for a year, but I did have the option of getting a restricted license that would allow me to get to and from work. And of course I would have to pay something like $2000 in fines. Excellent.

I was not free to go after this ruling. Instead I was led to an office off the side of the court room where a thirty-something woman sat behind the desk. I had the misfortune of being coupled up with a fifty-something year-old man who brought his seventy-something year-old mother with him. I was pretty sure that he still lived at home with her too. After the woman behind the desk shot us looks that told me she thought we were trash, she proceeded to deal with the elder of us sleaze balls first.

The fifty-something year-old man was chuckling as if being found guilty for DUI was some colossal joke for some hidden-camera television show. "I don't know why I'm here," he chuckled.

The woman said, "You were found guilty for DUI."

"I know," he chuckled some more. "But I don't know how. I was drinking iced tea!" He looked back over his shoulder at his mother. Chuckle. Chuckle. He was literally a chucklehead.

"What was in the tea, sir?" she asked.

"I don't know. Nothing really. Some sugar, some lemon." God, this guy was getting on my nerves. I have a soft spot for underdogs and well-meaning losers, but losers in denial need to shut their pie holes. Or in this case, their iced tea holes.

Desk-lady moved on in the conversation. She went over what the rules were when we went to the correctional facility. "Do not bring anything to the correctional facility except what is on this approved list." She gave us each a copy of the list. "You can bring two paperback books and one blank notebook, but it cannot have a spiral binder. You can bring two pens." She went on to explain that no toiletries were allowed. I was horrified. No brushing of my teeth for *two days*? I wasn't disturbed by not bathing for two days because I'd rather be dirty than naked when it came to prison. "Your underwear must be white cotton. Bras must be white cotton and cannot have an underwire. If you wear anything other than white cotton, it will be confiscated."

My fellow defendant chuckled again. I couldn't understand why this situation was a joke to him. I was simultaneously scared and thankful that I did have a few white cotton bikinis in my lingerie drawer as well as a white cotton sports bra that had no underwire. Not only did I not want to be naked in jail, I definitely did not want to go commando in jail either.

"You will be required to go to one eight-hour DUI School which is held on Saturdays. You have to pay seventy-five dollars to attend the class. Now when can you serve your time at the correctional facility?" she asked us.

The fifty year-old chucklehead shrugged and said, "I don't have any plans. I can go right now." Loser! Desk-lady agreed with that and an officer escorted him and his mother out of the room. I wondered if he realized that his mother wouldn't be able to go to jail with him.

"I can't go right now," I clarified. "I have a job. But I am off on Sundays and Mondays. I could go on a Saturday after five o'clock or so.

"OK," she said. We sorted out when I would attend DUI School (in two weeks) and then I would go to the correctional facility the beginning of May. She gave me a small stack of paperwork in return for my time in court. She highlighted the fact that I would need to be at the correctional facility at 6:45 p.m. because I would be admitted at 7:00 p.m. She told me to eat dinner before I came because the evening meal would have already been served. (Even if I had arrived in time for the evening meal, I still would have eaten before I came.) I paid my DUI school fee, took all my paperwork, and was finally free to leave the office.

Although I was carrying a larger burden now than when I arrived, I still felt relieved to walk through the courthouse and into the cold outdoors. Freedom felt good, even if it were only temporary. I was dreading the next few weeks, but was also looking forward to getting them over with.

31

When the Saturday morning of my DUI school came around, I was pleasantly surprised to find that the class was held directly down Dayton Boulevard about two miles from my house. Theoretically, I could walk there from my front door. If I hadn't had a ride via Tod, I would have had to walk there because I had not gotten a restricted driver's license yet.

I was a little nervous as we approached the facility, wondering what we were going to do for a whole day at DUI School. Write, "I am a horrible and terrible person who deserves death by a MADD firing squad" on the blackboard 1,000 times? Go out into a field and find a thick, thorny switch and have the Chief of Police spank us with it? Smack ourselves in the head with a board until we render ourselves unconscious or brain dead, whichever comes first? What exactly would the judgmental, watchful eyes of Society like for us to do to degrade ourselves fully for their satisfaction?

When Tod pulled into the parking lot, I did find a little humor in the situation because I had never seen so many adults getting dropped off at once. As I got out of the car, I told Tod bye and reminded him when this lame-ass "class" would be over with so he could pick me up on time. He nodded his head and wished me luck. As I shut the door, I hardly thought I'd need any luck. All I had to do was sit in a classroom and veg out for the allotted amount of time. As long as I kept my mouth shut and didn't fall asleep, everything would be fine.

When I opened the front door, I saw that a line had formed. I sighed as I waited for the formality of checking myself in so I could get credit for attending DUI School. As I drew nearer to the front of the line, I was horrified to realize that we were being breathalyzed! Why the hell were we being breathalyzed? I stepped out of line and walked over to the Coke machine trying not to panic. Since I didn't have to work today, Tod and I stayed up late drinking. Last night I figured that today was like having a day off. Although I didn't feel drunk, I knew that I still had alcohol in my system. I slipped some coins into the machine and bought a Coke. I entertained delusions that drinking a Coke would be enough for me to prevent the machine from detecting alcohol in my breath. It was a long shot, but it was worth a try.

As I sipped on the soda, I remembered a rumor from high school that if you put coins in your mouth, the metal residue would throw off the reading of a breathalyzer. Unfortunately I had just used all of my coinage for my Coke. Then again, if a police officer saw me sucking on coins, I was as good as busted anyway. After downing the soda, I stepped back into line and hoped for the best. When it came my turn I was nervous. I stepped up and blew. They read the meter and paused. I failed. The person was decent enough to let me blow again. I failed again. I was told to enter the room where "class" would be held, and sit down on the raised platform up front.

Great. I was now sitting at the front of the classroom like an example for others to learn from. Fortunately I was in a room of my peers who probably didn't pass too much judgment on me. A couple of other people came to join me on the stage as well. An overweight police officer in civilian clothes with a bulging abdomen usually reserved for women pregnant with multiples stepped over to me and looked down on me, literally and figuratively. He shook his head from side to side as if I were the sorriest soul on earth.

"You just had to have a drink, didn't you? Just had to have one more drink. Just couldn't go one night without a drink," he lamented condescendingly on my behalf.

I was pissed. Yes, as a matter of fact, I could go without a drink. Had I known that I would be breathalyzed at eight a.m. on a Saturday morning, I would have gone to bed stone cold sober instead of thinking that I had an extra night to party.

I really loathed this fat-ass cop. What I really wanted to say after looking at his fat gut and thinking about all the gargantuan worms writhing inside of him was, "So you just had to have one more doughnut. You just couldn't go without one more fucking chocolate-covered, cream-filled doughnut." Needless to say, I did not speak this thought out loud. Freedom of speech in the United

States of America does not extend to potentially hostile conversations with police officers. One arrest was enough.

After everyone had been breathalyzed, the few of us on stage got one more chance. One guy passed and got to join the rest of the DUI students sitting in their desks. I blew again and failed again. I was not allowed back into the classroom. I was not credited for showing up for DUI School. I was sent back home after paying $75 for the crappy class that I wasn't even allowed to attend. I would have to reschedule to take another class and I would also have to pay another $75.

I was quite unhappy. I did not have my cell phone with me, but fortunately there was another one of those phones attached to the wall for the free phone calls that were becoming a habit of mine in police stations. Actually just being in police stations was becoming a habit of mine. Since Tod had moved out of Ted's place and in with me, I called him both on his cell phone and at my house, leaving messages that I was kicked out of DUI School for failing the breathalyzer. I told him that I was going to start walking home, but would he please come pick me up as soon as he got my message?

I walked across the parking lot and headed for the shoulder along the road. As I passed the entrance to the trailer park next to the police facility, I kicked a tuft of grass, "Loser!" I chastised myself out loud. "Loser, loser, loser," I muttered with disgust under my breath as I continued along the shoulder, kicking a stray rock here and there with my Volatile sneakers with the red and yellow flames down the side.

I'd felt so good when I woke up this morning. I'd dressed in my long sleeve Tuff Muff shirt; put on my cool black Volatile shoes; had thought that I was going to check off the first of my DUI offender duties from my list. But now I was worse off than I was before. This sucked! How had I become such a loser?

I looked back on the years after leaving law school. I had worked as a sales associate, a server, a bartender, and now an esthetician. Although I had liked my post-law school jobs, some more career-oriented people my age were successfully kicking ass and taking names. Apparently I was just fucking up and wearing a nametag.

My feet were starting to hurt, but not from kicking myself while I was down. Volatile sneakers were so cool, but they were not made for treks down the shoulder of a two-line highway. The shoulder got narrower so I decided to cross the street to face oncoming traffic, which, now that I think about it, is what one is supposed to do. So I crossed and continued to be lost in my thoughts of self-degradation. Suddenly, I was startled back into reality when a red Jeep Cherokee pulled up beside me, facing the wrong side of the road.

"Need a ride?" the driver asked me with a smile. I took one look at the sixty year-old man who looked like Mr. Magoo's son and chills ran through me, my hairs standing on end. Although he was rather harmless looking with his bald head, white tufts of hair on the sides, round wire-framed glasses, and a fluffy white dog on his lap, my skin prickled relentlessly. I suddenly felt so alone on the side of the road. I surreptitiously looked around and was thankful to find that I was standing in the driveway of a fire station. Two firemen were taking a smoke break out front, no further than ten yards from me. I felt secure that I could run or call for help if I needed it and merely responded with a polite, "No thanks."

"OK," he smiled at me again and he and his dog drove away. My body was shaking after he left. I stood in the driveway for a few more moments so I could take some deep breaths and calm down. I never distrust my instincts (unless they're dating instincts) and my instincts told me that man was Satan's Little Helper. When I looked into his eyes, I knew without a doubt that he had a dungeon in his basement where he would rape and murder me. As much as my life sucked right now, it did not suck bad enough to suffer that fate.

After a few more moments, I regrouped and felt okay enough to continue my trek down Dayton Boulevard. After just taking a few steps I was so happy to see Tod's car approach. Never had I been so happy to see him and I gratefully opened the car door. "Hey," he smiled as I fastened my seat belt. "So what happened?" While enjoying the moment of feeling safe, I felt happy and at peace as I shared my breathalyzer story. Although my morning at DUI School had not gone the way I had planned, I was so thankful, grateful, that it hadn't turned out worse.

32

April

A few weeks later, I was awakened to my windows rattling at five a.m. As I rubbed my eyes and focused on the situation, I realized that my house was shaking. As impossible as it seemed, Chattanooga was experiencing an earthquake. I sat up alone in bed since Tod had flown to Toronto on Saturday to visit his mom and explore possible job opportunities. He would be back on Friday so he could take me to the correctional facility on Saturday. Monday we would go together to the DMV so I could get my restricted license. After the house stopped shaking a few moments later, I curled up under the covers and went back to sleep.

As Donna and I walked to work, we talked about how crazy it was that we'd had an earthquake. Roy and Tippy were on their usual bench and we stopped to speak and pet the little dog.

After we arrived at Mercury and got settled in, Lindy and Donna waited for their first clients to arrive and I sat behind the reception desk. Kitty, of course, was already working away on her regulars. As Lindy and Donna chatted, I got lost in nervous thoughts about my upcoming weekend. I was glad that I was going to get it over with once and for all, but it was going to be the longest week of my life. I had already bought two paperback mystery novels and a blank notebook and had them set aside for my "trip." However, I did feel a small sense of relief in the fact that I had now completed DUI School.

After getting kicked out the first time, I had rescheduled for a few weeks later and arrived sober and somber for my eight hours of retribution. I sat quietly in my desk as we watched a video series about real-life stories and reenactments of drunk drivers who had killed themselves, others, or both while operating their vehicles under the influence. It was terrible yet contrite. Even so, it reminded me of hokey movies we'd had to watch in high school warning about drugs, alcohol, and driving under the influence.

Although I was a bit cynical about the video, I was grateful that those drivers' fates had not been my fate. I once again thanked God for allowing me to learn my lesson without me or others suffering such dire consequences for my irresponsible actions.

Of course the video was not complete without the appearance of a smug MADD representative. I discreetly rolled my eyes and sniffed in disdain at her holier-than-thou attitude. She claimed the video was made because MADD wanted to help "people like us," but she was much too condescending for me to believe her. Kindness and forgiveness rather than self-righteousness would have been a better tack.

As the day progressed, I was pleasantly distracted from my own problems by the number of walk-ins that came into the salon. Apparently the Opera was in town and the actors were staying across the street at the Read House. A couple of groups of women came in for manicures, pedicures, and brow waxes.

I was also pleasantly surprised when a handsome guy about my age came in for a brow wax. He was very gregarious as I led him back to the facial room, telling me his name was Kevin and that he and the other actors were from New York City. He seemed like a friendly guy and I thought it would be interesting to hear more about his acting life. Turns out, he was more interested in my life, or what he perceived to be part of my life, down here in the South.

"So," he began. "Why are people down here so hung up on the Civil War? It only ended over one-hundred years ago."

"Well," I began as I applied wax to his skin, "now I know why we had an earthquake this morning. Damn Yankees are in town." He didn't know I was being dryly sarcastic because I was sure he thought that all Southerners actually referred to people from the North as *Damn Yankees*. We don't. In fact, I never even think about people from the North, much less speak of them, unless they are annoying me with their stereotypical, potentially offensive questions about the South.

His silence was deafening. I could hear the wheels in his brain turning, wondering if I were the direct descendant of a bigoted redneck cop. "That was a joke," I pointed out. "I was *kidding*. But what exactly are you talking about?"

"There are all these Civil War battlefields and monuments and stuff around here."

"Yes," I confirmed. "It's part of our American history. What would you like for us do with them? Pave them over with asphalt and build Wal-Marts?"

"It just seems kind of backwards down here, all the reenactments and stuff."

"You're awfully ballsy for a guy lying on a table getting his eyebrows waxed," I said. "I'm not into reenacting the war myself, but I don't care if other people do it. I am pretty sure that up North y'all have reenactments of the Revolutionary War."

"Yeah, but that's different."

I snorted. "Yeah, it's different because it's *you*. This may come as a shock to you," I commented dryly, "but the SEC stands for Southeastern Conference, not secession."

He laughed. "Touché."

I smiled, warming up a bit. I was actually enjoying this little game of tit for tat with him. "Actually, now that I think about it, the only time I have conversations about the Civil War is when some *Damn Yankee* brings it up. The last Civil War conversation that I had was in 1989 after a friend of mine had moved back to Ohio after living in the South for a few years and told me that all the South wanted to do was 'rise again' because that's what her Northern friends thought; not because that's what we Southerners actually think." In fact, my recollection of Civil War details was so dusty, I couldn't even remember if the South wore the blue or the gray. Unfortunately, the uniforms pictured in the Read House looked bluish-gray so they were of no help. I continued. "So why do Northerners think that Southerners are ignorant when it's actually the other way around? Since you now stand corrected about the Civil War, maybe you can go back home and educate your peeps about a few other things. Let them know that we have indoor plumbing, telephones, and electricity. We're also literate." Well, most of us.

"Ohio's the Midwest," he pointed out.

"Is it above the Mason-Dixon Line?" I asked, knowing full well that it was.

"Yes," he admitted.

191

"Then it's the North."

He sat up and I handed him a mirror so he could check out his brows. He was pensive, thinking of another counter-attack, I was sure. "The lobby of the Read House has portraits of General Lee and other Civil War soldiers on the walls."

"Yes, it does," I agreed. "Did you know that the Read House is on the Historic Register because it was used as a hospital during the Civil War?"

"I did hear something about that."

"Did you also hear about the Read House ghost?"

"Yeah, but I didn't believe it. So she's real?" he asked.

"That's what I hear. Of course I've never stayed there so I don't know for sure. It's rumored that she was a nurse who took care of the soldiers." No need to slander a ghost with an unfounded rumor of prostitution.

"Interesting," he said.

Something else dawned on me. "Actually, Point Park is also part of a Civil War battlefield. In fact, the monument in Point Park honors both the Confederate and Union soldiers who fought in the battle. A statue of a Confederate soldier shaking hands with a Union soldier is part of the monument too. It is the only monument of the Civil War in the country that honors both Union and Confederate soldiers and symbolizes the two sides coming back together. Now that I think about it, the Union soldiers honored were from New York."

"Really?" he asked, surprised. "I might have to check that out while I'm here."

"You should," I agreed.

He surprised me, pleasantly so, with his next question. "So, would you like to go to dinner tonight?" Boy would I ever. I had enjoyed the banter and conversation with a handsome guy who could both dish it out and take it.

"I can't," I said. "I'm dating someone." As soon as I said those words, they tasted bitter to my mouth.

After Kevin paid and left (he gave me a nice tip, I might add), I was feeling a tad morose again. I wasn't thinking about my DUI situation this time, but rather my lackluster relationship. I knew I wasn't really trapped in it, but I was feeling kind of confined by it and the rest of my circumstances. Yet, I wasn't exactly ready to find a way out; I was still a bit muddled on whether or not I could trust my instincts about relationships yet. I kept my thoughts to myself and did my best to shove them to the back of my mind. That process got much easier when one of my favorite clients, Dr. Lauren Alcott, stepped through the door.

Lauren was a beautiful, nice woman who was a pediatrician, a wife, and a mother of two little boys. She never made an appointment, but would drop by after work when she needed me to perform the simplest of tasks: waxing her lip. The service only cost ten dollars, but she would always leave me a twenty for a tip. I liked her whether or not she left me a big tip. However, in my financial situation, her generosity was greatly appreciated.

"Hey Lauren! Are you stopping by before picking up the boys from The Bright School?" I asked as I stood up from a chair in the waiting room. Lindy glanced up from the *People* magazine she was reading.

"Hi Vandelyn," Lauren greeted me in return. "No. David picked them up earlier. Do you have time for me?"

"Sure! Come on back." She followed me to the facial room and I quickly waxed her lip. When we returned to the front she handed me cash for the service and tip and breezed on out the door.

"Wow," said Lindy in awe. Lauren really did have a presence about her; I could tell that people were just drawn to her. "She's so pretty," Lindy added. I agreed as I put the money for the service in the drawer and slipped my tip into my pocket. Donna's last client had just left and she was sweeping the hair into a dust pan while Kitty was in the back shampooing a client. I sat down next to Lindy in the reception area as she continued. "So her kids go to The Bright School? She must have money."

"She's a pediatrician. I think her husband is a doctor too." As I spoke, Donna relaxed into a chair across from us. "She is really sweet and a great tipper, which is nice." She was the complete opposite of Mrs. Donovan, that's for sure.

Lindy seemed to be genuinely impressed by Lauren. Her eyes were bright and a cheerleader's smile spread across her face as she chirped, "Wow! She's so classy for a colored lady!"

A second of silence ensued as Donna and I registered what Lindy had just said. Then we verbally attacked her like barracudas on chum. When Lindy's eyes were watery and looked like they were on the verge of overflowing with a torrent of tears, we stopped. In some ways, we may have been too hard on her because Lindy didn't have a mean bone in her body. Since we had already ripped Lindy for all the reasons why her sentence was so insulting and wrong, I softened my tone as I also reprimanded her on her choice of word.

"Lindy, you were born in 1983. How do you even know the word *colored*?" It was kind of a silly question since it is part of the NAACP (had Lindy even heard of the NAACP?), but I was still surprised. "That word hasn't been in use since before you were born."

"Really?" she asked tearfully. "I thought it *was* the correct term!"

I had no answer for that. However, a vivid memory flashed into my head as I recalled being a small child and walking with my grandfather through the neighborhood I lived in now. "Colored people live there," he had said with a nod of his head towards a particular house. I was so excited! I had always believed that colored people were real, but had never seen any in person, just on *Sesame Street*. "Really?" I had gushed as if he'd just told me we were going to Disneyland. When I realized that he was not speaking of orange, blue, yellow, and green Muppets, but of black people, I was deflated and confused. Why had my grandfather bothered to point out where black people lived? Didn't he know that I'd seen black people before?

Donna was not feeling nearly as forgiving as I, which was obvious as she glared at Lindy and then stomped off to grab her purse. Fortunately, it was time to leave for the day so Lindy and Donna could go their separate ways and regroup. I said good-by to Lindy; then Donna and I headed to her car which was at a meter out front.

"I am so angry!" Donna spat.

I wisely remained quiet. It was a beautiful, warm spring day and I wasn't in a big hurry to get home and sit around. "You want to grab a beer or something?" I asked.

"Sure," Donna said. "Where do you want to go?"

"Tundra has an outdoor patio," I suggested.

"The lesbian bar?" she asked. "OK."

I laughed. "Why does everyone call it the lesbian bar?"

"Because a lesbian owns it," she explained.

Donna drove the few blocks to the bar and was able to find a spot immediately out front. We hopped out, grabbed a couple of beers from the bar, and relaxed in the afternoon sun while sitting at a wrought iron table. Since we were the only ones on the patio, it was quiet as we sipped our beers. Then someone selected Def Leppard's *Pour Some Sugar on Me* from the jukebox inside and music blared from the outdoor speakers above our heads.

I broke our silence by saying something that Donna might find irritating, but something that I thought needed to be said. "Although what Lindy said was insulting, you know she doesn't have a mean bone in her body. I'm not excusing what she said, but she spoke from a place of ignorance, maybe even cluelessness. She's not really the sharpest tack, you know. Remember? She thought Darth Vader's name was *Garth* Vader. Then there was that day she swore that there was a bridge that spanned from San Francisco to Hawaii. Oh, oh, oh! Remember when that Canadian client came in and mentioned that Canadian Thanksgiving was in October and Lindy asked her when Canadian Christmas was?"

Donna gave me a look. "Is your defense that Lindy's a moron? Aren't *all* racists morons?" Good point. "Do you know why I left Michigan and moved down here?"

"Not for greater racial tolerance, I'm sure."

"I had to get away from my mother."

"I know you said she was crazy or something."

"I can deal with loony-tunes crazy, but not her kind of crazy. Although she is bi-polar or something, she said something so reprehensible that I took Derrick and left."

I was shocked by the revelation, wondering what Donna's mother could have possibly said.

Donna continued. "When Tony and I were having marital problems and I felt that we needed some space away from each other, the simplest, most economical thing was for me to take Derrick and move in with my mother. She lived in the same town as us and she could help take care of Derrick when Tony and I were working. Well one night when Derrick was in the next room watching TV, my mother said to me, 'You're just a *n*****-lover.'"

The hyphenated term Donna spoke *uncensored* and *out loud* mortified me. My cheeks flushed and my ears burned with someone else's shame. I surreptitiously glanced around to see if anyone was nearby. Last thing I needed after my conversation with Kevin was a gaggle of Northerners thinking they were in the midst of *Mississippi Burning*. I was grateful to see that we were still out on the patio alone and that no one, Yank or otherwise, was walking down the sidewalk. Clearly no one besides me had heard what Donna had said.

"Your *mother* called you that? I didn't know anybody even said that anymore! And Derrick was in the next room? Did he hear?" I was still in shock. Tony was African-American, Donna was white, and Derrick, obviously, was their son.

"No, thank you God! But I quietly cussed her out then and there, packed up our things, and left her house that night. I called Tony and told him what had happened; he was pretty shocked too. I took Derrick over to his house, our house, and I spent the night at a friend's. I never let on to Derrick what had happened other than his grandmother and I had a fight. And my mom really must be plain crazy or something because she really does love Derrick and Tony. I just can't have Derrick in that kind of environment, *ever!* It horrifies me to think how hurt he'd feel to hear his grandmother, or *anybody*, say something like that! That's why I'm so pissed at Lindy. I know she doesn't have a mean bone in her body, but neither does my mom and look at what she said! Ignorance and insanity aren't excuses for that kind of talk; they don't make words of hate any less hurtful."

We both sat in reflective silence. *Pour Some Sugar On Me* had finished. I was immersed in thoughts about what a weird day it had been. First, an earthquake; then a conversation about the Civil War followed by an ignorant comment that was sadly intended to be a compliment; and now a story about a mother insulting her daughter with a hateful term. What exactly was going on? Had the quake unearthed bigotry and ignorance that I had mistakenly thought was long gone? Just because my family and friends did not think like that, had I mistakenly assumed that the rest of America was the same?

As we sat together quietly on the patio, I noticed that a fuzzy white noise was beginning to tickle the back of my subconscious. Suddenly a voice boomed from above. Surprised, Donna and I looked around for the voice. *Wait a minute. Had it just called me a sistah?*

A second later, the voice boomed again, shattering our air space by shouting out the word, *n*****!* Shocked, our jaws dropped. My cheeks flushed with embarrassment once again as Donna and I stared at each other, dumbfounded. Then the voice continued

196

spewing racial slurs which echoed shamelessly above our heads: whities, crackers, Jews! This voice surely wasn't the voice of God. Then I was worried for a moment: *was it?* Finally the booming voice assured us that if there were a hell below, we were all going to go. The voice then let out a scream.

Donna and I didn't move. We couldn't move. We just stared at each other in disbelief, mouths hanging open, until we heard funky music coming through the speakers and realized this was part of a song. Then we busted out laughing so hard I thought we might wet ourselves.

"What the—?" was all I could get out as my body shook with laughter.

"Oh my god," Donna said as she wiped her eyes. "I thought for a moment that might be the voice of God or something."

"I know," I agreed. "I was worried for a second." We endured another bout of giggles. I took some deep breaths, trying to regain control of my lungs. "How did that happen? I mean, we were just talking about racism and that song comes on? And nobody else has been out here. Nobody has even passed by!"

Donna and I were silent for a moment as we wiped our eyes and tried to breathe normally. When we heard the voice melodically sing about sisters, brothers, blacks, and crackers, we immediately doubled over with laughter once more.

When we finally started to regain control of our emotions again, I focused on the song. "You know who this is, don't you?" I asked her. She shook her head. "It's Curtis Mayfield! I love Curtis Mayfield." I had a greatest hits album of his at home. I mainly listened to *Freddie's Dead* and *Superfly*, but I couldn't wait to see if this song were on it.

Donna and I finished our beers and returned to the car. During the ride home, we would occasionally burst out in giggles that would last for a number of seconds. As soon as we thought we had them under control, we'd burst out laughing all over again.

"Donna, I hate to ask this, but could we stop by your house before you take me home? I have to pee so badly and I don't think I can wait much longer." Donna's house was about a mile before we got to my house. Normally, I could wait the few extra minutes to get to my house, but today after all that laughing and drinking that beer, my bladder couldn't take much more.

"Sure." A few minutes later we were pulling into the driveway and parking in front of the mother-in-law apartment. As Donna pulled the keys out of the ignition, she inhaled sharply as she focused on the yard behind the main house. I followed her eyes and saw Derrick and Jamal happily running around the backyard with Teepee. Then I saw a man sitting on a bench watching the boys as they played. He turned to smile at us as we parked and I knew it had to be Donna's husband, Tony.

Donna was still staring at Tony as she removed the keys from the ignition. "The door is probably unlocked, but this one's the house key just in case you need it."

"Thanks!" I said as I grabbed the keys and took off to the apartment. The boys were oblivious to me as they laughed and yelped playfully in the grass. Tony glanced my way and I waved and called out "hi" to him as I passed. He returned the greeting as I flung open the front door—it was unlocked—and headed for the bathroom. Of course I was curious about what was happening with Donna and Tony, but my curiosity was going to have to wait until after I peed, which might take a few minutes.

After washing my hands and heading towards the front door, I dropped Donna's keys on the kitchen counter in plain sight. As I stepped outside, I made sure that the door had no chance of accidentally locking itself behind me.

I walked down the steps to the driveway and stopped, watching the familial scene from a slight distance. Jamal and Derrick were still playing in the yard with Teepee alongside. Donna and Tony were sitting next to each other on the bench watching the children play.

Donna and Tony looked content, but I could tell from Donna's body language that she was still keeping a wall up between them. Tony's body language was much more relaxed and open. Teepee took off towards the main house, yapping as he went, and the boys happily chased each other in circles.

Suddenly Jamal said, "Look out!"

Jamal dropped to his knees and gently extended his arm out to prevent Derrick's involvement in a potential tragedy. Derrick knelt down on the ground next to Jamal and examined what Jamal had noticed just moments before: a pretty fuchsia flower blossoming undisturbed in the near-trampled grass. As Jamal rubbed a velvety petal between his fingertips, Derrick gingerly extended his fingers towards an adjacent blossom.

Jamal looked up at his cousin to exclaim in awe, "It's so soft!"

As the boys appreciatively rubbed their fingertips across the velvety petals in silence, Tony tenderly caressed his finger over Donna's hand.

"Yes," he said. "Yes, it is."

33

I stood there silently wondering how to excuse myself from this touching scene, pun not intended. I didn't even want to interrupt to say good-by, but I knew I couldn't just disappear without a word. Plus, I couldn't leave the premises without being noticed anyway and that would be totally awkward too. I waited until Donna seemed to remember that I had ridden in the car with her.

She looked around and called out to me, "Vandelyn, what are you doing standing quietly over there? Come on over and let me introduce you to Tony!"

I joined Donna and Tony at the bench and let Donna formally introduce us to each other. After a few cordial moments, I told Donna, "It's such an awesome day outside; I'm just going to walk the rest of the way home."

Donna frowned at me. "No you're not. I'll take you home." She turned to Tony, "It'll take just a second. Vandelyn only lives a mile away, if that far."

"No, seriously, Donna. You and Tony and Derrick and Jamal hang out and enjoy the afternoon. I really want to walk home. Really."

"Are you sure?" Donna asked doubtfully.

"Positive. Oh, and your keys are on the kitchen counter." Once I convinced Donna once and for all that I really did want to walk home, I said good-by to everyone and headed on my way. Walking through Donna's neighborhood towards Dayton Boulevard uplifted me. I loved seeing the spring flowers and inhaling the scents of rebirth and renewal. As I walked up to the sidewalk and headed past the small businesses, my cell phone rang. It was Mitchell Overton.

"Hello?" I asked.

"Hello, Vandelyn!" he bellowed. "How are you?"

"I'm doing well," I said. "How are you?"

"Doing great," he admitted. "I never heard back from you about your court date and wanted to ask you about it."

"Well, it went," I muttered. "I actually go to serve my forty-eight hours this weekend."

"Why didn't you keep fighting it?" he asked. I guess a good defense attorney would ask that.

"Because I didn't have an extra seven hundred-fifty dollars to pay Mr. Peters and it just didn't seem worth it."

"What do you mean, *an extra seven hundred-fifty dollars?* I talked to him earlier and he told me that he offered to keep defending you for free, but you didn't want to do it."

I stopped in the middle of the sidewalk. "James Peters told you that he offered to continue defending me for *free?*" I couldn't believe what a scoundrel that guy was. I started walking again. "That is such a load! If he'd offered to continue defending me for free, of course I would have accepted it! But he didn't. He told me that I would need to pay him an additional seven hundred-fifty for his continuing legal services. I just couldn't afford to do it." What an asshole. Correction. What a sniveling, lying cocksucking bastard.

"Really?" Mitchell Overton seemed genuinely baffled by my statement. He was probably wondering which one of us was lying to him: his protégé or his former law student? It really wasn't hard to figure out. The lawyers are the liars; there's probably a Foundations in English Language course that can verify that both words come from the same root.

"It's OK, though. I've just got to get through this weekend and I'll be done with it; except for paying off the fines, of course." And getting my restricted driver's license; paying for three years of SR-22 insurance; and having DUI First Offense on my record until the day that I die. We chatted for a few moments more and then spoke our friendly good-byes. I made sure to tell him that even though I still had to go to jail, I did appreciate his taking time to help me with the situation and for giving me a call.

By this time I had arrived at my kitchen door. I unlocked it, threw my things on the counter, and picked up a mewing Mack from his perch on the table. I petted him as we headed into the dining room so I could grab my Curtis Mayfield CD. I plopped Mack on the floor and scanned the song list on the back. I was joyous when I saw the title, *(Don't Worry) If There's A Hell Below We're All Going To Go.*

I hurried over to the CD player as Mack watched me with curiosity. After the song's spoken intro segued into the funky music, Mack scattered out of the room suspecting that I might want him to be my dancing partner again. Mack remained scarce as I moved around the room to the music, an occasional giggle sputtering from my lips when Curtis Mayfield sang about the crackers and the whities.

I repeated the song again before switching to En Vogue's *Free Your Mind* in honor of the day's events. After strutting around the living and dining room to the music (something that I now only do when I am alone since Marais and Jarrett shamed me at the club by pretending to raise the roof for me while chanting, "Go George. Go George. It's your birthday." Apparently my moves were less Michael Jackson and more George Jefferson.), I grabbed my cell phone so I could call Marais and tell her about my day.

After she answered, I dramatically said to her, "You'll never believe the day that I've had."

Since I wasn't one known for dramatic statements, Marais was intrigued. "Really?" she asked with curiosity. "What happened?"

I started with the earthquake and didn't leave out one detail until the moment that I arrived home.

"Are you serious?" Marais was a bit stunned by the day's events. "First of all, that lawyer you had *sucks!*"

"Tell me about it!" I agreed.

"But all that stuff throughout the day about racism, stereotyping, and the Curtis Mayfield song? That's really bizarre. And it just keeps reminding me that no matter how much progress is made, there will never be a black president, at least, not in our lifetimes."

I could almost see Marais shaking her head from side-to-side. Her strength always amazes me. I can self-destruct from anger and frustration in two seconds flat, but Marais just stands tall in the face of adversity. I think that's because she has a tight-knit loving family. I am strong too, but in that fend-for-yourself-aggressive-junkyard-dog kind of way that comes from surviving the pain of childhood hurts including a splintered family.

Although I knew what Marais said was true, I was

disheartened to hear her prediction about a black president. Not too long ago, Marais had told me a story about when her older sister, Michelle, was in school back in Philadelphia. Michelle had a learning disability and the DuBois' were concerned about their daughter's education. When they met with Michelle's teacher, who was white, she was blasé about the matter. "Don't worry about her scholastic career," the teacher had nonchalantly told Dr. and Mrs. DuBois. "Your daughter's future will be fine because Michelle can sing and dance very well."

Although at the time Mrs. DuBois had fantasized about impaling all ten of her fingernails into the teacher's face, she had maintained her self-control. But it raised a serious question: could it really be that no matter how many pretty pictures of students of different ethnic and racial backgrounds grace the covers of college applications, latent (or was it blatant?) racism and sexism still exists?

Just then an optimistic thought, actually a person's name, popped into my head as a possible black presidential candidate that might actually have a chance of getting elected. I shared it with Marais. "Thomas Sowell?" I offered hopefully.

A moment of silence passed. In a weird voice Marais asked, "Is this in response to my statement that we won't have a black president in our lifetimes?"

"Yes," I said. What was so odd about my suggestion? I thought she would have agreed.

The weird voice continued. "And you are suggesting Thomas Sowell, the conservative columnist, as a possible black presidential candidate?"

I slapped my palm to my head. "Did I say *Thomas Sowell*?! That's not who I meant. I meant Colin Powell!" My cheeks flushed.

Marais could not control herself any longer. Peals of laughter ricocheted through the phone. I could hear her stomping her feet on the floor as she convulsed with hysterics. "What is this?" she asked between giggles. "Black People White People Like?" She was rolling. "Did you get them confused because they're both black and their names rhyme?" More howls. I had no response so I just remained quietly on the line while she practically peed her pants. "Oh Vandelyn!" she gasped when she finally quit laughing long enough to come up for air. "I'm sorry, but that's just so *white* of you!"

34

May

Saturday afternoon finally arrived and Tod and I drove to Silverdale Correctional Facility in silence. As Tod and I drove up to the guard gate of the correctional facility, my stomach flip-flopped. Although I was nervous as I spoke to the guard, I still felt like 100 percent of a human being (a percentage that would diminish over the next thirty-seven hours or so). I smiled. He smiled. He asked me about the approved items I had brought. I showed them to him. He told me that the pen I brought was not allowed, but he switched my contraband pen with his approved pen and sent us on through the gate. It was all very pleasant. Maybe jail or prison or whatever wasn't going to be so bad after all.

Just as I was waxing optimistic as we pulled into a parking space, Tod cheerily said, "Don't get raped!" I stared at him. He smiled. To say that I wanted to give an Executive Order by shoving my fist into his oval orifice (pick one) was an understatement. Although I exercised self-restraint, I did bear my teeth and growl. It also helped me to remember that I was inside the gate of a correctional facility. Since I never wanted to go to jail again, it was not advisable to break the law right now, even if the assault and battery were justifiable.

I grabbed my things and got out of the car as Tod called out, "Good luck!" What an asshole. As I entered the facility without looking back, I debated on whether I should upgrade him to a cocksucking bastard.

The interior of the facility was as expected: commercial tile flooring, benches along the walls, and a long counter where the guards were stationed to greet the incoming prisoners.

I stepped up to the counter. "Hi," I chirped to the guard

with forced gaiety, still waxing optimistic about my upcoming experience although my nerves were atwitter. "I'm here to serve my remaining time for DUI First Offense." I couldn't remember the exact time I had left, but I wanted him to know that I had less that forty-eight hours left. "I think it's around thirty-seven hours," I clarified, peering down at his computer screen although it was angled away from me.

"Name?" he asked. I told him. He checked his screen and verified my remaining time. I was relieved. I did not want to have to spend any more time in here than necessary. I remained standing at the counter and chit-chatted politely with the guard. He politely chit-chatted with me until he had an epiphany of some sort.

He turned to his fellow guard and exclaimed with surprise, "I can't believe I'm sitting here talking to a *prisoner*!" I felt that now was a good time to sit down on the bench. I was no longer a whole human being. I was now at least three-fourths human being since being degraded and demoted to rank of "prisoner."

I sat there quietly with my two paperback murder mysteries (I was now wondering if murder mysteries were a good idea for prison), my blank composition book, and my newly acquired pen. I was wearing my white cotton bikinis and my white cotton no-underwire bra underneath my jeans and T-shirt.

I wore no makeup because 1) I wasn't allowed to bring any toiletries to remove it, and 2) who cares about looking good in prison? Especially in light of Tod's comment. But I already knew that rape didn't occur because of how hot women look, no matter how much society wants to blame the victims. Rape is a violent crime of power and control.

Although I was offended by Tod's comment for all the obvious reasons, I was also mad because I actually was afraid of getting raped in prison. Up until a few years ago, I had thought that only men got raped in prison. It never occurred to me that women would commit the same act of violence on their own kind. I naively had thought women were more civilized that that. *No woman wants to be raped, so why would one woman rape another?* I had innocently asked myself. It wasn't until after a *Lifetime* docu-drama that I learned that women do in fact rape each other in prison. (Thanks so much for sharing, *Lifetime*.) So underneath my optimistic exterior, I was all too aware that I was about to be incarcerated at a medium security facility instead of a more harmless, low security armory gymnasium where I could play *Chutes & Ladders* without the fear of someone sneaking up behind me and forcing her ladder up my chute.

Were these medium security inmates capable of rape? was the obvious question. My eyes narrowed and my brow furrowed as I pledged to myself that if I were raped while serving my remaining hours for DUI First Offense, I was going to be the most litigious, pissed-off, former-inmate Hamilton County and the State of Tennessee had ever seen. I'd be madder than MADD could ever be.

My thoughts of possible vengeance were interrupted when the door opened again. All hateful thoughts fled as I saw an older Hispanic man enter the facility. In his hands were items someone had lovingly packed for him: a folded towel and washcloth, a new bar of soap, and his toothbrush and toothpaste. His eyes were wide and he looked vulnerable and bewildered as he hurried up to the counter. His broken English broke my heart.

"Oh no. He doesn't realize they are going to take all his toiletries away from him," I noted silently. I thought about the kind person who had made sure he had the basic necessities of home so he could care for himself while in jail. He looked even more bewildered and vulnerable than before when the guard took his items from him and would not give them back. Then, a different male guard joined the Hispanic man and walked him down the corridor.

I sighed. A few minutes later a female guard just a few years older than I was approached me. I smiled. She didn't. She stopped a few feet away from me, motioned with her hand for me to get up off the bench, still not even bothering to speak. I stood up and acted like my normal self.

"Hi," I said, smiling at her again.

She gave me a look of disdain. Whatever I had been or had accomplished in my life before entering Silverdale (which, let's face it, wasn't a whole heck of a lot) was of no interest to her. What did matter to her was that I was a prisoner and prisoners were obviously without any redeeming value.

"Come with me down this hallway," she ordered. We walked down the hallway. "Stop." I stopped. She unlocked a door and held it open for me, waiting for me to enter. I entered. It was a room longer than it was wide. Along the wall by the door stood wire racks with navy blue jail uniforms, blankets, and pillows stacked on them.

She grabbed a shirt, pants, and shoes for me and ordered me to strip.

"Take *everything* off?" I asked. I was definitely nervous now. Why did I have to get naked? I did not want to get naked. It was a direct violation of my don't-get-naked-in-jail policy.

"Yes." I removed all my clothes including my approved white cotton bra and underwear, mentally making notes for my future don't-fuck-with-me lawsuit against Hamilton County if not the State of Tennessee. "Turn around."

"Turn *around?*" I repeated. I was confused by this direction because why on earth did I need to turn around? But I did. Now my backside was facing her. This had better not be a game of *Chutes & Ladders*.

"Now squat." I didn't even bother repeating this order. I squatted. "Now pull your cheeks apart and cough." *WTF?*! I did as I was told. If I thought going to the OB/GYN had been embarrassing at the age of seventeen, it was nothing compared to this. This was humiliating *and* degrading. "You can stand up and put on your bra and panties now. Hand me the rest of your clothes."

"Why did I have to do that?" I asked as I dressed, my irritation apparent.

"Some people smuggle drugs into the jail that way," she answered as she took my shirt and jeans and handed me my prison garb.

As I put on my navy pants, shirt, and shoes, I wondered what kind of idiot, especially one in for DUI First Offense, would try to smuggle drugs into jail. As far as I concerned, I wanted my relationship with the Hamilton County Police Department and Silverdale Correctional Facility to be the equivalent of a one-night-stand. So what kind of moron would choose a long-term relationship with Hamilton County's Department of Corrections by being a repeat offender?

We continued down the hallway until we reached an area with a guard station in the center. Four glass doorways and four large picture windows faced each other and the guard station. The signs up above the doors told me that these were Pods A through D. The guard station consisted of a pentagon-shaped desk so the guard on duty could see into each of the pods with a mere swivel of his rolling chair. The guard on duty nodded at my escort and watched us as she led me into one of the rooms.

As we entered Pod C, I noticed that the noise level was low. Some women were sitting in groups talking to each other; others kept to themselves; a few sat at one of the four high-school-lunchroom-style cafeteria tables; some were reading; others were lying on their cots, presumably asleep.

The hostile prison guard led me over to a wooden slab that was permanently attached to the floor. Its edge was slightly raised to hold some sort of mattress, but no mattress was present. I looked around at all the other wooden slabs and they all had mattresses on them. The prison guard was unconcerned about my plight. She tossed my folded blanket and flat, flimsy pillow onto the hard wooden slab and turned to leave. No way could I sleep on a hard wooden bench with a raised edge, but no way was I going to ask this guard about it either. She had to know I needed a mattress. However, when she began to walk away as if she were done with me, I began to panic inside. As I turned to watch her leave and hopefully muster up the courage to ask for something I was entitled to even as a lowly prisoner, another young woman came to my aid.

"Hey!" she called out. "She needs a mattress. You have to bring her a mattress." The guard stopped and turned to look at my naked wooden slab. She sighed with annoyance. Then she turned back around and headed out the door. Although she had made no comment about returning with the mattress, I was confident that she would.

I was grateful to the girl who helped me, but I wasn't exactly sure about how to respond. Did I say "Thank you" like I normally would? Good manners so far had not helped me in jail, at least not with the prison guards. I glanced over at the girl, but she was animatedly talking to her fellow inmates again as they sat on their cots. Saved from prison-etiquette concerns (would Martha write a book on it?), I decided to familiarize myself with the rest of the room.

Basically it was an open, square space except for an interior wall that made up one side of the showers. Of course there was a back wall and the exterior wall to create the second and third sides for the showers, but there was no privacy from the front. The showers and the toilets faced each other. And the toilets weren't private either because they had no doors and were surrounded only by half-walls on the other three sides. I could lie on my cot and see women sitting on the toilets if wanted to (which I didn't). All the walls were made out of smooth cement blocks. Fortunately they were painted the color of sweet potatoes instead of remaining their standard industrial gray color. Behind the toilets were the sinks and the sinks were adjacent to the eating area which was in front of the cots.

In my perusal, I did notice a few very important things: First, no toilet paper *anywhere*; second, no hand soap; third, no paper towels. Not only was I not allowed access to my own toiletries for thirty-seven-plus hours, Pod C, although immaculate in presentation, was one-hundred percent without any state-supplied toiletries which translated to me as 100% unsanitary. Where was the Health Department? People ate food in here didn't they?

When I worked as a server and a bartender, the Health Department considered it "unsanitary" if an employee with shoulder-length hair didn't have it pulled back in a pony-tail. So what was up with not being able to clean your hands before eating or after wiping your ass? Wasn't that an infraction of some kind? Or was it because prisoners are considered to be less than human and deserve whatever flesh-eating disease they get from lack of proper sanitary conditions? I figured I already knew the answer.

By this time my unfriendly prison guard had returned with my "mattress." She dumped it onto my wooden slab and then turned and left. *What?* I wanted to ask. *No complimentary fruit basket? No mint on the pillow?* Thankfully I kept my smart ass comments to myself. As I straightened out my mattress, I realized that "mattress" was a very liberal, very indulgent term. Long, flat, sandbag-type object would be more accurate. Still, it was better than the equivalent of a closed wooden coffin with a raised edge.

I then draped my thin, very thin, wool blanket on top of it. This blanket sucked. Why exactly was the government so inept when it came to buying supplies? This blanket had the thickness of paper, the texture of a Brillo pad, and probably cost more than a comfy, cotton, twin-sized blanket from a department store.

The pillow couldn't be flatter even if everyone in Pod C jumped on it. Hadn't the government ever heard of Big Lots? At Big Lots, you could get a nice, fluffy pillow for a few dollars. How much had the government paid for this pillow? And what company made this crap for government institutions? Was it publicly traded?

If so, I might want to invest. God knows it wasn't going out of business and the returns had to be great since the product was so cheap and had to be over-priced.

I doubted these blankets were even made in the United States. So why didn't the government talk manufacturing with Malden Mills and give American tax payer money to Aaron Feuerstein's *American* company? Wouldn't that make sense? Then again, when did common sense apply to whom voters elected into positions of power? Not too long ago, Hamilton County had a politician run on the platform of "Pro-Gun, Pro-Life." Where was the sense in that?

At that moment in time, I had no idea that Silverdale wasn't run directly by the government. It was actually run by a company that claimed to create solid employment opportunities, rehabilitate inmates, give back to the community, and bring innovative security measures to correctional facilities. The corporation boasted that it did all this *and* saved the tax dollars of hardworking tax payers.

Did I mention that this corporation actually *is* a publicly traded company? I could buy stock and become an investor in the corporation that incarcerated me. I mean, how much more American capitalist can you get? I also had to wonder how a for-profit corporation with a Board of Directors installed to protect the shareholders' interests (as opposed to the taxpayers' interests) could really be concerned with saving the tax dollars of hardworking Americans.

35

This train of thought got me thinking about *my* hardworking tax dollars that went to support the Silverdale Correctional Facility. Inspired by my fellow inmate's successful demand for a mattress, I decided that I was going to ask for toilet paper. I was entitled to toilet paper and I was going to get some toilet paper!

I walked over to the glass window and stood there, waiting for the desk guard to look up at me. He didn't. I could tell that he sensed that I, a prisoner, was standing at the window, but he didn't want to acknowledge my presence. As he continued to deliberately not look over at me, I made it harder for him to ignore me.

"Hello," I called out through the window I was sure was sound-proof and possibly bullet proof. (Then again, bullet proof might be a bad idea.) No response. I began waving my arm and repeating the word, "hello" in a variety of quasi-sarcastic, sing-song versions. Finally he could no longer ignore me and looked in my direction.

"I need toilet paper," I told him through the glass.

"What?" he said. We couldn't hear each other so it was more like a game of lip reading.

"Toilet paper," I repeated. He stared at me. "Toilet paper. I need TOILET PAPER." I wasn't yelling, but I was overly enunciating. I was not rude, but I was not nice. Mainly, I was annoyed.

When he finally understood (or finally stopped pretending not to understand me), he placed his hands on the counter, rolled his chair backwards, and looked underneath the desk towards his feet. Seeing no toilet paper in the vicinity of his toes, he rolled his chair back into place, gave me a shrug letting me know that he had no toilet paper to give me, and either went back to reading *Snuffy Smith* or thinking about how much his company's bottom line and stock would increase since they stopped wasting valuable dollars on prisoners' toilet paper, hand soap, and paper towels.

I turned my back to him with narrowed eyes and a curled lip and headed for my cot. *Thanks for the thorough search for toilet paper, asshole.* I was pretty sure that the guards' bathrooms were never without toilet paper. I imagined that roll after roll was stacked up to the ceiling, ensuring that the guards had plenty of quilted softness with which to wipe their asses. I sat down on the cot and picked up one of my paperbacks. I opened to the first page, but couldn't focus on the words because I was thinking about how prisoners were treated by the guards. When I noticed that my heart was beginning to harden and shrink into a little stone, I was pretty sure that the Grinch, whose heart was two sizes too small, had once been incarcerated at Silverdale in Pod C.

A little bit later, after finally being able to get into my murder mystery, the same unfriendly guard returned to do the headcount. Everyone sat on their cots while she counted. My cot was at the end of a row. The girl next to me had been lying down, presumably asleep, since I had arrived. Now she was sitting up, waiting for the guard to finish her count. As she stared out into the room with her knees pulled to her chest, arms wrapped around her shins, I noticed how young she was; around nineteen if I had to guess. Her long, brownish-blond hair was pulled back into a ponytail and she looked so frail. She lay back down on her bed and reached underneath her cot. Sliding out a footlocker, she pulled off the lid and pulled out a photo. Lying on her stomach, she held the photo with both hands and stared at the image, as if willing it to appear before her. Out of the corner of my eye, I glanced at the photo. It was of a baby boy, maybe a year or so old. Silently she started to cry and buried her face in the crook of one arm while clutching the photo tightly against her chest. Her pain broke my heart.

After the guard finished her count and confirmed that we were all still present and accounted for, she shouted, "Lights Out!" and turned and left the room. The room dimmed, but a few security lights remained on. I placed the book I was reading on the floor by my bed. My neighbor stared at her son's photo one last time in the dim lighting and then replaced it in the footlocker, closing the lid.

I snuggled under the blanket, no longer too concerned about

rape. I had been relieved to note that everyone had been more of the mind-your-own-business type and less Bend-Over-I'm-the-Alpha-Dog-of-Pod-C type. Instead, my thoughts focused on the young girl next to me. I didn't know her, but she seemed so fragile. She was obviously a young mother who desperately missed her son. How had such a tender soul ended up in a place like Silverdale? Since I had no answer, I tried to get comfortable on my sandbag mattress and hoped to quickly fall asleep.

36

The next morning, the lights flicked on at jail-thirty, which is about the same time as the crack-ass-of-dawn. Although I'd had plenty of sleep, I was still a bit ornery at having to wake up so early. Those of us who chose to eat breakfast staggered to form a line once the guard on duty let us know that it was our turn at the trough.

As I slowly progressed through the doorway to grab a tray and be served from the portable cafeteria style set-up that had been temporarily erected by the guard station, I was curious as to what would be served. I was sure that as most state institutions, the focus would be on the food pyramid and The Four Basic Food Groups.

After noting the lack of privacy in Silverdale, I knew that my food focus would revolve around the fact that I had no desire to use the facilities any more than I had to. More specifically, I knew that there was no way I was doing Number Two anywhere walls, doors, and toilet paper were not present. (Peeing was more acceptable. Worst case, I could hover and drip-dry.) Therefore, I simplified The Four Basic Food Groups into my two basic food groups: the pee group and the poop group.

As I took my tray of eggs, sausage, toast, and pint of milk to a seat at one of the cafeteria tables, I started my inventory with the easiest foods first. Milk: pee. Sausage: poop. Eggs: debatable; which meant that today they went on the poop side. Toast: also debatable but I felt good about the chances it would convert into pee. So I ate my toast and drank my milk. When a table mate asked me for my sausage, I gave it to her with a thankful prayer that my cot was on the end of the row farthest away from the toilets. I dumped the remaining food and empty milk carton into the garbage and placed my dirty tray in the appropriate spot.

I stepped over to the sinks and rinsed each hand under the

faucet, irritated again by the lack of supplies. I shook my hands to remove the excess water and then patted them dry on my shirt. Then I walked back over to my cot, sat down, and grabbed my mystery novel. I also noticed that my young neighbor was also returning from eating her breakfast too. We unintentionally made eye contact and I smiled at her. She smiled and said, "Hi." I returned the greeting.

"What are you in for?" she asked as she sat cross-legged on her bed with the blanket pulled over her lap.

"DUI," I said. "You?"

"Felony Arson."

"Really?" I asked, my surprise evident. I wasn't sure who seemed like the Felony Arson type, but I was pretty sure it wasn't her.

"Yeah," she sighed, heavy with a burden. "I was with my boyfriend, my ex-boyfriend, when he blew up a fireworks factory."

I didn't know what to say to that. I mean, what *could* I say to that besides, *That sucks?* The first thing I thought was, *What a crappy boyfriend*, but then again, who was I to talk? The next thing I thought was, *What a bad decision.* And again, who was I to talk? Every woman in Pod C was incarcerated for the sole reason that she made a bad decision (even if Tennessee Code Annotated has a proper legal name and number for each of those bad decisions). Maybe I should also take a survey and see if we all had crappy boyfriends (or girlfriends). I was pretty sure that was a no-brainer. If The State of Tennessee had a handy codes book that none of us had abided by which blatantly outlined right from wrong, I was pretty sure that our much more subjective choices in dating partners had been just as foolish. I mean, could you really have great taste in men (or women) and still find yourself in jail?

"So what's your name?" I decided to change the subject.

"Missy," she said. "What's yours?"

"Vandelyn. So, Missy, what's up with the lack of toilet paper?"

"They didn't give you any toilet paper?" she asked.

"Nope. I tried to ask the guard for some last night, but he claimed not to have any."

She leaned over the side of the cot and grabbed her foot locker. After sliding off the lid, she pulled out a nice big roll of toilet paper. "Anytime you need toilet paper, just grab it out of my foot locker, OK?"

"Thanks!" I was genuinely appreciative. "Do you mind if I take some now?" She handed me the roll and I tore off a section and placed it with my meager belongings. I returned the roll to her and she placed it back into the locker, sliding it back under her bed. Then she turned away from me, pulled the blanket up over her shoulders, and, I assumed, went back to sleep.

I returned to reading my book. It was a pleasant escape from my present circumstances. My bubble burst when I closed the book cover and realized that it wasn't even lunchtime yet, just late morning. I only had one book left and all too many jail time hours from which I would want to be distracted. This ratio was not good. As a result, I decided that the best solution would be to pepper my reading with sleep. Or maybe it would be more accurate to say, pepper my sleep with reading. I snuggled under the blanket, pulling it above my head to block out the fluorescents, and napped out of boredom and the need for escape.

37

When I awoke, it was time to eat again. I continued my good hygiene charade by rinsing off my hands before getting into line and then waited my turn for eats. Lunch consisted of a fried chicken patty (poop), green beans (pee), roll (pee), two generic vanilla-flavored sandwich cookies (nasty), and milk (pee). After offering my chicken patty and cookies to two other inmates, I finished off my pee food-groups and wondered if I were on to something. Maybe I could solve my money problems by making a bundle off of a new diet based on my pee and poop food classifications? I could call it the *Two Basic Food Groups Diet Book*. Of course, I'd have to lose my love handles first, but not before I take my "Before" picture for the inside cover. I disposed of my trash, returned my tray, and headed back for my cot.

I had to admit that I was quite impressed with my jailhouse food philosophy because it seemed to be working. I had no need to poop and I'd managed to go without peeing for quite a while. Unfortunately, the pee thing was catching up with me. I grabbed the folded tissue from beside my bed and reluctantly headed for the toilets while no one else was using them. I could imagine nothing more embarrassing than sitting next to someone using the facilities and having the ability to make eye contact with them; actually, having the ability on making eye contact with anyone in the whole room.

I covered the seat with tissue so I didn't have to hover and tried to maintain as much dignity as possible while simultaneously trying to render myself invisible. When I was done, I continued my personal hygiene façade by rinsing my hands with water. Out of consideration for my fellow inmates, I turned the faucet with the hand that had not been involved in the wiping process to help maintain the illusion of being sanitary. Of course, the reality was that it was pretty disgusting to think about how many of us wiped, then touched the faucets with no real chance of our hands being clean. *Ever.*

After wiping my hands this time on my pants, I returned to my cot. I was so bored that I did not even feel motivated to read. I lay down on my stomach, folding the pillow in half so I could use it as a prop under my chin, and observed my surroundings. One girl was doing lunges as she made laps around the room. I admired her desire for physical fitness. If I had been in here long-term, I think I might have been motivated to do the same. As it were, I just wanted to pass these hours as effortlessly as possible, willing them to hurry up and be time-served.

The girl who came to my mattress rescue the night before was now calling out to the rest of us in the room. "Hey everybody, listen up!" Somebody mumbled, "Shut up," but it went unnoticed or ignored. "Why don't we work together and buy extra toiletries for inmates who haven't had the opportunity to get them yet?" One of her friends backed her up in agreement while the rest of the room made quiet rumblings, good or bad, I couldn't really discern. A couple of women got up from their cots and went and sat next to her in apparent support of her proposition and conversations resumed about how to achieve this goal.

I had a moment of dawning enlightenment: so *that's* what the deal was. Inmates had to purchase their toiletries from the correctional facility. As the discussion increased in enthusiasm, I heard yelps of how many VO5 shampoos would be recommended for purchase. I gave a wry smile. VO5 shampoo reminded me of the 1980s, maybe even the 1970s. At one time, I think it had been a brand people wanted, but was now relegated to discount store shelves. In the culmination of my Bargain Basement lifestyle, I'd been to Fred's, Big Lots, and Dollar General. I think they all sold VO5 for about a dollar. I wonder how much the correctional facility charged for a bottle? I'd guess for a bit more than a dollar; probably added a 100% mark-up, if I had to guess.

Now I was curious as to *how* inmates went about paying for products during incarceration. Obviously, they didn't have jobs. No jobs equaled no income. So if you have no income, how do you buy things? Maybe some inmates earned money by serving meals, cleaning the pods, or doing the laundry, but only a few were trusted with such privileges, which meant that the majority of inmates had to figure out other ways to get money. The obvious answer would be that their families gave them money. I knew that if I were in here long-term, my family would donate money to the purchasing of my basic necessities. However, if I had to guess, I'd say that many of these women came from poor families who didn't have much disposable income for extras of any kind. But I guess if you're poor and your family needs something, you find a way to get it for them.

I sighed and flipped over onto my back as a guard entered with a new prisoner. A new inmate was of mild interest to the room, but by the time she made it to the empty cot on the row behind me, most in the room had moved on to thinking or talking about other things. I wasn't much interested in the new girl either until she started talking loudly behind me to a girl on the cot next to hers.

"So we was just having a party and like there's a knock on the door so I go to answer it and there's the two cops standing there. Then they's like, 'Are you Tina?' And I's like, 'Yeah. Wassup?' And they like, 'We've got a warrant for your arrest. You violated your probation.' So I's like, 'Well, let's go.' So I had to leave my own party!" Tina gave a laugh as she paused in her story. "But I'm sure they shut the party down. Prob'ly brought in the dogs, too, ya know?" She laughed again. "But if they brought in the dogs, ain't none of that shit mine, ya know? But I'm sure they'll *say* it's mine, ya know what I'm sayin'?

"I mean just last month, I'm mindin' my own business and the cops stop by and tell me that I missed my court date or somethin'. I told them that couldn't be right unless they changed it on me and if they changed it on me, nobody gave me notice so it was like their fault not my fault so I shouldn't have to go to jail—"

At that point I did my best to quit listening because Tina was annoying the shit out of me. I'd just encountered the moronic repeat offender who was doing her best to have a long-term relationship with the Department of Corrections. Actually, not only was she forging a long-term relationship, she was forming a *kinship* with DOC. When she talked about her criminal history, she spoke about the police as if they were her distant cousins come to visit instead of law enforcement come to arrest her for yet another violation.

I lay there thinking about all the freedoms that we have, all the legal things we can do to play, frolic, and have a nice life. Yet she is one of many who can't live within the boundaries. *Quit acting like a loser, Tina!* I wanted to tell her. *Why didn't anybody tell you that there's a world of beautiful opportunities out there, Tina? Of all the things you could do with your life, Tina, why is being a repeat offender the career path, the* life *path, you choose?* Not to mention, her repeat offender status was based not on being an active criminal, but just on the basic stupidity of missed court dates, hanging out with people she shouldn't associate with, and for doing things she wasn't supposed to do while on probation.

Of course, I was a total hypocrite. I was in jail too. But I never, ever, wanted to return. I had pushed outside the boundaries, gotten caught, and I knew that I did not want to be out-of-bounds again. What I didn't understand was why Tina didn't mind coming back to jail again and again? If getting arrested wasn't a life changing event for Tina, if it wasn't a wake-up call, then what would be?

Thinking about wake-up calls made my thoughts segue to the biggest wake-up call in my lifetime: September 11, 2001. I had been getting ready for work for my job as a bartender and I happened to be channel surfing. Normally I had the station set to MTV or VH1 so I could listen to the Top 10 video countdown while I dressed. That day for some reason, I changed my routine. I clicked onto a national news channel just in time to see an airplane slam into the World Trade Center. *Live!* It was shocking. I remained focused in disbelief on the images I was seeing and listening to the commentary as the events unfolded. When a second plane crashed into the other tower, it was like a slap in the face to someone who was in shock. I hopped up and grabbed the phone and called Jarrett. She didn't answer so I had to leave a message.

"Oh my god! A plane just crashed into the World Trade Center. And then another one crashed too. Turn on your TV and call me!" I was pretty sure that Jarrett was over at her boyfriend's place asleep. I had the phone number, but I debated on calling it. Although this was serious stuff, it wasn't immediately clear what or why this was happening. Her boyfriend might be pissed at being woken up after a night of partying to hear about news in New York City.

When I got to work in the morning, we were glued to CNN. The towers were smoking. One of our degenerate employees, a twenty-something whose life revolved around getting fucked-up and doing the least he had to do to get through life, walked in through the front door and stared at the TV screens. He had no idea what was happening. When one of the towers collapsed, we gasped. Except him. He laughed.

I turned to him with a snarl. "You're laughing?!" I demanded. "You think that's *funny*?!" It had been a horrifying image to witness, even if only through the lens of a camera. I could not imagine how devastating it would have been to live in New York City and witness it live. Or even worse, to have been trapped in the towers.

He looked a little startled by my anger and said, "Oh. That's real? I thought it was a joke." Then he walked back to the kitchen, clocked-in, and began his work day, business as usual.

A few days later, we remained glued to CNN, watching New York City Mayor, Rudy Giuliani, warn the public about scam artists claiming to be victims of September 11 for financial gain. I was appalled and disgusted to hear that people were trying to profit off of a tragedy, especially this tragedy. About two hours later, towards the end of my shift, the front door opened and a guy in his mid-to-late-twenties stepped in. After working in the service industry for a number of years, especially as a bartender, I had learned to pick up vibes about people. The vibes this guy sent off were unnerving. The way his eyes darted around the room, unfocused, caused the thought, "This guy is crazy," to pop into my head. It wasn't a literal assessment, but it was just my brain telling me that there was something definitely off, definitely not right, about this guy; something that told me he was mentally disturbed.

When he slid onto a bar stool, I was leery. "Hi," I greeted him. "What can I get for you today?"

"I'd like a draft beer. I was in here last night," he began, "and the manager let me have beers for ninety-nine cents because I was in The World Trade Center on September eleventh."

"I'll have to ask," I told him and I left the bar area and walked over to my manager. I was disgusted. The Trade Center had collapsed only a couple of days ago and this guy was in Knoxville, Tennessee trying to use it to get cheap beer? Mayor Giuliani was right; this was reprehensible.

As I stepped over to my manager, I explained the situation in a low voice, letting my skepticism show. "It's OK," my manager told me. "He was in here last night. Go ahead and give him the beers for ninety-nine cents."

221

I was surprised by my manager's response, but it wasn't my call. I went back to the bar, checked the guy's ID (it said he was from Kansas), and poured him a beer. After sliding it in front of him, I did my best to casually ask about his circumstances. "Your ID says you're from Kansas, but you were in New York a couple of days ago?" I definitely wondered why he was now in Tennessee too.

"Yeah," he said. He pulled out a folded program from his pocket and handed it to me. "I was in New York for some training at The World Trade Center." I glanced down at the now unfolded paper in front of me. It was an itinerary stating the days' events for a finance conference at The World Trade Center dated for this week, including the date of September 11. I was shocked to realize he was telling the truth, but did my best to hide it. He continued. "A friend and I were standing outside the building, taking a smoke break," he said. "A minute or so later, the first plane hit the building."

"Oh my god," I said. No wonder I had gotten such a weird vibe about this guy when he had entered the bar. No wonder I had thought he was mentally unstable. He was still reeling from the reality of escaping a horrifying death. "So what are you doing here in Tennessee?" I asked.

"My girlfriend is in graduate school here. I came straight down to see her. She's supposed to meet me here in a few minutes." A few minutes later as I was clocking out, I saw his girlfriend slide up next to him and wrap her arm around his shoulders.

Back in August 2001, a month before the attacks had occurred, I had picked up a server shift at our sister restaurant in the airport. As I greeted a table of two good-looking guys in their thirties, one of the guys said to me, "Nice Docs," referring to my Doc Martens. That guy had blond hair, fair skin, and blue eyes. His friend had brown eyes and thick black hair that complemented his dark complexion.

"Thanks," I said, my guard slightly up. After working as a server and a bartender for a few years, I had gotten used to guys trying to work me. I had the edge on them, though, because I wasn't going to be taken in by two hot guys thinking they were All That.

"Do you recognize him?" the blonde asked me pointing to his friend. *Here we go. Bullshit Central.*

"No, I don't," I said, slightly annoyed that these guys apparently mistook me for a star-fucker. "Do you recognize me?

I'm Vandelyn, your server, and I'm here to take your order."

They were amused and undaunted. I had to admit I was feeling pretty cocky myself. "No, seriously. You don't know who he is?" I shook my head. "Do you ever watch the show, *Mysterious Murder*?" the blonde continued as he pulled out an article from the paper. I glanced at it. It showed a picture of these same two guys sitting in front of me.

I began to look at the two men in a new light. "No," I said. "Actually, I hate Reality TV shows, but that was actually one that sounded interesting to me." That was the truth. I'd despised Reality TV ever since MTV had introduced *The Real World*. And *Mysterious Murder* had appealed to me because I do like murder mysteries.

"Well, we're the two final contestants. I'm Ryan and this is Luis." Once I realized they weren't a couple of bullshit artists, I was charmed, I admit it, and I let down my guard.

"So, you don't know who's won yet?" I asked.

"Actually we do," Luis said, "but we can't say because the final episode hasn't aired yet."

"That's cool. So what are you doing here?" I asked, referring to the happening metropolis of Knoxville, Tennessee.

"I'm from here," Ryan said. "Luis and I got to be good friends after being on the show together and he came down to visit me."

"I live in New York City," Luis added.

"Yeah," Ryan chimed in. "Luis is a New York City Firefighter." I nodded my appreciation and realized that I needed to get on with getting their drink orders.

Turns out Ryan and Luis were actually really likable guys instead of the cocky guys I had presumed them to be. Not only were they befriending me, but their table neighbors as well. As Ryan and Luis headed for their gate, they stopped to speak to a family of four whom they had befriended. As I passed by to deliver drinks to an adjacent table, I heard the jovial father say to Luis, "So, you're a New York City Firefighter?" When Luis confirmed that he was, the man bellowed with genuine admiration and sincerity, "Thank you! Thank you for all that you guys do!"

The final episode of *Mysterious Murder* aired on September 4, 2001. Luis had been the winning contestant. Exactly one week later on September 11, 2001, Luis was one of the thousands who died in

The World Trade Center attacks. Although my heart was heavy at this news, one thing brought me some comfort: the kind words of appreciation spoken by the man sitting with his family, showing his thanks to Luis and civil servants everywhere by saying, "Thank you! Thank you for all that you guys do!"

38

After September 11, I realized how little I actually knew about the Middle East. I remembered when I was a young child that my mom had always wanted to go see Baghdad, Iraq; she spoke of how beautiful it was; or maybe how beautiful it used to be. In the simplistic way that children have for solving problems, I said, "You should go to Baghdad then." She was quick to contradict me by stating it was a time of unrest in the Middle East. That's when she mentioned something that I had also heard in the news: "The Shah of Iran has just gone into exile." I was fascinated, not by the unrest, but by The Shah of Iran going into exile. The whole sentence sounded so intriguing to my young ears.

"The Shah of Iran?" It was such an exotic thing to say. I mean, what was *The Shah of Iran* and (as I would later learn) *The White Revolution*, if not a great band name? After all, *Exile* was the name of a 1970s band. "What's the Shah of Iran? And what does it mean that he is in exile?"

"He was the leader of Iran, but he was ousted. He and his family had to escape Iran for their safety." *Escape from their country for safety?* These were foreign concepts to me since nothing like that ever happened in the United States. At that time my mom happened to be reading a book called, *Monday the Rabbi Took Off*. From that day on, I took the unusual political circumstances of the Middle East and simplified them by forever linking them to that book title: *Monday, the Rabbi Took Off; Tuesday, the Shah of Iran Ran.*

A few weeks after the World Trade Center terrorist attacks occurred, one of my lunchtime regulars, Jeff, sat at the bar to eat his chicken fingers. "So," he said by way of introduction to his subject matter, "do you think the terrorists are going to Hell?"

"No," I said and gave him a puzzled look.

Jeff looked at me as if I had just claimed that Osama Bin

Laden were actually the Messiah instead of Christ. "You don't believe that the terrorists are going to Hell?" he demanded.

"Not really," I said, wondering when I'd been upgraded from bartender to St. Peter's nefarious sidekick who damned others to Hell. "I'm not even sure that there is a Hell." I actually didn't believe there was a Hell with fire and brimstone and a red devil with horns and a pitchfork. I mean, was I really supposed to believe that?

Now Jeff looked at me as if I were one of Beelzebub's little minions. I really wasn't trying to piss him off. I just didn't know anything about Islam. So I told him what I suspected about the matter. "If the hijackers did what their religion, their God, told them to do, why would they go to Hell?"

I didn't actually think there were five different gods vying for our attention in heaven or nirvana or wherever. I just thought it was arrogant of one religion to think its people were going to heaven and all the other major religions' followers were going to Hell. We all believed in the same entity, after all, but we were just playing a religious version of *Who's Your Daddy?* Jesus, God, Brahma, Yahweh, Allah? Apparently Jeff thought I was offensive, idiotic, or possibly both. Although he did tip me, he walked away from his empty plate without another word.

I did become a little more educated on Islam when I met a Palestinian woman at the Dollar General store. We had met each other's eyes and smiled as she and I both examined the plastic wrap. She was an older woman, but I couldn't tell how much older because she was dressed in her traditional garb including a hijab. As I was gathering up my dollar-priced version of cling wrap (I had learned from experience that it worked better than the name-brand wrap), I saw her reach for the designer brand.

"Actually, the generic brand works better. I've tried them both," I told her.

"Really?" she asked, glancing over at me.

"Oh yeah," I said. "*Much better.* And it's only a dollar per roll."

On my recommendation, she replaced the name-brand wrap on the shelf and placed the generic version in her shopping cart. "Thank you," she said. "My daughter likes name-brand things, but I will tell her that this brand works better."

Just then, the aforementioned daughter stepped over to the

cart and placed some items in it. She frowned at the generic roll of cling wrap.

Anticipating her daughter's comment, the Palestinian woman defended her choice. "This woman here says it works better than the other brand."

"It really does," I said as I put my roll in my basket. The daughter accepted my recommendation and then told her mother that she was going to look at the kitchen wares.

Feeling chatty, I smiled at the woman and asked, "So, are you visiting your daughter?"

"Oh no," she said. "She is visiting me from Atlanta." Somehow we started talking about her life history. She told me that she and her husband were married at the age of eighteen, not long after the end of World War II. Apparently, the U.S. government was handing out U.S. citizenships back then and they decided to move to the United States for a new start. My companion did not mention it, but I knew that in 1948 times were changing. Israel had recently been created and the controversial British White Paper of 1939 had been rescinded, finally allowing Holocaust survivors a place of refuge; a refuge that Jews had been denied by many countries, including the United States, when they had tried to escape anti-Semitism in Nazi Germany *before* becoming prisoners and (if fortunate) survivors of concentration camps.

I asked her if she had dual citizenship. She said no, but that she had a visa. She said she had to be very careful when she went back home to visit her family. Visas were only valid for a limited amount of visitation time. If she were to stay until the last day of her visa and then was delayed beyond her permitted time by circumstances beyond her control, such as a delayed flight, her visa would be permanently revoked.

She then spoke of the horrible car bombings that were occurring. Apparently it was being reported that people were packing bombs in their trunks and performing suicide missions after passing through checkpoints.

"No!" she said with dismay. "I know a family whose car exploded after passing through a checkpoint. They were good, kind people who would never harm themselves or others. The checkpoint guards are planting bombs in the trunks without the passengers knowing."

The thought that people entrusted to protect were actually causing harm, if not death, was one of complete evil. No one wants to believe such things occur, but I know they do; *we* know they do. *Everywhere.* Just ask the civil rights workers of the 1964 Mississippi Freedom Summer Project; the activists that weren't murdered by corrupt, racist policemen, that is.

Our discussion then segued into September 11 and Islam. "People claim that what happened occurred because of religion, but that is not so," she said. "No true religion would advocate hurting other people." I nodded in agreement. Then she smiled at me and said, "Jesus was a good, kind man, yes?"

A little startled, I smiled and said, "Yes. Jesus was a good, kind man."

"God is not about hurting others. God is about love." Although I knew nothing about Islam, I knew what she was telling me: Islam was about love, not hate.

"So true," I said as we suddenly yet instinctively reached our arms out towards each other. As we embraced in the cling wrap aisle of the Dollar General store, this kind Palestinian woman kissed me on the cheek. "Love you," I said, startled to hear the words come from my mouth.

"Love you too," she replied. When we released each other and continued on our way, I discovered that I was beaming and my heart was bursting. I knew immediately that *that* was the work of God.

39

Even though The White Revolution and The White Paper of 1939 happened a long time ago, thoughts of them continued to meander through my brain. Although The White Revolution was a bloodless revolution, The White Paper of 1939 was drenched with the blood of those who were killed for no good reason (actually, is there a good reason for killing?). It was Death by government; Death by politics; Maybe better yet, Death by politicians.

Despite my wandering thoughts, my brain felt as if it were turning to mush. I was at the point of wishing that I had brought an algebra or Spanish textbook with me so I could work math problems or relearn Spanish; do *anything* to keep my mind stimulated. As it were, I had just finished dinner and had decided to live on the edge since the end of my sentence was drawing near. I had opted to eat half of the Salisbury steak (definitely poop) that was served with my peas (poop) and applesauce (pee).

Over the course of the afternoon, I had read numerous chapters of my book, saving the last few chapters in case I experienced a desperate outbreak of intolerable boredom. (I was sure I had already figured out who-done-it.) Missy and I had talked a little, but it was hard for me to get to know her too well because our circumstances were so depressing; her situation was also a lot more dire than mine. None of the usual get-to-know-you conversational starters were useful here.

In our first chat, I had learned a lot: she was young, unmarried, had a baby boy, a terrible ex-boyfriend, and an uncertain future regarding her felony arson charge. I could tell her family wasn't wealthy; presumed that she would have a public defender; and felt confident that her case would be plead to the court with the same zeal that a Puritan has for discussing orgasms.

The most tragic of her circumstances was her relationship with her baby boy. She loved that little boy so much. Every time she looked at his picture, her heart broke. Missy wasn't ignorant and foolish like the prisoner who had come in earlier this afternoon. Instead, she had been naive and trusting. She had made a mistake, a terrible mistake, and had to pay for that mistake. I could tell that all she wanted to do was get out of jail and be a good mother to her little boy. If loving and caring for her baby was all she ever did in life, she would be so happy. I said a little prayer for her because that's all that I had the power to do.

In order to think of happier thoughts as well as urge time to pass more rapidly, I closed my eyes and envisioned that I was in my dining room getting ready for my Sunday night dance party. I imagined that I was partaking in my usual activities: pouring myself a glass of wine; loading the CD player; listening and dancing to my line-up of core dance songs. I tried to imagine everything in real time, but that is impossible. My whole fantasy lasted probably no more than a few minutes. I sighed, but revisited it once again. This time I tried to hear every verse of every song that I loved, but of course I could only remember a few lyrics here and there which surprised me. How could I have spent those Sunday nights singing along with every song and now not be able to remember all of the words when I needed them as entertaining diversions?

I kept my eyes closed and did my best to pretend I was somewhere else having a good time. After a while I was pleased to realize that it was finally time for a head count. I sighed when I thought of which prison guard was going to enter the room and remind us that we weren't people, but nameless inmates planted on cots, attaching numbers to our heads because we weren't worth knowing on any more of a human level than that.

I was shocked when the door swung open and a vibrant woman in a prison guard's uniform cheerfully called out to us, "Good evening, ladies!" She addressed us like she really knew us, liked us, and was a friend of ours. My shriveled, hardened rock of a heart began to soften around the edges.

"Good evening, Miz Williams!" the women pleasantly hollered back. I looked around the room, still stunned by this guard's attitude compared to her co-workers' attitudes toward us.

"How are you ladies doing tonight?"

This question received a less uniform response. Some whooped and hollered with happiness, some grumbled, but the grumblings were just honest responses, not grumblings towards Ms. Williams.

Ms. Williams addressed us again, maybe a little inspired by the grumblings. "Ladies!" she shouted out to us enthusiastically. "God loves you! This does not have to be your life! When you step out of these doors here, I hope you know that you can make a change in your lives! You can make a positive difference not only in your lives, but in the lives of others!"

Ms. Williams then began her head count. As she counted, I noticed that my heart was becoming downright soft and squishy. I felt as if someone had given me a great big hug when I needed it most. I wasn't the only one affected. Women had shouted out "Amens" or whooped and hollered in agreement. It was awe-inspiring: Our usually sullen, MYOB-type inmates of Pod C were downright upbeat. I even discovered that I had a smile on my face. I hadn't smiled in days. I glanced over at Missy. She wasn't smiling fully, but her face expressed a little more hope than I had seen in the past twenty-four hours of knowing her.

When Ms. Williams finished her head count, she said, "Good night, ladies!"

"Good night, Miz Williams!" everyone shouted back. I was a little surprised and maybe a little embarrassed to hear my voice amongst the others.

"Remember ladies that you can thrive! You don't just have to *survive!*" More whoops and hollers of hopeful enthusiasm. She left the room and the lights dimmed. I snuggled on my sandbag, got comfy on my flat pillow, wrapped myself in the pathetically thin blanket and felt better than I had in days.

40

The next morning, the fluorescent lights powered on at the crack of dawn once again. Irritated by the brightness at the early hour, I decided that I'd just skip breakfast and keep on resting. The covers were pulled over my head in a futile attempt to block out the light. As I continued to lie on my cot, I could hear my fellow inmates stirring and moving towards the door in order to form a line for breakfast. A little while later, I felt someone shaking me to wake me up. It was Missy.

"Hey," she said in a low voice. "It's time for breakfast."

Since it was so kind of her to think about my needs, I pulled the blanket off of my head and made an effort to rise.

"I didn't want you to miss breakfast," she explained.

I smiled at her. "Thanks," I said. The line was dwindling and most of the inmates had already eaten. I hurried over to the cafeteria line and accepted a plate of bacon (poop) and eggs (poop). I was living on the edge because soon enough I'd have access to a private toilet. I ate a little of the food and drank my carton of milk and reveled in the fact that I had only a couple of hours left. However, I did worry a little that maybe it wasn't of serious concern to the guards to release me on time.

I returned to my cot and opened my book, glad to have a couple of chapters left to occupy my time. Turns out that I was right about who did it which both pleased me and annoyed me. I always enjoyed trying to figure out who did it, but appreciated the author who could trick the reader into thinking that she knew who the murderer was, but in reality the culprit was somebody else.

For the remaining time, I continued to lie on my cot and wait until the guard came in to tell me it was time for me to go. I wasn't sure how much time had passed before that moment occurred, but I was truly elated when a guard entered the room and called out my name. I was also glad to note that the guard came for me at the exact time my sentence had been served.

As I hopped off my cot, a couple of inmates spoke to me. One woman on the row in front of me who had spent most of her time over the weekend reading the Bible asked me for my blank composition book and pen. I was happy to give her them to her. Next, the outspoken girl who got me a mattress asked me for my two mystery books. I was all too pleased to let her have them too. I also added a little stipulation. "Please share them with the other women when you are finished," I said as I extended them towards her.

"I will," she said and we smiled. I walked back to my cot where Missy lay under the blanket. I shook her awake and she peeked out from under the blanket. She knew it was my time to leave. We hugged.

"Take care," I told her.

"You too," she said.

I hurried over to the guard, bringing my pillow and blanket with me. The guard leading me to my freedom was not Ms. Williams from the night before, but just another nameless, faceless body who probably viewed me the same way. I handed over my blanket and pillows and she led me to the room where I could change back into my regular clothes.

I was then led back out into the same waiting area that I had been in on Saturday night. All I had to do to get to freedom was be escorted out the locked door that led to the parking lot. Unfortunately, it wasn't going to be that simple.

I was instructed to wait on a bench because three guards were in the process of transporting another prisoner. The prisoner was a young male, probably twenty years-old, and obviously psychotic. His hands were cuffed; his ankles shackled; and unfortunately he had been ordered to face the wall where I sat while the guards stood near him. When the prisoner and I made eye contact, he smiled the creepiest, I'm-going-to-rape-you-and-rip-your-face-off-with-my-teeth grin I had ever seen. It made the encounter with Mr. Magoo's son in front of the fire house seem endearing. I knew it had to be my imagination, but this guy's teeth seemed to be sharp and pointed and slick with saliva. I looked away, freaked out and irritated that the guards weren't more observant about this guy's intense stare directed at me. All I wanted was to leave this place and here I was stuck in reception with Norman Bates' grandson.

After what seemed to be another eternity, the guards finally loaded up the prisoner into the paddy wagon and I was able to be escorted out into freedom. Thankfully, Tod was already parked in the lot. I was happy to see him, mostly because I was thankful that he was going to drive me away from this place and take me home. A smile fluttered across my face as I remembered that he was also going to take me to get my restricted driver's license.

"Do you want to grab something to eat?" he asked me as I fastened my seatbelt.

"That would be great! But first I want to go home and shower before doing anything else." Tod complied with my request. As he drove his car through the open chain link gates topped with barbed wire, I smiled as I realized that I had survived Silverdale and could now put it behind me. My life wasn't perfect. I still had a long way to go, but life was definitely getting better.

41

orty-eight hours after my pronouncement that my life was getting better, Chattanooga was flooded, my electricity was out, and Tod and I were stuck in my house, bored out of our gourds. (Two good things: I did have my restricted driver's license and SR-22 insurance.) Presently we were in my kitchen with the door standing open in order to let as much natural light into the room through the storm door. I had been sitting on the floor by the door reading a book for entertainment, but Tod had protested because he had nothing to do. I was irritated, but I shut my book.

It was still pouring rain outside. Turns out, it would rain for four days straight, flooding Chattanooga and giving no reprieve. Last week: an earthquake; this week: a flood. What would happen next week? Locusts? "We could play cards," I suggested. I grabbed a deck and we sat down at the kitchen table. We played a few hands of War until we got really competitive and irritated with each other and quit.

"How about we go sit out on the front porch?" I suggested, clearly out of options. I did love sitting on the comfy glider and watching the world go by.

"And do what? Watch the pouring rain?"

Tod was getting on my nerves. "Well, it's not like we can watch a movie or listen to music or anything. At least we'd get some fresh air and not be cooped up inside."

He acquiesced. As we walked through the dining room and living room and headed for the front door, I glanced over at a box pushed off to the side. I had noticed it before, but had just ignored it until now. "What is that?" I asked.

"It's just a box of my stuff that I didn't know where to put," he explained.

"We can stick it in the back bedroom and get it out of the way," I offered as I walked over to it. I bent over to pick it up and realized it was pretty heavy.

"Let me get it," Tod said.

"What's in there?" I asked.

"A mixture of stuff," he answered noncommittally. I peeked in the box and focused on one item I immediately recognized: a school annual.

"What's this from?" I asked as I reached for it. Before he could answer, I saw that it was from his freshman year at Bean Field High School back in the 1980s. "Oh! This is great. Let's go outside and look at it."

Lacking any other interesting thing to do, Tod agreed and we stepped out onto the covered front porch and got comfy on the glider. "I can't wait to see what your hair was like," I laughed. Then something else dawned on me. Taylor would be in this annual too. Bonus! What would *her* hair look like?

I opened to the first page and started flipping through. "Are you in any of these beginning pages?" I asked as I perused.

"I don't remember," he said as he looked over my shoulder at the photo collages. I decided to flip straight to the freshman class and looked for his name. Finding it, I counted the appropriate number of faces over and touched my finger to his photo. He looked like a much younger version of the man he was now. I had to admit that he was cute despite the butt-cut that feathered to each side of his face. He had that sweet little-boy freshman look to him. He looked like the type of guy I would have had a crush on in high school, so why wasn't I crushing on him now? I checked out his team sports pictures and school activities before deciding it was time to check out Taylor.

"So Taylor would have been a senior, right?" I asked as I flipped to the graduating class. All the photos were in black-and-white.

"Yeah," he confirmed. "She's on—"

I could tell that Tod was about to point her out to me so I quickly cut him off. "No, don't tell me. I want to find her myself." First thing I did was quickly scan for her first name because I did not know her maiden name. I was a little puzzled when I was unable to locate her name. Maybe she went by her middle name or something.

"Did she go by her middle name?" I asked Tod. "I'm not finding her."

"She didn't go by *Taylor* back then." Tod gently took the annual from me and flipped to a page. "She's on this page right here." Tod pointed to one side of the annual.

"OK. No more hints." I was ready to find Taylor on my own again. I looked over the young, female faces and then looked over them again. I was so laughing inside because the girl that I thought might be Taylor had really dark brown hair styled in long Farrah Fawcett feathery layers. The photos of girls with blond or light brown hair contrasted with how dark Taylor's hair really was. (Why would a girl with such pretty blond hair dye her roots black, indeed!) Of course, I knew Taylor colored her hair, but I had no idea how in the closet she was about her natural dark brown hair color, *if* I had picked the right girl.

"Is this Taylor?" I asked, pointing to that particular face on the page. Tod leaned over and looked at it.

"Yeah," he said. He was unaware that I felt as if I were profiling a criminal; putting pieces together to figure out who this abrasive woman was and what made her tick.

"Nice dark brown hair," I commented snidely. I counted faces and names to figure out what name Taylor went by in high school. When I read it with my own eyes, I screeched with glee. Tod looked over at me, surprised. "Taylor's real name is *Tammy Dawn Clampett*?!" I squealed. "Tammy? Like the hillbilly girl in the movie, *Tammy and the Bachelor*? And Clampett?! As in *The Beverly Hillbillies*?! *Really*? That's so great!" My laughter was perverse.

I glanced closer at her black-and-white photo and examined her eye color. In some photos I could easily tell that some of the students had blue eyes because I could see the light and dark contrast between the iris and the pupil. Tammy "Taylor" Dawn Clampett's eyes were not so clearly defined. She could have blue eyes or she could have brown eyes and now wear blue contacts. I shook my head. Could she really be that screwed up to wear fake-colored contacts?

Having confirmation that Taylor actually was the insecure fraud who enjoyed putting others down to make herself feel better gave me a sick sense of pleasure. It wasn't nice to make fun of others, but she was such a wench, that I felt she deserved it. I have compassion for others, but as I've mentioned before, I have no compassion for bullies. And she apparently was one of those bullies who hated where she came from, hated what she perceived herself to be: second-best because she grew up in a poor, rural area; second-best because although her birth name actually *was* Hollywood (in the worst way), it sure wasn't glamorous or sophisticated; and apparently she decided she was also second-best because she had dark brown hair instead of the blond hair that she told her daughter was the most desirable color. What a freaking loser! It wasn't a kind thought, but I so wanted her to be exposed for the fake that she was.

Tod must have been clueless that I was totally enjoying deconstructing Taylor's contrived image because he innocently offered up more ammo. "This guy here," he pointed out a face on a following page, "was Taylor's first husband."

I glanced at the guy who was OK looking in a cheesy, early 80s, I-wear-a-gold-chain-over-my-turtleneck, kind-of-way. "Really? What's his name? Jethro?" When I read his first name, I clapped my hands together. "Carl! His name is Carl!" Happy! Happy! Joy! Joy! "Tammy loves Carl!" I mocked. "How long were they married?" I asked.

"I don't know. Maybe four or so years? It was until she met her second husband, Chad."

Wait a minute; wait a minute. Was he saying what I think he was saying? I pinched myself. Could I seriously be dreaming? Had I hit my head during the torrential downpour and flooding much like Dorothy had during the tornado? Was I in my own colorful Land of Oz abloom with psychological ammunition on my personal Wicked Witch of the West?

"Hold on," I said. "Are you telling me that she married Carl —" I glanced at his last name and was amused yet again—"*Gross*? Seriously? The most offensive woman I know once had the last name of *Gross*? How appropriate. And are you telling me that while she was married to Carl she met her second husband? Brittanee's dad?"

Now Tod looked a little uncomfortable. "She was already going to divorce him, I think."

"So she starts dating her second husband while she's still married to her first?" Tod did not confirm nor deny which meant that my inference was correct. "Does that mean that she started

238

dating her third husband while she was still married to the second?" Tod was still quiet. My jaw dropped. "OK. Somehow she convinces a man to marry her then a few years later she cheats on him with the next guy that she ropes into marriage? And *she* goes around calling unmarried single women *whores?*" I was indignant. "She's on her third marriage by the time she's in her early thirties and she goes around calling *other* women whores?!" I could not believe it. I still could not articulate my feelings to my satisfaction, so I tried again. "She goes through marriage licenses and surnames like other women go through toilet paper and *she's* the one who acts morally superior? My fellow inmates in Silverdale have fewer aliases and more integrity than *Mrs.* Tammy 'Taylor' Dawn Clampett Gross—" I glanced over at him. "What's Chad's last name?"

Tod had only just now realized that I was gathering munitions. His expression revealed that he didn't want to be an accomplice to my stockpiling, but he recognized that it was already too late. He was already guilty by association. He squirmed. "Christian."

"Christian?" Now that was a hoot. "Christian? At one point in her life her name ended in *Gross Christian?*" Ain't that the truth. "So let me try this again: Tammy 'Taylor' Dawn Clampett Gross Christian Kazakov? She is totally a serial bride and only forty years-old." I wonder if they give the death penalty for that. I could only hope.

42

June

It was a beautiful Friday morning, almost to the point of inspirational, when Donna and I found ourselves with a little downtime. We were sitting in the reception area, enjoying the sunshine penetrating the large window, when one of Donna's clients, a woman named Caroline, popped in.

"Donna, I am so glad that I caught you!" Caroline beamed. She struck me as the happiest person on Earth. "I have a present for you." The woman extended her hand and held out a wrapped gift that looked like a book.

Donna was surprised, but accepted the gift. "Thanks," she said looking over its shape and size.

"Go ahead and open it!"

Donna did as was told (it was a book) and then read the title out loud, "*The Purpose Driven Life.*" I had not heard of the book before and I could tell that Donna hadn't either.

"It's an awesome book!" Caroline gushed. "It changed my life! I just wanted to share it with you too!"

"Well, thanks, Caroline. I'll look it over."

Caroline continued beaming and called out good-by as she hurried out the door. I stood up and went over to sit by Donna as she flipped to the first page, was quiet for a moment, and then became irked. "This book says it's not all about me." I peered over her shoulder to read the first sentence when Donna announced, "The hell it's not!" and slammed the book shut. She tossed it off to the side and said, "No way am I reading this book," and went on to complain about people bringing unsolicited religious texts into her life.

Although I feared self-proclaimed Christians the way others

fear the boogeyman, I noticed that Caroline hadn't dropped the C-word ("Christian") at all. Besides, I didn't think the first sentence was so bad. I mean, if it were all about me, what an incredibly screwed-up world we would be living in. The tip of my iceberg of life involves a small penis, HPV, multiple dysfunctional relationships, a lot of alcohol, and jail time. If that doesn't support the argument that there has to be a Higher Being, I don't know what does.

Since Donna was now in a rotten mood, I returned to my original seat and picked up the paper. As I flipped through the pages, I came across an article about an outbreak of Hepatitis A amongst the male inmate population of Silverdale. I sat up straighter as I read the reported account. According to the story, the Warden said he was taking control of the situation by not allowing inmates to share soap (there's a bad joke hidden in there somewhere) or other toiletries while incarcerated. I was indignant and made a squawk of disbelief. Donna came out of her funk enough ask, "What?"

"This article!" I yelped. My pulse was racing and my blood pressure was rising at the injustice of it. "There's an outbreak of Hepatitis A in Silverdale and the Warden says it's because of inmates sharing toiletries. So he's not going to allow inmates to share toiletries anymore!"

Donna was listening and waiting for me to make the connection of why this was important and so infuriating to me.

"When I was in Silverdale, I was not given toilet paper. I was not given soap. They didn't even supply paper towels for crying out loud! And now there is an outbreak of disease and inmates without toiletries are not allowed to use other inmates' soap. Disease does not come from cleanliness. Disease comes from a *lack of* cleanliness!" I tossed the paper aside and continued in a quieter voice. "People are using the restroom in a communal area and are not able to properly cleanse their hands." Donna was repulsed.

I wasn't sure how Hepatitis A was transmitted, but if the Warden thought it was transmitted through toiletries, I thought it was transmitted through the lack of toiletries. I was frustrated and angry, wondering what I could do about the situation. Then it dawned on me. "I'm going to go call this reporter and tell him what the real deal is." Don't all journalists idolize Woodward and Bernstein? Don't they have a thirst for The Truth and a desire to unearth The Real Story? This guy was going to be eager to expose Silverdale's dirty little secret and bring some justice, I just knew it.

Donna uttered some words of encouragement as I grabbed the paper and went to the back to make my phone call. After getting the phone number from the front page, I called and asked to speak to the reporter who wrote the article. When he picked up the line, he spoke with such apathy I thought I might be speaking to a sloth instead the zealous journalist I was hoping for.

"Hi," I began with enough energy for the both of us. "I am calling about the article you wrote about the Hepatitis A outbreak."

"Yes?" he asked, his voice emulating the same amount excitement I felt while watching C-SPAN.

"Well, what the Warden said about no longer sharing toiletries, it's not going to solve the problem. It's going to make it worse," I explained as if I were a representative from the Centers for Disease Control. "I was incarcerated in Silverdale and there was no soap, no toilet paper, and no paper towels! Disease does not come from cleanliness; it does not come from sharing soap. Disease comes from a *lack* of cleanliness! And there is a lack of cleanliness when inmates cannot properly wash their hands after using the restroom or before eating a meal," I pointed out. Although I was sure that my admission that I had once been an inmate in Silverdale would diminish my credibility in most social circles, I was less concerned when it came to a reporter. Weren't reporters more open to the insights of those outside society's parameters?

"What about the inmates?" he asked with a little more interest. "Are they dirty? Is there a lot of garbage strewn around?" Was this guy deaf? The problem wasn't with the inmates; it was with those in power denying inmates access to basic necessities.

"No!" I said. "The inmates are very clean! In fact, one of the inmates was kind enough to let me use some of her toiletries since I did not have any." No need to explain my toilet paper conundrum. "Inmates removed garbage from the pod every night and cleaned the sinks, toilets, and showers daily too."

"Mmm," he mumbled, with renewed disinterest. "OK. Thanks for calling." Then he hung up. I stared at the phone then returned it to its cradle. So much for my quest for justice.

43

Later that night, Tod and I opted for a low-key evening and decided to rent a movie. I had mixed emotions about movies. As a female and former English major, I was so sick and tired of the same old movie plots and characters. The female characters were especially aggravating to me. The blockbuster movies had women of two types: good-girls-next-door vs. hot-fuckable-bad-girls. It was such bullshit. I had beautiful, kind, smart, sexy, smart ass, cool female friends and I never saw a one of them represented in main-stream movies. So when Tod and I were choosing movies, we had a rule: it had to be off-the-wall in some sort of way. A few weeks ago, I'd chosen *Keys to Tulsa;* then Tod had chosen *Trees Lounge*; and now it was my turn again. As Tod and I wandered down the aisles, I knew what I was looking for: *Kissing Jessica Stein*. I smiled when I found it and removed the DVD case from the shelf.

"*Kissing Jessica Stein?*" he asked. I glanced over at him because he sounded nervous about it.

"Yes," I said. "I've wanted to see this movie for a while now."

"Why?" he asked. I noticed he was fidgeting with the hem of his shirt. Good Lord. Bring on the homophobia. He was the one guy in America who wasn't into potential girl-on-girl action. (Then again, maybe it was because this movie was smartly written from the female perspective instead of being from the bring-on-the-orgy male perspective.)

I sighed. "Because it's a different perspective on life. I think the main actress in it is funny and the plot sounds interesting to me."

"Isn't it about lesbianism?" He was definitely nervous now.

"It's about a girl who gets tired of dating guys and decides to try dating girls and see how that goes," I explained. I knew that this

243

explanation was not really putting Tod at ease. A few days ago, he had received an out-of-the-blue phone call from one of his close guy friends, Vick. After catching up for a few minutes, Vick revealed the reason for his call. I hadn't heard the announcement myself, but had watched Tod's face go from tan to pasty white. I had thought someone had died. When Tod finally got off the phone after an awkward and stilted conversation on his end, I had been curious and a little worried about what had happened.

"What's going on?" I had asked.

"That was a friend of mine from Canada. A guy named Vick. We've been good friends since we were kids." He paused and I waited a little nervously to hear the traumatizing news that Vick had imparted. Was he dying? Did he have cancer? What? "He just wanted to let me know that he was gay."

When I heard the "devastating" news, a breath and a little laugh of relief escaped from my lips. "Oh. Is that all? Thank goodness. By your reaction, I thought he might be dying." When Tod didn't look at me, I thought that he might have rather heard that his friend had cancer than learned that Vick was gay. That really bothered me. "I'm confused," I said. "You're still going to be friends with Vick, right? You're not *not* going to be his friend because he's gay, right?" Although I was doing my best to steer Tod in the right direction, I've learned that you can lead a homophobe to a gay bar, but you can't make him drink.

"I don't know," he mumbled.

I gasped. I guess I wasn't very sympathetic to Tod's perspective. Maybe that wasn't fair of me. It's just that if Marais or Jarrett or Toronto Jen called me up and said, "I'm gay." I'd say, "OK. Cool. Tell me about her."

Tod still didn't look at me, but waved his hands in the air as if trying to swat down my judgment of him. "This is hard for me!" His face was contorted with emotion. "I'll probably get over it, but it's just that Vick and I used to chase girls together. He was such a ladies man; he got action all the time. I am just having a hard time reconciling the guy I knew with the guy who now says he's gay."

Although I still thought that being gay was no big deal, I realized that maybe I was being too hard on Tod. After all, I knew nothing about what it felt like to be him in this situation. So I kept my mouth shut. However, my judgmental feelings towards the situation still lingered in the back of my brain.

I should have picked a different movie. Tod was extremely uncomfortable with characters making conscious decisions to change their sexuality from hetero to homo, especially when one of the characters, Helen, reminded Tod of a female version of Vick: Helen was very attractive, had no problem picking up the opposite sex, and by the end of the movie was gay.

Tod and I watched the movie in uncomfortable silence. I knew he was ill at ease and he sensed my unspoken condescending judgment towards him. The wine we had been drinking had not helped to alleviate the tension either. It only exacerbated it. After the movie ended and I ejected the disk, Tod sat in silence, as if in deep thought.

I sighed. "Are you thinking about Vick?"

"No, I was thinking about your HPV. What's the deal with it again?"

Apparently he was interested in tossing some condescending judgment my way too. I narrowed my eyes as I snapped the DVD case shut. "I told you. HPV is what causes precancerous cells and cervical cancer."

"It *is* an STD, though." I hated that he pointed that little tidbit out because those were the three initials that nobody wanted associated with them, including me.

"Technically, yes!" I snapped. When I said "Technically," what I meant was that I had no symptoms. It wasn't like Tu-Tu was foaming at the mouth or anything.

"HPV means you have warts."

"What? I don't have warts! Where'd you get that information?"

"From that pamphlet you got from the doctor." I furrowed my brows. I had brought back a pamphlet that they had given me and stuffed it on a shelf on my bedroom. I stomped to the bedroom and found the pamphlet. I had never bothered to read it because I knew all I wanted to know about HPV or so I thought. As I read the information, I saw that some HPV viruses caused warts while others caused cervical cancer. I was relieved to learn that I had the high-risk type that could possibly kill me with cancer rather than the low-risk type that would grow warts. Warts were nasty; death by cancer was respectable. I quickly realized that my screwed-up thought process about this subject was not unlike Tod's homophobic logic regarding Vick. That gave me pause. But I quickly shifted gears and went on the offensive.

"I don't have the wart kind!" I told him waving the pamphlet in the air. "Not to mention that men can be carriers. I told you about this a while ago and told you to get tested for it too. You could have HPV just as easily as I do and you could keep spreading it to others! I've had three surgeries to eliminate the abnormal cells. The least you could do is go and get checked out too."

"I did go to the doctor to get it checked out. He said they would stick a closed-umbrella type device into my penis. Once it was inserted, they would open it up and scrape the inside of my penis. He said it would hurt."

"The doctor said it would hurt and that's why you didn't get tested?" Guys were such pussies. In fact, people need to stop using the word "pussy" and start calling wimps "penises" instead. "What kind of doctor discourages a patient from getting tested for an STD because it might hurt?" Although Tod had no response, I had learned a valuable piece of information. Next time I ordered a fruity drink, I was keeping the little cocktail umbrella.

As much as I wanted to keep fighting with Tod, I knew that I needed to go to bed because I had to be at work in the morning. We brushed our teeth and got ready for bed in silence. I wore pajama pants and a long-sleeve top to bed and curled up into a fetal ball. I was relieved when we both chose to turn our backs to each other because the thought of any romantic involvement between us made my skin crawl. That might not have been a symptom of an STD, but it was indicative of a greater problem between us.

44

The next night Tod and I went out to Tundra. We ignored the fight from the night before and pretended that we didn't find each other to be aggravating. I had hoped to sit out on the patio since I enjoyed warm, summer evenings, but by the time we arrived, the outdoor patio was already packed. So we went inside and grabbed a table for two near the jukebox.

"You want a Wild Turkey and Sprite?" Tod asked as he headed up to the bar.

I started to agree and then thought better of it. "No. Actually I'd like a Mai Tai." Tod was surprised by my request but came back with my fruity drink and his beer. I removed the cocktail umbrella, held it in front of my face, and enjoyed sliding it open and shut. Tod and I barely spoke. I sighed and placed the cocktail umbrella on the table. Sometimes he seemed like such a dolt. I mean, was there nothing of interest that he could bring to the table as stimulating conversation?

Apparently not. After a couple more drinks, I introduced some traditional ice breakers to get any type of conversation started that might develop into something interesting. They quickly dead-ended. Then I decided to tell Tod about a place I often fantasized about being able to travel: the Greek Islands (any of them). In order to encourage Tod to fantasize about some really cool or exotic place he'd like to visit, I waxed poetic about the sparkling blue seas, the white-washed buildings, the unique architecture, the sun-drenched beaches, and a country steeped in history. I thought for sure Tod would come up with some equally detailed response. "So where would you like to go?" I asked, eager for any verbal discourse.

Tod just shrugged and said, "I don't know. The Greek Islands sound pretty good."

Rather than bang my head against the table, I slurped the remainder of my drink through my skinny little straw. I slurped even harder when Tod's cell phone vibrated on the table. Oh Lord. Here comes the Calvary. Tod's Calvary. Not mine. In fact, somehow I had managed not to be around Taylor since she had egged my car. That issue was still unresolved as far as I was concerned. If she were to come out tonight, I wasn't sure exactly how I was going to handle the situation.

Just then a song began to play from the juke box. It was Blondie's, *The Tide is High*. I glanced over at the juke box and saw a couple of girls standing by it, equally as thrilled as I was to hear the song. I loved Blondie and this particular song brought back joyous memories of me being in fourth-grade. It also reminded me of hanging out with Toronto Jen. One bar we had frequented would play Blondie upon request and we requested it often, our favorite song, *One Way or Another*. When I saw the girls dancing together, I, slightly inebriated, hurried over to join them.

"I love Blondie! Did y'all play this?" I asked. They nodded their heads in confirmation as they sang and we started serenading each other with the lyrics. A thought quickly occurred to me and I told the girls I'd be right back. I hurried over to the table, grabbed the three cocktail umbrellas, and returned to the two girls.

"Here," I said. I handed each girl an umbrella and we each put one behind our ear as we sang. When the song finished, the girls and I hugged quickly and laughed because, yes, we were a bit drunk. But it had been fun for me to act a little silly with some girlfriends, even if they were only filler girlfriends. Even though I did communicate often enough with Marais, Jarrett, and Toronto Jen, I really missed my best girlfriends so much!

When I returned to the table, I was disappointed to see Taylor sitting in my chair, talking animatedly to Tod. When Taylor observed my presence, she looked up at me with a smile and said, "Hi, Vandelyn. How are you?"

Was she joking? Only a true fraud can look up at someone she hates and smile and pretend to be her friend. I was no fraud.

"Don't 'hi' me," I said. "Don't act like you're my friend after you egged my car."

Taylor snorted and rolled her eyes. "I didn't egg your car."

I once knew a girl who strongly suspected her boyfriend was

cheating on her. She needed to hear him admit to the deed so she asked him point-blank, "Did you sleep with her?" He looked her in the eye and said, "No." She repeated the same question to him over the next few days. His answer was still the same: "No." Then a week or so later, it dawned on her. "Did you do it in the car with her?" she asked. "Yes," he answered. If Taylor thought she could play me with semantics, she'd have to think again.

"OK, then. Your friend Gina egged my car while you drove."

"Whatever, Vandelyn." Bingo! "Wasn't that like *months* ago or something? Get over it."

"I really like it when someone goes out of her way to cause me harm and then tells me to 'Get over it,'" I said.

Taylor stood up. "You are so psycho!" Ah yes. Let's start with Phase II of cheap tricks used to discredit women. If you can't get the "whore" label to stick, start up with the "psycho" label. It seemed like a good tactic so I went with it too.

"You don't have much self-awareness, do you? Psychos usually don't, do they, *Tammy 'Taylor' Dawn Clampett Gross Christian Kazakov?*"

Taylor leaned into my face, glowering at me as if daring me to speak again. I dared. "Actually, is *Tammy 'Taylor' Dawn Clampett Gross Christian Kazakov* just *your* name? Or is it a combination of your multiple personalities? Or should I quit mocking you and try to hone on the actual truth? You were raised in a small town with small town values. You grew up poor and hated it. Maybe your dad was a failure or your mom drank too much and you hated that too." Jeez! Who the hell did I think I was? Hannibal Lecter in *Silence of the Lambs*?! "So you decided that you were never going to be poor ever again. So you got a good job and probably stepped on people to get to the top. You do realize that it's not considered shattering the glass ceiling if you sucked dick while climbing the corporate ladder, right?" Holy shit! Why was I being so mean?! And why couldn't I stop?! "The really sad part is that you still couldn't shake your small town's values that to be successful as a woman, you had to be married. And apparently while you might be good at sucking dick, you are pretty inept at being married. In sum, I just wanted to let you know that you are an inspiration to women everywhere." My voice was dripping with sarcasm with the last statement.

To realize that I was still standing at the end of my diatribe was shocking. Certainly Taylor would have punched me already. What I hadn't focused on was the fact that while I was going "psycho" on her, she had been going "psycho" on me, cursing me up and down and calling me names as well. We probably hadn't heard a single insult that the other had said since we had been much too self-absorbed in our counter-attacks. What I did begin to notice was that a bouncer was standing next to me, trying to intervene.

"Ladies, you are causing a disruption. You need to leave."

Taylor slung a few more insults before the bouncer started to man-handle us. He grabbed us by each of our biceps and led us to the door. Tod scrambled behind me with my purse. One of Taylor's friends came to her aid as well. When we got outside, Tod and I went one way, Taylor and her friend another. When we arrived at Tod's car, he finally spoke. He was so upset that his voice was shaking.

"I knew you were a lesbian!" he blurted out.

"What?" I asked.

"You and those two girls over by the juke box!" he explained. I just stared at him, dumbfounded. "See?" he said again as if it were all clear. "I knew you were a lesbian!"

Now the dolt comes up with a provocative ice breaker. Go figure.

45

"**Y**ou are such a moron," I told Tod as we started the drive back to my house.

"I am not a moron!"

"Yes, you are. You just witnessed me and Taylor getting into a verbal fight and then getting thrown out of a bar and the event that sticks out to you is me singing *The Tide is High* with a couple of girls I don't even know? You could see everything that we were doing. We were just girls having fun, not girls getting it on. Why is this so hard for you to recognize?"

Then something dawned on me. Was it possible that Tod was now insecure about his own sexuality? Was he seeing homosexuality at every turn because he was beginning to question his own sexuality in light of Vick's revelation and Tod's dysfunctional relationship with me?

I was sitting in the passenger seat, shrouded in dark thoughts about the night's events. Some people think that cutting down your enemy to her face is the greatest accomplishment ever. It's not. Even if Taylor had not heard a word I'd said, I was still ashamed. Don't get me wrong, I was still really pissed off, but I couldn't ignore the shame I was feeling. Thank God I was no face-eating Hannibal Lecter, but let's face it (*pun!*), he did have one thing that I didn't have: an actual knowledge of psychiatry. I had been guessing, or more accurately, making shit up about Taylor and her family and her reasons for being who she was. I called her father a failure and her mom a drunk. How incredibly mean (not to mention, ridiculous) was that?

I knew how much it hurt to have people make fun of me and my family. It had caused me deep-seated pain and anguish; so deep in fact that I was still struggling with those issues at age thirty. And yet I had just done the exact same thing to Taylor. If I had learned anything from my sessions with the psychologist it was, *Hurting people hurt people.* A whole bar had just witnessed two women who were

251

hurting, hurting each other. Yes, I know it conjures up a memory of a 1970s Carpenters' song, but here's the deal, it's true.

Even worse, I was appalled to discover that I was no different than male chauvinist pigs acting like the only way a woman gets ahead is by giving head. What the hell was I doing?! I had ragged on the panel at *The Voices* for acting like only certain women count and certain women don't. Here I was guilty of the same thing: degrading a certain woman and acting like she was only successful for one very derogatory reason; an alleged reason of which I had no actual knowledge. Why was there such divisiveness between some women? What exactly threatened us about each other?

By the time we had pulled into the driveway, I was more irritated than ever. I slammed the car door, hurried up to the side porch, and unlocked the kitchen door. I let the storm door slam shut before Tod could get to it.

"Thanks," he grumbled, jerking the door open. "You didn't have to let it slam shut on me!"

"Hey. You called me a lesbian. Did you expect me to politely hold the door open for you?" I said as I stomped into the bedroom to throw my purse on the floor and kick off my strappy heels.

"Well, you act like a lesbian!"

"How exactly am I acting like a lesbian?" I asked as I returned to the kitchen where Tod was standing.

"You and I haven't had sex in a really long time."

If my repulsion to your spindly fingers and spider monkey penis makes me a lesbian, so be it, was what I wanted to say, but I held my tongue. "Yeah, we haven't and it's got nothing to do with me being attracted to girls." Although at this point in time, I'd rather hook up with a girl than hook up with Tod.

"Then what's it got to do with?" asked Tod.

Did he really have to ask? Did I really have to explain it to him? Was he that obtuse? "Are you that clueless?" I snapped. "Are you really that dumb?"

His face twitched in a way that let me know it might crumble. "You call me stupid all the time." His voice wavered. I was alarmed. "I really try to think about things before I say them; I really try not to say stupid things—" his voice broke. My heart broke. What kind of monster was I?

"You're not dumb!" I told him, reaching out to gently touch

his arm.

"I really try to do things that will make you like me more."

This conversation was horrible. "Tod, that's what our problem is. We shouldn't have to do things to *make* this relationship work. Our relationship *doesn't* work. It hasn't worked in a long time." Had it ever worked at all? "That's the problem. We're not happy. I'm not happy. You should never be with someone who makes you feel like you're dumb. I'm so sorry that I ever made you feel like that." I was truly sorry. It's terrible to realize that you've been destructive to someone else. At least, it was terrible to me. I was tossing out all my unhappiness onto him instead of doing what I should have done a long time ago: broken up with him.

"Are we breaking up?"

"Yes, Tod. We have to. Don't you see? You deserve to be with someone who treats you well." And I deserve to be with someone who gets me.

I guess I hit a nerve because Tod's demeanor changed from sad to arrogant and angry. "Well," he said. "If you hadn't slept with me so quickly, I would've dumped you a long time ago."

I just stared at him. It was such a cheap shot, tossing out the "whore" card like it was the wild card in a game of poker. When I didn't respond, he gave a mean laugh and added, "Well, it's true. I was just looking to get laid and you were there."

"I spoke too soon, Tod. You actually are an idiot. Get out of my house."

"No," he said and he made a move around me as if to get ready for bed. I followed him to the bedroom.

"I told you to get out of my house."

"No," he said. "I don't have any place to go tonight. I'll leave tomorrow."

"Hell, no!" I shouted. "You'll leave tonight." We were both standing by the bed. He looked a lot calmer that I felt. He also looked smug. "Get out," I repeated.

"No. I'll leave in the morning." He stood in the center of my bedroom, arrogant in the thought that he was going to win because he was a guy and I was a girl. I lunged for him and tackled him onto the bed. I had the advantage because my knees were on his chest, my hands around his upper arms. Although we were wrestling, WWF style, I did draw the line at slamming a folding chair over his head.

While Tod and I were grunting as we wrestled each other (I'm pleased to announce that it was a pretty even match), I thought about how much I wanted him out of my house and out of my life. The balance of power started to shift to Tod's favor. In between his grunting he giggled like this was all a big joke. That made me growl even deeper as I wrestled him back down onto the comforter. Advantage, me.

"I hate you," I snarled. *I want you out of my life now and forever,* is what I added to myself. I really did hate him right now. All I wanted was for him to go; for my life to be completely my own once again, yet, for some reason, this asshole was fighting me for it. I tried to figure out a way to throw him onto the floor. Or better yet, haul his ass out of my house. Unfortunately it wasn't possible because we were basically the yin and yang of wrestling. Neither of us won; our power struggle was completely balanced. What broke us apart was exhaustion.

"You need to leave. Now," I told him as I panted. "Go sleep at Ted's house. It's renovated and devoid of virgins and other company. Ted won't mind." Tod stood up, grabbed his keys, and started for the kitchen door. "Hold up!" I yelled after him. I quickly followed him into the kitchen. He wasn't slowing down. "Leave the keys you have to my house behind."

"No!" he yelled. "Not until I come back and get all my stuff." He yanked the door open, pushed open the storm door, and let it slam shut behind him. I didn't argue because I knew it would be futile and I just wanted him out of my house. I also knew that the only keys he had were to the storm door since I rarely locked the wooden door when I went out. At night, though, I locked both doors and knew that Tod wouldn't be able to reenter my house, keys or no keys. The front door was secure too because it was so old that it required a skeleton key. He wasn't coming in that way either.

I leaned back against the wooden kitchen door after locking its deadbolt and sighed. I was so glad to be broken up with him. I wasn't completely free, though. He still had to return to get his belongings, but I could help expedite that process. I collected all his clothes and put them in a garbage bag. I pushed the few boxes of his belongings by the kitchen table. Then I grabbed the hamper and threw our dirty clothes in the washing machine. I was all too happy

254

to wash his clothes if it meant him getting out of my house quicker. When he came by tomorrow, there would be no dilly-dallying, no searching for stuff and delaying his tenure at my house. This time tomorrow, I would be free.

I had a ritual when a relationship ended. I would play music that reflected my mood. With Thibodeaux, I mostly played Dido's, *White Flag*, and Alicia Keys', *Fallin'*. After our final demise last year, though, I had listened to Porno for Pyros', *Kimberly Austin*, because the next person I dated, I wanted him to think of me like that. Maybe Tod had thought of me like that. What I hadn't remembered to consider was what type of man *I* wanted and needed my next boyfriend to be.

For this ended relationship, though, I knew exactly what song would be apropos: The Jesus & Mary Chain's, *Nine Million Rainy Days*. I went over to my CDs and found a mixed CD that Toronto Jen had made for me that had the song on it. I pulled it out of its case and inserted it into the CD player. Once the song began to play, I sat down on the sofa in the living room and pulled my legs into my chest. Mack surfaced from wherever he had been hiding and joined me on the sofa. Although I realized that Tod could just as easily play this song about me, I still couldn't help directing the lyrics towards him and agreeing that all my time in hell was spent with him.

46

I n my mind, I had fantasized about Tod coming over late Sunday morning, calmly retrieving his belongings, and then leaving my life once and for all. I even kidded myself into thinking that he and I might part on friendly terms. Unfortunately for me, none of that happened.

When I hadn't heard from Tod by noon, I gave him a call. "Hi, Tod. It's Vandelyn. I need you to come by and pick up your stuff. Call me when you get this message." It was a beautiful, bright sunny day and I had intended on enjoying the summer afternoon with my newfound freedom. Now my quasi-psychotic ex-boyfriend was throwing a wrench in my plans.

When I did not hear from Tod in an hour (as you are aware, Tod is always in touch with his friends via cell phone), I knew he was deliberately screening and ignoring my calls. I called him again and left another message.

After another hour had passed without hearing a response from Tod, I picked up the phone and left a rather impatient third message. "If you don't come now and get your things, I will throw them in the garbage can. Pick-up is first thing tomorrow morning."

My phone rang about fifteen minutes later. "Don't you throw away my belongings!" he spat into the phone. "I am on my way. Can't you give me a reasonable amount of time to get to your house and get my stuff?" He was acting as if I were the unreasonable one.

"I've called you multiple times and you've refused to answer your phone or call me back. I know you've received my phone calls; you're always with your phone."

"I was out playing golf with Bruce!"

You were out playing golf with Bruce?! Was I supposed to feel compassion for this? He was out enjoying his Sunday while I was sitting at my house with his boxes of crap waiting for him to get the hell out of my life? I wasn't sure who I was madder at, me or him. "Well, you should have thought of what's more important to you, your belongings or your golf game, before you played a round with Bruce. Or you could have called to tell me what time you were planning on coming by because there are things that I want to do today too!" With that, I hung up the phone.

Although Tod had assured me that he was on his way, he didn't actually show up at my house until an hour later. I was really irritated and relieved at the same time. I just kept reminding myself that soon enough, he would be gone. I stepped out onto the kitchen porch and saw that Ted had brought him over in his small SUV.

Tod and I barely spoke. "Where's my stuff?" he growled.

"It's right there!" I snapped, pointing at the collection on my kitchen floor. He stepped by me and stared at the large black garbage bag.

"What's in the garbage bag?" he asked.

"Your clothes!"

He turned to me, apparently just wanting to pick a fight. "You put my clothes in a garbage bag?"

"Yes. What did you expect me to put them in? And by-the-way, you're welcome! Everything you left over here is clean and in that bag."

"You could have folded it and put it in that luggage that I gave you for Christmas."

"What? I'm not your fucking valet! I did more than I should have done for you as it is. But if you want your luggage back, I'll gladly give it to you. Just start taking your crap out to Ted's car and I'll get it for you!"

I did not want Tod anywhere in my house except the kitchen. And I actually didn't even want him in that room either. Tod grabbed the plastic trash bag filled with clothes and carried it out onto the porch. I turned and went to one of the back bedrooms to grab the luggage. When I returned to the kitchen, Ted was picking up a box off the kitchen floor as Tod was headed back for another load. I waited for Ted to leave, then I waited for Tod to grab another box, and then I followed them out with the luggage.

I stood on the patio by the driveway holding the luggage while Ted put a box in the tailgate area and Tod put a box in the backseat. When they both stepped away from their loading areas and turned towards me, for some reason, Ted's hands reached out gingerly towards Tod while Tod's hands were reaching out towards the luggage I was holding. As I watched their bodies as if they were moving in slow motion, I saw the craziest thing happen. Ted's hand touched Tod's and it was as if an electric current zapped the air. Even though nothing tangible happened, I could still perceive the current. We all could. Ted was at ease with the unseen *zing!* I had witnessed, but Tod looked startled and a bit flustered. He quickly moved his hands towards the luggage, taking it from me while Ted remained facing Tod. Ted's gaze lingered on Tod's face. Tod threw the luggage in the back seat and hurried back up to the house. I followed him, intrigued by what I had just witnessed.

Although Tod had looked completely ill at ease, I was wondering about the interaction. I had never thought that Tod was gay, but I suspected that Ted was. I was sure now that Ted was gay, but wondered about Tod. Was Tod closeted too? Was that why he was so freaked out about Vick? Or was Tod's heterosexual personal life just a lot more dysfunctional than even mine?

When Tod picked up the last of his belongings, I was so glad that I was practically chipper. I felt like saying nice things to Tod and wishing him well even, just as long as he got the hell out of my house. "So that's everything," I commented.

"Let me just look around and double check," he grumbled. But apparently he wanted to double check after running the last load out to Ted's SUV. I waited for him to return inside. When he did, I followed him around as he looked for any remaining belongings of his. Finding none, we returned to the kitchen. His eyes lingered on the refrigerator.

"Food," he said. "I want to take the food that I bought."

I tossed him a grocery bag and said, "Knock yourself out!" I hoped he hadn't bought the last round of batteries for the remote control because he'd probably want those too. He grabbed some meat out of the freezer and peeked in the fridge. Apparently realizing there wasn't much for him to retrieve, he slammed the door shut and turned towards the kitchen door.

"My keys," I reminded him. He put the bag of meat on the counter, slid the keys off of his chain, and slapped them in my palm. "Did you make extra copies?" I asked.

He glared at me. "No." And then he stomped out the storm door, letting it slam shut behind him. I looked at the keys in my hand. I asked him about a duplicate set because I wanted to see what he would say; see if he would lie about it. I didn't think he was lying about it, but you can never be too sure. I knew that I would have to get a locksmith out tomorrow to change the lock. I also needed to figure out how to change the alarm code.

I remained behind the storm door as I watched Ted and Tod finally back out and drive away. When the SUV was out of sight, I shut the kitchen door, headed over to the CD player, scrolled to a different song on Toronto Jen's mixed CD, and hit play. As Primal Scream's, *Movin' on Up*, filtered through the speakers, I felt uplifted as I changed into shorts, a T-shirt, and my running shoes. I had an epiphany that moment: being alone isn't lonely. But being with the wrong person is the loneliest, most depressing feeling in the world.

As the song ended, I felt as if I were shedding scales. I was a new woman. I could do anything I wanted; the world was open to all possibilities for me and my life. Although I had dug a hole for myself, I could see my way out. If I had gotten to this point by making left turns, all I had to do now was make right turns. And if I kept on making right turns, right decisions, I would be completely out of darkness and into the light.

I grabbed my music, ran outside, crossed Dayton Boulevard and started to jog. I would have loved to drive downtown and walk along the Greenway by the Tennessee River, but my restricted license precluded me from doing so. Since I never wanted to go back to jail again, I thought I shouldn't push my luck by violating the terms of my restricted license, the license I was all too grateful for. Instead, I was going to let the beauty of the town of Red Bank, churches and all, embrace me and engulf me as I walked and ran. For the first time in my life, I was excited to be a woman without a boyfriend or a love interest in sight. Life wasn't just good, it was great.

47

July

Today was the Fourth of July. It was a Friday and Kitty was open for business as usual. Kitty was busy, but the rest of us were slow, as we should have been on Independence Day. However, Kitty's regular clientele were a different breed from the younger generation: they had standing appointments for roller sets. Come hell, high water, or Fourth of July, Kitty's clients were getting their hair done, especially before the weekend hit. I personally disagreed. The Fourth of July is made for lake parties and cookouts, not roller sets and backcombing.

So Donna and I were planning on celebrating The Fourth on the fifth. Donna had invited me over for a cookout with her, Tony, Derrick, and her sister-in-law's family tomorrow afternoon after we got off work. Since tomorrow was Saturday, we'd get off work at four and meet over at her house around five. I was really looking forward to it, especially since my social life had come to a halt after Tod and I broke up. Honestly, though, I didn't really miss it since hanging out with Tod and his friends brought me misery more than anything else.

Sometimes Donna and I would go out for a beer after work (if she were driving), but that was the extent of it. It was just as well because now that I had monthly court costs to repay, only thirty dollars per week remained from my paycheck to purchase gas, groceries, and entertainment. It's a shame that Sav-A-Lot, Fred's, and Big Lots don't sell gas or beer.

Although I had never regretted my decision to leave law school, my middle-class poverty forced me to question my decision. Should I have become a lawyer just to make more money? When I thought of the asshole I could have become, I shook my head. Neil

Armstrong once said, "One small step for man, one giant leap for mankind." He was speaking about moon travel, but I thought it could've easily applied to my decision not to get a J.D.

When I got home from work, I made some bean burritos and curled up on the couch. While having to work on The Fourth was a bit of a downer, I was also bummed out because when I parked at the Choo-Choo this morning, I discovered that the Nick's Liquors sign was gone; dismantled when I least expected it. I had always promised myself, "Tomorrow," when it came to photographing the sign. Now tomorrow was much too late.

My mood improved, though, when I turned to PBS and discovered a Fourth of July special starring John Schneider and Tom Wopat (otherwise known as Bo and Luke Duke). Who knew that they could also sing and dance? I hadn't known what had happened to Bo and Luke after *The Dukes of Hazzard* had ended, but I was pleased to note that if they were starring on a PBS Fourth of July special, they had to be doing just fine.

I continued watching PBS until the sky started to darken and I heard the sound of fireworks. I grabbed a blanket and headed out the front door, spreading the blanket over the grass. After I got comfortable on the soft fabric, I watched the homegrown fireworks display. To my delight, it seemed every other house in Red Bank was sending off starbursts into the night air. Soon enough I was surrounded by a smoky haze.

I decided to go back inside and get something to drink. I opened the fridge and pulled out a can of Pepsi and poured it over a large cup of ice. (I preferred Coke, but now drank Pepsi because I could buy a six-pack for a dollar at Sav-A-Lot.) As I walked through the kitchen, I heard my cell phone ring. I hurried into the den, grabbed my purse, and quickly found my phone.

"Hello?" I asked.

"Hi," the voice purred in my ear. "I used to have a *friend* named Vandelyn, but I haven't talked to her in a long time. I wanted to let her know that I miss her. How are you?" I recognized the voice immediately. It was Thibodeaux.

"I'm fine. How are you?" I asked. I cannot tell a lie. Hearing his voice warmed the cockles of my heart and a place lower on my body as well. However, hearing him refer to me as "friend" brought me back to reality because it brought to mind Cake's song,

Friend is a 4-Letter Word. It reminded me that he would never be what I needed and I would never be what he wanted which made my heart ache for just a moment.

The ache quickly went away, though, when I reminded myself of the New Deal that I had made with myself a few days ago, apparently just in time for this phone call. Obviously Thibodeaux had no knowledge of my New Deal and would have been surprised to realize that it also involved an unlikely accomplice, my NIV Student Bible.

One day, I noticed it sitting on one of my shelves and observed with it the same trepidation one reserves for opening Pandora's Box. When I finally did dare to open it, it fell open to where the marker had been placed: Ecclesiastes. I was surprised to see headings such as, *Wisdom is Meaningless, Pleasures are Meaningless, Toil is Meaningless.*

Not only was I elated and encouraged to learn that there was a disillusioned smart ass in the Bible, but to also hear confirmation that everything in life was meaningless, including lawyers, insurance companies, and politicians. However, it wasn't until I flipped through The New Testament and came across the *Love is patient; love is kind* verses of 1 Corinthians that The New Deal was created in my head. I was quick to realize that 1 Corinthians 13:4-7 was a lot more helpful than all the Tennessee Codes Annotated could ever be.

"I'm fine," Thibodeaux said, pronouncing the words in a way that was quite cute, I had to admit. I also had to admit that the thought of one last romp with Thibodeaux was tempting. I could use a good time with Thibodeaux. I could almost taste the salt of his skin as I imagined licking his tribal tattoo just one last time.

No. I had the New Deal and I was sticking to it. Even the thought of frolicking with a big dick after a really small dick wasn't going to get me to change my mind.

"So, how's Chattanooga?" he asked. "You got a boyfriend?"

"Chattanooga's great and, no, I don't have a boyfriend. But I do have a New Deal. Want to hear about that?"

"What's your New Deal?" he asked.

"My New Deal is that I deserve better than anything that you or any other past guy has given me relationship-wise."

"Ah," Thibodeaux said.

"Yes," I agreed. "*Ah.*"

"Well, good for you," Thibodeaux said. I could feel him smiling through the phone.

"Yes," I agreed. "Definitely good for me."

"I just thought I would give you a call and see if you'd like to have a weekend visitor."

"Thanks," I said, "but I already have a weekend visitor. She'll be visiting into early next week too." It was a bad joke referring to my period.

Thibodeaux laughed. "OK. So I guess you don't have any room for me now that you've got FDR and The New Deal going on."

"Right," I said. "And don't forget that Eleanor is visiting this weekend too." As soon as those words were out of my mouth, I wished I'd never uttered them. Not only were they lame, they made it sound as if my period were a determining factor in my refusal of his advances. It wasn't. "But that's not really a factor," I corrected. Then I paraphrased FDR's presidential nomination acceptance speech. "It's just that I pledged to you, I pledged to myself, a new deal for Vandelyn Devanlay."

"Well, I'm glad to hear that." And he was. I could tell. "You deserve good things."

"Thanks," I said as I smiled. "I agree."

"And remember, the only thing we have to fear is—"

"Bad relationships."

He mocked offense at my terminology. "Were we *bad*? I thought we were good."

"There were good times," I acknowledge with a smile. But there was also plenty of heartache, at least for me. "Maybe 'bad' isn't the best term. How about unhealthy or dysfunctional?"

"Nah. I'll stick with 'good.' Well, you take care of yourself, Vandelyn. I hope your New Deal works out for you."

"Thanks, Mark. You take care too," I said and meant it. Then we hung up the phone.

I grabbed my Pepsi and returned to my spot outside on the blanket. The smoke from the fireworks was still hanging thick in the air, but the starbursts and icicle-shaped explosions popping in the dark night sky made the thick haze beautifully worthwhile.

I smiled as I realized that there was no more Great Depression for me. (Or so I hoped.) I had a New Deal and by talking to Mark tonight, I had begun to make peace with my painful past. Apparently peace came from relinquishing my pain, letting it go free into the night air. I still had other hurtful memories to deal with, but at this moment I felt liberated.

Words from Dr. Martin Luther King Jr.'s *I Have a Dream* speech resonated in my head: "And as we walk, we must make the pledge that we shall always march ahead. We cannot turn back." As I applied those words to my own quest for positive change, I realized that for the first time in my life, I was moving forward; no longer was I confined or defined by my past. I smiled as I remembered that cold day in January on Lookout Mountain, pleased to realize that the words Dr. Abraham G. DuBois shouted out for all of us to hear could also apply to a Southern white girl like me: *Free at last. Free at last. Thank God Almighty, I am free at last!*

Made in the USA
Lexington, KY
24 April 2015